About the Author

The author was born Gerald Morgan at 15 Brook Street, Llanfyllin, on 17 October 1938. In 1946 his father was released from captivity in a Japanese POW camp, and in the June of that year, at the age of 7 years and 8 months he attended the wedding of his parents at Whixall, Shropshire C of E house of our Lord and suddenly he became William Gerald Thomas. His education continued at Whixall Primary C of E School, and then, having passed 11 plus at 10 years of age, he attended Adams Grammar School, Wem, Shropshire. Joining the Royal Navy in December 1956, he trained at HMS Raleigh where some aspects of naval training were carried out aboard the battleship 'Howe' and the frigate 'Venus'. After three months' sea training aboard the carrier HMS Ocean and a Seaman Gunner's course, he was drafted as Ship's Company to the battleship HMS Vanguard.

Training completed, he served full commissions aboard a destroyer and two frigates. In the latter end of 1977 HMS Matapan had completed its work and the author was drafted to HMS Collingwood, the naval electrical school, and took over Admin and Regulation for the Collingwood Maintenance Unit. During 1978 he had the letter from the naval drafting commander inviting him to remain in the Royal Navy for a further five years; however Mrs Thomas had other ideas having brought up five children virtually on her own for long periods over the last 19 years so, in November 1978, he saluted the ensign for the last time in Royal Naval Barracks Portsmouth, and walked through the main gate as an apprentice civilian.

Note: The essential discipline of service life and the good times are worth remembering, as is the camaraderie and the sense of belonging.

D1638454

Published by

MELROSE BOOKS

An Imprint of Melrose Press Limited
St Thomas Place, Ely
Cambridgeshire
CB7 4GG, UK
www.melrosebooks.com

FIRST EDITION

Copyright © William G. Thomas 2007

The Author asserts his moral right to
be identified as the author of this work

Cover designed by Jeremy Kay

ISBN 978 1 906050 08 5

Printed and bound in Great Britain by:
CPI Antony Rowe, Bumpers Farm, Chippenham,
Wiltshire, SN14 6LH, UK

THAT'S LIFE
IN A
BLUE SUIT

William G. Thomas

This statement is to verify that William G. Thomas is the author of this work. Where jokes and songs have been added, I have kept to the rules of copyright just in case there is someone out there who has written claim to any copyright.

Typical Naval humour (usually passed on by word of mouth) stems quite widely from wartime service done by people of celebrity status, who used their wit to create a definitely pornographic style of theatrical humour, normally displayed during a Ships Operatic Dramatic Society (SODS) evening either aboard ship, or in a 'Stone Frigate' theatre. Many of the dirty songs partially written in the text have different words according to which branch of the British Military has included it in their dirty song itinerary.

All names in this novel are fictitious. As mentioned in the Foreword, some of the places visited by the Fourth Destroyer Squadron during its 1957–59 commission have been revisited in this book as a means of giving continuity to the yarn. The exploits of sailors in these ports relate to no one, and are merely a result of the author's attempts to make the story believable.

DEDICATIONS

TO MY WIFE MARIAN
Once again your help and support have proved invaluable.

TO CHARLES AND JUNE BIDMEAD
and all our other friends at the Kalymnos Caravan Park,
Governor's Beach, Limassol, Cyprus. Our 'prime time' get-
together on Saturday nights certainly charged the batteries for the
following week's work.

AND FINALLY
To every British Sailor who served aboard one of these dashing,
daring Greyhounds of the sea.

DEDICATIONS

CONTENTS

CONTENTS

ACKNOWLEDGEMENTS

THE HOLY BIBLE

B.R. 67(2/51) MANUAL OF SEAMANSHIP VOLUME TWO

BY COMMAND OF THEIR LORDSHIPS

PEARS CYCLOPAEDIA 74TH Edition 1965–66
Editor: L. MARY BARKER. BSc.Lond

TEACH YOURSELF JUDO By ERIC DOMINY, this impression 1958.
Printed in Great Britain for the English Universities Press Ltd,
London by Elliott Bros & Yeoman Ltd, Liverpool.

The above books assisted the author in ensuring that dates and
other details were correct.

ACKNOWLEDGEMENTS

FOREWORD BY THE AUTHOR

For the purpose of this novel, I have brought many, now scrapped, Royal Navy ships of the 1950s back to life again.

The Fourth Destroyer Squadron consisted of HMS *Agincourt* Captain 'D', HMS *Barrosa*, HMS *Corunna*, and HMS *Alamein*. These four destroyers form the basis of this novel, and I have used some 'visits' during the 1957–59 commission to give continuity to this yarn.

HMS *Vanguard* is the starting point for the story, because she was moored in Portsmouth Harbour in 1957, and she was my first ship after training as Ship's Company for a few weeks whilst I and others waited for the commissioning of the Fourth Destroyer Squadron. The old Destroyer *Vigo* was gunnery training ship at HMS *Excellent*.

HMS *Birmingham*, HMS *Sheffield*, HMS *Kenya*, HMS *Jamaica* and HMS *Bermuda* are presented as the five Cruisers playing the role of lead ships to a convoy of Merchantmen in my fictional NATO exercise 'Biscay'.

The Cruisers HMS *Ceylon* and HMNZS *Royalist* are mentioned in context with their actions during the Suez War. The Carriers HMS *Ocean,* HMS *Theseus* and other Carriers are included in this part of the story.

The Aircraft Carrier HMS *Warrior* towers over HMS *Barossa* in Portsmouth Harbour, while the Carriers USS *Saratoga* and HMS *Eagle* play a leading part in 'Biscay'.

The Destroyers HMS *Broadsword* and HMS *Aisne* are mentioned in conjunction with fishery protection duties.

Bringing all these old ships together in this novel is a result of the author's imagination, and in no way follows a pattern of orders that may have issued from Admiralty. In all cases, only enough naval procedure is added to give the reader an impression of reality.

William G. Thomas

The elusive and very speedy Russian Submarine introduced into the story gives an element of truth to the cold war brinkmanship that was consistently going on between major nations opposing each other in peacetime.

The four young men who form the basis of the story, joined the Royal navy in 1956 during the Suez War. Each one of them joined the navy to avoid national service in the army, favouring the service that they had all dreamed about since boyhood.

Upon finishing basic training they all find themselves aboard HMS *Vanguard*, the last and biggest of all Great Britain's 'Battlewagons'. It is here that their real service life begins, and it is here they have their first experiences of the lower deck pecking order. Up until this moment everyone they had come into contact with had to be called 'SIR', and that included all non-commissioned ranks above them.

Ship's Company life does not start well for the four lads. First the acidulous Petty Officer Hancock puts them all in the rattle, and as a result of this they find themselves at the defaulter's table for the first time in their young careers. Later, Ordinary Seaman 'Dusty' Miller has an adversarial confrontation with Able Seaman Smith, which sets the ball rolling for the obsessional Smith to keep popping up in the story even to the unexpected outcome of the final chapters.

All is not bitterness and 'bollockings' though. A Petty Officer physical training instructor notices the lads having a sporting afternoon at Pitt Street Royal Naval swimming pool on a Saturday when all the pubs are open. This impresses the instructor and he approaches them in an heartening manner. His actions and the encouraging conversation he has with them leaves the four shipmates feeling much better about their lowly situation just because they had shown some ability in their chosen sports.

Lieutenant Jeremy Forrester, Korean War veteran and Navigating Officer, reads their service documents and discovers all four have a Captain's commendation for prompt action. Service life begins to improve for them. Quite naturally a story about the Senior Service cannot be told without lashings of text involving the fairer sex, therefore they all meet nice girls; and of course, not so nice girls.

That's Life in a Blue Suit

Two of the pals are drafted to HMS *Vigo* so that they can continue improving their sporting talents. The story then goes on to follow the adventures of 'Dusty' Miller, and 'Wiggy' Bennett who is 'Officer Material', right up to the conclusion of the fictional 'Exercise Biscay'.

The language used in the narrative is typical of the lower deck. Descriptions of sexual encounters are blunt and to the point. Encounters in brothels are part of the text, as are actions of good time girls in the pubs of Commercial Road, Portsmouth.

W. Thomas.

1

JOINING ROUTINE

The Bedford truck rattled to a stop at North Corner Jetty in Portsmouth Royal Naval Dockyard. The left hand cab door opened and a diminutive figure dressed in the number two rig of a Royal Naval Petty Officer stepped out, rear first. His left arm carried three red chevrons surmounted by crossed anchors. The red stripes signified twelve years of unblemished character, or twelve years of undetected crime, according to the level of cynicism with which they were viewed.

The Petty Officer reached back into the cab of the truck, and his right hand emerged grasping a ticking off board with a few documents held in place by the metal clip affixed at the top of the board. 'Right, pay attention you lot!' he shouted officiously as he came round the back of the canvas covered truck. 'Miller, Bennett, Wright and Knight, out you get with your kit, and fall in, in front of me 'ere.'

The tailboard of the truck clanged down, and the four ratings jumped from the truck and formed a line in front of the Petty Officer.

'Pass these along,' he ordered, shoving four slips of paper in Miller's hand. Peter Miller took the flimsy with his name on it, and passed the three remaining to Ronald Knight. When all four had their draft chits safely stowed away, the Petty Officer indicated a Battleship moored across to the Gosport side of the harbour. 'There's your 'ome for the next couple of months until they commission the Fourth Destroyer Squadron,' he said disinterestedly as he tucked the ticking off board back under his left arm.

The four men strained their necks to get a glimpse of the ship he had indicated to them. The huge grey mass was moored between two harbour buoys, one forrard, and one aft. The huge chain links, and ship to buoy shackle that secured each cable end to the buoy, were as thick as a man's arm. Their eyes swung back to the Petty Officer as he said 'wait ere until the PAS boat picks you up, then report to the Regulating Office as soon as you get aboard.' Without further ado, the Petty Officer jumped back in the lorry which moved hurriedly away with a cloud of cigarette smoke billowing from the driver's open window. Shouts of farewell echoed from the remainder of 218 class, who would be spread around other ships forming the reserve fleet under the famous name of HMS *Bellerophon*. Tomorrow morning they would find themselves carrying out all the menial tasks specifically reserved to test the patience and the stoicism of all youngsters at the bottom of the naval pecking order.

Fifteen minutes later the PAS boat swung into North Corner steps, and reversed to a stop, wicker fenders absorbing the shock of contact with the harbour wall. The four young sailors held back, allowing Dockyard Mateys and other passengers to board first. Peter Miller jumped aboard first and caught and stowed all his mates' kits as it was thrown to him. The boat moved quickly away under the practiced hand of a dockyard coxswain who had no doubt seen service aboard the very ships he now delivered to.

'Bloody 'ell! Look at the size of that!' Arthur Wright expressed the view felt by all of them as they neared the crew's accommodation ladder positioned starboard side amidships. The PAS boat bumped the Catamaran, and was quickly secured forrard and aft before the young sailors jumped onto this floating landing stage and piled their kit up in one heap ready to pass up the ladder. It made quite a pile consisting of four kit bags, four hammocks, four large green cases and four small brown cases. Hat boxes were no longer a compulsory part of kit, but it still represented quite a pile of personal gear.

The duty hands of the day, backed up by two 'side boys' helped the four to get their kit up to the deck of the mighty ship, and then carried on with getting the sack of mail, and the milk and bread for the day inboard.

Fresh out of training, and having completed a training cruise aboard the Aircraft Carrier HMS *Ocean*, followed by a seven week basic gunnery course to the grade of Seaman Gunner Q, their quick eyes picked up all the little nuances of seamanship pertaining to an accommodation ladder.

'D'yer see there aren't any 'Tide Spars' rigged, and no 'boatrope' forrard or aft,' Ronald Knight just had to say, having noticed the deficiency during a cursory glance at the rigging normally associated with an accommodation ladder. 'That's because of this Catamaran,' he added knowledgeably.

'Okay then smartarse,' piped in Arthur Wright. 'What sort of ladder would it be in a position that was too rough for an accommodation ladder?' Ronald Knight looked at his pal, and retorted mockingly 'a bloody jumping ladder you daft dick'.

'Keep silence down there!' A voice roared from the deck above them.

They all froze and gaped upwards. The Petty Officer of the day was glowering down at them from the weather deck, his face puce with anger. 'Up here at the double!' he screamed.

They all flew up the accommodation ladder and stood to attention alongside the Quartermaster's desk. The Petty Officer glared at them for a few seconds, taking in the dishevelled sight of the four unfortunates. 'What is the first thing you do when boarding one of Her Majesty's warships?' The anger in his voice had not abated as he glared at them threateningly. Not waiting for a reply, he answered his own question, 'you face the quarterdeck and salute, as a matter of respect. None of you oafs saluted, did you?' He glared into each face in turn, mentally registering that Ordinary Seaman Bennett stared impassively ahead of himself, not in the least bit flustered. He turned to Arthur Wright. 'And you, you unshapely excuse for an OD, were doing all the talking.'

Arthur Wright's face was beetroot red, but his eyes glowed with repressed anger. His lips pursed meanly as he stood and let the Petty Officer's tirade bounce off him.

'Look at the bloody state of all of you. You all look as if you have just dived out of a China Station whorehouse window… follow me!' He ended abruptly, turning on his heel and heading for the screen door which gave access to the mighty ship through the superstructure.

'Leave your kit there!' he yelled, as they all made to pick it up.

He led them down one deck, and then along the Burma Way. Minutes later he stopped at a door on the port side off the passageway with the words 'Regulating Office' hand painted in gold on a richly varnished strip of marine ply beaded around the perimeter.

'Another four Jim,' he said conversationally as he slid open the door, then turning to the four Ordinary Seamen shouted 'in 'ere you lot'. The four young men stepped briskly through the door, and lined up expressionless in front of the office counter.

'Draft chits,' the Regulating Petty Officer said firmly, holding out his hand to receive the four documents. The RPO checked all four to ensure he had all details correct, then appended the four names to sheets of paper marked 'joining routine'. The card attached to the paper had several squares across its surface each with a name of an office or department. The sheet of paper told them which compartment an office or store could be found, and also bore some advice for new ships' company just joining. The two most popular squares were marked 'Pay Office' and 'Victualling Office'; once these two squares were stamped a sailor knew he would be on the pay roster, and victuals would be supplied to the galley for him. The navy may have its priorities, but Jolly Jack had a few of his own.

'Officer of the Days report for all of them,' the Petty Officer of the Day added imperiously.

'What's that for?' the RPO looked up as he replied, the hint of an annoyed frown creasing his brow.

'Failing to salute upon coming aboard, and being improperly dressed.'

The RPO looked up at the four faces peering back at him. Three of the faces seemed slightly pensive, but one face was set firmly from the line of the jaw to the determined gleam in his eyes. His momentary scan of the four faces paused long enough to register the general bearing of Ordinary Seaman Bennett. Satisfied that the look was not insubordinate, merely showing an acceptance of his fate, the RPO looked across to his colleague at the disciplinary section of the office. 'Hey Jock, another four for Officer of the Days report.'

The disciplinary RPO glanced up from the pile of charge sheets he had placed in order. 'Back here at 1030 hours,' he ordered firmly, and then staring directly at the Petty Officer of the Day continued, 'stay behind and give me the details, Petty Officer Hancock.'

The first RPO spoke again, 'get your kit down the mess sharpish, and be back here in thirty minutes, off you go!'

'What mess are we in RPO?' Arthur Wright asked politely.

'Look at yer bloody joining card,' came the terse reply.

They followed their tracks back to the gangway, and by the time they had got all their kit through the screen door, Petty Officer Hancock's face appeared above the hatch combing. 'Hey Wallace,' he shouted as the remainder of his body cleared the hatch.

A fresh young face appeared through the screen door. 'Yes PO,' the sixteen year old replied.

'Take these four idiots down to five mess.'

The Boy Seaman rushed to obey the order, picking up a case to be helpful.

'Nobody said anything about being a railway porter Wallace, put that bloody case down.'

Young Wallace dropped the case as if it had burnt his fingers, then hurried down the hatch to two deck saying, 'follow me lads'.

It took two journeys to get all their kit to the messdeck they had been allocated, this involved descending two decks, then going forrard along a passageway decorated with every type of handwheel, fire fighting and damage control equipment, to make a fighting ship capable of sustaining its fighting ability. Having dumped their kit in five mess, they just made it back to the Regulating Office in time to be lined up by the Disciplinary RPO in the passageway to the left of a small desk just wide enough to hold a couple of charge sheets. Petty Officer Hancock appeared and stood at ease, his back to the bulkhead.

A few minutes later, a tall thin officer with one gold ring on each cuff suddenly appeared behind the desk. The RPO turned to the line of defaulters and shouted, 'Defaulters Hoe.'

Everyone to the front of the desk sprang to attention. The RPO turned smartly to face the Sub Lieutenant, and saluting said, 'Defaulters mustered sir.'

'Very well RPO, first defaulter please.'

'Aye aye sir.' He turned to the four young sailors and having used the necessary orders to line them up in front of the desk, shouted 'Off Caps,' and then proceeded to read out the charge. 'All four are charged with failing to salute when coming aboard at 0930 this morning the tenth of September 1957. They are also charged with being slovenly dressed in appearance and improperly dressed.' He then quoted the appropriate order from Queen's regulations and Admiralty instructions, and for good measure included the appropriate order from 'Ships Standing Orders'.

'Thank you RPO,' the Officer replied, then asked, 'who has brought these charges against these four men?'

'Petty Officer Hancock,' the RPO bawled.

The Petty Officer of the Day marched smartly to the table and saluted. The Sub Lieutenant listened with an air of concentration as the Petty Officer of the Day laid the morning's events out in detail, ending with a loudly delivered 'Sir.'

'They were in the process of joining, were they not?'

'That's correct sir.'

'Thank you, Petty Officer Hancock, that will be all.' The young Sub Lieutenant turned to the four offenders saying, 'what on earth made you forget to salute as you came aboard?' His face showed a hint of surprise. 'Don't you realise it is the first elementary mark of respect that all of us learn?'

Three of the young sailors looked at him numbly, a bit surprised at the young Officer's statement. One of them however was not chastened by this whole affair.

'In mitigation sir,' Ordinary Seaman Bennett spoke up politely. 'I think we had all rushed to obey Petty Officer

Hancock's first order, and omitted to show the proper mark of respect.'

All eyes behind the desk swung instantly to the open face of Ordinary Seaman Bennett. The Officer of the Day seemed flustered for a moment, but quickly regained his composure.

'So you all admit to the Offence,' he asked hurriedly.

Three of the young men said 'yes sir,' in unison, but once again the polite unhurried voice of Ordinary Seaman Bennett put their admittance more succinctly. 'Under the circumstances, yes sir.'

His demeanour and his delivery were not insubordinate. Behind the desk was an array of superiors who had the full powers of the naval system at their fingertips; his eloquence under duress had surprised them, but it had not given them a reason to jump all over him.

Looking at the RPO and then back to the four defaulters the young Officer said with a sternness that still needed practice, 'I will deal with the first offence now; I will not pass it on to First Lieutenant's defaulters.' He paused for a second, gathering himself, whilst staring at the charge sheet. Finally he looked up. 'Two days number fourteens for the first offence. The second offence I have decided to pass on to your Divisional Officer, he will no doubt ensure that you get enough kit musters to ensure that you abide by the naval dress code at all times in the future.' He glanced sideways at the RPO again, who repeated the first punishment loudly, 'Two days number fourteens…on caps… about turn…quick march.'

'Right you lot.' Petty Officer Hancock halted their retreat. 'You will all muster at the gangway at 1630 hours when 'Men under Punishment' are piped to muster. You will then be put to work until 1830 hours when 'hands to supper' is piped. You will also carry out the same procedure tomorrow. By the way,' he added with a crooked grin. 'As you now know, I am Petty Officer Hancock, and I am your divisional Petty Officer. When you have finished your joining routine you will report to me at the 'Top part of Ship', I'll soon get you lot sorted out, off you go sharpish and get your gear stowed away. My 'Hooky' Leading Seaman Wilson will be along shortly to make sure you put your kits in the lockers designated to you, and that you stow your hammock in the netting allocated to you.'

The four new members of the Ships Company jumped to obey the Petty Officer's orders without breaking into a run. Briskness is the order of the day in the RN, but running can be dangerous aboard ship, so therefore is not expected.

A tall skinny, fair haired Leading Hand met them as they descended the ladder to three deck. 'You lot the new lads for five mess?'

'Yes Hooky,' Bennett answered for them all, being the nearest.

The Leading Hand lost no time in getting them sorted out. Immediately they entered the mess he pointed each man to his locker, hammock stowage and case rack. He continued fussing around them as they began to stow their kit in the appointed lockers. 'Leave all your tropical kit in your green cases; you won't be needing that in Portsmouth Harbour. Fold your kit bag up and put that in your case also, all that lot will be consigned to the forrard baggage store.'

The Leading Hand was interrupted by the blast of a bosun's call from the tannoy, followed by the order 'Hands of the mess for rum.' Almost simultaneously a weather-beaten three badge Able Seaman dashed into the mess, grabbed the rum fanny, and disappeared again briskly.

'Grab your cases and follow me,' Leading Seaman Wilson ordered. 'We just have time to get these stowed before the bosun gets back with the rum; come on then,' he urged. 'I've got to be back here by the time the rum bosun gets back or all the mess pissheads will be seeing little green spiders.'

The Leading Hand was in charge of the forrard baggage store so he kept a key at all times, permanently loaned to him as a responsible person. All four cases were hurriedly but tidily added to the other cases in the store, the door was re-locked and all five hurried back to the mess. Another blast came over the tannoy, only this time it continued for an extended period of pips and trills, and highs and lows followed by the verbal order 'Haaaands to dinner.' By this time the rum bosun had returned to the mess with the rum ration for all those men entitled over the age of twenty years, who were not 'temperance'. All those who were 'under age' kept well away from the little ceremony that brightened the day of every able bodied sailor clustered around the end of the messdeck table in a tight group. When every man had quaffed his tot there was generally some left in the rum fanny. This residue was called the 'Queens', and came about by the bit of over spillage that always occurred at issue. It was always added to by the bosun putting one or two fingers into the tot measure when tipping it into the recipient's glass. The 'Queens' usually represented an extra mouthful of rum per man, and the glass was passed around to all entitled.

The standard issue of 'grog' was three eighths of a pint per man; this consisted of one eighth of a pint of neat rum, mixed with two eighths of a pint of water. Chief Petty Officers and Petty Officers received a neat tot which was kept in a private bottle until the end of the working day by many senior rates. Totally illegal of course, but as the navy grew more technical many people in the technical branches would do this, even going as far as keeping it until a day in harbour. Grog on the other hand was vile if bottled, even for a short length of time, so all concerned preferred to 'get it down their throats' immediately.

'You lot had better get up to the dining hall and get your scran,' Leading Seaman Wilson advised his new messmates, as he took up his position beside the rum bosun.

'Have a wet,' an old Able Seaman ordered the rum bosun, a little disgruntled at the moment's delay whilst the Leading Hand spoke to the four lads. The bosun carried out the request, touching the glass to his lips, taking the smallest of sips, and then handing it to the eagerly waiting seaman. He drank it in one long swallow, and then stood for a moment smacking his lips before swilling the glass in the washing up fanny, and then placing the glass upside down on the mess cloth laid at the end of the table for that very purpose.

'I see that basterd Hancock has put the four new lads in the rattle before they'd even got their bloody kit aboard,' the old AB started the daily conversation.

'Some buggers goin' to 'ave 'im one of these days, you mark my words,' another messmate chipped in, 'and I want to be there to turn me back on it and pretend it wasn't 'appenin',' he added, putting his glass to his lips and downing his tot in one.

'Ow the fuck d'yer work with that basterd?' another piped in, turning the question to the Leading Hand of the mess.

'I just do me job and keep out of 'is way. 'E never tries ter get me into a conversation, so I just look after me lads, and try ter make sure they don't get in the shit.'

The conversation around the rum fanny was totally insubordinate, but was a fact of messdeck life. If a sailor hated someone, the whole of his mess knew it, but it never went out of the mess, and a sailor's likes and dislikes, and the way he expressed them, were always reserved for this private moment during the daily grind.

The time had come now when the four new messmates would no longer be Pete Miller, Ronald Knight, Donald Bennett, or Arthur Wright. They would have been baptised with their new nicknames during training, but now on their first ship as 'Ships Company' they would always be known by their peers as Dusty, Bogey, Wiggy and Shiner. Of course their real names would be known in the mess from 'cooks of the day' rosters and the 'mess list', but those Christian names would never be used, and so it came about that a smiling messmate, an Able Seaman, said 'Come on Dusty and mates, I'll show you the routine.' He led them up to join the dining hall queue saying, 'I'm one of those odd buggers who likes to eat before 'avin me tot,' he explained with a grin.

They all joined the rear of the queue, which shuffled forward quite quickly as food was thrown from servers' ladles onto the compartmentalised metal tray that served as a multiple course plate.

Soup and bread were on a separate table within the dining hall.

The five of them reached the duty Leading Hand standing poised with his meal ticket clippers. 'Meal card,' he snapped, glowering at Dusty.

'They've only just joined, and 'aven't been issued meal cards yet,' Slinger Woods sang out from the rear.

The Petty Officer of the day stepped forward. 'Names,' he asked, then appended the names to his notebook.

'Come on past them!' The PO in charge of the servery called out to the men behind.

Slinger Woods came to the front of the queue saying, 'you'll be okay now,' then shuffled from ladle to ladle as the food was dolloped onto his tray.

'Tell the victualling office to clip out today's dinner when they give you your card,' the Petty Officer ordered.

'Come on then you lot!' the servery Petty Officer shouted at them, as they appeared a bit unsure about rejoining the queue.

They collected their meals and spread themselves around any seats that were vacant. Cafeteria messing was pretty new aboard ships at this time, and of course no space was big enough to take the whole of the lower deck junior ratings at one sitting, hence the term 'eat it, and beat it.'

'Men under punishment to muster,' the tannoy blared out, startling the four Ordinary Seamen.

'Does that mean us?' Bogey Knight turned and asked Dusty Miller at the next table.

An older Able Seaman looked up from his tray. 'What uv yer got?' he asked Bogey, fork poised in mid air.

'Two days number fourteens,' Bogey replied, his tone suitably respectful, his eyes searching the old salt's face.

'Just two hours extra work then, 1630 hours until 1830 hours.' Then returning Bogey's direct stare he added sarcastically, 'that's arf past four till arf past six this evening for green ODs, still wet behind the ears.'

Bogey coloured slightly at the old AB's lightly delivered sarcasm. He was being helpful whilst still demonstrating the pecking order. 'Done yer joining routine yet 'av' yer?'

'Nah! We only joined three hours ago,' Bogey replied respectfully.

'Christ almighty! And yer in the shit already, what's that for?'

'We didn't salute at the top of the gangway, and our number twos were scruffy from carrying our kit.'

The three badgemen nodded knowingly, glancing at Bogey's crumpled state of dress. The blue collar and silk were all a bit awry. 'So yer fell foul of 'is nibs 'ancock did yer, that's nothing new; what's yer name by the way?'

'Bogey Knight,' he replied, warming to this senior lower decker.

'Well, Ordinary Seaman Bogey Knight. Before both watches are piped at 1315 hours, get out of number twos and into number eights, otherwise all you lot are going to find yourselves deeper in the shit for being out of the dress of the day.' So saying, he picked up his tray with the cutlery balanced on top in the soup plate, and strolled over to the scullery hatch. He deposited his load on the aluminium counter and sauntered off nonchalantly, hands thrust deep in his number eights trouser pockets. The four young seamen followed his lead, and then returned to the mess.

No one paid a blind bit of notice of them as they opened their lockers and proceeded to get changed into the dress of the day. Nobody moved to give them more space, so the changing procedure had to be carried out in the foot that separated the lockers from the messdeck tables. The lockers were stacked two high, and needless to say the bottom row was reserved for ratings of less importance in the mess, namely those below the rate of Able Seaman.

Bogey Knight, a fellow of seventeen stones, did not have enough room to change, and kept nudging the Able Seaman at the table behind him.

'Get yer fat arse out of my face,' the AB shouted, his face a picture of surliness. 'Fuck off in the passageway, there's plenty uv room out there.'

Bogey scooped up his clothes obediently and continued changing where he had a little more room to swing his ample posterior.

A sudden blast from a trumpet over the tannoy rose above the noise of the fans and hull and fire pump noises that formed the ambient noise level of anywhere below decks. The single blast was called the 'G', the bugle call itself enough warning for the hands to ready themselves for an afternoon's work. Five minutes later as all the hands were making their way to the upper deck, the bosun's call preceded the order, 'Out pipes, both watches of the hands fall in.'

Major warships, cruisers and above, carried a Royal Marine detachment, so big ship routine orders were preceded by a bugle call. Some smaller vessels carried a RM detachment also, but it usually depended on the area a ship served in, and if the area may need the assistance of a land force with a bit more specialised ability than a landing party made up of sailors.

Both watches of the hands fell in by parts of ship either side and in front of 'A' Turret. The four new lads joined the 'Topmen' standing at ease beside the starboard barrel of A Turret. The fifty foot length and massive diameter of the sleeve of the barrel where it protruded from the gunhouse dwarfed all who stood near it. Today, only thirty sailors formed the seaman branch, and that number fluctuated daily as men joined to await their next draft, and others left as their draft date arrived. HMS *Vanguard* at this time was acting as a convenient base as part of NATO Headquarters in the UK. She was in fact a useful conference HQ, well separated from prying eyes, and listening devices. This being the case, only a skeleton crew was kept aboard, just enough to keep her clean and tidy, and ticking over. All unused compartments were locked off, and she was kept alive by shore power through 'shore supply' cables. Just one diesel generator was kept on stand by, in case of a shore supply failure.

Leading Seaman Wilson stood at ease in front of seven Able Seamen, and four Ordinary Seamen. The eleven men had fallen in two deep, six in the front rank, and five in the rear rank, with the blank file on the left. With such a small number of men, a quick glance proved that all were present, and it was not necessary to call out everyone's name as would happen in a conventional muster of a large part of ship.

'Topmen Hoe,' Petty Officer Hancock shouted, calling his men to attention in the time honoured manner. After pausing for a second he turned right and marched up the forecastle deck to report his men 'mustered and correct' to the Chief Boatswain's Mate.

'Stand them at ease,' the Chief ordered with practiced terseness. When all parts of ship had reported to him, the Chief Boatswain's Mate roared, 'Both watches of seamen hoe,' then turned about and marched further up the forecastle to come to attention in front of the First Lieutenant.

'Both watches mustered and proved correct sir,' he reported firmly, having saluted first.

'Very good Chief, turn them to by parts of ship please.'

'Aye Aye sir,' the Chief replied loudly, then turning right and marching a few paces forward until he was facing aft, he shouted, 'Both watches turn to by parts of ship; Diiiiisssmis.'

All hands turned right, dwelt a pause of two marching paces and broke off, shepherded to parts of ship by Petty Officers and Leading Hands.

'Right! Miller, Wright, Bennett and Knight,' shouted Petty Officer Hancock, then paused, grinning broadly, saying to Leading Seaman Wilson, 'almost sounds like the first line of a poem don't it.'

Wilson raised his head in a quick 'ha ha' then continued walking, flicking his eyes skywards with disparaging effect, unseen by his superior, but noted by Slinger Woods who was alongside him. He too had glanced sideways at the Petty Officer, quickly turning his head back so Hancock would not see his look of contempt.

Petty Officer Hancock turned to the four Ordinary Seamen again, his face changing from stupid grin to frowning glare, as if to lend weight to the order he was about to give. 'Get on with yer joining routine, and report back to me on completion.'

'Aye Aye PO!' they shouted in unison, and then proceeded briskly to collect their joining cards from their respective lockers.

The Pay Office, Victualling Office, Naval Stores Office, and Loan Clothing Store were all adjacent to each other more or less, so in ten minutes they had completed four sections of the joining card and had the four stamps to prove it. The Sick Bay and Dental Surgery were together, so having had their mouths stared into, accompanied by the seemingly indifferent 'any teeth problems?' they had only the Divisional section to complete. The seeming disinterest of the young Lieutenant in the Dental Surgery was not an act of negligence; during training no young men are better cared for than naval trainees. Medically one is cosseted from the day of entry until the day one joins the fleet, and even then annual checkups are promulgated, and a sick bay is always close at hand wherever one serves.

Thirty minutes later the four lads were back in the Regulating Office standing in the section panelled off as 'The Ship's Office'.

'Come back later,' the Leading Hand ordered them, as he took their joining cards. 'I haven't had time to do your ship's company card and your station cards yet. Don't worry though, I won't put you in today's duty watch.'

While the four ODs were finding their way around the system Petty Officer Hancock had paid a visit to his boss Lieutenant Jeremy Forrester, who was top part of Ship Divisional Officer.

Lieutenant Forrester was an ex public school boy who had specialised as a Navigating Officer. He had completed Naval College in time to serve on one of a squadron of Algerian Class Minesweepers during the Korean War. This afforded him an early baptism of fire during very dangerous mine-sweeping operations preceding the arrivals of the men and machines to fight the series of savage battles that prevented the loss of freedom of the South Koreans.

'Have you got time to see them this afternoon sir?'

'Yes PO, nothing pressing on at the moment, wheel them in any time you like.' His manner was deliberately offhand; jobs like this were very boring for ambitious young Officers who hated being pushed into a backwater until their turn for real service came round again. At twenty-seven years of age he knew he was well up the ladder towards Lieutenant Commander, and that's where the real battle for promotion began.

'I was Petty Officer of the day until 1200 hours today sir,' the Petty Officer continued, ignoring the offhand answer to his question. 'I had to put all four of them in the rattle for failing to salute when coming aboard, and being slovenly dressed.'

'Yes so I heard PO, you take care of the kit muster, and let me know when I am to inspect them; just to keep it official, will that be okay?'

'Very good sir,' Petty Officer Hancock replied a little sourly. His boss knew he was rationed ashore which meant he got away at 1615 hours every day when he was not duty. His boss also knew that kit musters were held outside of working hours. For once his ardency in keeping a constant queue of defaulters at the First Lieutenant's table had rebounded on him somewhat.

'Will that be all for now PO?' Lieutenant Forrester asked, the mere hint of a smile etched across his face.

Having replied in the affirmative, Petty Officer Hancock closed the door behind him as he left, and then allowed his face to fully reflect his inner chagrin. He walked forrard along two deck, his features remaining set in the peeved expression that showed he was not at all pleased at the outcome of the meeting with his superior officer.

Lieutenant Forrester watched the departure of his Petty Officer, allowing the blossoming smile to spread across his face as the door closed. 'Let's see if that cools your eagerness to drop everybody in the shit, Petty Officer bloody Hancock,' he muttered to himself, quite pleased with the way he had turned the tables on this over officious non-commissioned officer.

By 1430 hours the lads had visited the Gunnery Office, and apart from collecting their station cards and ship's company card, only the divisional office square required a stamp and signature. They ignored the pipe 'stand easy', preferring to wait at the top part of ship for the Petty Officer to return after his cup of tea. This was the first moment of relaxation since they had rushed aboard this mighty vessel, and it gave them a feeling of unease. Wiggy Bennett in particular, by nature a very aware and observant fellow, had caution in mind at this moment. 'I suppose we could look around to see if the PO is elsewhere, he does seem to have a propensity for dropping people in the shit at the drop of a hat.'

'Sit tight, Wiggy,' Shiner said reassuringly. 'He was on this spot when he ordered us to report back to him.'

Bogey Knight added his piece, 'stop bloody panicking, Wiggy; we are in the right place.'

Wiggy grimaced at his pal. 'It's not a case of panic, Bogey, I just don't trust the man, and I certainly did not join this man's navy to be continually glancing back over my shoulder.'

At that moment Petty Officer Hancock appeared through the adjacent screen door onto the upper deck. 'Come on then,' he ordered. 'I'll take you down to meet your divisional officer.'

He led them down a deck, and aft past the Regulating Office, then told them to wait outside a door marked Top Divisional Office, the words written in bold letters at eye level. He knocked lightly on the door, and opened it. 'All here sir,' he was heard to say. There was a brief pause.

'Ah yes PO, bring them all in please, might as well see all four together.'

'Ordinary Seamen Knight, Bennett, Miller and Wright sir,' Petty Officer Hancock introduced them as they came through the door, caps in hand.

'Well men,' Lieutenant Forrester greeted them, indicating a bench seat set against the port bulkhead. 'You created quite a stir with your arrival. Not to worry though, the next few days will see your problems behind you, and then we can continue the work of making sailors out of you, instead of giving you the wrong impression of this career you have ahead of you.'

Wiggy Bennett, ever perceptive, reacted to the short pep talk. 'Quite sir,' he said in that well mannered way of his. 'I really began to think I was not welcome here.'

His reply visibly startled the Lieutenant. He stared searchingly into Wiggy's face. The words he had just heard were spoken in an educated accent; for a moment the Lieutenant wondered if he was being mocked. The openly pleasant and sincere expression on Wiggy's face assured him that he was not, and after a second he smiled by way of reply.

Petty Officer Hancock's face betrayed his momentary astonishment.

'Your service documents preceded you by twenty-four hours, so I have had some time to get to know a little about you.' He paused for a moment, looking down at a series of papers spread out before him. 'Your 264 ratings history sheets hold quite a revelation, as does your individual S.1245 gunnery history record. I see you were involved in that terrible disaster when that twin four inch blew up some weeks ago killing four of the crew and the camp dog. You Miller, and you Bennett actually pulled two of the nearby injured out of the resulting inferno. You Knight, and you Wright quickly manned a fire hose. All of you may like to know that apart

17

from the excellent write up in your 264s, the Captain of HMS *Cambridge* has personally written a commendation in your gunnery history sheets.' He picked up the documents and carefully made sure he placed the right ones in the appropriate folder. He looked up at the four again and said, 'you join us with excellent records.'

The four pals were not prepared for this aura of respectability that suddenly surrounded them, but Wiggy had no qualms when replying politely, 'thank you for saying so sir. We did what we were ordered to.' His statement, although polite was delivered in a matter of fact manner. 'We simply carried out the orders of our Gunnery Instructor.'

'Well Bennett, nobody knows better than you that the four who were killed could have risen to six if you had not reacted so promptly. Few things are more devastating in the world of gunnery than having one's own people killed by a round cooking off with a half closed breech. It is the circumstances under which you followed your instructor's orders that make your actions commendable. Before leaving training you have witnessed the horrors of an event that is just as horrible as losing a guns' crew from enemy action; you were faced with the results of a terrible incident and were not found wanting. I am proud to have you in my division, although it is only until the fourth destroyer squadron commissions.'

The four young seamen sat looking at their superior, well aware of the fact that he was adding his appreciative words to the line of superior officers who had already commended their instant reaction to the orders of the God like figure who was their Gunnery Instructor.

As the Lieutenant finished speaking he turned to his Petty Officer. 'I believe you are putting them to work in 'B' Turret, and 'Y' Turret as gun sweepers.' His tone suggested that this was an order, and had not been previously discussed.

'Er-um, yes sir,' Petty Officer Hancock replied, caught unawares by his boss' veiled order. The manner of his reply assured all present that this was the last job he would haven given four young Ordinary Seamen who until now had been likely fodder for his overbearing and insidious style of authority. Cushy numbers like that were usually reserved for badge men of a little seniority on big ships.

'Now, these kit musters,' Lieutenant Forrester took the conversation forward. 'I am Officer of the Day on Thursday, which means I shall be doing evening messdeck rounds. Have your kits laid out in any convenient positions close to your messdeck by that time, and I shall inspect them as I go through. I think that is the most convenient way to complete that matter under the circumstances. Leading Seaman Wilson can offer help and advice...don't you think so?' he added, turning to his Petty Officer with a knowing smile.

'O yes sir!' came the reply, the Petty Officer's face suddenly brightening as it dawned on him that he would not have to stay behind on two nights, inspecting his men's kit in preparation for his Officer's inspection.

'Well that's about it then,' Lieutenant Forrester brought the meeting to an end, holding his hand out with a smile. Nobody rushed to grasp his hand. Once again it was up to Wiggy to lead his companions. Naturally, he did not push himself to the fore, but the instant he realised that some form of leadership was required, he thrust his hand forward, and taking the proffered hand gave it a firm but respectful shake, realising that his oppos were not quite ready for this form of familiarity. Nothing in an Ordinary Seaman's early career prepared him for touching contact with a superior officer. Permanent apprehension became a way of life.

'Sign their joining cards PO, then they can be on their way. Right chaps, I shall look forward to seeing you happily at work in your new jobs when I walk round our part of ship...cheerio for now.'

The four pals walked out of the office a little stunned. Somebody had treated them like human beings. 'Hey, ee's awright as a DO innee?' Bogey Knight broke the silence as they walked down the Burma Way to the Regulating Office door. 'Did yer see the look on 'ancock's face when the DO gave us the gunsweeper jobs, friggin' gobsmacked wasn't ee?' Bogey's face held the wide grin of the subordinate who had just found pleasure in seeing his taskmaster taken down a peg or two. They walked into the Regulating Office, their faces having assumed a look of solemnity as each of them stepped over the dwarf bulkhead that prevented ingress of water to the office. The Leading Hand behind the desk of the Ship's Office section stamped their joining cards. He then told them to return the following morning for their station cards and ship's company cards. He offered no explanation for their delay, and none of the four posed the question. They handed their joining cards to a Leading Regulator and departed the office.

In the meantime, Lieutenant Forrester had invited Petty Officer Hancock to take a seat. 'Lucky I phoned the Pay Office to see if their documents had arrived after we had met earlier, otherwise I would not have known the true facts about these young men,' he began. 'It has also occurred to me that they have had quite a day joining this ship. They seem to have encountered nothing but hostility since they set foot on the accommodation ladder. The Navy needs young men like these. They are not habitual skates; they give the definite impression of being future leaders. I think their actions serve to confirm the excellence of good naval training. What a shame to give them the wrong impression of life in the fleet before they even serve their first commission.' He paused a moment.

'Will that be all, sir?' Petty Officer Hancock rose to his feet as he spoke. The Lieutenant's words had gone completely over his head.

'Sit down Petty Officer Hancock,' Lieutenant Forrester ordered, a distinct edge in his tone of voice as he continued purposefully. 'I can see I am going to have to spell it out for you. Have you ever stopped to consider how bitter a young man becomes when he finds himself at the First Lieutenant's table for a paltry, very minor offence that could have been effectively dealt with by giving a sound bollocking? Have you ever considered what the First Lieutenant may think, having to support you at the defaulter's table very often; in fact most often,' he emphasised, 'for a piddling thing that only in its most remote consideration could be said to be "against the good order of naval discipline".'

The Petty Officer had never paused to think such a thought, not ever. The look of total incredulity that gradually spread across his face as his boss laid it on the line confirmed what many of his peers said about his leadership qualities behind his back: 'he leads from behind with the overbearing attitude of one who uses Queens Regulations and Admiralty Instructions to bolster his own ineptitude.'

All of his men on the Top Part of Ship feared and despised him; they worked willingly under oppression. As one of his senior Able Seamen had been heard to grumble, 'I served on a few ships during the war, where the likes of him might disappear at a convenient opportunity!' This statement summed up the general dislike of every subordinate who had come in contact with him. Many times whispers had reached the ears of higher authority, and Lieutenant Forrester had just been delivered the most opportune moment to bring Petty Officer Hancock to account for the acidulous way in which he conducted his shipboard duties.

'That will be all PO. Think well upon what I have said.' Lieutenant Forrester turned back to the papers on his desk; a blunt indication that this meeting was over.

'Very good sir,' Petty Officer Hancock replied, his voice confirming the look of stunned acceptance on his features.

He went through the door, the stunned look set like stone in his features. He made his way to the Petty Officer's mess, the words of his superior officer ringing in his ears. Still in a daze, he poured a cup of tea, his pursed lips and black frown leaving his messmates in no doubt as to his inner feelings at that moment.

'Bloody 'ell Tony,' a messmate spoke up, using his nickname. 'What's up!? Has some bugger trooped you for a change?'

The jokily delivered statement raised a titter from the gathered mess members. Petty Officer Hancock bit back a caustic reply, and chose to ignore the quip. The barb had struck home however; he sat thoughtfully sipping his tea, whilst the buzz of mess conversation continued around him.

The faces of many of the men he had lumbered with petty charges returned awkwardly to his mind at that moment. He had never given it a thought before, but within five minutes of each other, his superior officer, and then a messmate, each in their own way, had given him cause for serious doubt. Their words left him seriously considering the real effect of his personality at that moment; the sudden realisation that he was universally disliked by all his shipmates was not an easy pill to swallow.

'Cooks to the galley!' The tannoy broke into his thoughts. Placing his cup on the table, he went to his kit locker and opened it. He changed from uniform to civilian clothes like an automaton. With his raincoat over his arm, he opened the mess door and went through. No one shouted 'cheerio', or any other words that might suggest a form of friendship, or recognition that he was leaving the mess.

'Hands to tea; libertymen fall in; free gangway is now open for senior rates!' the tannoy blared.

He closed the mess door behind him, and placed his peg in the 'out' position on the Petty Officers' leave board bolted to the mess door, and walked to the gangway. Junior Rates were lined up being inspected by the Second Officer of the Day before being allowed ashore. They would be the last to board the liberty boat.

Petty Officer Hancock, like many of the Ship's Company on this first liberty boat was 'rationed ashore' (RA). This meant that when he was in his home port, living with his wife, he was paid an allowance to feed himself ashore. This of course meant that he was not entitled to any victuals whilst on board, unless he purchased a meal. He was also paid marriage allowance in keeping with his station in life.

The PAS boat slipped its fore and aft lines and chugged the short distance across Portsmouth Harbour to 'Welcome Jetty', its first stop. It was only a short walk from here to the dockyard main gate, and the nearby bus stops.

Back on board HMS *Vanguard*, Dusty Miller and his three oppos were enjoying a mug of tea and a cheese sandwich in the dining hall.

'Christ, it's nice to relax for a moment, isn't it?' Dusty said, his mouth full of masticated cheese and bread.

'Shh…you'll wake me up from this dream,' Bogey Knight replied, closing his eyes with a dreamy expression across his rosy cheeks.

Shiner Wright looked at his watch then said, 'make the most of it Bogey, you're about to get a rude awakening.'

As if in answer the tannoy roared out, 'men under punishment muster starboard side of the Fxle.'

'Ah shit!' exclaimed Bogey. 'I was just beginning to enjoy that.'

They all gulped their tea down, leaving plate and mug on the scullery counter as they passed. Five minutes later they were all back again having been ordered to report to the duty Leading Cook.

'You two – scullery,' he ordered Dusty and Shiner. 'You two in the galley, get tomorrow's spuds done,' he ordered Wiggy and Bogey.

Wiggy Bennett and Bogey Knight joined the regular galley party taking the eyes out of potatoes that had been through a machine that rubbed the skins off by rotating the potatoes in a drum that had a rough lining. The four of them were quicker than the drum could peel, so whilst waiting they peeled and quartered the potatoes by hand. All work was finished by 1800 hours, so the duty chef rewarded them all with a pot of tea and a few ship's biscuits each. 'Don't look so bloody surprised,' he grinned. We're not all arseoles yer know, just wash yer 'ands and yer all first in line for supper.'

'Don't we have to get into night clothing first?' Wiggy Bennett asked, ever cautious.

'Nah! The Duty Po knows yer under pun, only a real shitouse like 'ancock forces the issue,' the cook answered with a wide grin.

The four pals looked at each other, each in turn breaking into a grin at the up front style of the Leading Cook.

'Yes! Don't we know it,' Wiggy said sourly. 'It is that man's hostility that puts us all where we stand at this moment…the bastard,' he added with uncharacteristic venom.

The Leading Cook gave him a quick glance. Wiggy's well schooled accent often invited such a response.

'Hands to supper, men under punishment secure,' the tannoy spoke pleasantly.

'Off you go!' The Leading Cook shooed them away, shepherding them to the front of the queue.

An hour and a half later, they were all sitting at the end of a messdeck table playing 'Nomination Whist.' They had all bathed, and carried out their immediate 'dhobying' needs, e.g. underpants, vest and socks, a daily habit common to all sailors. They were now dressed in night clothing which consisted of blue trousers from their number two suit, a clean white front and 'flip flops' the latter being allowed below decks in the evening.

By 2130 hours some of the mess members were slinging their hammocks. The best slinging positions belonged to the Leading Hand of the mess, and then senior Able Seamen in descending order. These were usually in positions where the hammock could be slung at any time without causing hindrance to the remainder of the mess, such as over messdeck tables. The four new members found themselves slinging their hammocks next to and along the passageway; the least favourable positions. As yet the four Ordinary Seamen had not had the chance to acquire a 'stretcher', this being a slat of wood with a notch cut in each end to place between the two outer 'nettles' of 'mackerel line' from which the main body of the hammock was suspended. This stretcher not only gave the pillow a higher position, but also prevented the hammock from hugging the user too closely. Many old salts customised this prize possession with different styles of ropework, indicating the experience of the owner elaborately.

The four new lads had never slept in a ship's company messdeck before, even though all their sea training had included use of the hammock. Quite naturally the personalisation of this important part of a sailor's kit is not included in sea training, so watching the actions of their new messmates provided an interesting addition to that part of a sailor's life that does not appear in the training manual.

'Christ! I'm glad to see today over,' Wiggy Bennett murmured as he swung from the hammock bar, and plopped into his hammock. Muffled replies from the other three hammocks confirmed that the feeling was mutual.

2

KEEP YOUR PLACE AS AN 'O.D.'

The four young servicemen had first met on 5th November 1956 when sixteen of them were formed into a class to be kitted out in HMS *Victory* Royal Naval Barracks Portsmouth (now HMS *Nelson*). Each of them had become eighteen years of age during the second half of 1956. Not unusually for naval entrants at this time, they had joined the navy to escape call-up papers for the army. Although Donald Bennett was the only one who could boast a naval ancestor who had served in the Royal Navy during the nineteenth century, all four had discovered at an early age that they had a yen for the sort of adventure that the navy could provide. Another dimension was added to this preference when the Suez problem erupted, and very quickly became classified as a war. The idea of being dressed in khaki and with no say in the matter becoming a number rather than a name, did not fit in with their individual ideas of a more selective service, as appealing as it may be to some. The four of them had discovered during group conversations that all of them had 'hot footed' it to their nearest recruitment office and signed nine years of their young lives away at the stroke of a pen.

Peter Miller was a Welsh lad, born in 1938 in the town of Welshpool. Having left school at fifteen years of age, his father had found him a job with a local firm of Carpenters and Joiners. He was taken on as an apprentice, so could quite easily have applied for deferral of his national service until his apprenticeship was completed.

It was no secret in the family that young Peter had strong thoughts on the navy. Many times he had pestered his Mum and Dad to sign the necessary papers to allow him to join the navy as a Boy Seaman. His Mum and Dad had resisted his appeals strongly, advising him to 'get a trade under your belt first'. Unfortunately for his parents, young Peter viewed life in civilian employment as sheer drudgery. He was a hard working lad; in his mind was but one dream, and adventure was the key word in that dream.

On the Monday after his eighteenth birthday, he had taken a day off work without his parents' knowledge, and visited the navy recruitment office in Shrewsbury. He took his first steps towards self determination with no qualms whatsoever. He was eighteen and the world was his oyster. His young mind had not yet considered the mastery of his destiny, but therein lay the appeal.

On the night before he left Welshpool for the main medical in Birmingham, he had a night out with his Mum and Dad and his pals from his local Judo Club. His girlfriend could not forgive him for what he had done, so did not put in an appearance. When asked of her whereabouts he shrugged resignedly, and said bluntly, 'she ditched me!' Two days later his adventure began when his party was ushered onto a train at New Street Station, Birmingham. It was then that he met Ronald Knight and Donald Bennett.

Arthur Wright had been apprenticed to a plumber. He too suffered the same desires as his future friend Peter Miller. The need for adventure; the need to establish his own future, in his own way. He just had to get out in the world, he was determined that that was where his destiny lay. Even a large bustling city like Sheffield with its various attractions could not hold him. His apprenticeship could have delayed his call-up, but the urge was in him, and he was compelled by his very nature to follow where his youthful dream took him. Perhaps, of all the four friends, Arthur was the one more likely to act on impulse. He was blessed with an outgoing nature and did not always heed the advice of his elders. They, like all parents watching their son throw away a worthwhile career to disappear into the unknown, were forced to react with strong advice. His mother in particular was heartbroken; she loved the little scamp who was her son dearly. The thought of him entering a service with all the inherent dangers of a life at sea, when he could have achieved a life of relative stability in his home city mortified her, but even her red-eyed pleas failed to divert Arthur from his destiny. His father was more circumspect. 'He's eighteen,' he said with a resigned nod of the head. 'We can't stand in his way.' Even the appeals of a girlfriend who seriously loved him were soothed by the words of this charmer, who quite honestly had never considered love beyond its capacity to provide for his immediate needs as a virile young man. In his final frantic last moments with this doting girl he promised faithfully to write every day, but the excitement of his pending adventure made his words sound unconvincing, and his perceptive girlfriend knew it. She bade him farewell the following day with all the passion of a lover, knowing in her heart that this fickle young man was disappearing from her life forever. Time alone would heal her sense of loss, and experience would guide her to a more stable romance, but this impulsive young man who had been her first lover would occupy a portion of her mind until the day she died.

Ronald Knight was the son of a tenant farmer. His whole life to date had been divided between the law of the land, which on one hand insisted that a portion of five days of every week of a lad's young life must be spent acquiring knowledge in the properly appointed place. On the other hand, the practical law of the land insisted that the requirements of domestic animals were a seven-day-a-week commitment. Being the son of farming stock was a full time job in itself. He often admitted to his friends that he 'could not wait to get away from this humdrum wedded-to-the-land existence fast enough.' All his close associates were aware of his intention to join the navy, although his parents were blissfully unaware of his desires; such was the intensity of a fourteen-hour day job on the land, idle chatter was not encouraged.

Ronald would later boast to his new friends, 'On the 28th of September I became eighteen years of age. By two o'clock of that very same day I walked out of Birmingham recruiting office a committed man.'

This, in truth, was exactly what happened. He faced his astounded parents with the news and immediately bade them farewell. 'The sad look of acceptance in their faces hit me like a bombshell. I was left with the feeling that they knew this day would come, and whilst I couldn't wait for it to come; they were dreading its arrival,' he added, then said wistfully, 'for the first time in my life I felt a real shithouse.'

Ronald had been brought up to be a well-behaved, hard-working country lad and member of the family, and hence the society that surrounded their country existence. He had rewarded his family by working for little more than a roof over his head, and a well spread table at every mealtime. His only break every week was to play rugby for his local town of Bridgenorth, and on completion of that he still had to help with evening milking; only then was a pound note slipped into his hand to reward him for a week's work. This small payment did allow him to spend a night out with his rugby mates, but very little else. In a very short time now, the new job that he had signed nine years of his young life away for would provide him with the princely sum of four pounds nineteen shillings per week all found, riches beyond his wildest dreams.

His only romantic involvement to date was with the daughter of a nearby tenant farmer. They had been pupils at the local primary, and then the local secondary modern, and for years had walked the same path together to and from school. To any onlooker it may have seemed obvious that such long term familiarity would develop into something warmer as nature forced their young bodies to realise the real reason for human existence. The furtive meetings on country lanes and behind hedges when the day's labours were completed for both of them drew them inseparably together in a pact of mutual loyalty to each other. Both knew, even at this young age that their futures were bound in an unbreakable union that would survive the separations of the near future. They had planned this moment, and kept it away from their respective families, even to the point of forming marriage plans, to be carried out when the time was right.

That's Life in a Blue Suit

Ronald Knight had no doubts as he left his parents' home, he had shrugged off the feeling that they would actually miss him, he now had two people to think of, and this was the start of their united dream. What he did not know as he boarded the train for London with his new friends was that the planned future would be joined by a very demanding additional responsibility within the next eight months.

Donald Wilfred Bennett's life was in complete contrast to the three who would become his best buddies. He was the son of a reasonably prestigious solicitor whose obvious wishes were that his son Donald would provide the fourth name on the brass plaque that boasted the profession of those beyond the wall it was mounted on. The very idea of this beautiful plaque bearing the names in order of seniority of this partnership was his dream for the future: Bennett, Thoroughgood, Morton and Bennett. The very thought of it filled his modest ego with pride. His intentions for his son became tied into his personal desire for the future of the partnership, and were tantamount to an obsession.

Donald had stayed in Grammar School until the summer holidays of 1956. He had recently completed 'A' levels in English Language, Mathematics, and European History; added to the six subjects that he previously gained at 'Ordinary Level', his lowest being a 'C' in Biology, made Donald Bennett a sure candidate for a university position.

On 20th July 1956 however, whilst celebrating his eighteenth birthday at a lavish party paid for by his doting parents, he hit them with the bombshell 'that he had that very day signed the papers that would very shortly gain him membership to that august band of heroes called collectively "the Royal Navy".'

'You should have seen their puce faces,' he had later told his new friends. 'It ruined the party for my parents sadly, but everybody else had a ball, it was a wonderful evening, got my leg over later, and did not arrive back home until twelve the following day. Poor parents were in an awful state, they could just not understand that I was so dreadfully fed up with the awful stiffness of such a predictable existence. I just had to get out, and get a life, do something different, become a man in my own right. The navy seemed to offer that very thing.'

When asked why he had not enlisted as an officer candidate; either 'Upper Yardman,' or straight in as a 'Midshipman', he would answer, 'not just yet old chap, I have a great desire to live the dreams of my childhood: *Boys Own*, Horatio Hornblower, Lord Nelson and all that, but I want to do it from the lower deck upwards; I'm sure no one will deny me that privilege. Anyway, my Great Grandfather was an old Able Seaman in 1875, and we have this ancient sepia photograph of him in the uniform of the time hanging over the mantelpiece in the parlour. I have this desire to at least emulate the old boy to honour his existence.'

━ • ━

'Call the hands, call the hands, call the hands! Wakey Wakey Wakey! Rise and shine! Hands off cocks on socks!' The loud voice of the Quartermaster of the morning watch roared out over the tannoy, adding, 'men under punishment muster at the gangway.'

It was 0630 hours and the day had just begun for all day work hands, and that included the four new members of the ship's company. Their first lesson of the day was the reaction of some of the older hands to the disturbing noise that had just emanated from the tannoy. Leading Seaman Wilson leapt out of his hammock immediately, whilst one senior Able Seaman hurled a flip flop at the tannoy. Another old hand cursed the Quartermaster vehemently, referring to the doubtful legitimacy of his forebears. Others found the reactions of a couple of their messmates amusing, and it was these messmates that set the general tone of early morning on a naval messdeck. Good natured badinage was the order of the day, those who had an axe to grind, or started the day wrapped up in their own shells were generally ignored; that is unless their lack of even temperedness overflowed into someone else's airspace. On these occasions the culprit would be told to 'fuck off and sleep in the tiller flat, if that's yer bloody attitude!'

On the whole though, the messdeck of the 1950s was a haven of good humour; most laughed at the sourness of others and 'took the piss' out of them unmercifully as they folded their hammocks into orderly lumps, then lashed them up with the appropriate number of marlin hitches that suited them. They weren't under training now so the odd extra marlin hitch made for a tighter lump.

The queue for breakfast on this second day aboard for the four new lads was fifty bodies long by the time 'hands to breakfast' was piped, and after devouring a tasty spithead pheasant, and a few slices of toast, everybody was ready to attack whatever the day may bring.

Leading Seaman Wilson took the four lads to one side, and asked them, 'Were you given your station cards yesterday?'

They all shook their heads.

'Right!' he said, 'All of you lot fall in when both watches is piped, and I'll get Petty Officer Hancock to let you have time off to collect them at 0-nine-dubs. You can't draw a pot and one from the paint shop without yer station card to leave as security.' He paused for a second. 'Also, check the details on yer ship's company card complies with the details on the watch and station bill.' He paused again. 'Have yer read daily orders yet?' He looked at them enquiringly, instantly realising by the blank stares that they had not. His face took on a slightly more serious expression. 'It's very important that you read daily orders before the day begins; there may just be something in them that includes you.' His face turned to stone. 'If you are absent from place of duty, you will find yourself deep in the shit,' he uttered sternly, then jerked his thumb at the mess notice board. 'There they are, read and inwardly digest NOW, before both watches is piped.'

The four lads crowded round the notice board as if their very lives depended upon it, the action bringing a titter from the more experienced mess members. They had watched with interest as the Leading Hand started his day by ensuring that his new charges got off on the right foot. His job was one that consistently saw good conduct badges and hooks disappear off a wearer's arm as a punishment for not being on top of the job.

'Both watches hoe!' The Chief Boatswain's Mate carried out his morning routine with relish. It was the highpoint of his day on this ship that would never see seatime under its own power again. Ten minutes later the tedium of keeping a grey funnel line ship spick and span was under way. Brightwork had to be polished every day, and you could see your reflection in the highly polished pussers grey paint that coated the bottom part of the superstructure, the other side of which was the NATO conference room.

'Show 'em 'ow to polish posh paintwork 'ooky,' Petty Officer Hancock ordered his Leading Hand.

'Aye aye PO,' Leading Seaman Wilson answered, and then turning to his charges said, 'right, let's get yuh fixed up with the cleaning gear.'

Five minutes later he stood before the four lads with a cleaning cloth draped over the index finger of his right hand, a tin of cleaning paste and a two gallon bucket of water at his feet.

'Now cast yer eyes along this length of superstructure,' he said, ignoring the suppressed mirth on the faces in front of him. 'You'll see that there's no need to throw water all over it and scrub it all, just look for the rust streaks, dab yer cloth in the water and then in the cleaning paste, and then delicately remove the rust streak only. ''Ave yer got that?' he asked turning to them after he had demonstrated.

'Yes hooky!' they all replied together, their faces still showing the effort of suppressing a damn good laugh.

'Right get on with it then, and if yer unsure about anything, I'm in the top locker compartment.'

The four oppos looked at the back of the disappearing Leading Hand, and as his backside reached the top of the screen ladder, their faces broke into wide grins as they relaxed their posture.

'Not very exciting stuff this, is it?' Wiggy Bennett said as he bent over the bucket to wet his cloth.

'Better than pickin' brussels sprouts on a frosty morning, I can tell you,' Bogey voiced his opinion with a definite air of preference.

'Oh Bogey! Please do spare us these retorts that describe earthy hardships, they are just as boring as staring at this sodding paintwork.'

'You chose the bloody navy...put up with it.'

'No, I fancy something a bit more exciting than this,' Wiggy replied, not in the least perturbed by Bogey's terseness. 'I think I am going to apply for a diving course.'

'WHAT!?' the other three retorted, utter surprise evident in their wide eyed retaliation. Then Dusty Miller who had recovered first said, 'but you didn't pass your swimming test at HMS *Raleigh*, you could hardly complete half a length in your overalls... so how can you become a diver?'

Wiggy gave them all a pained look before replying, 'what is the relationship between not being practiced enough to swim a long way on the surface of the water in overalls, and working underwater breathing compressed air?' The reply in the form of a question caused them all to pause in their work. Dusty looked at Bogey as if to say, 'can you answer that'. Finally Shiner Wright broke the momentary impasse.

'You're absolutely right, Wiggy,' he said supportively. 'You can swim, so all you need is a bit of practice in a pool to build up your stamina, and improve your breathing technique. What say you and I visit the navy pool at Pitt Street? Swimming is my sport so I can give you a hand and get a bit of swimming in myself at the same time.'

Wiggy's face brightened visibly, not given to strong language yet, he replied simply, 'what a flipping good idea Shiner, I will take your offer up gladly.'

The presence of Petty Officer Hancock broke the conversation up abruptly. 'Off you go,' he ordered. 'Just put yer cleaning gear in that washdeck locker, it'll be there when yer get back.'

'Something's changed!' Wiggy whispered as they walked along the Burma Way. 'Did you notice his attitude? He was almost polite in giving that order.'

'Don't be too eager to give 'im a good name,' Shiner whispered in reply. ''E's still a basterd at heart.'

'No, Shiner,' Dusty broke in. 'I noticed a change in attitude. A man like 'im doesn't change from out and out basterd to youth leader overnight. I think somebody has whispered in his ear, probably something to do with the Skipper of Cambridge writing in our docs. Think how he would look in this man's navy if we slapped in to buy ourselves out, and he was known as the cause, plus all of us were within four marks of the top qualifier at Cambridge.'

'I never thought of it that way,' Shiner conceded as they reached the Regulating Office door.

'Excuse me RPO,' Wiggy said as they walked through the door, then waited politely until the Regulating Petty Officer acknowledged their presence. 'We were told to report here this morning to collect our station cards and ship's company cards.'

'End desk, yuh know where it is,' came the reply, accompanied by a terse nod.

Wiggy led the way to the end desk, and then they all waited for the Leading Hand to finish writing on a huge sheet fixed to an even bigger notice board on the bulkhead facing them. Wiggy noticed at a glance that all details were applied to this large sheet lightly in pencil.

'Ah! The four new blokes,' the Leading Hand greeted them, throwing two green cards and two red cards on the counter in front of them. As they picked up the cards, he tossed four ship's company cards onto the counter. 'Check all the details on the watch and station bill outside on the notice board, and if there are any differences tell me immediately, or sooner, and don't worry about the sections with a line drawn through them, this ship ain't going to war, ever,' he emphasised with a knowledgeable air.

They walked out into the passageway and studied the huge broadsheet, searching for their names. Wiggy passed a red card each to Dusty and Shiner, who found themselves to have been put in the first part of port watch. He and Bogey were in the first part of starboard watch so had green cards, the colours being representative of the port navigation lantern which gave off a red light, and the green of the starboard navigation lantern.

'Here we are!' Dusty pointed to the part of the big sheet marked 'Top Part of Ship', and the section marked 'First Part of Port Watch'. 'It doesn't tell us anything we don't already know does it,' Dusty went on, his tone tinged with disappointment.

'No old boy it does not,' replied Wiggy. 'But then, we are not in the real fighting navy yet, are we?'

His voice also had an air of disappointment about it, as he viewed the lines drawn through the 'Battle Stations' part of the sheet. The dreams of his boyhood, the vision he had of himself serving aboard a fully commissioned Battleship policing the seas of the world, never to become a reality. 'Well, everything seems to be in order,' he added resignedly. 'I suppose we had better return to our high priority job of ship's husbandry,' his eyes flicked upwards scornfully as he spoke his mind.

'Hang on a minute!' Dusty's words made them stop expectantly, all eyes turned to him enquiringly. 'We don't know which part of watch is duty today,' he said, his eyes already scanning the huge notice board for the Daily Orders.

'Here they are,' shouted Shiner, the index finger of his right hand stabbing at the far end of the board. 'Second part of starboard watch,' said Shiner, his finger tracing the words on the daily orders sheet. 'When does that make us duty?' He turned to his three pals with brow creased. Nobody answered immediately.

'We...ell,' said Wiggy thoughtfully. 'If this ship follows normal routine, the duty watch sequence in harbour is first of starboard, first of port, second of starboard, second of port.'

'So that makes second of port duty tomorrow, Wednesday?' Bogey interrupted, keen to show he had paid attention, and looking at Wiggy for confirmation as he spoke.

'And we will be duty on Thursday,' Wiggy assured him. 'You two will be duty on Friday,' he went on, turning to Dusty and Shiner, then added with a grin, 'That makes us all free on Saturday night, anyone for a run ashore?'

'Ah shite, blank week!' Shiner replied. 'I'm as broke as a fart, just enough for goffers.'

'Don't worry mate, you can borrow a quid off me until payday, it's the least I can do for my new swimming coach,' Wiggy offered good-naturedly, his face wearing a broad grin.

With that last remark brightening up the day, they returned to their buckets and cloths.

2030 hours on Thursday evening found the four pals putting the finishing touches to their kits, which were neatly laid out in kit muster order on their spare hammocks.

Leading Seaman Wilson was fussing over them like an old hen, because of course the Lieutenant did not want to find any fault. Should he find a glaring fault he would have no option but to order a re-muster. Many smaller items had to be folded to the size of a navy paybook, and it was usually these items that a fussy inspecting officer would select as being too big or too small; anything to further harass a young sailor who had truly done his best. Leading Seaman Wilson of course was wise to all the nuances of a kit muster that reach beyond just laying it out clean and tidily. To this end it was almost comic opera watching him going from man to man, and back again, measuring, adjusting, advising, and generally instilling in his subordinates an attention to detail for which the navy is famous.

Night rounds started at the forrard end of the ship, and as the Quartermaster piped 'stand by for rounds, men under punishment and stoppage of leave muster at the gangway,' the Officer of the Day glanced at the miscreants who had been standing waiting to fall in. His Petty Officer of the Day called them to attention, reporting them 'present and correct', and the Officer of the Day walked the length of the stony faced line ordering his Petty Officer to 'dismiss men under punishment Petty Officer Hargreaves,' as he stepped through the screen door into the superstructure preceded by the bosun's mate warning everyone that night rounds were approaching by blowing a straight blast on his 'bosun's call'.

As the night rounds party neared five mess, Leading Seaman Wilson reported his mess ready for rounds, then stood by each of the four lads' kits as Lieutenant Forester's keen eye swept over each man's kit in turn. He knew it was the strict supervision of the Leading Hand that had created this excellent layout, and showed his appreciation for not having to criticise, by saying, 'fine turn out Leading Seaman Wilson. Well done…carry on!'

As the rounds party disappeared to the fading blast of the Bosun's Mate's call, Shiner looked from the Leading Hand to his pals and just had to say, 'Is that it then, we spend all that fuckin' time tartin' this lot up, and it's all over in minutes.'

Leading Seaman Wilson grinned at his subordinate's expression. 'Would you rather he had have ordered a re-muster tomorrow night then?'

Shiner's expression changed instantly. 'No fuckin' fear!' he answered grinning back at his mates as they enjoyed this moment.

'Thank God for that!' Wiggy sighed loudly. 'All the bloody trouble that we stumbled into on Monday is behind us. I'll tell you what though; this little episode has taught me one very valuable lesson. Never drop your guard when you are a lowly

Ordinary Seaman. Bearing the brunt of some of our superiors' natural sourness could really turn one against this man's navy, especially when a swift bollocking would have done the job in the first place.'

'So you won't be slapping in to buy yourself out then?'

Wiggy looked at his mate Bogey and grinned as he said, 'No Bogey my old pal, I think I'll give them another chance.'

'I bet you lot are ready for a can of beer now,' Leading Seaman Wilson said, a knowing smile spreading across his face.

'I think we've bloody well earned it hooky,' Dusty answered, piling kit on his right arm to return it to his locker.

'Leave yer cases out here till termorrer then, I'll open the baggage store first thing in the morning.'

The sound of cans of beer being punctured mingled with the ambient noise of the messdeck.

'Bloody 'ell I'm enjoying this!' Bogey smacked his lips noisily as he crushed his first empty can between sausage-like fingers. His messmates laughed at his greedily expressed confession, accompanied by the loud noise of satisfaction. He belched loudly to give added effect, and gained a frown from Wiggy for his bad manners. It was no secret; Bogey loved his beer, and had the reputation of being something of a 'pisshead' amongst his peers. He was always the only one standing after a good session and still reasonably sober; this gave added kudos to his already substantial reputation.

'Take your time Bogey,' Wiggy advised. 'The gangway's closed and you can't get ashore for any more.'

'Suppose I'll just 'ave ter 'ang on till shaturday night then, won't I?' Bogey grinned, slurring his accent theatrically.

'I'm bloody glad tuh see this last four days over,' Shiner said with a fervent edge to his voice, bringing the conversation back to the reality of their situation.

His pals all nodded vigorously, leaving Wiggy to air his feelings on the matter. 'I'll never be caught like that again, I will never put myself in a position where a turd like that man Hancock can express his distaste for me by using the authority that in my opinion was wrongly invested in him. Arseholes like him should never be given superiority over anyone.'

They looked at the determined set of his features. 'Sounds as if yer mean it Wiggy,' Dusty said, looking at his oppo.

'As I said previously: never drop your guard if you are a lowly Ordinary Seaman,' Wiggy replied, his face holding its serious expression. 'I now know that the real navy is geared up in such a way as to keep you constantly on your toes. So be it! If that's what makes one a good sailor, it must be a tried and tested method, maybe that is why we are part of the best navy in the world.'

'Christ Wiggy, yer beginning to sound like a bloody recruiting poster,' Shiner piped up, a broad grin stretching his mouth.

'Maybe I am Shiner, but the way I see it, I can either end up as a right 'Jack me tickler paper' or I can meet it head on and go for it, and have a good career; or just take the easy way out and piddle along just keeping my nose clean. I would suggest that you, my hearties, do the same, and make this an interesting and worthwhile career. We have another eight years to do, why not make it a worthwhile eight years.'

Leading Seaman Wilson and Slinger Woods could not help but overhear Wiggy's well spoken views and looked at each other knowingly. Slinger mouthed silently at the Leading Hand of the mess, 'officer material.'

On Friday morning after both watches of the hands had been dispersed to parts of ship, Dusty and Wiggy found themselves part of a four-man working party under the charge of Leading Seaman Wilson. The ship still carried gunnery spares for her eight 5.25 inch gun mountings, four each side of the superstructure. This was known as the ship's secondary armament, the 'Main Armament' being her four twin fifteen inch turrets, two forrard and two aft.

'Right lads,' Leading Seaman Wilson started a brief outline of the job. 'We've got ter get a Newton Ridley hydraulic pump and its electrical drive motor from the gunners store on 3C deck, up to the deck 'ere and onto a boat from Priddy's Hard Armament depot. They'll be in two boxes so shouldn't be too 'ard ter sling.' He turned to Dusty and Wiggy. 'Now I want you two to pay particular attention to the safety side of the job; I know you 'ave been taught all the seamanship side of the job, but this'll be the first time you'll 'ave bin involved in a slingin' job on a ship. Just don't do anything unless I tell you, but watch everythin' closely.' He paused to ensure that his little lecture had sunk in. He was met by two pairs of eyes glowing with youthful enthusiasm, and two heads that nodded in unison saying eagerly, 'Aye aye hooky.'

The Leading Hand turned to one of the two Able Seamen in his work party. 'Smudge, you get a two inch sling from the locker, and I'll bugger off and draw the key. Slinger you get a two fold purchase and a couple of heaving lines too.'

The Able Seaman called 'Smudge', alias Able Seaman Roger Smith sauntered off with a surly expression clouding his face followed by Able Seaman David Woods, alias Slinger. Dusty and Wiggy fell in behind the two experienced seamen and followed them to the 'Top Locker'. 'Ere y'ar, Wiggy, grab this block and tackle,' said Slinger pleasantly, handing the equipment through the locker door. They all trudged off across the deck to the ladder leading down to the screen door into the superstructure. In front of them all Smudge Smith suddenly turned round and threw the rope sling at Dusty. 'Ere O.D., you carry this barsterd,' he sneered scornfully.

Dusty was momentarily taken aback by the inflammatory statement. He caught the rope sling, and growled, 'the name's Miller, and watch who you're throwing things at!'

'Oh yeah, O.D., and what are yuh going ter do abaht it, fancy yer chances on the fxle d'yer?'

Smith walked right up into Dusty's face as he spoke. Dusty flinched in readiness as the foul stench of last night's beer and this morning's tobacco reached his nostrils. He stared defiantly into the eyes of the aggressor just as Slinger Wood's arm shot between them. 'Lay off Smudge,' he yelled. 'What the fuck's up with yuh man, picking an unnecessary fight right 'ere on the upper scupper, are yer still pissed or something?' He hauled Smith roughly away from Dusty as he spoke.

'Ah! The cocky barsterd needs teachin' a lesson, standin' there smug and proper while I am ordered to get the fuckin' sling,' Smith hissed nastily, then added, 'e needs a fuckin lesson in respect, 'e needs teachin' 'ow ter keep 'is place as a fuckin' O.D.'

Able Seaman or no, this was getting a bit too much for Dusty, his arms shot out striking Smith sharply in the chest. Slinger Woods caught Smith in his arms before he fell to the deck under the impetus of the shove. 'Hey! Hey now, that's enough!' he yelled, hanging on to the writhing man in his arms. Wiggy had walked up to Dusty and laid a hand on his shoulder. 'Come on Dusty,' he said. 'Leave it at that before it gets out of hand.'

Dusty backed off at the advice of his friend, but his dander was up, and the anger showed ripe in his face. His eyes glowed, indicating he was not satisfied with the outcome of this needless provocation. Able Seaman Smith had made himself an enemy. Dusty was an unknown quantity to the Able Seaman, but not to his pal Wiggy. Only he of the group had witnessed Dusty's well executed defence of himself in the compulsory 'Milling Contest' at HMS *Raleigh* during training. It had taken him twenty seconds of the one minute bout to totally demolish a buff stoker of similar size. Wiggy himself had taken the full minute, but it was his arm that the POPTI had raised immediately the sound of the bell indicated the end of this unusual ordeal.

'Ease off now Dusty,' Slinger Woods ordered, raising one hand from his grip on Smith, and pressing his palm flat on Dusty's chest.

Dusty obeyed instantly, whipping his eyes away from Smith's glowering face, and turning his back on him. His sensible move allowed the party to make their way to 3C port flat without drawing the attention of any passing crew members. Smith sat down on the hatch cover and stared angrily at the deck, his thoughts full of revenge for this affront by an Ordinary Seaman.

The two of them were of similar height and weight, around five foot eight, and about 175 lbs. Both of them had the physique of a good middleweight, and it had just been proved that neither of them would back down, although Dusty did have the good sense to obey a directly given order. His strict Judo training had also taught him restraint, so he would not use that ability unless forced to. His experiences as a young freestyle wrestler though was a different thing altogether. If Smith attacked him again, the aggressor could find himself at a distinct disadvantage.

Able Seaman Smith on the other hand, came from the rougher area of Rotherhithe, London. He had been brought up to believe that everyone from the north of the river Thames was a foreigner. The result of these common differences was usually compounded on a Saturday night by a good old street punch-up. His was a tough area that provided a tough upbringing, and hence his toughness was a result of weekend gang warfare. Politeness, nor any other overt correctness were not in his blood; revenge, however, was, so even in this well disciplined arena, the law of the streets had just raised its ugly head.

Wiggy kept Dusty at the forrard end of the Gunners Store flat, whilst Slinger Woods stood beside Smith in such a way as to block the protagonists from each other's field of view. Ten minutes later Leading Seaman Wilson appeared jangling a set of keys in the fingers of his left hand.

'What's up?' he asked, a puzzled look creasing his face as he looked from one group to the other. 'Somebody shit themselves!' He walked over to the hatch and inserted the key into the large lock. 'Shift yer arse Smudge, and get those clips undone,' he ordered tersely when Smith made no move to ease over.

Slinger Woods jumped to and gave Smith a hand with the hatch clips then they both grasped the lip of the hatch and lifted it ninety degrees until it clicked into its retaining clip. This done they inserted a drop nosed pin to ensure the hatch stayed safely in its upright position with absolutely no chance of being accidentally loosened.

'Come 'ere you two,' Leading Seaman Wilson ordered, beckoning Dusty and Wiggy to his side. 'This is where you start to become real sailors. Rig that block and tackle from that eyeplate,' he beckoned to the deckhead above the hatch. He watched as the hook of the tackle slid through the large metal eyebolt then said, 'now, what do we do to make sure that the hook of the tackle does not jump out of the eyebolt?'

'Put a mouzing around the hook of the top block,' Dusty replied, unable to avoid eye contact with Smith as he looked at the Leading Hand. The eyes that met his held the message, 'just give me the chance O.D. and I'll have you!'

Leading Seaman Wilson reached down to the lanyard that his 'pussers dirk' hung from and unhooked a length of one eighth inch diameter seizing wire specially made for the purposes of 'mousing' any hook to close of the jaw of the hook as an added safety measure.

'Here,' he said to Dusty with a smile. 'You mouze that hook.' He turned to Able Seaman Smith saying, 'just watch him, and then inspect his work, if he gets it wrong he must do it again...come on you two,' he beckoned Slinger and Wiggy, 'we'll go down and pull the boxes to the bottom of the hatch while they're doing that.'

They disappeared down the hatch to the Gunners Store. Dusty waited until the last head had gone below the hatch combing, and then straddled the open space with one foot on either side.

He had already bent the seizing wire double, so reached up and passed the two ends around the back of the hook, and then through the loop of the wire. He had just pulled it tight when Smith saw his opportunity with no one else near. He just could not control himself any longer. 'Gimme that fuckin' seizing wire arseole, that's a job for an Able Seaman,' he hissed savagely, snatching at Dusty's wrist. Dusty lost his balance momentarily, and cracked his head on the bulkhead as he overbalanced trying to save himself. His hat went flying through the open hatch bouncing off the Leading Hand standing right underneath at that moment. Dusty found his feet, and quickly corrected his balance, his face white, eyes glaring madly. He lunged at Smith carrying him six foot forward with the force of his momentum. Smith twisted around and threw a punch which grazed along Dusty's right ear reddening it instantly. Stinging from his knock on the head, and now smarting from the effect of the glancing blow, he did not allow Smith to fully regain his balance. He seized Smith's right fist in his left hand and with his right hand pushed Smith's elbow up just as they hit the deck with a crunch. Smith was instantly winded, and Dusty took full advantage of the situation, and really applied the pressure to Smith's right arm, which now took the form of an inverted 'V' down the side of his head, with his fist somewhere in the vicinity of his right shoulder blade. Smith gasped for air, and then screamed hoarsely as the pain from his distorted right arm racked through him.

Leading Seaman Wilson's head appeared above the hatch combing. 'What the fuck's goin' on 'ere?' He scrambled towards the two men writhing on the deck. The whole section of the ship echoed to the howls of pain mingled with frustrated anger as Smith tried to wriggle and squirm his way free of Dusty's determined wrestling hold. Wiggy and Slinger Woods joined the Leading Hand's attempts to separate the pair; but while there was still madness in the man below him, there was no way Dusty was going to release his assailant.

'Let the fuckers be!' Leading Seaman Wilson walked from the fray, lips pursed. Wiggy and Slinger stood back urging the two to 'give up.'

'Dusty,' Wiggy yelled into his friend's ear. 'Hooky Wilson is ringing for help, come on man, you will be up to your neck in it.'

'Nope,' Dusty gasped. 'I'm not letting this mad basterd up while there's still fight in 'im.'

Wiggy threw his arms in the air in worried exasperation. He envisaged all sorts of character assassinating punishments that his oppo would undergo, just for reacting physically to obsessive provocation.

Leading Seaman Wilson pulled out the handset of the sound powered telephone fitting bolted to the bulkhead. He flicked the selector switch marked HQ1 which would get him the Regulating Office in its new peacetime capacity as a group of administrative offices. He wound savagely on the hand generator call up handle.

'Reg Office,' a stern voice answered.

'Is that you Jim?'

The reply was affirmative.

'Get a couple of Crushers and the Duty Hands down to 3C port Gunners Flat. I've got two blokes down 'ere goin' at it 'ammer and tongs, I just can't separate 'em.'

'Tell this barsterd to get off me 'ucky,' Smith yelled.

'Okay Dusty,' the Leading Hand shouted. 'Let him up, come on now! The Crushers are comin', let's not make it look any worse when they get 'ere.'

Dusty eased back on his hold cautiously. Smith remained groaning on the deck, but made no move to continue the fight. Dusty sprang to his feet still prepared to react violently, but Smith was only concerned with getting some life back into his dead arm. Slinger Woods bent over and helped him to his feet. Venom returned to Smith's eyes as he said, 'there'll be another time O.D., and the next time you won't get a chance to use a fuckin' wrestlin' 'old!'

Leading Seaman Wilson reacted loudly to Smith's venomous statement. 'Pack it in Smudge, I don't know what the hell started this, but it ends 'ere, d'yer understand?' He stood over Smith and added, 'let's get back ter work, it's over, and I've still got ter get that pair of boxes onto the ferry for Priddy's Hard.'

The first box was on its way up when the Leading Regulators and the four duty hands of the day's duty watch came down the ladder in a rush.

'Where's the trouble Tug?' the first regulator looked around the section as he was asking the question, and then his face broke into a grin as he said, 'Ah! Come on yer cunt; don't tell me it's an exercise to check reaction times.'

'Nope!' Leading Seaman Wilson, alias Tug to his familiars, grinned back. 'Two of my lads decided to 'ave a little wrestling match. We couldn't get 'em apart; but as soon as I phoned you they came to their senses.'

The Leading Hand played down the problem purposefully, he had done what was required of him, and his men were cracking on with their job. All of them knew that the Captain would have no option but to send a proven aggressor to detention quarters for at least thirty days. DQ's at the time was run by a huge Royal Marine Sergeant famously referred to as 'Tiny'. He was renowned for doing his job thoroughly, only fools went back for a second dose. The food was sufficient but uninteresting. The work was terminally monotonous, and the physical exercise ensured that the transgressor came back to the fleet fit enough to be selected for the Olympic Games.

'I'll 'ave ter take 'em up ter see the jossman, 'avin' bin called out,' the Crusher said.

'Okay then, let's just get these two boxes through the hatch onto two deck, d'yer mind if the duty 'ands give us a lift to the gangway, I've got ter get this lot onto a ferry by 1100 hours.'

'Nah, course not!' The Crusher turned to his men. ''Ere lads, lend a hand.'

He paused a moment while the duty hands jumped to help their shipmates, then turned back to Leading Seaman Wilson. 'Right Tug, which of these is comin' with me to say "good morning" to the Jossman?' He then added as an afterthought, 'And who saw the start of it all?'

'Me, I did,' Slinger Woods stepped forward from behind Wilson, having first laid a lightly restraining hand on Wiggy's wrist. This was an instantly clever reaction on Wood's behalf. Wiggy was well spoken, and quite unintentionally he could have been blatantly honest and dug a hole from which Smith would have not been able to extricate himself. Slinger Woods had the lower deck experience, which would tell the truth in a completely different tone, thereby leaving the disciplinary branch alone to sort out the maliciousness of the moment or otherwise. Everyone knew this, and it was very rarely that the authorities did not extract the total guilt of an offender. The whole truth had a habit of rising to the surface; hence justice was always seen to be done.

The Leading Regulator waved a set of naval manacles in front of them both. 'I don't want to 'ave ter put these on,' he said firmly, but with just enough menace in his voice to make the possibility distinctly clear.

'Big punch up then?' the RPO called Jim asked as they passed his desk on the way to the Master at Arms office which was at the far end of the compartment.

'Nah, just a scuffle by all accounts,' the Leading Regulator answered.

'Wait there,' he ordered tersely, indicating a space by the bulkhead. Knocking on the office door, he entered as a firm voice called, 'Come in.' Ten minutes later he exited the office saying, 'In you go Woods, he wants to see you first.'

The men outside became aware of the hum of conversation from within. Smith's ears could be seen twitching as he strained to discern what was being said. A few minutes later Slinger

Woods came out of the office, his face a blank. 'Your turn Dusty,' he said, replacing his hat as he walked along the compartment and out through the door.

The buzz of conversation continued again in the office, and it was noticeable to all those outside that the Master at Arms had not raised his voice once, that meant that no one as yet was getting the benefit of his feelings on the altercation. Dusty had sat there for ten minutes politely and respectfully answering all the questions put to him.

'That will be all, Ordinary Seaman Miller, return to your part of ship, I won't need you for anything else. Ask Leading Regulator Foster to come in as you go out.'

Dusty left the office, and passed the message to the Leading Regulator. Walking along the passageway he did not know whether to be relieved or apprehensive. Where did the matter go from here? Was he in trouble up to his eyeballs? Was the talk with the Master at Arms the end of the matter?

The working party, backed up by the duty hands, was just lifting the boxed electric motor through the screen door onto the upper deck as Dusty returned. Leading Seaman Wilson raised his body from over the box saying, 'Cor flippin' 'eck, I'm getting too old for this humping shit; 'bout time my bloody PO's rate came through.' He groaned theatrically, making the pretence of using a walking stick.

'You're soon back young fellah,' he said, grinning in response to Dusty's appreciation of his theatrics. ''Ow did yer get on?'

Dusty related the main points of the questioning, and then looked at the Leading Hand quizzically. 'What happens now? Am I in the shit or not?'

'Nope,' Wilson replied. 'The Jossman would 'ave told yuh there and then if he was going to pass it on to the Jimmy…Slinger 'ere reckons it's just goin' ter be a bollockin' for Smudge,' he added, jerking his finger towards the smiling Slinger. 'Smudger acted like a cunt provoking a scrap like that. The daft basterd should know better, 'e's bin in the fuckin' navy long enough.'

'So I'm in the clear then?'

Leading Seaman Wilson looked into Dusty's unbelieving face. 'Course you are yuh daft git,' he confirmed unable to contain an assuring laugh. 'The DO will probably want to 'ave a word with you. But if the Jossman has decided in his infinite wisdom that this affair goes no further, believe me that is the end of it. The DO will only see how the incident has affected you... if at all.'

Meanwhile at the Master at Arms office, Leading Regulator Foster had assured his superior that by the time he arrived on the scene, all the men were at work again. 'They gave me the impression that this had just been a minor altercation Master,' was his finishing sentence.

'Well Foster, I think I have the picture now. Neither Woods nor Miller actually incriminated Smith while they were in front of me, but in the light of knowledge that I have acquired through our own department, I have no doubt in my mind that Smith was the instigator of this spot of trouble. Miller came over as a typical Ordinary Seaman just trying to get by from day to day without incurring anyone's displeasure. He has only been with us five days and already he has run foul of Hancock.' He raised his eyebrows meaningfully as he mentioned the Top part of Ship Petty Officer's name. 'Now he falls foul of this idiot Smith, bloody good job he is a resilient young fellow isn't it? Okay, send him in; let's get this over and done with.'

'Your turn Able Seaman Smith,' Leading Regulator Foster said, indicating the door with a backward motion of his thumb.

Smith rose to his feet slowly and sighed resignedly under his breath, 'Oh fuck! 'Ere goes nothin'.' He walked smartly into the office and stood to attention in front of the Master at Arms. The huge man was on his feet leaning slightly forward, the fingers of each hand splayed across his table, taking the weight. His size and his permanently stern features helped to make him well suited by personality for his job. He was totally aware of his status in the navy and knew full well that the thought of a confrontation with him kept all would-be skates in line during the working day. He did not have the powers of punishment, but he did have the power of decision. His fierce delivery had sent many a lad scurrying from his office fully convinced that all the fires of hell were waiting to consume his miserable body. The outcome of this psychological approach to his job was to keep down the queue for

First Lieutenant's defaulters to a huge degree. His capable way of dealing with minor infractions kept a long line of possible clients from clogging up the passage outside the Regulating Office waiting pensively to be presented to the First Lieutenant. His direct action saved a lot of unnecessary time wasting.

'Well, Able Seaman Smith,' he opened, his eyes boring into the man before him. 'So now you have to cause a punch up on my war canoe. Aren't you satisfied with the rumbles you get into ashore? Oh yes Smith,' he nodded with hooded eyes, as he noticed the flicker of surprise across Smith's face. 'We know every time you have created a war zone. It's not just the odd mouse under the eye, nor is it the odd cut around the eyebrows and cheekbones that you strut around with proudly. You may also think that getting changed into civilian clothes at Agnes Weston's hides your real occupation in life. Well it does not young man! Out there on the streets of Portsmouth and Southsea every night are some of my colleagues in civvies, and they know all about you. It is very fortunate for you that you are just a piss artist, and cannot resist a punch-up. If it was robbery, mugging, drugs, or any other scum-like offences of that nature, you would be banged up in that most notorious of all Army Prisons, Colchester, long before now.' He paused, his eyes boring into Smith, whose facial expression showed him to be dumbstruck.

'So, Able Seaman Smith, now that you know that the regulating branch has you dead to rights, I would suggest that you curb your natural tendency to have a poke at anyone who displeases you. It will also serve you well to remember that an attack on a subordinate, if proven to be delivered with the intention of causing 'Grievous Bodily Harm' also deserves a fixed time of punishment in Colchester army prison. Believe you me! Some of those Sergeants and Corporals are equally as serious about the rehabilitation of 'Hard Cases' as Tiny is in the Royal Naval Detention Quarters in Portsmouth Dockyard. Now, get out of my office before I get really angry!'

Able Seaman Smith flew out of the office, his mind a jumble of thoughts. The revelation that he had been under surveillance when ashore came as a definite shock. Were the Crushers told to keep an eye out for him, or did they just keep their eye on him if they happened to bump into him ashore? As his mind settled down, the old arrogance started to return. A feeling of self importance surged into his being. 'So I'm good enough ter be watched am I?' A confident smirk returned to his battle scarred features. The instinctive feeling of relief he had felt when he realised that he was not going to be punished beyond the Master at Arms warning had dispersed already, a cocky grin now took over from the stunned look of his recent revelation. His mind turned to his new enemy: Dusty Miller. The black hatred welled in him, causing his lips to purse, and his eyes to narrow determinedly. The hatred that surged through him was now joined by an animal awareness that urged caution. If anything, Smith had now become more dangerous and unpredictable, as a result of his narrow escape from punishment. 'I'll get yuh, yuh barstard, mark my words this ain't finished yet!' He was still muttering under his breath as he climbed the ladder to 01 deck and reported to Leading Seaman Wilson.

'What've yer got fer me now 'ucky?' A false smile flickered across his face for an instant, Leading Seaman Wilson hesitated a second, a bit surprised by the unexpected appearance of Smith. 'Er um, go down the Naval Stores Office and get the paperwork to go with the pump and motor,' he ordered, glad that something had sprung to mind.

'He's soon back,' Petty Officer Hancock said, 'Seems a bit bloody cool about it all to me, what d'you think?

'I've a feelin' the Jossman just dished out a bollockin',' Wilson replied, and then felt he had to go a bit further. 'I had them all back to work by the time the Crushers got there. In fact I think I may have been a bit hasty in calling them to the scene. Perhaps three of us could have separated them, but not without joinin' in ourselves.'

'Don't fret yerself Tug, with Smith's reputation as a knuckle bosun, if it 'adn't been terday it would 'ave bin another day, and oo knows, it could 'ave bin worse. Strange innit though,' the Petty Officer went on. 'E's always bin nice as pie up 'ere. Never creates any fuss about a job, just cracks on with it. Never ever adrift, always on time, but 'e can never steer clear of a punch-up,' he followed Leading Seaman Wilson to the crane as he was speaking.

'Well let's 'ope that that's an end to it,' Wilson said wishfully as he eased himself into the operator's seat and started checking the controls. 'Are they ready to connect up the motor down below?'

'Stand by below there, the jib's comin' over now,' the Petty Officer yelled down to the men below. He then took up a position where Leading Seaman could see him clearly, and he could watch the positioning of the crane hook in exactly the right place. He raised his left arm at right angles to his body, index finger extended from a closed hand. Leading Seaman Wilson reacted to the signal by moving the crane to the left until his controller turned to face him with his right arm raised, palm of hand towards him in the signal to stop. This signal was followed by the 'top down' order as Hancock with his right arm at forty-five degrees to his body pointed at the deck with his index finger. Wilson lowered the jib until the signal to stop. The next order was to lower the lifting hook, the weight of the 'ponders ball' keeping all the specially made lifting wire taut as it was lowered. Petty Officer Hancock's right arm went up and down with a flat hand until he gave the signal to stop. The men below, on the main deck quickly put the sling on the first box, and stood by using two heaving lines to steady the load while the crane went through the motions of loading the box onto the boat. When both boxes had been loaded, and there was no further requirement for the crane, the Petty Officer turned towards his crane driver and raised both arms with palms of hands extended outwards facing the crane operator in the signal to secure the crane. In the meantime, Dusty and Wiggy were coiling up the heaving lines while Slinger Woods rolled up the 'shot mat' that had been laid out to protect the deck against scuffing.

'Hands of the mess for rum,' the tannoy blared out. The working party was close enough to the Quartermaster's position to hear the pipe in stereo. No sooner had the pipe ended than Petty Officer Hancock's head appeared over 01 deck guard rail shouting, 'Ave yer finished down there? Get all that gear returned to the top locker.' He turned to his Leading Hand. 'All secure Tug?'

'All secure Tony,' Wilson replied crawling out of the operator's seat. The familiarity was not abnormal between a Petty Officer and his Leading Hand on a face to face basis.

'You get off to rum issue then, I'll make sure everythin' is in order 'ere.'

Able Seaman Smith's body appeared at the top of the ladder, an envelope with stores return notes in it clutched in his left hand.

'Give 'em to the Coxswain of the boat, then secure for dinner,' the Petty Officer ordered, the terseness having returned to his voice.

There was always a bit of a bottleneck at 'heads and bathrooms' when both watches of the hands secured from duties at the same time. This caused a queue with a towel over one shoulder and a block of 'pussers hard' wrapped in a face cloth in the other hand. It was not uncommon to see two men sharing a pistol in the urinal, and then sharing a bowl in the bathroom to wash their hands.

Dusty arrived back in the mess and stowed his toilet gear away. Wiggy, by this time, was sorting through the mail placed on the end of one of the mess tables. Able Seaman Smith was just collecting his tot from the smaller of the two tables as Dusty started to flip through the letters. He came to one letter where the name was not immediately clear to him due to the scrawled handwriting. He peered closely at the letter, only to have it snatched from his hand with the remainder of the pile. 'D'yer wanna read the fuckin' thing,' a voice hissed. Dusty turned to face Smith's sneering glare, noticing his lips were still moist from the tot he had just downed.

'It's a dangerous 'abit, reading anuver matelot's mail,' Smith growled, removing the letter with the barely discernable name, and tossing the remainder on the table.

Dusty ignored the provocative act and picked up the pile. Smith brushed past him, his body language increasing the provocation as the determined aggressor moved to the other end of the table.

Only Bogey Knight of the four new lads had a letter. Upon picking it up he had immediately left the mess and walked up to the Fxle to read it; news from his beloved Margaret was best read in private. He had not yet included this part of his life in any conversation with his pals or anyone else. They had no idea that their huge, gentle minded, extremely powerful oppo was actually the father of a young lad now six months old. They could have questioned why he was always broke by the weekend preceding Thursday payday, but they always put his lack of finances down to his huge thirst. Not being married he could not claim marriage allowance, so naturally that left him a bit short after sending four pounds a fortnight to Margaret.

Shiner Wright looked at Dusty and Wiggy. 'Don't you know anyone who can write either?'

By way of reply they both laughed, then Wiggy said, 'Where's Bogey?'

'Ah you know he always tries to get down first to see if he's got any mail.'

Just then Bogey walked back into the mess, no visible sign of his letter evident.

'D'yer know anyone who can write Bogey?' This was Shiner's way of trying to draw his oppo to glean a bit of knowledge about Bogey's mail time habits.

Bogey returned the grin that accompanied the question, but then boxed clever with his reply.

'My Mum's the writer in our house; when she can catch a goose.'

It took a moment for his mates to catch on, but it got a round of titters as a final response.

Dusty changed the subject. 'We're duty watch tonight aren't we Shiner? What time's the first muster?'

'Seventeen hundred hours for the duty hands, and 1800 hours for the whole part of the watch,' Wiggy answered as Shiner got up to look at the daily orders. 'We're not duty hands so it's 1800 hours for us,' Shiner said, sitting down again.

Slinger Woods joined the conversation. 'It's Friday today, so sometime after secure this evening they are bound to call out 'fire and emergency parties' for a fire exercise, so keep your ears open. If you miss that one you'll be spending next week's spare time painting ship for a couple of hours every night; so be warned!' he added with an air of seriousness.

It was then that Dusty noticed that Slinger had taken a seat between himself and Smith on the same side of the table. Tug Wilson had put himself on the other side of Smith, and engaged all at the table in conversation. 'Time for scran, Dusty,' Shiner said as he noticed his pal's eyes lock with Smith's. 'The dining hall queue will have shortened by now.'

3

SHORESIDE CONFRONTATION

'Fire Fire Fire! For exercise, fire in the galley. Fire and emergency parties muster in the cafeteria,' the Quartermaster yelled down the tannoy, his voice inspiring the duty part of the watch to get to the cafeteria with all possible haste.

Dusty glanced at the mess clock as he grabbed his hat. 'Seventeen forty-five; come on Shiner,' he yelled, striding out of the mess with his pal hot on his heels.

The duty Petty Officer Mechanical Engineer (usually referred to as 'pomie') who was in charge of the fire party of Mechanical Engineers (Stokers), bustled around ordering hoses rolled out, and glancing at breathing apparatus wearers as he selected seamen from the duty watch to carry out necessary assistance as dressers and fire hose handlers. Other men were carrying out their jobs as emergency party, stretcher bearers, first aid, and pumping party. Seamen were detailed off to provide and stand by to use two gallon gas and water, and two gallon foam extinguishers. Other men were standing by holding nitrogen extinguishers for low voltage electrical fires. Men were hopping around getting into fire suits, which as effective as they were against burns, were terribly cumbersome to put on and to wear. The breathing mask, when it was added, with its long breathing hose did not allow for any agility, so the wearer stood his ground in front of a blaze feeling very hot and uncomfortable, and not able to see anything very clearly. His breathing hose holder had the job of holding the hose end through a porthole, or in a space that hopefully had clear air. This job usually went to an experienced seaman, and sometimes, sailors being what they are, he would put the hose between his legs and break wind; but only in an exercise of course.

By 1830 hours all duty watch commitments had been completed. Duty Petty Officers of sections, having ensured that all equipment was correctly stowed away, dismissed their men.

'Hands to supper, men under punishment secure,' the tannoy blared its routine pipe. Dusty and Shiner could now wash their hands, grab a bite of supper, and then get their bath and dhoby completed before they had to muster for night rounds. With a bit of luck their day would end at 2115 hours, when a blast on the Quartermaster's call would indicate that night rounds were completed. They would not be able to totally relax however; many big ships required the duty watch to append their slinging billets to the 'shakes book' before turning in, just in case an emergency occurred. After a long day, it was a relief to be able to sling hammocks, and gratefully fall asleep.

By midnight the mess was reverberating to the loud insistent snores of Bogey Knight, mingled with all the other below decks noises. Wiggy was stretched out with the feet of his six foot two inch frame resting in the nettles at the foot of his hammock, wrapped in sheet and blanket. Not a sound came from Dusty and Shiner, after this long day they were deep in the arms of Morpheus, and dead to the world.

A shadowy figure staggered along the passageway, made more eerie by the blue police lights which reflected dully off the figure's white hat. The eerily illuminated body pulled open the curtains and staggered into the mess; unfortunately, to do this, he had to bend under Wiggy's hammock. In his well oiled state he barged into Wiggy's hammock, sending it swinging from side to side. The force of the bump roused Wiggy immediately, and his head appeared over the lip of his hammock saying sleepily, 'steady on there,' as his eyes tried to focus in the blue haze.

'Up yer guts; yuh toffee nosed barsterd!'

The voice was slurred and drunkenly aggressive as a head belonging to the voice rose to the level of Wiggy's face. At the same instant that Wiggy recognised the face, the fetid breath of the owner saturated the air between them with the stench of stale tobacco and alcohol. Wiggy flinched as Smith hissed directly in his face, 'gerrin line college boy, your turn'll come when I've finished with that Welsh twat Miller.'

Wiggy was wide awake now, he didn't need telling that this could turn into a nasty situation at the least inflammatory inflection in his voice.

'Get turned in Smudger please, I don't want any trouble,' he whispered, the tone of his voice placatory, attempting to diffuse the situation in a polite manner.

'Aw! There's a nice college boy,' Smith leered scornfully, his right hand coming up and stroking Wiggy's hair for a moment. 'Wants ter be oppos nah, peraps yer'd like ter get yer laughin' tackle around this?' He indicated his crotch by grasping his trousers and genitals in his left fist and shaking it up and down.

Wiggy's eyes narrowed defensively as he stared at the evil expression on Smith's face; made even more ugly by the reflections of the blue Police light that cast shadows and made hooded eyes look like cadaverish hollow sockets. He surprised Smith by grabbing the neck of his white front savagely, pulling the leering face closer to his own.

'If I get my laughing tackle round your pox ridden dick, you'll never piss through it again, you can be assured of that,' he spat out loudly, with a venom that had never come to light at any previous time.

'Get turned in there,' Leading Seaman Wilson said loudly, having been brought out of his slumbers by Wiggy's anger. 'Cut the cackle and get turned in,' he ordered again, assuming it was a couple of messmates returning from shore leave a little worse for wear.

Smith ducked out of sight through the curtains at the sound of the Leading Hand's order. A few seconds later he could be heard hauling his hammock out of the netting, and dragging it further up the passage to unlash it and spread it out on the deck. He got down on it wavering drunkenly, grunted a couple of times and then lapsed into loud snores in a matter of minutes.

Wiggy breathed a sigh of relief, and wrapped himself in his sheet and blanket again; but sleep did not return for ages as his mind ran over this unpleasant episode in his chosen career.

Dusty looked sideways at Wiggy next morning as they were lashing up their hammocks, and asked, 'What was that cunt on about last night?'

'Oh, he was inebriated, and suggested that I should provide sexual relief for him through the medium of oral sex,' Wiggy replied, his face splitting into a grin.

'You mean he wanted a chew,' Dusty said, also grinning like a Cheshire Cat.

'Well, if you must be so crude...precisely,' Wiggy went on with an affected haughtiness that provided them both with an early morning guffaw.

'Half day today,' Shiner shouted across happily. 'Fancy a swim this afternoon Wiggy?'

'Business or pleasure?'

'Wadyer mean?' Shiner's face screwed up in puzzlement as he looked at his pal across his tightly lashed hammock.

'Well, do I take my overalls to practice for my swimming retest, or do we just enjoy a swim?'

'Oh gotcher! What say we start off in overalls for a while, and then enjoy ourselves for an hour, it's all good practice anyway?'

'Glad we sorted that out,' Wiggy grinned, cuffing Shiner playfully on the head over the top of his hammock.

Bogey glanced at Dusty as they were stowing their hammocks in the netting and asked conversationally, 'watter we goin' ter do then, Dusty, while these two water babies are getting rusty?'

Dusty thought for a moment, then answered bluntly with a grin, 'get rusty with them I suppose.'

'Then out on the piss tonight?' Bogey followed up with a gleeful chortle.

'Oh yeah,' Wiggy said with lip smacking relish.

'That will make this Jack shit a happy sailor,' Shiner broke in, and then elucidated, 'A bit of work, a bit of sport, and a lot of pleasure.'

'Right on maaan,' Dusty piped up grinning, whilst trying unsuccessfully to imitate colloquial American, which sounded even worse tinged with a Welsh accent.

57

Two hours later the four of them had nothing to laugh about. They were stretched out line abreast on hands and knees. Slinger Woods was playing a fire hose across the deck from a seawater hydrant, and the four pals were scrubbing backwards and forwards leaning heavily on the pusser's deck scrubber with both hands.

'You would have thought someone would have patented a long handled scrubber by now wouldn't you?' Wiggy voiced his feelings passionately.

Slinger Woods heard him and laughingly shouted back, 'Oh they have! I've got several stowed away in the top locker, but if I got them out to scrub the quarterdeck, it would spoil some sadistic basterd's idea of a Saturday morning.'

The tone of his interjection raised a laugh from the young Ordinary Seamen, and momentarily served to ease the discomfort of cold hands, feet and knees. The quarterdeck awning hid any effect the weak and watery sun may have had, and further served to channel the light harbour breeze along the wooden decks, adding to the chill factor.

'You know that swim we're going for this afternoon,' Bogey said looking sideways as he spoke.

'Ye…ssss Bogey,' Wiggy answered, staring sideways at his oppo, curious to hear what gem Bogey would come out with.

'Well, I'm fuckin' rusty enough already, all we 'ad to do this morning was put on our swimming cossies, and we could 'ave killed two birds with one stone.'

'Yeah!' Dusty shouted from the other end of the row. 'But that would hardly satisfy all the oglers on the day trip boats who have paid two bob a nob to get a glimpse of the Royal Navy at work first thing in the morning. I mean where else could they get a glimpse of four daft basterds providing a jolly scene like this?'

'Get on with it Dusty,' Slinger Woods shouted good-naturedly.

'Fuck the oglers!' Shiner's teeth were chattering as he spoke. 'If they want to know what it's like wankin' this scrubber up and down just let 'em come aboard and form a queue behind me, they can 'ave this basterd gladly.'

Slinger Woods grinned knowingly. He had got them working, and talking, and bantering whilst keeping the rhythm, all serving to ease the monotony and the discomfort. Just like all sailors do as they get used to the idea of being hard done by, they aired their grievances with a good old drip about it. The forenoon disappeared in a cloud of jolly banter, and the four pals had been given a taste of Britain's old navy, urged on by a senior Able Seaman who had cut his teeth on commissioned Battleships.

'Well you lot, what 'ave yuh learnt this mornin'?' he asked looking from one to the other of his morning's charges as they stowed the deck cleaning gear in the top locker.

'That it is not much fun being an ordinary seaman,' Wiggy answered with airy humour, then added, his grin broadening. 'But at least this morning has served to cure me of the boyish dreams of life aboard a British Man-O-War, and any other masochistic ideas that may have passed through my infantile mind,' he continued with humorous enthusiasm. 'I think I shall have to strive gainfully to reach the exalted state of Able Seaman, that's where the real power lies in this man's navy. They seem to have the ability to leap Royal Naval Barracks in a single bound; cross Portsmouth Harbour in a single stride, while the remainder of us mortals hop off kerbs and play around in puddles.'

His companions were already showing their appreciation of his affected wit as he reached the final word of his theatrical delivery, the seasoned Slinger laughing as loud as anyone. His face distorted in mirth, he brought up an important point at that moment. 'Beer issue is earlier on a Saturday because it's the big night of the week in harbour. Make sure the beer bosun has your money, because until he has an agreement with you, he will only bring down the ale he has been paid for, and that means you would have to go and queue up for your own.'

Wiggy glanced at him, his face still wearing the mirth of the last few minutes. 'What do you mean by agreement?'

'Well some mess members pay for the whole two weeks in advance on payday,' Slinger said, then went on to explain further. 'If he knows you are regular and reliable, and pay each day in advance, there is no problem. But if you want to pay when you get your ale, he has got to be sure you will not be broke. In other words it's all about reliability. He charges an extra halfpenny a can, which allows him to build up a bit of a float of course, so he can always pay up front for a messmate he can trust. Also, don't forget, he could drop himself in the shit for getting a man's beer when that man is officially ashore or on some other twenty-four hour assignment that takes him off the ship. So you can see, the old beer bosun has to be on the ball. On the whole though, it's better to pay him up front at tot time every day, you both know exactly how you stand then.'

By this time they had reached the mess so they all grabbed their toilet gear, had a quick wash, and proceeded to the dining hall. Dinner over and done with, they joined the queue for beer issue, and stowed the two cans each in their kit lockers to be enjoyed later after their exertions at Pitt Street Navy swimming pool.

Wiggy pulled his rolled up number two suit out of his locker and then paused thoughtfully. 'Do you have to wear full number ones to go to Pitt Street?'

'Nah Wiggy, it's just number twos negative collar, lanyard, and silk; unless you're going straight ashore afterwards,' Leading Seaman Wilson answered helpfully.

'Thanks hooky,' Wiggy said, and then joined his three pals getting dressed, and packing their little brown cases with swimming trunks and towel, not forgetting to roll up his blue overalls and tuck them under his left arm.

'D'yer know the best way ter get to Pitt Street from 'ere,' Leading Seaman Wilson asked.

'We know where it is because we went there after we kitted up last year,' Dusty answered.

'It's best to get off the boat at Excellent Steps,' Wilson advised. 'From there it's only a short walk to Unicorn Gate, turn left and you're on Pitt Street in no time. By the way,' he added, his voice taking on an advisory inflection. 'Don't amble through the dockyard, and certainly not when yuh get out of the gate. Look purposeful, the whole bloody area is swarming with Crushers on a Saturday…and a Jossman or two may be out and about as well.'

Ten minutes later they had fallen in with Liberty men at the gangway to be inspected before going ashore. The Officer of the Day commented on their duty rig; he did however smile encouragingly when told the destination and reason for a sporting afternoon.

'Bennett, isn't it?' he paused and asked.

'Yes sir,' Wiggy replied, unable to hide the element of surprise in his voice.

'Have a successful afternoon,' the officer said pleasantly, 'And try to complete your personal survival test before you leave us for deeper waters.'

'Yes sir, I shall do my best,' Wiggy replied with service aplomb.

Later, as they walked through the dockyard towards Unicorn Gate, Shiner said to Wiggy, 'looks as if your name's done the rounds in the wardroom. It's that posh accent that gives you away.' He grinned at his pal as he stated the obvious.

'Rather nice of him though, don't you think,' Wiggy replied, and then added with sincerity, 'he could have been a stuffed shirt, but he showed interest, I find that very encouraging after the hostility we encountered at the beginning of the week.'

'Hey watch it Wiggy,' Bogey joined in. 'You'll begin tuh like bein' an O.D. next!'

'Oh God! Never, Bogey!' Wiggy's expressive features affected a look of pure agony. 'I just cannot wait to reach the exalted status of Able Seaman.'

Dusty broke his silence saying with a sly note to his tone, 'this thing you've got about jumpin' over RNB in one mighty leap, and stridin' across Pompey Harbour. Does it include swimming a length with one stroke?'

'You bitch Dusty!' Wiggy stopped in his stride, affecting an injured look. With his hands on his hips he lisped, camping it up, 'you really know how to hurt a girl.' The action looked funnier because of the brown case in his left hand, the awkwardness of it made his arm slump downwards as his hand slipped off his hip. 'Oh shite! Can't even do that properly!' he laughed, and his pals joined him in a good laugh as they continued to Unicorn Gate. The humour died as they approached the gate. A few patrolmen were positioned prominently outside the gate in the road, but their presence was preventative rather than punitive. Any sailors in the area would be on their best behaviour immediately, at the sight of the Crushers in their white belts and gaiters with trenching tool handle hanging in a slot on the belt.

'You lot going to the PT school?' The Leading Regulator glanced at their uniforms and the brown cases, taking in Wiggy's overalls automatically.

'Yes Leading Patrolman, we are going to the swimming pool for a couple of hours,' Wiggy answered respectfully, and then they continued on their way as the leading patrolman gave them an acquiescent nod.

'Dunno what this navy's comin' to,' the patrolman said, turned to his colleague.

The colleague's face turned from bored indifference to puzzled semi interest. 'Wadger mean?' he asked, his indifference only slightly dented.

'Dabtoes goin' for a sportin' afternoon when the pubs 'ave been open for an hour now. Bet they go on church parade termorrer mornin' as well; and kneel in front of the sin bosun with the smokey 'andbag.'

'Yeah,' the colleague answered, a flicker of a grin crinkling his pretensively stern gaze. 'Goin' tuh hell in a shit cart innit?'

They both tittered at the momentary break from the terminal monotony of their Saturday afternoon vigil.

Wiggy had a good start to the afternoon. After a few attempts interspersed with a rest, he managed to propel his long frame, bedecked with sodden overalls for a whole length of the pool, much to his own surprise. It was however, as he gratefully stated to his pals, 'Only your stupendous encouragement that got me there; even you, you great white whale,' he teased Bogey, whose seventeen stone of solid muscle created quite a splash as he practiced his elephantine like dives.

'Gerunder there!' Bogey reacted with his phenomenal strength, pushing Wiggy beneath the water. The unready Wiggy burst to the surface again, coughing and spluttering, grabbing desperately at the poolside. A couple of helping hands grabbed him by the buttocks and heaved him onto the side of the pool gasping for air. He lay there for a second floundering like a beached whale, and then gave them all a laugh with a pretence of swimming, acted out on the poolside, his overalls clinging to him like some sodden wrinkled second skin; this gave an added effect to his actions.

'All yuh need is a blowhole on yer 'ead, and yuh wouldn't 'ave to act out the part,' Shiner shouted, laughing loudly at Wiggy's antics.

'No that's at the other end old boy,' Wiggy laughed back. Then, the mixture of his previous efforts added to the strength of his mirth, made him break wind loudly, as if on cue. His pals all rushed away from him in mock horror. 'You smelly basterd Wiggy,' Dusty gasped, creased up with laughter. 'If you 'ad done that in the pool, you would 'ave done that length in arf the time.'

The laughter did not abate as they helped Wiggy to climb out of the clinging overalls, and only reduced slightly as the Physical Training Instructor walked over to them. Absolute silence descended on the group as the Petty Officer spoke.

'G'dafternoon lads, enjoyin' yerselves?'

The momentary tension that had interrupted their badinage disappeared immediately as they all realised that this Petty Officer was smiling at their jollity.

'Yes Clubs,' Dusty replied, as they all nodded their heads.

The Petty Officer's gaze swung to Wiggy, and he said pleasantly, 'It's obvious you didn't pass your swimming test at *Raleigh*, would you like me to put your name down on our backward swimmers list?' He gave Wiggy another look up and down, appraising the long limbed youth candidly, before asking, 'What's yer favourite sport?'

'Well, er, cricket is the only sport I ever excelled at to any degree of competence,' Wiggy replied politely, then added, 'possibly because it was played at a more leisurely pace.'

The Petty Officer did not quite expect the eloquence that reached his ears, but his momentary surprise was quickly replaced by a look of interest. 'Like to do a trial in the nets before you leave, it'll only take about twenty minutes?'

'Sure Clubs, love to.' The look on his face showed surprise in return as he expressed his willingness.

'And you big fellah,' the Petty Officer said, turning to Bogey. 'Muscular frame like yours must have been developed on the rugby pitch.'

Bogey reddened slightly. 'Yeah, Clubs, but I didn't 'ave the time ter train properly; lived on a farm yuh see,' he answered truthfully.

'Ah!' the Petty Officer exclaimed. 'That's what really accounts for the build then. Like ter 'ave a trial with us, would yer? It gets yuh Wednesday afternoon off work, and furthermore, if yuh prove good enough we put yer in the Portsmouth Command second team, and that gives yer an automatic reserve position. We 'ave ter do it this way because lads are not always available…shipboard duties, on leave, sick, et cetera. This means I can virtually promise yuh a game every month. How's that sound?'

Bogey's reddened face was now topped with a look of wonderment. His sparkling eyes and jolly smile seemed a bit out of context with what he was being offered. To a young lad straight out of the hayfields such an appraisal of his physique by a navy professional was a huge boost to his status as an Ordinary Seaman. The Petty Officer Physical Training Instructor took one look at the eagerly smiling face and said with a grin, 'see yuh Wednesday at 1330 hours then. I'll be in touch with yer Clubswinger, and inform him of the details…all right son?' He gave Bogey an encouraging slap to the shoulder as he turned to Shiner.

He had just opened his mouth to speak, when he suddenly changed his mind, and turned back to Bogey. 'D'yer like a pint?'

The question raised an instant laugh from his three pals. The Petty Officer glanced at them, a comic grin spreading across his features as he asked, 'Does that mean yes?'

'You'd better believe it,' Wiggy answered for them all, his head nodding up and down with wide eyed emphasis.

'Good!' the Petty Officer said emphatically. 'We have a bit of a 'Yorkshire' afterwards, everybody chucks in five bob, and we go to the 'Home Club' for a couple of pints. Afterwards, the navy bus drops us off, starting at the dockyard main gate.'

He turned to Shiner again. I watched you swimming closely. You've had more than a little practice, would yuh like ter train fer the navy?'

Shiner stood dumbfounded. Quite uncharacteristically he was lost for words. His pals started grinning at his unusual silence. Bogey nudged him. 'Come on yuh daft git, say something tuh the man!'

Shiner seemed to burst into life. 'D'yuh think I'm good enough?' The words fell from his mouth in an excited burble.

'Be here at 1330 hours Wednesday and find out. Personally I think you can lick the arse off our best, come and 'ave a go, yuh've got nothing ter lose,' the Petty Officer answered, his face turning deadly serious.

Shiner stood transfixed, incredulity etched into his face.

The Petty Officer turned from him, his face slowly changing to a grin, he said, 'prop 'im up you lot!'

'Now young man,' he said, turning to Dusty. 'I can't place your forte...no don't tell me, I like to have a stab at guessing a well-built young fellah's sport. Er...um...er, you look to be wiry enough, good muscle definition, but not through body building.' He paused, contemplating Dusty's form with apparent serious concentration. 'I think it's something that requires strength and agility, but not gymnastics, your upper arms and shoulders are not quite thick enough. I think a full contact sport...er... something like Judo.' He reached his decision quickly as he broke off speaking. 'Am I far off?'

'Bloody 'ell, Clubs, that's a good guess. Judo is my favourite sport, but I also like freestyle wrestling, it livens things up a bit for me.'

'Like to continue your sport would you?'

'Yeah, why not, I've got another eight years to go in this man's navy, might as well brighten it up with something useful. Keep me out of the pubs wunnit.'

'Fourteen hundred hours Wednesday at the gym in RNB. Royal Marine Sergeant Tommy Watkins is the instructor, I shall inform him that he has another Dabtoe to throw around...okay.'

The Petty Officer made it sound like an order, which impressed Dusty.

'Ows about that then,' the Petty Officer nudged him, then added in a less serious tone, 'you'll enjoy it, 'e's an 'ell of an instructor, 'ard as bloody nails, typical bootneck.'

He turned to Wiggy still grinning at the look on Dusty's face. 'Right, let's see what you 'ave tuh offer. We've only got enough room for bat and bowler, but at least it gives keen individuals a chance to practice. Right, 'ave a shower and get into arf blues, you other three can stand at the back of the bowler, to the side, there's no room down the end where the nets are. You take the bat first Wiggy.'

Twenty minutes later Wiggy took the bat and managed to get a few good whacks into the nets. 'Nice straight bat yuh've got there,' the Petty Officer complemented him.

Two overs later, Wiggy and his instructor changed places, and after a couple of balls he was surprised to find that the ball reacted quite well to the coir matting.

'Okay let's 'ave some fast ones now,' the Petty Officer ordered.

Wiggy only had ten yards to run up in, but his arm came over in a blur and the ball hurtled to a spot just wide of the off stump. The delivery caught the Petty Officer completely unawares as the ball hit the matting with an audible thump and changed direction towards the middle stump. The three stumps in their wooden block hit the floor with a thwack and skidded into the back of the net. The surprised look on the Petty Officer's face stayed there for three overs, by which time the wicket had skidded into the nets at the back three times.

'Enough Mr Bennett,' he called to Wiggy as he managed to stop the eighteenth ball. Very impressed, he walked up to Wiggy and put an arm around his shoulder. 'One week from today,' he started. 'The Portsmouth Command Royal Navy Cricket Team take on the Royal Marines in the final blood match of the season, and you, young man, will be part of the navy team fielded that day.'

'Bloody great Wiggy,' the other three shouted encouragingly, then laughed at Wiggy's expression, which this time was not put on for their benefit.

'That's not all,' the Petty Officer interrupted the back slapping. 'It's followed by a dinner and dance at the Royal Marine Barracks; how does that sound to yer? Every bugger who is anybody will be there, so your number one suit had better sparkle; oh, and by the way,' he added, just a hint of authority creeping into his voice. 'Practice nights are Monday and Thursday, be there prompt at 1630 hours. We provide the whites on Saturday, so don't bother to break out your tropical trousers, bell bottoms won't suit this occasion, but do bring yer white canvas tropical shoes.' He turned to all of them as he finished speaking to Wiggy. 'I have to let your ship know, so that the Reg Office and the rest of the admin side know that you are required to train for official sporting occasions, the only effect it will have on you is that it becomes a duty as well as enjoyment, okay.' He thrust his hand out, and the four surprised young men shook it in turns.

'Cheers, Clubs,' they all said, then Wiggy added, 'we don't know your name Clubs!'

'Geoff Mitchell,' he replied, and then added with a grin, 'it's a pleasure to rescue four likely lads from off duty time absolutely saturated with hedonism.'

Five minutes later the Petty Officer Physical Training Instructor said 'cheerio' to the four pals and shut the door behind them.

Nobody spoke for a full two minutes as they walked up the road towards Unicorn Gate. Finally it was Shiner who broke the silence.

'What's hedonism?' he asked, looking at Wiggy, who in turn looked at him slyly and whispered, 'it means pissing up, and bagging off at every opportunity.'

'Oh I'll 'ave some of that! Fuck sport, and other strenuous things. Watter yuh called if yuh do this hedonism?'

'A frigging hedonist you twerp,' laughed Wiggy.

'Then that's what I'm goin' ter be, a fuckin' hedonist... instead of crossed guns on me right arm, I'm goin' ter 'ave crossed penises over a tot glass.'

The roars of mirth that followed this light hearted moment were quickly extinguished as they neared the dockyard gate.

'Did yer 'ave a good afternoon then?'

'Unbelievable,' Wiggy answered the patrolman. 'Absolutely fantastic afternoon, it will be a regular habit from now on.'

The patrolman looked sideways at his colleague, and then raised his eyebrows skywards. 'What did I tell yer? We'll all be takin' electrocution lessons before long.'

His partner looked puzzled for a moment. 'Don't you mean elocution lessons?'

'Fucked if I know what I mean, but it's a shockin' state of affairs.'

His partner afforded the statement a strangled giggle, and then they both resumed their boring state of nothingness.

'Christ, do they 'ave to stay out there all day? They were in that same spot when we went out of the gate,' Bogey said.

'Nah, they're watchkeepers, twenty-four about,' Dusty answered, then elaborated. 'They're afternoon, first, and morning. Their opposite numbers will be dog's middle and forenoon.'

'Must bore the arse off them,' Bogey replied. 'Who the fuck would join the navy as a regulator?'

'You can't join as a regulator,' Wiggy corrected. They recruit from suitable applicants from other branches.'

Shiner looked puzzled for a moment. 'D'yer mean, if I wanted to, I could show two fingers to the seaman's branch, and become a regulator?'

'Not quite so simple old boy, I believe one has to attain a certain level of competency in one's original branch, and then apply for selection if of good character,' Wiggy answered knowledgeably, and then added, 'you could never join anyway Shiner.'

'Why not? I'm as good as any other bugger,' Shiner retorted, showing a hint of indignation.

'They don't take hedonists,' Wiggy replied, laughing, and then started running as Shiner took a swing at him with his brown case.

The wind had risen slightly, and swung northeast, making the harbour waters a bit choppy. As others sought shelter in the boat's hold, which was converted into a rough passenger cabin, the lads found shelter behind the wheelhouse. The spray sent up from the prow was caught by the wind, and whipped across the deck with stinging fury. The PAS boat swung to port as it cleared North Corner jetty, then came alongside the steps with a jolt. Nobody disembarked, and only one Dockyard Matey leapt aboard. The boat powered away into the choppy waters once more, and very shortly eased alongside the catamaran under HMS *Vanguard*'s accommodation ladder. The four pals ran up the ladder and with great sense of purpose faced the quarterdeck and saluted. They collected their station cards, and made their way below decks.

Only Tug Wilson and Slinger Woods were in the mess, a few empty beer cans alongside them, and a Cribbage Board to the other side. They looked up as the lads entered the mess, nodding pleasantly by way of greeting, and then continued their game. 'Gotter 'ave a beer,' Bogey groaned, as he opened his locker enthusiastically. 'Why not have a bath and dhobs first,' advised Wiggy. 'You'll enjoy it more then, it's nigh on two hours until supper, and sure as hell I am not going ashore on an empty belly.'

Bogey went along with his friend's advice, and very soon all of them were raising a lather in their wash bowls, rubbing 'pusser's dunghampers' vigorously with a block of pusser's hard.

'Don't swing around without warning, will you Shiner,' Dusty said with a wide grin, nodding down towards Shiner's pendulous flaccid penis, which was by this time frothily anointed with soapy lather. Everybody chortled lightly at the observation, and then Wiggy added, 'you can tell how his mother hauled him out of the bath as a baby, can't you?'

The chortles grew to mild laughter.

'That reminds me of a joke I haven't told you,' Bogey said as he laughed with the rest of them.

'Years ago a young fellow was tramping across the moors on a dark night hoping he would soon find an inn to rest for the night. Suddenly, as he crested a gentle slope, he saw a large building looming ahead in the mist. He walked to the huge front door, and pulled on a metal handle which caused a cluster of small bells to tinkle inside the mansion. The door creaked open and a hooded figure greeted him politely. The young man asked for shelter for the night, and the figure ushered him through the door saying, 'my master will welcome you sir, at this moment he is preparing for the evening's entertainment, meanwhile may I offer you some refreshment.'

The young man ate and drank his fill, and then nodded off by the large fire. Some time later he stirred, and realised he had been woken by a drone of voices coming from somewhere below. He shook the sleep from his body and followed the direction from which the drone was coming, suddenly realising that the sound was actually a group of male voices droning 'settle on me, settle on me' repeatedly. The young man opened the door from which the sound was coming and was immediately greeted by the same hooded figure. 'Welcome sir', the hooded figure said, 'would you like to join the entertainment?'

'What is the entertainment?'

'Well, you can see that all the men are standing around a table with huge erections on display. You cannot fail to notice also that there is a naked maid lying invitingly on the table, and a field bee is buzzing around the room.'

The young man took all this in and said, amazed, 'surely not all of those present are going to have their wicked way with that young woman?'

'No, no!' The hooded one hurriedly assured him. Only the prick that the bee settles on will service the young maid.

'Well what about that fellow tied and gagged over there in the corner,' the young man asked, puzzled.

'Oh! He cheated; he put jam on his prick.'

Bogey's pals looked at him, letting the surprise punch line sink in, then Shiner said with mock exasperation, 'Fuck off with yer shaggy dog stories,' and cupping his hands dipped them into his bowl and heaved frothy water at Bogey. The other two joined in, and amongst howls of laughter, Bogey was drenched from head to foot in frothed up pusser's hard.

'Hey, I've got one I've never told you,' Dusty shouted over the mirth.

'A matelot and a pongo walk into a brothel, and were surprised to see two doors, one marked big cunt and the other marked little cunt. 'Weigh-hey me lad, that's the one for me,' the pongo said marching towards the door marked big cunt. He opened the door; and found himself back on the street.'

Har-har-har, the laughter continued.

'What d'yer call a Glaswegian having a shit behind the hedge?' Shiner yelled out above the din.

'I don't know, what do you call a Glaswegian having a shit behind the hedge?'

Shiner paused momentarily for effect, and then with eyes popping he chortled, 'A bloody Squatsman.'

The roars that greeted this daft joke were typical of young sailors becoming acclimatised to bathroom humour. Sometimes totally silly humour was the norm; it acted as a relief valve from the tedium of menial tasks. In many cases, the old saying 'If I didn't laugh, I'd cry,' was never more true than when associated with the terrible monotony of daily tasks for young sailors keeping Britain's Grey Navy free from rust and sparklingly clean.

By the time the dhobying was finished, and they had all had their three minute shower (a minute to wet, a minute to wash, and a minute to rinse) the mirth had reached its peak, and was in the descendent. The mood however, was set for a good run ashore.

The four pals climbed into best bellbottoms and white front before enjoying the first of their two cans of beer. Bogey had sucked his dry in seconds.

'Like feeding buns to an elephant, isn't it,' Wiggy remarked, grinning widely at the insatiable Bogey. By way of reply Bogey grabbed each end of the can in a meaty paw and twisted. He finished off the manoeuvre by interlocking the fingers of each hand around the can lengthways, and flattened the can to about one inch in length between his field hardened palms.

'Tst, you brute,' Wiggy lisped. 'Remind me never to let you squeeze one of my zits.'

Silliness reigned once more, until it became time for supper, by this time they were all fully dressed, and ready for this much looked forward to run ashore.

Slinger Woods gave them a cursory glance, and uttered an old navy saying, 'Shore like a troubadour, back like a stevedore.'

The lads had never heard the saying before, but Wiggy clicked on in an instant. He enlightened a puzzled Bogey, 'A lyricist of possible knightly rank, as opposed to a dockyard matey.' He adjusted Bogey's blue jean collar as he spoke, adding, 'Personally, I think you have a greater resemblance to the latter before we go ashore…you very strong gentleman,' he added hurriedly in an act of preventive pacification as Bogey made a grab for him.

'Have a good run,' Slinger shouted as they paraded out of the mess. 'And stay clear of the Pompey Ladies, they'll 'ave yer balls as well as yer paybook!'

An hour later, having put a pound each in a Yorkshire, they were having their first pint in the 'King and Queen' just outside the main dockyard gate.

'Cheers Wiggy, thanks fer the quid,' Shiner said, raising his glass as he spoke.

'You're welcome shipmate.'

'Take yer bloody time Bogey,' Dusty urged, and then turning to the others said, 'Christ he's like a fuckin' drain isn't he. If we try to keep up with him we'll all be well pissed by half eight, and as usual he'll be the only bugger left standing.'

They all gave a titter at the sound of exasperation in Dusty's voice. Bogey screwed up his lips, and pointed his nose in the air, pouting pretensively. They all laughed at his antics.

'Fancy a stroll down Commercial Road after this one?' Shiner looked from face to face as he asked, then added, 'we 'aven't been in the Lennox since we left Pompey to go to Raleigh.'

'That's a fuckin' mile up the road,' Bogey complained. 'We'd be losin' valuable drinkin' time.'

'Yeah…we know Bogey, but all the fanny's up that end on a Saturday night, and what sort of a night would it be without a bit of fanny?'

He had made his point, so they all drained their glasses and placed them on the bar alongside Bogey's.

'Shall we 'ave one in the Home Club first?' Bogey nodded across the road as they approached the bright lights of Commercial Road.

Shiner could not wait to get amongst it in the Albany, and let Bogey know his feelings bluntly. 'Fuck off Bogey, the bloody Albany's just around the corner, and that's where it'll all be 'appenin.'

Bogey shrugged his shoulders resignedly, and moaned, 'It always takes five minutes to get served over there, there's never a queue in the 'ome club.'

'Aw! For Christ's sake Bogey,' Dusty joined in with a wide grin, stepping off the kerb and heading across the street.

'Come on you lot, I'd hate to be partly responsible for this cunt dying of thirst.'

Shiner threw his arms in the air in mock exasperation.

'Never mind old mate,' Wiggy clapped an arm around his shoulders as he spoke. 'If any of the Dolly Birds have seen what you've got dangling between your knees, they will be waiting for you breathlessly.'

The laugh the crude compliment raised lasted them until they approached the bar.

'Look who's at the table at the end there,' Wiggy nudged Dusty, and indicated with his head nodding towards the other end of the bar room.

Dusty cast his eyes in that direction casually. They became steely bright as the sneering face, and narrowed eyes of Able Seaman Smith met his own.

'Look away Dusty,' Wiggy advised, stepping back from the bar to block the two enemies from each other's view.

The barman picked up the cash, checked it, and turned away. They all picked up their pints, and made for a table just inside the door that was vacant, and far enough to one side to be hidden from Smith's view. As if by unspoken consent, Dusty's three oppos took seats that left Dusty the nearest seat to the wall, and therefore out of the line of sight of Smith and his cronies.

'So that cunt's 'ere; so what! If 'e starts anything we'll 'ave 'im through the door and on his arse one-one-two,' Shiner said determinedly, throwing a glance at Smith's table as he spoke.

There were four at the table, all dressed in civilian clothes. The haircuts and general dress style said without doubt that the three at the table were also matelots, but from which ship or base could not be discerned. Smith was talking, and his companions were leaning towards the centre of the table the better to hear what he was saying. Smith looked up, and his eyes met Shiner's full on. The look assured Shiner that he and his companions were the subject of the discussion.

Shiner turned to his pals asking, 'What's that cunt's non-sub?' This referred to whatever badge he carried on the right arm of his uniform.

'Radar Plot,' Wiggy answered. 'Why do you ask?'

'Aw, it's those cunts with 'im. Now you've said that, I reckon they're from HMS *Dryad*, just over Portsdown Hill.'

'Could be,' Wiggy answered. 'I reckon we would have seen them by now if they were on the *Vanguard*. Well dressed so and so's,' he added, perhaps with a hint of envy. 'That's about as close to Edwardian style you can get, without being called 'Teddy Boy'.'

Dusty, sitting in the corner against the wall, could not see what was causing the discussion between his two pals. Bogey, who was alongside him, had to lean out to get a glimpse of Smith and his friends.

'Ah, they're fuck all, if they push their luck, we'll ruin their hair styles, and ruffle up their pretty suits,' he said cheerfully with an assurance backed up by his large muscular frame.

The quick laugh that followed his confident statement broke the tension that had put an edge on the conversation. They all downed their pints and leaving the glasses on the table, got up and strolled nonchalantly through the door into the chill night air. They rounded the corner into Commercial Road, and strolled towards Portsmouth Town Station railway bridge. They waited a moment and then joined a throng of people crossing the road as the traffic eased momentarily. The Criterion was the first pub as they crossed the road, and next door to it the Albany, or the Club Albane as it was sometimes called in naval conversation. The bar at the Albany was three deep in good natured sailors, typical of a Saturday night, many of them waving their glasses over their heads trying to attract the attention of the hard pressed bar staff.

'Gis some money,' Bogey said to Wiggy, shouting to make himself heard over the din of the jukebox, and fifty voices all trying to get served at once. Bogey used his seventeen stone gently but persuasively, and reached the bar. The girl at that end finished serving a customer, and noticing Bogey was a fresh customer served him at once. She placed four pints on the bar, and, pausing in her mastication of a piece of chewing gum, said, 'want a tray luv?'

Bogey smiled and nodded, then used his seventeen stone of 'arsehole' to thrust his way carefully backwards through the throng of straining, shouting, and seemingly insatiably thirsty blue clad customers.

'There's a bit of space down at the other end,' Dusty said, nodding in that direction. They all grabbed their pints, and followed by his three pals they made their way to the far end of the bar. They all glanced at an old dear in floral dress that hung all the way down to her naval gym shoes. The old girl was writhing semi rhythmically to the sound of Bill Haley's 'Rock around the Clock'. It was proving a bit hard for her to retain the rhythm of this most popular of 'Pop' songs of the period, but at least her antics provided some amusement for the hand clapping onlookers. Shiner couldn't hide a cheeky grin as he gaped at the shapeless old dear in her even more shapeless dress.

'Get yer eyes off 'er, she's old enough ter be yer granny,' a familiar voice yelled to them from a corner.

As one, they all swung around. 'Hello Hooky,' they shouted in unison as they recognised the grinning face of Leading Seaman Wilson.

'Pompey Lil's not for you young lads, she'd much rather 'ave a bottle of stout and a bag of chips these days.'

They all laughed at the expense of the old dear enjoying herself in a space cleared for her by the surrounding servicemen.

'She resorts to a shuffle later on, when the stout gets to 'er, but she's well looked after here, part of the furniture you might say,' Tug Wilson informed them, his face still cracked wide open in permanent grin. 'That's Cardiff Rose over there,' he went on nodding towards a buxom wench playing darts with a bald headed Able Seaman. The big lass with her is Belfast Betty, loverly friendly ladies both of 'em. Sailors are their total reason for living; they have never been known to turn away from a sailor whose needs verge on the desperate.' His good humour continued as he educated his young mess members concerning the star studded cast (as far as sailors were concerned) of players in Commercial Road pubs on an average Saturday night.

Shiner could just not resist making a reply in his somewhat blunt fashion. 'Christ, I'd 'ave tuh be more than desperate tuh shag that,' he said, a slightly awed look enhancing his youthful countenance. He gaped at Cardiff Rose as she turned round having plucked her darts from the dart board. 'Christ!' he blasphemed again, 'she's got a fuckin' snake tattooed on 'er tits!'

His pals joined him in giving her cleavage a thorough looking at, the ample bosom of the savage looking lady was barely contained by the outsize low cut blouse. Then…too late, they could not avert their gaze in time to avoid the dark burning eyes that bored into the still gawping young sailors, with Shiner standing dead centre, his mouth gaping so widely he looked like an empty space.

Cardiff Rose crossed the space in three strides, seized Shiner at the back of the neck, and with a determined pull buried his face in those mountainous breasts.

'Have a real close look sprog,' she hissed. As she did so, her right hand shot down to the region of his groin. Trousers, genitals, pubic hair, nothing escaped that Amazon's determinedly placed hand. Her face suddenly changed to a look of astonishment. 'Jesus-H-Christ!'

It was her turn to gape widely as she uttered her blasphemous statement. She began to laugh as she ran her hand down Shiner's thigh. 'What have we got here, my well rigged little darling,' she chortled dragging a hapless Shiner to her chair.

The crowd had now cottoned on to what was going on, and gathered around to show appreciation to whatever may befall this young man securely held in the grasp of this very big lady.

'Whip it out Rose, lets all 'ave a look,' a voice yelled from the crowd, accompanied by other loud exhortations to increase the young fellow's embarrassment.

Shiner appeared to be in a trance as Cardiff Rose pulled him onto her lap as she dropped into her chair. Before he could do anything to stop her, his fly was unzipped and her meaty hand dived in, foraged for a second, and then pulled Shiner's penis out to a huge roar of laughter from the crowd.

'Ooooh, look at that lovely thing,' she crooned, smacking her lips suggestively as she waved Shiner's manhood at the howling throng, and then, not as an act of mercy, but realising that she had gone far enough, she made an elaborate act of putting everything back where it belonged. She hugged Shiner ferociously, her huge hips gyrating against his body in a stand up assimilation of sexual intercourse. 'Any goddamn time you like, it'll always be a freebie for you,' she uttered huskily, pulling sensuously on his buttocks.

The crowd had found a new star, and Shiner staggered to the claps on the back from the appreciative audience. No one guessed he had been so stunned by the swift abuse of his person to even consider putting up any kind of resistance. He edged his way back into the comparatively safe surrounds of his friends. Bogey handed him his pint back, which he had only just managed to rescue as Shiner was grabbed by his buxom tormentor.

'Fame for life,' Wiggy said, clapping him on the back, and then added with a sly grin, 'would you like another pint here, or would you prefer to try the Lennox, while you can still boast a set of balls?'

Shiner drained his glass saying ruefully, 'remind me to keep my gob shut, and stand at the back of the crowd next time, will you? A man's toggle and two aren't his own in this place.' He rubbed the area of his fly gingerly asking with mock horror, 'did you notice if she put everything back safely?'

They all shouted cheerio to Tug Wilson, who by now was heavily involved with a long legged young woman at a corner table. They edged their way through the door to the pavement, and then took the few paces to the Lennox still in great good humour.

The drinking area in the Lennox was not as large as that in the Albany, so was densely packed due to the notoriety of the public house. Pleasure seekers of all persuasions, and all sexual inclinations frequented this pub, due mainly to the high numbers of sailors who chose it as their favourite watering hole. Portsmouth is only a couple of hours down the A3 from London, and consequently was very often visited by celebrities from the 'Big Smoke'. They generally came down at weekends to enjoy the freewheeling attitude to life of off duty sailors. The Albany, Lennox, and the Sussex Hotel just past the Town Station railway bridge were favourite haunts for Saturday night revellers out to have a great time and socialise with complete strangers.

Bogey used his weight advantage to get to the bar, and not surprisingly was served quite quickly.

'D'yer know what Bogey,' Shiner said as he grasped his pint pot, and removed the brimming vessel from the tray. 'Yuh may be a big lumbering ever thirsty basterd, but at least you're useful in a crowded bar; you lovely fellah,' he added, as Bogey waved the tray as if to belt him.

Somebody with a great deal of talent was playing the piano at the other end of the bar. Whoever it was, he or she had gathered an appreciative crowd around their person, giving a totally expert rendition of 'Poor People of Paris'.

Bogey took the tray back to the bar and asked the barmaid, 'Who's that on the old Joanna?'

'Russ Conway,' she answered disinterestedly.

The look Bogey gave her insinuated the reply, 'gerroff, yer pullin me pisser!'

He edged his way back to his pals, and said unconvincingly, 'you'll never guess 'oo that is takin' a turn on the Joanna.'

They all looked at him expectantly.

'Russ Conway,' he said, as if imparting some lost memory in a conversation.

They all swung round, craning their necks in the direction of the piano. Wiggy, the tallest in the group caught the back of a well groomed head, then the shoulders and the left profile. The handsome contours were as unmistakable as the music. 'You're right Bogey,' he confirmed, his voice raised against the tune.

The solo performance ended with a flurry of notes, and the spectators burst into appreciative applause. The famous pianist rose from the piano stool, and a space opened up for him. The ever present smile stayed on his lips as he nodded gratefully to his admirers. He had obviously taken the stool at the behest of his many fans in the pub, because, as he made his way back to his companions at the table in the nook of the bar, the regular pianist dropped back into his seat, having first placed his pint on a coaster on top of the piano. His first choice, after flexing his fingers above the keyboard was the Irish favourite 'O Danny Boy'. A rich tenor quickly took up the melody, and between them they made a good job of this popular song.

The four pals finished their pints, and by mutual consent headed off down under the railway bridge to the Sussex Hotel opposite the Guildhall square. The huge stone lions stared across the square at them, sitting like great inert sentries glaring through the mixture of light and eerie shadows created by the lamps that illuminated their outlines to varying degrees of luminescence.

Both main bars at the Sussex were bursting at the seams. Drinkers in the lounge bar had spilled through the door onto the pavement. The floor show that night offered some scantily dressed young dancers that attracted both the navy and civilian revellers who always scrambled for the tables nearest the stage on Saturday night.

'We'll never get served in there,' Bogey said, matter of factly.

His companions agreed, and they all walked down past the Yorkshire Grey, and decided to have a pint in the Great Western.

'All the talent must 'ave found another venue ternight,' Shiner complained.

'Watter yer on about yuh fussy basterd, yu've already bin 'andled once tonight,' Bogey laughed, teasing Shiner.

'Aw shit man,' Shiner replied grimacing. 'I'm talkin' about something I can make love tuh, norra bloody Amazon who would wear me bollocks as a trophy. Did yuh see the size of that fuckin' snake tattooed on 'er tits? Fancy starin' that fuckin' thing in the eyes whilst yer pokin' the fire – brrr...,' he shuddered theatrically, 'puts a nasty taste in yer gob just talking about it.'

They all laughed with Shiner as Wiggy passed the beers along the bar. Later, having given Cardiff Rose and Belfast Betty a thorough, and definitely slanderous talking about, they moved off down to the 'Immoral' (Balmoral) for a quick one. From there they meandered along past Elm Grove, and on through the lawns of Southsea to the Sea Horse bars alongside Billy Manning's funfair. They all mustered at the bar together, and then took their individual pints to an empty table with four chairs.

Three girls sitting at the next table gave them a thorough looking over in the manner of the not too experienced predatory female. Their glances indicated that if anyone cared to ask, 'yes we are on our own,' and, 'no we are not waiting for anyone in particular.'

Shiner, always way ahead of his oppos when it came to ice breaking, stared back cheekily at the pretty dimpled brunette, who was very attractive in a podgy sort of way.

'I'd buy yuh a drink, but it's blank week for us navy guys,' he opened the conversation, his eyes roving up and down her frame suggestively.

'I've got one, thank you very much,' she retaliated a little nervously.

Her ruby lips had formed a slight pout as if unsure of just how to handle this blunt advance. Her eyes danced across Shiner's grinning face, making her look all the more innocently attractive.

'Where are yer from then?'

His eyes locked on mercilessly, enjoying her timidity.

'Ryde, the Isle of Wight,' she answered, transfixed by Shiner's stare.

'What, all of you?'

Shiner was slightly taken aback as his mind instantly envisaged the distance and awkwardness of the journey back if he did manage to trap this lovely plump little thing and take her home.

'Yes, all of us,' she replied, her eyes locked wonderingly on his.

'D'yer come over 'ere every Saturday night then?'

Before she could reply, one of her friends broke into the conversation. 'Beryl!' she said sharply, the words emanating from her pinched lips in a slightly shrill manner. 'You know we have to catch the eleven o'clock ferry, we should be going now.'

Both her companions looked at her, and then Beryl glanced at her watch as if undecided. She gave Shiner a hopeful glance, hoping he would understand the unspoken look which said she wanted to see him again. Shiner was not slow, he knew that look.

'Next Saturday okay, will you be here?'

Beryl blushed at the hurried question; she had not been prepared for the blunt interest in his tone. She was also very aware that none of the other lads had made a pass at her friends. Her thoughts were interrupted by Wiggy saying to Shiner, 'First of port is duty next Saturday.'

Shiner slapped his head with open palm in an overt act of exasperation, and then quickly recovered. 'If I come over on the ferry to Ryde next Friday will you meet me there at six o'clock?'

Beryl blushed again and looked at her two friends as much as to say, 'should I?'

They however, were rising from their seats with the attitude of the ignored female. Beryl glanced at Shiner. He was instantly struck by the hopeful innocence in her eyes as she blurted out, 'yes!'

Four pairs of eyes followed the rear end of Beryl as she hurried to the door in pursuit of her two friends. Their eyes took in the slightly twisted seam of the black nylons that swept attractively upwards, and down to the top of the heel section of a well turned ankle.

'Phooeey,' Shiner let out a noisy sigh of delight. 'Roll on next Friday night!'

He rubbed his hands together in anticipation of his carnal intentions.

'Bloody cradle snatcher,' Bogey said, a broad grin spreading across his face. 'None of them looked over sixteen to me.'

Shiner grinned back at his big oppo. 'Ah yer only sayin' that because yer trappin' valve is jammed shut. I reckon Beryl is seventeen at least, and the other two dogs were getting on fer twenty I'll betcher. Anyway,' he continued with sullen pretence. 'Why didn't any of you make a move on the other two?'

'Not my type old boy,' Wiggy answered matter of factly, draining his pint. 'Anyone for a refill?'

'Here, I'll get these,' Dusty said loudly realising that Bogey had been up to the bar twice that evening. Wiggy pulled a pound note from the kitty money in his belt flap, and handed it to Dusty.

'Bit of a witch, that tall skinny bitch, wasn't she?'

Bogey's sincere, if somewhat harsh criticism of the girl with the shrill voice was turned into a laugh as he said to Wiggy, 'I wouldn't touch her with yours!'

Amidst laughs all round Wiggy replied, 'You country born, thistle kicking, sheep shagging hayseed, how dare you even infer that mine could get a hard on for such a harridan. Did you see her eyes? They were spitting cinders at us...no I really couldn't raise any interest in that one; mind you, that cuddly little thing Shiner latched on to was worth a second look, if you like a bird with an arse four feet across.'

'Three foot eleven inches if you don't mind,' Shiner retaliated loudly, laughing at Wiggy's unusually coarse delivery, which was now fuelled by the evening's ale. After that the conversation took a definite turn for the worse as they sunk their seventh pint.

If the three girls who had not long left had heard the crude banter toing and froing across the table, Shiner's chances with the cuddly, dimpled Beryl would get no further than a quick slap in the mouth.

Wiggy shook his head as if to clear his brain of the fuzziness that was taking over.

'Hey you lot,' he slurred, a bit drunkenly. 'Fancy a stroll through the funfair, I need some fresh air.'

His request took a moment to register; only Bogey reacted with some haste.

D'yuh mind if I wait for yer 'ere and 'ave another pint? Not out of the kitty,' he hastened to add.

'I'll stay as well if yuh don't mind Wiggy,' Shiner spoke up as well. 'I've still got three quarters of a pint ter see off.'

'Are you coming Dusty?'

Dusty looked at Wiggy, and seeing the drooping lower lip, and glazed eyes, made an instant decision. 'Yeah, come on then, a bit of fresh air will do me good,' he said, realising that it was not wise to let his pal go outside by himself.

'Here, you see this off,' Wiggy slurred, pushing his half empty glass across the table.

Bogey grabbed the glass quickly as it tilted under the momentum of Wiggy's somewhat drunken thrust. 'Oops, nearly spilt that diddle I,' he spluttered with a lopsided grin, his loose face showing he had imbibed quite enough for the evening.

Dusty steadied him through the door, where Wiggy instantly dragged in a deep breath of fresh air. The breeze coming off the Solent ruffled his hair, making him struggle awkwardly in his befuddled state to tuck an unruly lock of hair under the rim of his cap. After a couple of attempts, he seemed to have achieved his goal, only to be told by Dusty laughingly that he was 'going astern' (his cap was on back to front). The continued struggle to get the cap and hair to do his bidding was comical to behold, more than one passer by had a good giggle at the expense of a wobbling Wiggy. Finally, unaware of the fun he had provided for a few, the cap seemed to sit where he had placed it, and the odd lock of hair only just peeped below the rim.

After five minutes or so of cool air Wiggy appeared to have sobered a little. 'Christ! That's better,' he said, apparently satisfied with the outcome of his struggle. At that moment a coconut shy caught his attention. He fumbled in his pocket for his own money, and handed a threepenny bit to the attendant. With exaggerated attention to the targets, he threw three balls with alarming accuracy at the space surrounding the coconut he had chosen. His magnificent effort was sarcastically applauded by both Dusty, and the attendant. Not to be beaten by this initial setback, he purchased another three balls, two of which found the same nothingness as the previous three. The sixth ball of the evening however, had been blessed by the God of probability, and smacked a coconut right in the centre, wobbling it off its perch. Dusty and the attendant erupted into a shout of acclamation, laughing like drains.

Seconds later Dusty was clapping Wiggy on the back with seven pint ferocity as the attendant handed Wiggy a coconut, and then, fumbling under his counter brought out a badge with 'Welcome to Southsea' written around the edge. The laughing face of Billy Manning looked up at Wiggy as he struggled to pin this gratuitous gift onto his suit, wincing with pain as he found the flesh underneath.

'Here!' said the attendant, signalling Wiggy to hand the badge over. 'Let me do it…there y'are squire,' he clapped Wiggy on the back. 'Ows abaht that then!'

The light hearted few moments over, they continued to weave their way through the fairground attractions, Wiggy's outlook improving by the minute.

Dusty stopped by a punch ball machine, and stared searchingly at the large clock face. As it was only a penny a punch, he fumbled in his pocket for small change, and selecting a few pennies from the handful, shoved the remainder back in his pocket. He slotted a penny in the machine and pulled down on the leather ball and chain. With the pennies clutched in his left hand, he stepped back, poised himself, and then let fly with his right fist with murderous intent. The ball reacted instantly to the attack, and flipped outwards and upwards; the needle however, which was meant to sweep around the clock face and indicate the force of the blow, just flicked abjectly at the bottom stop, and moved no further.

Dusty and Wiggy stared flabbergasted at the stationary needle. 'Here,' said Wiggy disgustedly. 'Gimme one of those pennies.'

He pushed the coin into the slot, and grinning foolishly at Dusty, pulled the ball down to its full extent. The drink affected blow he threw at the machine only served to make the needle flicker slightly. They both gaped at the stubborn needle, and then at each other. The humour of the moment suddenly hit them, and they both descended into a fit of gibbering laughter, well suited to their drink-enhanced mood. Dusty fed another penny into the slot, cocked his ear comically, and nodded his head as the penny was heard to drop into the machine. He stepped back with exaggerated purpose, and leaning back slightly, lined his fist up. The blow that exploded from his shoulder as his body came forward would have felled an ox if appearances were anything to go by. The ball bounced a bit, the needle waved at him momentarily, and settled once more at its bottom stop.

'Hey, this is getting serious!'

Dusty set up for another wild swing, as the pair of them laughed loudly; by now a small crowd had gathered, and they too were enjoying the spectacle.

He had just pulled the ball down to the ready position, when he was pushed savagely aside with such force that he went sprawling along the tarmac surface.

'Out uv the way, yuh fuckin' useless O.D., let an Able Seaman show yer 'ow it's done!'

Dusty had just rolled over and was on the way upright when his gaze fell on Able Seaman Smith throwing a solid straight right at the leather ball. The needle had just reacted to the action applied to the mechanism by the chain, and swung fully round the clock to the stop on the right hand side of the dial as he regained his feet. The readiness of his stance told Smith that Dusty was about to retaliate savagely, so like any aggressor he threw another punch, hoping to get his victim before he was prepared. Dusty had just regained an upright position in time to angle his body to one side allowing the punch to graze his chest. As the punch reached the full extent of its forward motion Dusty was bending forward over the punch into a slight stoop, at the same time his tightly clenched fist started coming up, and found its mark with unerring precision on the left side of Smith's jaw. That was the end of the viciously enacted few seconds, Smith's brain switched off as the flash of light that surged through it closed down all his awareness faculties. He lay stretched out on the ground, arms extended upwards as if appealing to some superior deity to accept him, his eyes were glazed and wide open as if not of this earth, but looking into another existence.

Dusty gazed down at his vanquished foe; Wiggy also was gazing down with awe at the outcome of that perfectly placed right uppercut. They both reared their heads together as Smith's friends of the earlier part of the evening ran over to survey the spectacle of their downed acquaintance; Dusty immediately assumed a defensive mode.

'Okay, okay lads, nothing to do with us,' the front one hastened to say placatingly, raising his hands, palms outwards, towards the victor.

An onlooker, who had seen how the fight started, spoke up, 'he got what he deserved, but I doubt if he expected that outcome.' A few people laughed awkwardly at the statement as Smith's acquaintances were lifting him to a sitting position, his back to the punch ball machine.

'Okay lads he's coming round now, you bugger off, we'll take care of this,' the same fellow spoke up, taking charge of the scene of battle.

The onlooker, who had commented on the outcome of the attack, thrust a card in Dusty's hand saying, 'If he tries any bullshit about what really happened here, you just tell whomever to give me a ring, I'll put them straight.' He shook Dusty's hand vigorously before he departed, his face holding the look of a person who had done his civic duty.

Dusty thanked him, his gaze flicking to and from the scene on the ground. Everything that had happened, and the sight of a groggy Smith gradually coming round seemed to be being played out in another dimension that he had suddenly become aware of.

His trance like look was disturbed by Wiggy saying, 'Come on Dusty, let's get out of here!'

The urgency in Wiggy's voice had the effect of pulling him back to reality. He reacted to the urgent tugging on his arm and followed Wiggy out of the funfair, but the effect of their night on the beer was still evident in their slightly waving gait.

Far at the back of the crowd that had gathered, two very serious looking individuals nodded at each other; one of them slipped a notepad and pencil into his inside pocket, and they both faded away into the anonymity of the remainder of the night's pleasure seekers.

4

WIGGY MEETS THAT SPECIAL GIRL

The following Monday morning, the Master at Arms of HMS *Vanguard* came bustling through the Regulating Office to a flurry of 'good mornings' from his staff. As he changed from his civilian suit into his service attire, his eyes dropped on a sealed envelope lying on his blotter pad. The Regulating Office runner, a young Ordinary Seaman, had left the Master at Arms a fresh pot of tea, milk and sugar, on a tray at the side of the blotter. He poured himself a cup of tea, added milk, and one spoonful of sugar, then stirred the brew vigorously clockwise for a few seconds, and then took a sip. His face brightened noticeably as he savoured the tea, and then after a gulp or two, he picked up the letter, and studied the front for a second. The top left hand corner had the words: 'CONFIDENTIAL, BY HAND,' written in large capital letters. The middle portion of the envelope was addressed:

Master at Arms Fullwood,

Regulating Office,

HMS *Vanguard*.

He slipped his letter opener into the flap of the envelope, and neatly sliced it open. Removing the sheet of signal paper, he studied the message thereon for some seconds. Finally satisfied that he understood the full import of the message he glanced at his watch, picked up the telephone and dialled three digits. He listened for a moment then said, 'Ah, good morning Lieutenant Forrester, Master at Arms Fullwood here sir, have you the time for a chat ASAP. Bit of trouble concerning one of your Able

Seamen, but I have to speak to you in person about it.' He listened for a while, and then said respectfully, 'very well sir 0830 hours your office.'

He replaced the receiver, and read the contents of the letter again while he finished his tea. Then, as if having reached a momentous decision, his face took on a stern look, and he slipped the message back into its envelope, opened his briefcase and slipped it inside. His face now had the determined look of a man who had reached a decision. That decision, if in interests of good order and naval discipline, would be supported by his superior officers whole-heartedly, such was the power of this man's position. He donned his cap, glanced into the mirror and squared it off, and then, picking up his briefcase he walked through the door and up through the Regulating Office.

'Foster,' he said to his Leading Regulator. 'Answer my phone if it rings, I expect to be gone for a couple of hours at least.'

'Aye-Aye Master,' his subordinate replied.

He walked along the Burma Way until he came to the ladder leading up to the Quartermaster's flat. He climbed the ladder and stepped through the screen door onto the upper deck and looked upwards towards 01 deck.

'Petty Officer Hancock, Leading Seaman Wilson, a word for a moment if you please,' he shouted up to them.

The top part of ship Petty Officer and his Leading Hand hurried down the ladder, and wished the Master at Arms a 'good morning'.

'I have just come to forewarn you that you may be called down to your divisional office in a short while,' he informed them sternly, and then proceeded to enlighten them without giving them the whole story. 'The reason concerns a message I have just received from the Provost this morning about certain actions by Able Seaman Smith last night at Billy Manning's funfair shortly after 2230 hours last night. That's all I can say for now, but I am sure both of you have an inkling of what occurred at the funfair. I won't have you piped for, I'll ring the Quartermaster and he will pass on the message to you, meanwhile, discuss nothing with anyone; understand?'

'Aye-Aye Master,' Petty Officer Hancock answered for the both of them.

Minutes later the Master at Arms knocked on the top divisional office door, and walked in. 'Good morning sir,' he said, removing his hat, and taking the proffered seat.

'This was waiting for me on my desk when I arrived on board this morning.'

He removed the message sheet from its envelope and passed it to Lieutenant Forrester. Two minutes later, having absorbed its contents thoughtfully, he said, 'so the provost's men keep a weather eye on Smith whenever he's ashore do they?'

Lieutenant Forrester gazed into the stern eyes of the man opposite him as he confirmed that he could read between the lines of the actual text.

'I hope you will understand sir, it did not start that way intentionally, of course,' the Master at Arms assured the Lieutenant. 'Smith just seemed to have a penchant for being in the middle of any ruckus that came to our attention through the local police, and our own undercover guys. Smith always changes into civvies at Aggie Weston's, and more often than not stays the night there as well, so he is never instantly recognised as being a sailor. Add that to the fact that he does a quick disappearing act as soon as the law appears on the scene, and you will realise how difficult it is to nail him down to any specific act of aggression. Anyone who does get their collar felt by the law will never implicate anyone else either by name or description, so you can see how difficult the job is for the police. It leaves them in a position where they can only charge those who they are quick enough to catch at the scene of a scuffle, even then the charge is rarely more than 'disturbing the peace'. Our Able Seaman Smith has never been caught in the act, so to speak, but his face has been seen so many times in the vicinity of these weekend battles it caused our men to keep an eye on him and find out where he comes from, and who he is. When he gets back aboard on Monday morning, his uniform is spick and span, and even the odd facial mark would not prove that he has taken part in a disturbance ashore.'

The Master at Arms stopped speaking as Lieutenant Forrester made a move to speak.

'So once again Smith is at the scene of a scrap,' he said, referring to the message. 'Young Miller gives him more than he had bargained for in an act of self defence, and no one of any authority is at hand to place charges.' The lieutenant paused. 'You know Master at Arms; this begs the question, why didn't your regulators in civilian clothes make an arrest?'

The Master at Arms remained silent for a moment. When he replied, he did so choosing his words carefully.

'The very reason for having a few carefully trained and selected regulators out on the streets in civvies is to catch drug pushers, and any users and abusers who have a service connection. They also take note of any service personnel who have a tendency towards homosexuality, who, if they become active in the world of homosexuals, can become a serious danger to the nation's security if compromised by foreign agents. Our men will not jeopardise their cover unless the situation really warrants it. They do however file reports on the activities of suspicious individuals they observe whilst doing their job. The actions of Able Seaman Smith fall into that category, and their report on Smith is a damning indictment of the man's serious intention to do harm to the young fellow he attacked without any provocation.'

A short pause followed the Master at Arms' statement.

'What's the bottom line here then Master at Arms? What is the ultimate action you recommend?'

The Master at Arms' eyes met the Lieutenant's level gaze.

'Smith must be removed from this ship,' he stated bluntly. 'Miller is the innocent victim of this man's obsessive vindictiveness. The very fact that Miller is quite capable of looking after himself has probably strengthened Smith's hatred of him, purely because he cannot subjugate this young Ordinary Seaman to his will. I can only recommend a draft chit to another command.'

The Master at Arms searched the Lieutenant's face for a reaction, and then added in serious tones, 'what if Miller gets it in his head that the only way to get Smith off his back is to do him serious harm? Even ultimately, kill him.'

That statement brought a shocked look to the Lieutenant's face. 'Good lord Master at Arms! Don't you think that is an assumption too far?'

'Not at all sir. This is a physical situation that involves unreasonable hatred. It is quite plausible, even at this stage to assume that if left to fester uncontrolled this could explode into a homicide situation. My advice...my strong advice, is to nip it in the bud at this instant. Get Smith as far away as is possible from this young man, otherwise the very fight that provides the witnesses required to prove the intention of 'grievous bodily harm', may be the one that leads to a case of murder, or at the very least manslaughter. The least we must do is get Smith out of five mess and off this ship today. I don't want to stand before a court martial and explain why I did not take the necessary steps to avoid a situation, when I had all the circumstantial evidence at my fingertips to separate the individuals concerned...neither would you sir.'

The final strongly-expressed four words jolted Lieutenant Forrester out of his thoughtful attention to the Master at Arms' words. 'Then we must present this to the Captain without hesitation,' was his instant response to the possible consequences engendered by the emotive words, 'court martial'.

The Master at Arms was prepared for this reaction to his decisive words. 'I have my Monday morning meeting with the Captain at 0930 hours,' he said. 'I think you should join me, particularly as you are Smith's divisional officer. A few personal questions are bound to be asked, and the Captain likes his officers to have personal details concerning their men at their fingertips.'

By way of reply Lieutenant Forrester made a grab for the phone. 'Ah, pay office, could you get one of your writers to deliver Able Seaman Smith's 264s to the top divisional office immediately... thank you.' He replaced the phone and turning to the Master at Arms said, 'they should be here in a minute, would you like a coffee while you wait?'

The Master glanced at his watch. 'The Captain's steward always provides tea and biscuits, and as it's only five minutes or so, I think I'll wait, but thanks all the same.'

An awkward silence reigned for a minute, and then Lieutenant Forrester posed the major question. 'Are you going to recommend that Smith is removed immediately?'

'Yes sir, I am, and for good reasons. On Friday of last week, I gave Smith a very strong warning that he must curb his aggressive behaviour. This warning followed a tussle between Smith and Miller in 3C port gunners store flat. Everyone I questioned pooh-poohed the incident as a momentary flare up, but when I had Smith in front of me I could not help but feel the underlying hatred he held for Miller. Miller, it appears, contained Smith's aggression with a common wrestling hold, rendering him incapable of further hostility. Had Saturday night's attack not occurred, I would be discussing Friday's incident with you at this moment, so you see sir, this thing will erupt again anywhere, and it is my fear that the next time he takes Miller from behind, it may be with far more serious intent.'

'Quite, quite,' Lieutenant Forrester answered, having listened intently to the additional part of the evidence. 'And you believe, with Miller's obvious ability to defend himself, he may have to resort to more brutal tactics to defend his person.'

'That's about the size of it sir.'

A knock on the door interrupted them.

'Come in,' the Lieutenant answered with raised voice.

'Able Seaman Smith's docs sir,' the young writer said, placing the folder on the desk.

'Right sir, we should be going now, it's almost 0930 hours.'

'Is it the Captain's day cabin we go to?'

'Yes, he always meets me in a working atmosphere, he likes to keep our meetings focused on direct events that can be dealt with the same day if necessary,' the Master answered as they left the confines of the top divisional office.

The Master at Arms knocked on the door to the Captain's day cabin. A greying Petty Officer Steward opened the door. 'Ah, good morning Master at Arms,' he greeted, smiling politely. 'Come in please, the Captain is all ready for you…ah, good morning to you too sir,' he added as Lieutenant Forrester appeared in the doorway.

A hint of surprise showed in the Captain's eyes as they fell on his top division officer.

'Hello Jeremy, have you been a bad boy?'

The greeting raised a polite laugh from his visitors as they settled into the leather armchairs indicated by the Captain.

'Now what brings two of you to my morning meeting with the 'Jaunty'?'

He used the popular wardroom pseudonym for a Master at Arms, the smile remaining on his face as he angled his seat towards his visitors.

The Master at Arms opened the proceedings, and began relating the events that lead to important decisions that would be either agreed by the Captain or otherwise. The interpretation of the facts as they stood was most important, and this was reflected in the Captain's undivided attention to every word that was spoken. The Steward brought in a silver tray on which perched a beautifully engraved coffee set brimming with all the essentials. He flitted unnoticed from guest to guest laying a two-third's full cup of coffee in front of each of them, leaving the cream and sugar within reach of both of them. He added cream and sugar to his Captain's cup, and laid the cup and saucer within easy reach. The business of the morning continued as if he was not in the cabin, such was the trust laid on his shoulders. Only discussions of a highly sensitive nature would require him to absent himself.

One hour later, the Captain, having been completely briefed, concurred with the recommendations put forward by the Master at Arms. He ordered, emphasising the word 'immediately', that Able Seaman Smith should be removed to the cells in RNB whilst the formidable amount of paper work was completed, and from there to another naval billet when Naval Drafting authorities reassigned him. The Provost of the Portsmouth Division would play a large part in Smith's reassignment; he would back his departmental colleagues to the full extent of his authority.

'This is a regulating matter now sir, if you so wish there is no need for divisional involvement beyond this point, I can take care of everything from here on.'

'Thank you Master at Arms, you carry on and do what has to be done. Your actions will certainly have more impact on this man if his departure, and therefore, his timely severance from this ship is carried out with cold abrupt authority, leaving him in no doubt that he is "persona non grata", do you agree?'

'I certainly do sir,' the Master at Arms replied as they parted each other's company at the Regulating Office door.

'Any messages?' was his first priority as he stepped inside his domain.

'The Provost rang, and asked if you could give him a bell ASAP,' Leading Regulator Foster answered him.

'Right, will do,' the Master at Arms replied, then added, 'Get your oppo Jenkins and come into see me after I've had a word with the Provost.'

After closing his office door behind him, he removed his cap and hung it on the peg behind the door, and then placed his briefcase beside his desk as he sat down. Before rushing into the job he had to do, he sat quietly for a few moments gathering his thoughts. Finally he picked up the phone and dialled; but not the Provost immediately. First he had to get his plan in motion.

'Ah Quartermaster,' he said. 'Pop up to 01 deck and ask Petty Officer Hancock and Leading Seaman Wilson to come down to my office, and then, in five minutes' time pipe the duty hands to report to the Reg office…okay…got that?' He sat in thought for a moment and then with a purposeful look of intent he braced himself against the back of his chair, and rang the Provost.

A stern voice answered the call.

'Master at Arms Fullwood here sir, you wanted to speak to me.'

After listening for two minutes, he gave the Provost a short account of his meeting with the Captain, and concluded with the words, 'so in approximately two hours' time Able Seaman Smith will be delivered to the Reg office at RNB, and from then on he is all yours to do with as you will, does that sort this one out?'

The reply was affirmative, so after a couple of minutes' light chat Master at Arms Fullwood said, 'goodbye sir,' and replaced the receiver, an inadvertent smile on his face. The smile disappeared as he got up from his seat and knocked on the glass partition indicating to Leading Regulators Foster and Jenkins that he was ready to receive them.

Having briefed his subordinates on their part in what was about to take place, he invited Petty Officer Hancock and Leading Seaman Wilson into his office. 'You're losing Smith,' he said bluntly. 'The Captain has just authorised his removal to the custody of the Provost. I want you both to understand that everything that happens from this moment until we remove Smith from this vessel must be done with cold deliberation. The both of you will accompany the two duty hands and clear all his kit out of his locker, and out of the messdeck. You are not to be fussy how his kit is packed, the quicker he is off this ship the more meaningful the action taken against him will appear. By 1230 hours I want him on the Police Launch across to Welcome Jetty, and from there by Provost's Vehicle to Royal Naval Barracks.

'Duty Hands report to the Regulating Office,' the Quartermaster's voice interrupted his briefing.

'They will be here in a couple of minutes, just remain seated while I get the ball rolling.'

He picked up the phone again. 'Quartermaster, Master at Arms Fullwood here. I want you to pipe Able Seaman Smith Ship's Office. Have you got that?...Yes, Ship's Office.' He replaced the receiver and glanced through the glass partition. Foster and Jenkins were standing ready at the counter of the Ship's Office section of the compartment. 'Right,' he said to Hancock and Wilson. 'Any moment now we go into action.'

Almost on cue, the Regulating Office door opened and Able Seaman Smith entered, a slightly puzzled expression creasing his face. He sauntered up to the Ship's Office counter, the puzzled frown now creating a deep furrow on his forehead.

'Yuh 'ad me piped for, why's that?'

Foster and Jenkins appeared silently at his elbows, and nodded to the Ship's Office Leading Hand, who, with eraser poised, removed Smith's details determinedly from the watch and station bill.

'Locker keys,' Leading Regulator Foster ordered sternly, holding out his hand.

'Wha...what for?'

Smith stuttered as he spoke, looking very confused, a hint of panic evident in his eyes.

'Give me your locker key,' Foster insisted, and then added with emphasis, 'immediately!'

Smith fumbled in his pocket, and laid a bunch of keys on the counter. While Foster removed the locker key from the ring, Jenkins thrust a hand in each of Smith's number eight shirt breast pockets in turn. He threw the green station card he had extracted onto the counter, watched by a very worried Smith.

'Right, off you go,' the Master at Arms ordered Hancock and Wilson, as Leading Regulator Foster indicated he had got Smith's locker key.

As Smith was ordered to a chair against the bulkhead, Petty Officer Hancock and Leading Seaman Wilson vacated the Regulating Office closely followed by the duty hands. The Leading Hand hurried on ahead to get Smith's green case out of the baggage store. He arrived at the messdeck just as hammock, boots and brown case were thrown onto the mess table. Whilst he cleared Smith's suits out of the ship's equivalent of a wardrobe and laid them in the green case, the duty hands were sweeping Smith's kit out of his locker into the gaping kit bag. Ten minutes later the kit was dumped unceremoniously at the gangway.

'Quartermaster,' Petty Officer Hancock ordered, 'give the Master at Arms a bell and tell him that all is ready at the gangway.'

The puzzled Quartermaster, surrounded by his equally puzzled staff obeyed the order immediately. Five minutes later Able Seaman Smith was pushed through the screen door, closely followed by the eviction party. Without ceremony he was hurried down the accommodation ladder and into the harbour police launch where he watched his kit roughly thrown aboard after him. Now, in a totally dazed state, and flanked on either side by Leading Regulators Foster and Jenkins, he was transported to Welcome Steps, and from there straight into the Provost Vehicle.

The whole lower deck buzzed with speculation as the removal of Smith spread around the ship. All sorts of reasons for this ignominious removal would now be invented, only to be spoiled when the true reason filtered through the buzz line. No one could allow such a juicy bit of knowledge to be passed onward without suitable embellishment, and in typical lower deck tradition two and two quickly became five. It would come as a great disappointment to the buzz mongers when the person responsible for disconnecting Smith's awareness circuit with one well placed uppercut was an unpretentious Ordinary Seaman who would not submit to the bullying tactics of the ship's punch up artist. Leading Seaman Wilson put the whole affair in perspective when after dinner he said to Dusty, 'you won't have to keep your eye on your back any more.' The look on his face as he made the statement indicated that he too had reason to be a little relieved to see the back of a potential messdeck problem.

The ship's physical training instructor, Reg Purcell, visited the mess during dinner break.

'Hi Tug,' he greeted his fellow Leading Hand. 'D'yer mind if I 'ave a word with your four sporting prodigies?' He indicated the four lads at the end of the table, grinning broadly at his own pretentious eloquence.

'Fill yer boots,' Leading Seaman Wilson answered, looking quizzically at his four charges.

All four vacated their seats and joined the ship's PT instructor in the passageway. He spoke to Wiggy first. 'You're excused the 1800 hours duty watch muster, I've also fixed it with your part of ship PO for you to secure at 1545 hours, that will ensure that you catch the first liberty boat. Don't waste this opportunity, you are our only cricket representative, and the Captain was extremely enthusiastic when the message passed through his office.' The smile on his face remained there as he said, 'All of you are cleared for Wednesday afternoon; which one of you is Ordinary Seaman Knight?'

'I am,' Bogey answered a little shyly.

The PT instructor gave him a quick appraisal, his expression showing he was impressed by Bogey's solid build. 'D'yer know where the United Services sports ground is, just opposite HMS *Vernon*?'

Bogey nodded saying, 'yes clubs.'

'Well that's where you've got ter be at 1400 hours on Wednesday. Carry towel and sports gear, 'ave yer got any boots uv yer own?'

Bogey shook his head. 'No clubs,' he said still showing a hint of shyness.

'Come round to my store, and I'll see what I can sort out for yuh, size tens do?'

'No, elevens clubs,' Bogey said, reddening slightly as he answered.

'No problem, I've got an old pair of elevens somewhere that'll do yer...Miller?'

He looked questioningly at Dusty and Shiner.

'That's me, clubs,' Dusty said firmly.

'No problem with you, the Judo club meet every Wednesday at 1400 hours, and they will no doubt introduce you to all their other training venues when they get to know you. They are a mixed bunch of all the services in the Portsmouth area, plus a couple of civilians who work for the war department. As of next week they have been allocated a corner of the gym in RNB as a regular training base, so that means less dodging around, and never being certain where the next week's session will be.' He turned to Shiner. 'No problems with you old son,' he said familiarly. 'If they put you in the team after your trial on Wednesday, I will fix it up for you to be excused duties whenever necessary, 'ows about that lads?' He finished speaking, looking at all of them in turn, his bubbly enthusiasm for his job a bit infectious.

'Absolutely fantastic clubs,' Wiggy spoke for his three pals. 'Thanks very much.'

The PT instructor left them with a thumbs-up sign, saying, 'give it all you've got lads!'

That afternoon Lieutenant Forrester found time to have a stroll round his part of ship. Dusty and Wiggy had been assigned to X turret as gun sweepers, and as their divisional officer hauled himself from the gun deck through the open door to the turret they wrenched their eyes away from the wondrously complicated hydraulic systems and the massive structure of the breech ring and continued wiping hardly noticeable flecks of dirt from the lustrous paintwork.

'Carry on Miller, don't let me disturb you,' the Lieutenant said as Dusty stood to attention. 'I just want to have a chat with you tomorrow morning at 0900 hours, just thought I would let you know beforehand. Petty Officer Hancock is aware of my wishes, so you just pop down to my office at that time.' He paused a second before climbing through the door, and added, 'by the way, word has got around of your sporting abilities, well done!'

'Aye aye sir,' Dusty replied, as his divisional officer turned towards the door. He had been expecting a call to appear before one officer or another, and in a way was slightly relieved that it was his divisional officer, and not the Captain or Executive Officer.

— ∙ —

In the meantime, at Royal Naval Barracks, Able Seaman Smith had been delivered to the cell block. He was not locked in his cell, because of course, no charges had been brought against him. He would be kept in this block, where he would not be able to fraternise with anyone who was not of the regulating branch. His escorts had not uttered a word to him, and the regulators of Royal Naval Barracks were not going to be any more forthcoming. Deep in thought, he sat on the edge of the palliasse on the metal framed bed. It was slowly beginning to dawn on him that he had not been charged with any offence, and while he puzzled that over he got up, and throwing his hammock on the palliasse that served as a mattress on this robust steel bed proceeded to unlash it and then lay his kit out atop of it. He winced noticeably as he saw the crumpled state of his kit; 'stroppy bastard' he may be, but strict training had made him fastidious with his personal effects, all matelots hate the term 'crabby bastard' inferring that one was not as clean and tidy as the service insisted one should be.

'Is there anywhere I can get an iron?'

His question was to the cell block staff in general, and no one noticed his painful reaction to the movement of his jaw as he spoke.

'This end 'ere,' the sentry indicated. 'Yuh 'ave ter bring yer stuff 'ere and do it,' he added tersely.

The work kept his hands occupied, but his mind could not help but dwell on the predicament he found himself in. Was he being chucked out into Civvy Street; or was he on his way to Army Prison? Whichever it was, neither appealed to him in the slightest. He liked the navy; he thrived on the pecking order of the lower deck. 'Shit on before you yourself are shit on; never give a sucker an even break.' The fact that he would never rise above Able Seaman whilst he continued with this aggressive style never entered his head. 'Better to be a good A.B. and sod the rat race, anyway, the waiting list for Leading Hand was a seven year long roster.' This was how his mind worked, he was said to have a chip on both shoulders whenever messdeck discussions referred to advancement, but lazy he was not. He was a good seaman and a good Radar Plot rating. He had to be perceptive to become that, it's not easy to write backwards. This was the enigma that was Able Seaman Smith.

If his work and his abilities as a peacetime sailor were in any way indicative of wartime capabilities, then Able Seaman Smith would undoubtedly be one hell of a fighting sailor, if he could discern friend from foe!

He took his time doing his ironing, the neat pile of whites growing steadily higher. His actions were automatic, the ironing only serving to keep his hands occupied. The mind, so quick to hate was elsewhere reliving the moment of contact between Miller's right fist and his jaw. Inwardly he was kicking himself for allowing such a sucker punch to connect. Ultimately he blamed it on the few beers he had consumed that night, but his mind held no remorse for the provocative attack he had made, his ego finding complete justification for his actions. 'If I'd uv kept me cool, I'd 'ave 'ad the barsterd,' he reprimanded himself. 'That's twice I've let the Welsh twat gera rise on me, if I geranuvver chance I'll make sure the barsterd don't gera lookin.'

At the same time that Smith had his next chance of attack in mind, the Provost was in touch with naval drafting authorities in Haslemere.

'Ah, good afternoon,' he greeted the civil servant in charge of Portsmouth Command Drafting. 'I want one of your little favours again. I have an Able Seaman RP2 whom I would like posting out of the way for a couple of years' cooling off period. My sources assure me he is a satisfactory worker, and believe it or not he has a pretty clean service sheet. He just suffers from a short fuse with subordinates, seems he has a bit of a superiority complex when it comes to Ordinary Seamen.'

'I will ring you back in five minutes,' the voice on the other end replied, then asked, almost as an afterthought, 'what's his full name, and official number?'

The Provost read off Smith's details, and then turned back to the paperwork in front of him.

Ten minutes later his phone rang, and the same pleasant voice made an offer. 'HMS Rooke, Gibraltar, could do with another watchkeeper. His duties would be spread between shifts in the Rock Radar complex, and any ships exercising in the area who need back-up in their Operations Room. I can arrange for him to be on the RAF flight from Brize Norton at 0100 hours Wednesday. You will have to get him there by 2200 hours Tuesday at the latest, does that suit you? I will have the paperwork on its way to you in one hour by dispatch rider if that is agreeable.' The pleasant voice broke off in a manner that suggested the owner was pleased to be able to help.

'That will do fine, thank you for your prompt help, much appreciated,' the Provost replied gratefully. 'Thanks again for your efficiency,' he added, knowing full well that civil servants had an unwritten code of absolute politeness in their dealings with the military end of their government service.

By 0130 hours on Wednesday 19th September 1957, Able Seaman Smith found himself sucking a boiled sweet provided by the RAF flight attendant as the Britannia RAF transport passenger plane clawed its way into the skies above Oxfordshire. He had been told nothing, only the 'Snowdrop' who sat beside him in civilian clothes knew what his orders were.

Able Seaman Smith had never flown before; the excitement of the moment was however lost to him as he sat sullenly looking at the back of the seat in front of him, oblivious to everything but his thoughts. The confusion in his mind, brought on by the total lack of awareness of where he was going made him angry, but there was no outlet for that anger other than in his own thoughts. The desire for revenge burned within him savagely now, distorting every thought that flashed through his tormented mind. His obsession verged on total paranoia as he lay back into his seat and wallowed in the unnatural hatred that consumed every fibre of his being.

The light indicated that seat belts could be removed; minutes later the Pilot took the opportunity to speak to his passengers, breaking into Smith's evil thoughts just in time for him to catch the word, 'Gibraltar,' and that 'a tail wind would ensure that they arrived on time'.

■ ▪ ■

Totally unaware of Smith's whereabouts, and not bothered in the least, the four young sailors were enjoying a Wednesday afternoon doing their level best to impress the Petty Officer Physical Training Instructor supervising their particular sporting interest.

Bogey was having a hard time getting used to being part of a scrum again, and was already suffering from burning ears, and a little mouse under his right eye. The POPTI in charge was changing everybody around every ten minutes or so, to give the new people a chance to show their forms. After forty minutes of strenuous scrum downs and lineouts for throw-ins followed by half field runs for tries everybody was blowing like wounded buffaloes and ready for a break. The man with the whistle would not let them rest idle though, he wanted to find a good penalty kicker amongst them. The men on the field were a mixture of Sailors and Marines all jumbled up together regardless of service connection; and not all were natural penalty kickers. When it came to Bogey's turn nobody was expecting a big lad of seventeen stones to be anything but a useful blocker and powerful scrum down pusher. His first kick went straight through the middle of the poles so the PTI gave him an awkward angle. He converted that shot, and the next long one, and waited for the Instructor's verdict, expecting to be given an impossible shot at the poles. The

PTI just took his notebook out, and after asking Bogey's name, appended it to his little book.

Meanwhile some of the navy lads were pulling another player's leg. 'Looks like we've got us a new kicker, Billy Boy,' one of them joshed, laughing as he spoke.

'Thank Christ for that! Some other basterd can take the blame for missed penalties now.'

Meanwhile back at Pitt Street swimming pool, Shiner had out-swam everyone that afternoon, and found himself in front of a very serious Physical Training Officer known by the pseudonym of 'Boss' by all his staff because he was not one for stuffy marks of respect during training sessions.

'I am not letting you escape young man,' he said taking Shiner to one side. 'Believe it or not you are an Olympic possible. It would be a shame if we did not improve your innate talent with that aim in mind. What would your answer be if I said I could pull a few strings, and get you a posting where you could carry out the necessary training to have a crack at it?'

Shiner was dumbstruck, he could not have been more speechless if the officer in front of him was a beautiful woman, and she had just said, 'I am first prize, and I am heavily into hedonism, particularly with someone whose 'cod piece' is as unnatural as yours.'

The Boss saw his hesitation and understood. 'You have a good think about it, you have the talent, all you need is the guidance and the necessary training to achieve success. Let me know your thoughts on the matter ASAP.'

Leaving Shiner with those words ringing in his ears, the Boss walked to the pool edge and started shouting encouragement to Wiggy, who, seeing the Boss' head hovering over his gasping body made one last massive effort to reach the end of the pool on his second length.

'There you are you see, you can do it,' Geoff Mitchell enthused, 'and the Boss is here to sign your form, how's about that?'

'Oh super clubs! Now piss off and let me drown in peace will you,' Wiggy gasped, perhaps being a little too familiar with his response.

Geoff Mitchell ignored the familiarity, and saw the funny side of the comment. 'Here,' he said, holding out a hand, and then, with Shiner hauling on the neck of the overalls they hauled him spluttering onto the poolside.

Shiner had watched the Boss and his senior rate's efforts to encourage Wiggy, and in that instant his mind was made up. 'Excuse me sir…er, Boss, I'm going to take you up on your offer, this is too good a chance to miss.'

'Well done young fellah,' the Boss answered, clapping him enthusiastically on the shoulder. 'Work hard and you won't regret it. We are here as guides, trainers, and arse kickers, work cheerfully with us, do as you are told, and you will gain all the attributes to put up a good show. Now, get in that pool, and finish off by showing us just how fast you can really do the 'Fly'' (butterfly stroke).

'Aye aye sir,' Shiner yelled in excited response to the order of a man well used to firing young men with enthusiasm. He dived into the pool, porpoised a couple of times, and raced up the pool in a spume of swirling water.

Dusty arrived at the Gymnasium in Royal Naval Barracks just in time to assist in laying enough mats out for ten training couples. Sergeant Tommy Watkins Royal Marines introduced himself, and chatted away lightly to Dusty, getting to know his new trainee. Dusty was the new man this afternoon, and looking around at the other people he realised that this was not a completely male dominated class; two attractive Wrens were laying their own mats out. The sight cheered him, and suddenly he had a feeling of being very much at home. His previous club at home in Welshpool included a female team.

'Right Dusty, lets find you a 'Judogi'; we all wear red belts for training, but you will soon find out all the other Judoka's grades; by the way what grade have you trained to so far?'

'Green, third 'Kyu'.'

'I'm black belt first Dan,' Sergeant Watkins replied, more as a statement of fact, than a statement of superiority. 'Like to aim for first Kyu would you?'

'If I can get the time and a bit of support with regular training.'

'We'll have to see about that then, but first of all would you like to start today at basics, and let us see what your breakfalls are like.'

They had moved to the locker room as they were speaking and as Sergeant Watkins opened a large chest in the corner of the room, he said, 'I keep a couple of Judogis for anyone joining us who does not have one, but it would be handy if you could get in touch with your home, and get your Mum to post yours to you.'

'Will do Serge,' Dusty replied as he grabbed the suit and belt.

After fifteen minutes of breakfalls they had a short break. 'Well you're ok in that department,' the Sergeant encouraged Dusty, 'now let's see what you're like in action for five minutes.'

The Sergeant turned to another pair. 'Jesse,' he called across. 'You and your training partner keep an eye on us two while I see what this third kyu can do.'

The man called Jesse blew the whistle he had been given, and Dusty grappled his opponent immediately, after the niceties of the sport had been solemnly done. His willingness to 'mix it' was countered by the Sergeant, and Dusty found himself falling to the mat under the impetus of his own opening move. With a quick twist he hit the mat face down then hunched up and rolled forward, coming to his feet again very swiftly. The Sergeant grinned. 'Good follow through!'

They both grunted as they came together again after Jesse signalled them to carry on. This time they both struggled for a telling hand hold on each other's costumes, and in seconds the purpose-built suits of both of them were hauled free of the red belt. Jesse blew the whistle as they wrestled over the boundary of the mats. They jumped to their feet, squared off their suits, and when ordered, met each other grip for grip again. They did not notice it, but all the other Judokas had stopped their practice in favour of the struggle going on, on the first Dan's mat. Dusty was doing well, and they were shouting encouragement from the sidelines. Amidst the verbal encouragement Dusty had contrived a hold that was causing the first Dan a spot of bother. The onlookers screamed advice at the Sergeant, who with a noticeable grin used his huge experience to dislodge Dusty, and surprised them all by wheeling Dusty across his shoulders and throwing him heavily to the deck whilst enhancing the move by keeping a tight hold on Dusty's right wrist, making sure that the left side of his body hit the mat heavily. Dusty recognised the throw a little too late which spoilt his breakfall. The result of this was that his heavy contact with the mat dazed and slightly disorientated him, as well as winding him. 'Christ,' he gasped as Jesse stepped in, 'I've seen that one before but never practiced it.' The grinning Sergeant helped Jesse to get Dusty to his feet.

'Why that throw?' Jesse asked, a faint grin on his face.

'It's the desperate instructor's throw when a third Kyu is proving better than expected,' the Sergeant grinned back, and then turning his attention to Dusty said, 'Are you ok son?'

'Yeah Serge,' Dusty replied, now fully recovered. 'I was just not quick enough to realise what throw you were applying, but, lesson learnt,' he added sportingly.

'I'm not letting yer 'ave that one Tommy yuh dirty git, it didn't start off with a judo move,' Jesse said with a broad grin stretching his face.

'Ok Jess I know the young feller was giving me a hard time, that'll teach me not to underestimate a third Kyu joining a new club, won't it?'

'Hey you nearly had him there sailor,' one of the young Wrens said to Dusty as they joined the group for a post mortem of the bout they had just witnessed. All the young enthusiasts were pulling the Sergeant's leg; one young marine joshed, 'what would you have done if the clever Dabtoe had a move up his sleeve to beat it?'

'Lie down and take it like a man, just the same as he did,' the Sergeant said, cuffing his subordinate lightly on the shoulder.

Dusty was beginning to feel at home with this crowd, and by the time 1600 hours came, and they all rushed into the men's showers, he was included in the hubbub of conversation, and the occasional loud ribaldry that accompanies young men of any sporting persuasion. What Dusty did not know at that moment was that he had gathered a young fan whose interest in him went a bit further than admiration of his judo skills.

'Did you catch that sailor's name?' the interested one asked her companion.

Her companion gazed at her with a knowing smile saying, 'Do I detect a spark of interest Christine; mind you he is dishy in a sailorish sort of way, isn't he? His nickname's Dusty by the way,' she added, her smile turning to a broad grin.

'Get yore eyes orf 'im Jane, I sore 'im first,' Christine replied, laughing as she put on an accent that suggested she may be chasing a bit of rough, and then changing the subject, she asked, 'are you joining the lads when they go to the home club?'

'You bet I am! That's the only reason I come to these sessions.'

It was later when they were all fully dressed that Dusty questioned the khaki uniform and naval beret worn by Leading Seaman Jesse Rhodes. 'I didn't know the navy had its own commandos,' he just had to say as he looked admiringly at the profusion of specialty badges adorning the uniform.

The answer he received, and the conversation that followed, lasted them through the side gate of Royal Naval Barracks, and the short walk up the road to the 'Home Club'. A seed of desire had been planted in Dusty's eager young brain; this chance meeting with this new acquaintance had kindled a glimmer of light concerning his future. He knew in that instant that he must find out more, and the questions he asked left the Naval Commando in no doubt as to where his young companion's mind was taking him.

'Come on you lot, lets 'ave yer four bob,' the Sergeant said good naturedly as they lined up at the bar of the Home Club. He opened the neck of a small string bag which he kept purposefully for the kitty, and all his Judokas chucked in their four shillings. Anything left over when they had consumed a couple of pints each would remain in the communal purse, and by mutual agreement every now and then a charitable donation would be made to St Dunstan's home for the blind; this was a favourite charity, and well subscribed to.

By 1700 hours they were all enjoying their first pint, when the rugby fanatics burst into the club all red faced and full of Bonhomie. They were quickly followed by the Pitt Street crowd, and soon the Home Club was alive to the loud chatter of Portsmouth Commands sporting fraternity.

Dusty spied Wiggy's tall frame, and before he got involved in a conversation dragged him over to meet Jesse Rhodes. Wiggy gaped in awe as he noticed the impressive array of badges, and before long Jesse was relating his journey from Boy Seaman at HMS *Ganges*, Ipswich, to his specialised job in a commando unit at present training at Horsey Island firing range, and based at HMS *Excellent*.

Bogey and Shiner worked their way towards Dusty and Wiggy, and very soon they also were showing great interest in the Naval Commando's exciting job. As the Leading Hand put it in dry terms, 'It beats a life of eternal boredom ensuring the cosmetic elegance of Britain's grey navy.'

The two wrens moved to the group, encouraged by the growing number of sporty servicemen obviously enjoying man's talk. The conversation quickly changed from idle chatter laced with the usual expletives to a discussion of the afternoon's sport. Christine had placed herself beside Dusty, and hung onto his every word, then said to attract his attention, 'Did Sergeant Watkins surprise you with that shoulder wheel throw?'

Her eyes said that she was not really interested in any answer Dusty would give, but wanted to engage his interest no matter what the subject.

Dusty laughed as he recalled the swift reversal of the bout. 'That's one I'll remember, I'll probably get a chance to use it back on him some day, the crafty sod!'

'He's the Portsmouth Command senior unarmed combat expert,' Jesse broke in. 'Honestly, he can kill a man with his bare hands in the time it takes you to snap your fingers.'

'Perhaps I won't use that move on him then,' Dusty said with a short laugh, then added, 'you must be adept at unarmed combat as well.'

Not to his level,' Jesse replied. 'But you're right, we are taught, and must be good at disarming a man from the front, and killing a man whatever the situation.' He grinned as he said the last words, obviously making light of a conversation that was getting a bit too serious. Before any of the youngsters could ask him the one question that he would not answer out of service etiquette, he changed the subject. 'Anyone for another beer while Tommy's at the bar?'

They were all in different kitty groups, but the money holders were all nattering at the bar, so they all had their pints bought at roughly the same time. As they moved away from the bar they broke into separate conversation groups again. Firstly, it was noticed, that the wren called Jane had latched on to Bogey, who, although delighted with her company, was just a bit uncomfortable. None of his pals knew about Margaret and his son. He had not shared that part of his life at any time.

Christine quietly angled Dusty away by tucking her arm under his right elbow, forcing him to change his pint over to his other hand. 'What do you do on Saturdays?'

The predatory question took him by surprise, but he quickly recovered and asked, with a wide grin, 'Why, are you pushing for a date?'

'Well, it occurred to me that you might not be seeing anyone. It also occurred to me that it would be a terrible waste of an opportunity, if you are not seeing anyone; so how about it sailor?'

'You're on,' Dusty laughed back, finding the cheeky grin on her face very attractive. 'What about here on Saturday at half six?'

'Great,' she beamed back at him. 'D'you mind taking in a film, *Brief Encounter* is on at the Odeon down the road, and I have never had the chance to see it.'

'Never heard of it,' Dusty grinned back at her. 'But we'll give it a go.'

— · —

Later that evening, the four pals were relaxing on the Fxle of HMS *Vanguard*, talking seriously about what the future could hold.

'I can't get that guy out of my mind,' Dusty had initiated the conversation.

'Who's that?' Bogey asked, because his mind had been elsewhere, thinking of a little lad, and his Mum.

'That Leading Seaman, Jesse Rhodes. I mean, you look at the sheer excitement of the career he suddenly found for himself.

Every moment of every working day spent perfecting his training for one specific purpose; parachutist, free swimming diver, small arms expert with top marksmanship expertise. Add to that his non-sub as a quarters armourer first class, able to use and maintain heavy armament and you have got one hell of a qualified guy.' He paused, then added with youthful determination, 'that's where I'm heading, fuck being a paint ship expert, as soon as I get my AB's rate I'm slappin' in for every God damn course that will get me those two little blue shoulder tabs.' He turned to Wiggy, adding, 'so it looks as if you and I are going to be divers together, doesn't it?'

Wiggy nodded soberly. He had taken in every word that Dusty had spoken.

'Hey! Are you two basterds serious?'

Shiner's face held a look of surprise, making his question sound a bit demanding. Dusty turned to face him, and with a dead pan expression said, 'You bet I fuckin' well am!'

Wiggy spoke for the first time, and surprised them all with a thoughtful statement. 'Saturday is the last cricket match of Portsmouth Commands season, so I had better look for a winter sport, hadn't I? That guy impressed me as much as he did you,' he nodded towards Dusty as he spoke. 'So next Wednesday I am going to ask if I can go Judo training with you my old mate.'

All eyes were now on him; this was not the impressionable eighteen-year-old who had walked through the gates of HMS *Victory* Royal Naval Barracks just over a year ago. This was a young man who now had a vision of the excitement of his boyhood dreams finding a suitable modern outlet.

Dusty looked into his friend's eyes, and saw the determination reflected in them. The slightly pursed lips, and the furrows lining the brow added to the overall appearance of a young fellow all fired up to become a man of some force of character in the near future.

Dusty held out his right hand, and Wiggy grasped it firmly as Dusty spoke two emotive words: 'Naval Commandos.' Their eyes stayed locked together as Wiggy echoed Dusty's words: 'Naval Commandos.'

Shiner watched the unfolding scene with a wannabe expression, as they made their pledge for the future. It was one of those things that comradely young men do, when becoming well tuned to a service career that has much to offer. A pang of regret rose in his mind, and as always, if Shiner felt it, it had to be verbalised.

'And there's me volunteering to be a navy swimmer when the time is right,' he said loudly and morosely. 'I can't back out of that,' he continued. 'So I'm stuck with it until August or September 1960.'

All three of his pals looked at him, but it was Wiggy who voiced the general opinion of all of them.

'What are you moaning about, you ungrateful so and so. Here you are, selected as an Olympic hopeful, and you're dripping about having to train for the next three years. None of us were given such an opportunity you know, we have to go with the flow of the talents that we have been given, which are nothing compared with yours; Mr Golden Bollocks,' he added uncharacteristically; but getting his point across to a slightly startled Shiner.

'Yes, but I'm goin' ter miss all t'excitement aren't I?'

Dusty and Bogey looked on amused, as Wiggy retorted knowledgeably, 'Are you hell, you daft sod! First you get your AB's rate, and that's only a matter of waiting now. Then you have to wait until someone thinks it's time for you to go through for leading rate, and all the time that is going on, they will also be deciding if you have what it takes to become a club swinger. Providing you are passed for Leading Seaman, they are going to grab you, an Olympic hopeful, as quickly as they damn well can.'

'Christ!' Shiner's blasphemy verged on the vehement, and continued in that vein as he added, 'that could take for fuckin' ever; I'm only in for nine years.'

'Well, there you are then,' Wiggy suppressed a grin as he replied. 'While you are training for 1960, you can slap in for anything that does not take you out of the Portsmouth area. I mean, even if you take a ship's divers course at Horsey Island diving school, you are still here to crack on with your swimming, Drafty is bound to give you some ship or other in the home fleet day running out of Pompey. You can't expect a shore base when you're straight out of basic training.'

Shiner brightened up visibly, the assurance of his pals always acted like a salve when he felt left out of things a bit.

'What about me?'

It was Bogey's turn to feel a bit left out of the picture. 'I can't leave you three basterds out there on your own; Christ knows what sort of bother you would get into without my guiding hand.'

'Bogey,' Wiggy said, clapping his pal on the back. 'Solid fuckers like you never have any bother, but just like I had a bit of a problem getting used to swimming in overalls, you have got to get your head down and pass your ETLR (Education Test Leading Rate). Once you have got that under your belt it takes you all the way up to Chief Petty Officer, and whatever you achieve in between is down to you. If you don't want to spend the rest of your time in this man's navy tarting up paintwork, look for something you can do that will lift you out of it.' Wiggy punched his pal lightly on the arm. 'You go for it Tarzan, it's all there waiting for you, all you have to do is find it.'

Bogey grinned, visibly cheered by Wiggy's pep talk, and punched him lightly in return as he said, grinning broadly, 'Just you remember your old mate when you're an officer, because there's no doubt that's where you're heading.'

The conversation dwindled as they all leant on the guard rail watching the harbour traffic plying to and fro, the Gosport ferries constantly criss-crossing one another as they plied between the two shores of the harbour with varying numbers of passengers. Nothing seemed to interrupt their clockwork movements back and forth across the harbour entrance. They were almost like some animate beings, imbued with the instinctive need to fetch and carry.

It was only a cold blast of wind hurrying up the Solent and seeking passage through the harbour mouth that reminded them all that they were only dressed in blue trousers and white fronts. They hurried below decks, to find the mess was empty so they hurriedly slung their hammocks whilst chatting absently about the day's events. Like all good messmates would do, they slung and unlashed Slinger Wood's and Tug Wilson's hammocks knowing that both of them returned on board regardless of what opportunities came their way ashore.

'How did you come to meet that bird who joined us in the home club?' Shiner asked.

'Her and her mate are the only two females in the judo club.'

'Did yer trap?' Shiner asked, giving Dusty a knowing grin.

'Mind yer own fuckin' business!'

They finished slinging Tug Wilson's hammock while Shiner prodded Bogey for information concerning the 'Jenny Wren' called Jane.

'Mind yer own fuckin' business,' Bogey echoed Dusty, giving Shiner a scolding look for his nosiness; but only in jest.

'What's up with you pair of fuckers,' Shiner asked, grinning just as broadly. 'Bein' a bit precious with what yuh've trapped aren't yuh?'

'I'm seeing Christine on Saturday night,' Dusty informed him, hands on hips in a theatrical stance. 'There, does that make yuh happy, yuh nosey cunt?'

Shiner looked at him, a bit puzzled. 'Are yuh sure it's Saturday yuh've asked her out?'

'That's what I said diddle I,' Dusty answered, his face now assuming a quizzical expression.

''Ave yuh forgotten yer duty watch with me on Saturday yuh daft basterd?'

The stupid grin fell away from Dusty's face as realisation suddenly hit him. The excitement of the day, and Christine's overt interest in him had made him forget.

'Oh shit!' he exclaimed feeling a bit foolish.

Bogey and Wiggy joined Shiner in a loud guffaw at Dusty's expense.

'Do you know what base she's from?'

Wiggy's question delivered through the loud chaffing of Bogey and Shiner caused him to think for a second.

'Yeah, she's a writer in the pay office at RNB.'

'Best you get in touch with her tomorrow then, ain't it mate,' Wiggy grinned at his pal, then gave some advice. 'You can get to her on the phone in the QM's flat, all you have to do is get the number of the pay office.' He laughed as an afterthought hit him, 'you had better hope she's not duty Friday because there's not much going on on Sundays.'

Bogey had lapsed into silence as his pals sorted out Dusty's love life.

'What the fuck's up with you?' Shiner gave Bogey a swift nudge, trying to keep the situation alive. 'Ave yuh made a fuck up as well?'

'Nah,' Bogey answered. 'I didn't make a date with her.'

Shiner's face took on a flabbergasted look. 'Yuh daft bugger you, all the bloody time we've been in the soddin' navy, and I've never seen yuh trap before. That wench was lookin' at yuh as if the sun shone outer yer arseole, and yuh didn't ask her for a date?'

Bogey looked at his pals, and decided that now was a good time for confession. He felt he owed them an explanation.

'Yeh, I can understand yuh wonderin' about me,' he started, and then gazed at each of them in turn. 'The fact is I've got a bird at 'ome. Even more to the point, she's got a kid by me, and that's why I 'ave ter send 'alf me money 'ome.'

The three faces staring back at him were limp-jawed with amazement. Even Wiggy, who was never at a loss for the appropriate statement was dumbfounded. Finally, Dusty scraped his throat and asked, 'How old's the kid?'

'Born in June,' Bogey answered, and then went on, 'we've arranged to get wed during Christmas leave, regardless of if I've got a ship or not. We've got the marriage banns organised so the Vicar can get them read as appropriate, he understands my situation yuh see.'

'Why on earth didn't you share this with us before?'

Wiggy had put a friendly hand on his oppo's shoulder as he spoke, and Bogey reacted to the matey gesture with a smile aimed at his friend.

'The time never seemed right,' he answered simply, his face taking on that shy look that strangers mistook for a form of weakness. His friends knew that his gullible look was just country boy shyness; it sure as hell was not a weakness.

Shiner came out of his state of shock saying, 'yuh bloody dark horse yuh,' he said with typical Shiner bluntness, and then smiling honestly at his pal continued. 'D'yer know yuh big soft sod, there was one time when I thought that yer maybe a bit on the queer side. Course that feelin' didn't last long as I got ter know yer, but the thought did occur.'

Bogey looked at his oppo, and seeing the sheer honesty, and the look of understanding, his face broke into a broad grin, and then, with a glint in his eyes he said, 'Are yer absolutely sure my dear!?'

He put a huge arm around Shiner and pulled him close, pursing his lips in front of Shiner's lips. 'If I was, it would only ever be you,' he lisped, camping it up to the huge amusement of Dusty and Wiggy.

'Go on! Slap the lips on 'im,' Dusty shouted.

Shiner began to struggle in the firm grip, giggling like a schoolgirl.

'Oh, I do like that sweetie,' Bogey teased waving his lips in front of Shiner's mouth.

''Elp!' screamed Shiner. 'Get this big lug off of me. I can't breathe yuh big sod, put me down.'

The laughter coming from his lips as he yelled made him red in the face, so Bogey relented, and, giving Shiner a big pursed-lips smacker on the cheek, let him go.

'Ahhgh, yuh big slobberin' basterd,' screamed Shiner, finding it hard to speak through his mirth as he tried to wipe the effects of Bogey's smacker off his cheek.

Everybody else was in tears. The other messdeck, just along the passage must have wondered what the hell was going on, but nobody poked their oar in.

The mirth slowly declined, and then Wiggy said something that made them all yell in agreement.

'Pity we all saw our ration off earlier, we shall have to wet the baby's head another day.'

— ∙ —

On Friday night, both Shiner and Dusty were aboard the 1630 hours liberty boat, and disembarked at Welcome Jetty. They strolled through the main dockyard gate together where Dusty turned left up Queens Street, and Shiner carried straight on to the Isle of Wight ferry terminal.

Some time later Shiner found himself on the jetty at Ryde gazing around to see if the object of his desires had taken him seriously. He walked towards some bus shelters, looking around expectantly, not realising that an amazed pair of eyes was watching him walk towards the main road. Beryl stepped from the bus shelter that had afforded her some protection from the chill wind that swept in from the Solent.

'Hi,' she called to him, attracting his attention with a small circular wave of her right hand. 'I wasn't sure that you would come,' she expressed her uncertainty as she walked towards him.

Shiner quickly recovered from his surprise; he too had not really expected anything to come of their chance meeting in the Seahorse Bars.

'Well, well, well!' His astonishment showed through a welcoming smile. 'So you came after all.' Before she could even think of objecting he planted a not too serious kiss firmly on her rich ruby lips. She tensed slightly, and then feeling his pleasant unforced grip reacted warmly in return. The second kiss was more like it although it still held a trace of uncertainty that told him that this young lady didn't give her all for the price of a first warm kiss.

They were both dressed warmly, but the cold wind made it somewhat uncomfortable to continue any discussion in the bus shelter, not to mention the interest shown by a curious bus queue.

'D'yer fancy a drink somewhere warm,' Shiner asked, keeping his arm around her waist.

'Mmm, yes,' she replied, and then shivered gently as she added, 'it is a bit cold out here. There's a nice little pub just up the road with a real coal fire in the lounge of an evening.'

'Sounds great,' he said, and then added with a cheeky grin, 'so you are eighteen?'

Beryl looked into his smiling eyes and said truthfully, 'not until October the third, but I had a sneak preview a couple of months in advance.'

'You naughty girl,' he chided jokily, tightening his grip on her waist as they walked across the road.

They walked a short way up the gently rising main street until Beryl pointed out a small public house. She led him into the empty lounge and selected a table close to the glowing fire. He watched her wriggling out of her coat in typically feminine fashion that accentuated the curves of her ample bosom and the seductive slope of her hips. All of this was not lost on Shiner as he hung her coat up. His mind was so distracted he forgot to remove his own hat and Burberry in his aroused state. He walked back from the bar carrying his pint and a babycham, and eased himself into the seat beside her. His face showed that something else was stirring, apart from the natural urges of a nineteen year old male body. Beryl's innocent actions, and the purely feminine way she had carried them out were now confused with another feeling of warmth towards her. He didn't analyse the feeling as he sat down with the drinks, but later he would realise that the first little flicker of love had occurred at that moment. The twin pleasures of the sexual urge combined with burgeoning affection made him feel quite heady, and it showed in his actions.

Beryl instantly felt his new warmth towards her, and in that uniquely feminine way she had read the message in Shiner's eyes, she instinctively knew that romance had just started to blossom.

He shuffled along the seat closer to her, and then suddenly realised he was still wearing his hat and Burberry. He laughed, half nervously, and said to her, 'see, you've got me all of a tiswas already.'

She noticed the huskiness in his voice, and gazed thoughtfully at his retreating lean frame as he walked to the door and removed his hat and raincoat.

Shiner plonked himself back down beside her, close, but not quite touching. They lifted their glasses simultaneously, Beryl taking a ladylike sip, and Shiner reducing his pint by a quarter. They began to chat, completely at ease with one another, the warmth between them deepening. Beryl, seemingly inadvertently, edged up close to him until their bodies were touching, and then lightly leant against him. Shiner reacted by slipping his arm around her waist possessively, and then for three hours they sat and talked, completely absorbed in one another.

Beryl's parents were both partners in the meat marketing business, her Dad doing the nuts and bolts of the job, and her Mum being the office side of the partnership. Beryl had left school with four ordinary levels, one of them being an 'A' in mathematics which she put to good use working for a local accountant.

Shiner tried not to show it, but he was very impressed with the short resumé of herself and her family. This warm hearted and cuddly young lady had qualities that went beyond 'kicking 'em off' at such a short association, so the closeness that had developed between them deserved nurturing, and not to be wasted by too hasty a declaration of base needs, whether by actions or words. Without dwelling on his thoughts too much he made an unusual decision to allow this romance to develop to whatever fate decreed would be its final destiny.

Later that night they strolled down to the ferry port, kissing and cuddling until the last moment. Both were now committed to taking this romance wherever it was going.

'What do I call you? All your pals call you Shiner, but I want to know you by your real name,' she asked, then added shyly, 'do I call you Arthur, or Art, or even Arty?'

Shiner grimaced, and then grinned at the simple question. 'Oh, God forbid! My second name is Samuel, so you call me Sam, or Sammy would be nice.' His smile became a quirky grin, and with a sly look he added, 'And I'll invent a suitably sexy name for you.'

They kissed, with real passion now, crushing each other's lips as if in some great osculatory competition. Shiner's hands crept down and clasped her under the buttocks, hoisting her up onto his thrust forward hips. She clung to him knowing full well that things could proceed no further due to the public nature of the ferry port. She would however be left wondering in virginal awe at the strength and rigidity, not to mention size, of Shiner's manhood.

They released each other and Shiner dashed for the ferry as a crew member urged people to climb aboard. She watched the ferry disappear into the darkness of the night, then, with romantic thoughts clouding her vision, she waited trance-like for her bus, her heart totally lost to the young sailor who had gone just far enough on this, their first date.

— · —

Shiner could not believe his eyes as he walked up past the bus stops to the main dockyard gate. There, strolling absently, lost to the world was his pal Dusty ambling down Queens Street, mind totally lost in a clinch that had occurred not ten minutes earlier.

'Bloody 'ell!'

Dusty gasped loudly as he caught sight of Shiner standing outside the gate gazing at him in disbelief. 'I do believe in synchronicity from this moment on,' he grinned as he approached his shipmate. In time-honoured tradition, the first words he asked were, 'did yer get a bit?'

'Nah,' Shiner laughed as he dropped in step with Dusty as they went through the gate. 'Quite honestly Beryl is a nice girl; I know our relationship will have to be a bit more secure before anything like that 'appens.'

'Christ!' Dusty blasphemed. 'Am I talking to the same bloke I left not six hours ago? Have you gone through some magic transformation? Or, wouldn't it stand to attention properly?' he grinned with a sly look.

'Fuck off, yuh daft basterd,' Shiner retorted, returning the grin, and the badinage.

'I was walking around three legged all night, but I knew that if I chanced me arm, that would 'ave been the end of it right there and then. Honest ter God, Dusty this is a good-un, I'm just goin' to 'ave ter take Cardiff Rose on if it gets as I can't keep it in me trousers any longer,' he laughed.

The bluff retort was only a foil to protect his macho bravado though; no matter how lightly he spoke of his feelings, Beryl was indelibly engraved in his mind, the tables had been turned. In naval terms, Beryl was the one who had 'trapped' that night.

The two pals talked about their respective dates as they continued their way to HMS *Vanguard*. Shiner learnt that Dusty would certainly be seeing Christine again, but no firm date had been set beyond judo training next Wednesday. They jumped off the PAS boat onto the catamaran and climbed the accommodation ladder, making a point of facing aft and saluting the quarterdeck. The Quartermaster handed them their station cards and they proceeded down to the mess.

'Hey, thanks you two,' Shiner greeted Wiggy and Bogey, both of whom were leaning over the side of their hammocks in anticipation of their oppos' return from their dates. Both Shiner's and Dusty's hammocks had been slung and made up, ready to leap into.

'Cheers lads,' Dusty followed Shiner's lead.

'Come on then,' whispered Bogey. 'Ow did yer gerron then?'

'Ah, it's a long story,' Shiner teased his pal. I'll 'ave ter wait until mornin' to remember it all.'

'Yuh got a bit then?' Bogey insisted, anticipation of a juicy story evident in his eyes.

'Weeeell, no, and yes,' Shiner continued the tease, and then grabbing hold of Bogey's ears over the rim of the hammock he grinned into Bogey's screwed up face and said, 'no, I didn't ger a bit, but yes, I got a bit older.' Then puckering up his lips he got his revenge on his pal and planted a slobbering smacker on his forehead.

'Aaaagh, yuh slobberin' basterd,' Bogey groaned in a muted loud whisper, his right arm appearing menacingly over the top of the hammock, and making a grab for his tormentor. 'Come 'ere, yuh sloppy git, I wanna kiss yer back.' He laughed as Shiner wisely dodged the grasping hand, and dived under Bogey's hammock to the other side. He jumped up on the edge of one of the messdeck benches, and just as Bogey swung round to meet him he grabbed Bogey by the ears again and planted another sloppy smacker on his forehead.

Bogey could hardly contain his muted mirth, spluttering almost maniacally now, he made a grab for Shiner, but his agile tormentor had ducked under the hammock again and was standing in the passageway puckering his lips at Bogey, and enticing him to come nearer.

Wiggy, who was enjoying the spectacle as much as the participants became a little concerned about the level of noise.

The remainder of the mess was ashore for the night, or taking advantage of a long weekend's leave, but the adjoining mess still had a few lads aboard.

'Keep it down you two; you'll be waking the rest of the ship up with your antics.'

Bogey reacted to the advice immediately and hauled himself back into his hammock, but not without first saying to Shiner good humouredly, 'I'll get yuh termorrer yuh fast little basterd.'

The skylarking died down, but a titter could be heard from Wiggy's and Dusty's hammocks as the pair continued their silly sailor banter for a while.

— ∙ —

The following Saturday found Wiggy seated in the cafeteria style dining hall enjoying an early dinner with the afternoon watch keepers. His presence was required at the United Services sports ground by 1230 hours to prepare for the first ball of the afternoon's cricket. Therefore permission had been obtained for him to have his meal in time to catch the 1200 hours Liberty boat.

Smartly dressed in full number ones, and topped by a cap that as yet showed no sign of bow waves on the sides, he strolled determinedly from Welcome Jetty to the main dockyard gate, his small brown case with toilet gear and tropical white shoes, grasped firmly in his left hand. He saluted a passing Lieutenant, who returned the salute whilst appraising the quality of the mark of respect, his eyes sweeping over the young sailor's attire purely by force of habit. Finding nothing lacking in the young man's appearance his arm swept down, and he continued on his way.

The dockyard policeman on duty eyed Wiggy's case suspiciously as he approached the main gate. He could not resist the opportunity to make his first check of the day for contraband, so slightly disgruntled at being informed by Wiggy, 'I do not smoke,' and finding nothing incriminating, he said tersely, 'off you go then!'

Wiggy made a point of tidying up his effects, and packing them into his brown case, and then smiling sweetly at the officer, said in his most well mannered way, 'thank you officer, good day to you.'

'Bloody smart arse,' the officer grumbled under his breath as he watched Wiggy's smart form striding past the bus stops outside of the gate.

His mind was far too involved with the anticipation of a good afternoon's cricket to dwell upon the natural surliness of a zealous dockyard policeman. He walked smartly under the railway by HMS *Vernon*, and on into the sports ground. Geoff Mitchell caught sight of the tall confident Ordinary Seaman and shouted, 'Over here Wiggy!'

'Hi PO,' he replied smiling.

'Here, try this white dress on,' Geoff Mitchell joked, passing a pair of white trousers and a white shirt to Wiggy. 'Did yuh bring yer tropical shoes?'

'All in here Clubs,' Wiggy said, raising his brown case a little.

'Right then, let's introduce yuh to the skipper of the navy team.'

Petty Officer Physical Training Instructor Mitchell put a hand on Wiggy's shoulder and guided him through the chatting groups of players to a tall distinguished figure dressed in immaculate cricket whites, with a personalised cricket bat tucked under his left arm, surrounded by what was obviously the navy cricket team. All of them were peering attentively at the tall figure addressing them, giving the impression that they were hanging on his every word. The truth of the matter was that this greying gentleman in his late forties was the Captain of HMS *Vernon*, the underwater weapons training establishment. Captain Godfrey Dunbar-Naismith had only recently taken over command of *Vernon*, having spent the previous two years in command of HMS *Manxman*, a fast minelayer.

'Excuse me sir,' Petty Officer Mitchell said politely. 'This is your new team member Ordinary Seaman Bennett sir.'

All eyes swung around to Wiggy as he suddenly became the centre of attention.

'Ah Bennett,' beamed Captain Godfrey Naismith. 'Glad to have you with us.' He thrust his hand out, his eyes appraising the fresh honest gaze, and the bearing of this young man, as their hands met for a moment.

'We are just having a pre-match natter, deciding the order of batting you know.' He hesitated for a second, and then continued, 'The royals have a strong team this year, particularly amongst their bowlers. Petty Officer Mitchell tells me you handle a straight bat so I have decided to make you fourth man, is that okay with you? If not don't be afraid to say so.'

'Ideal sir, thank you; be nice to get my teeth into a good game again,' Wiggy replied with polite deference that was just sufficient for the occasion. His choice of reply, his demeanour, and his delivery brought a glance from the Captain that did not go unnoticed by the remainder of the team. Anyone watching, with the ability to weigh up men's reactions would immediately sense the one sure fact of the moment. The Captain's quick glance said 'Officer Material.' That is how Wiggy would be judged this day. Not on his bowling, or batting ability; even if he made a complete pig's ear of today's chances, it would be his attitude, his instant reactions, and his qualities under game pressure. Whether he manfully accepted defeat, or graciously accepted the plaudits of a winning knock, could very well have lasting effect on his future by the end of the day.

With typical service punctuality, the first ball of the match was delivered at 1300 hours, and the game got under way with the Captain receiving the first wildly delivered ball. Having won the toss, he had elected to bat first.

By the time Wiggy took his turn at the crease as the fourth man, the score stood at sixty-three for two, the Captain having made a very creditable half century.

The umpire lined Wiggy up on his favourite position of the off stump. Wiggy smacked the ground a couple of times to make his mark, and glancing down at the mark appeared satisfied.

The bowler waited patiently, ready for his run up. Wiggy stood erect, and cast his eyes around the field with an air of enthusiasm. As his eyes swept past the stand, they alighted on the Captain taking a seat between two females. In that instant his mind registered the beautiful girl sitting to the left of the Captain. For two seconds Wiggy was distracted, and his heart did a little flip. The beautiful form of this delightful blonde became indelibly imprinted on his young mind. He tore his eyes away from the vision, and completed his assessment of the field. The couple of extra men at slips assured him he was facing a fast bowler, possibly with a long delivery hoping he would snick a ball into their waiting palms.

The sight of the Royal marine bowler hurtling towards his release point at the other end erased the vision of Felicity Dunbar-Naismith from his mind. The savage looking fellow chose to bowl around the wicket, and his first delivery had a bit too much angle to it, nevertheless Wiggy made a pass at the ball by putting his left leg forward but his bat stayed slightly raised as he made no attempt to attack the ball as it hurtled past him at a rate of knots. He took a crack at the next ball, and broke his duck with a 'one'. Off the crease now, it gave him a little time to settle in and have a good gaze around. The next ball delivered was neatly snicked into the ready hands of the third slip, who looked down at the ball clasped in his fingers as if unable to believe his good fortune. A second later he leapt joyously into the air, and upon landing accepted the macho plaudits of his team mates who rushed to congratulate him. Meanwhile, a hapless navy batsman made his way back to the pavilion for an early cup of tea.

Wiggy soon found himself facing the bowler again, and got at a ball that just managed to beat a fielder to the boundary for a four. His keen eye and youthful vigour soon got the measure of this particular bowler, and during the next two overs Wiggy knocked two sixes and a four. With another couple of twos, pushing his luck a little, his score now stood at twenty-one. 'Pretty good in three overs,' passed through his mind. The crowd also was warming to him, and no one clapped more vigorously than Felicity Dunbar-Naismith, a fact that did not go unnoticed by her father.

The game proceeded apace, not played with the familiar caution of test or county cricket, because every ball that presented itself at the batsman's end with a slim chance of being belted anywhere in the field was taken. Hence, the only thing that saved many batsmen from instant dismissal was the inaccuracy of the bowling, and the fact that the fielders were off target when hurling a ball back at the wicket. Nevertheless, batsmen were taking courageous chances of ones and twos, and this was how

Wiggy left the field, run out, after his fellow batsman had called for a run after a very chancy tap to mid on, who had to swivel on his toes and dive full length at the ball as it dawdled past him. Wiggy grinned as he gazed at the apologetic look of his team mate. 'Hey! Don't worry,' he shouted above the applause. 'It's a damned enjoyable game, the pace is very exciting.' He raised his bat to the acclaim of the crowd as he strolled off the field. They had enjoyed his courageous knock of forty-two, and were showing their appreciation for his sporting innings, and by the time the last navy wicket fell for 138 all out, he had been introduced to many of the spectators and their ladies.

Teatime was all the more pleasant because everything had been provided and prepared by the wives of the players who had all mucked in together with a will, regardless of their husbands' status, or lack of it. Wiggy poured himself a cup of tea from a large white pot with floral designs breaking up the pristine surface. He added cream and one spoonful of sugar, and while gently stirring, cast his eyes over the abundance of sandwiches, buns, cakes and biscuits that proved just how diligent the ladies had been in their culinary preparations. After a short but appreciative perusal of the bounty sitting on the two trestle tables which almost hid the elegantly decorated table cloths from view, he decided on a cucumber sandwich, a neat wedge of current cake, and three rich tea biscuits.

Placing his cup and saucer on a convenient side table, he joined the boss, and Petty Officer Mitchell. The conversation started with a discussion on the exciting pace of the game. The Boss brought his feelings on the game into the conversation with the ease of a professional. 'Not a bad score; considering that our time at the crease only provided three sixes and ten fours. Everybody did a hell of a lot of running, and don't you think the bootnecks fielded very tightly; mind you, that's what you would expect from that ultra fit lot, so I think our finishing total was pretty damned good.'

'Mind if we join you?'

The Captain and his daughter appeared at the table, and immediately joined the conversation. 'Good knock you had there, Bennett. For a while I thought the honour of highest knock was going to you. I think maybe you would have achieved that goal had you not been called to make an impossible effort.'

'Very enjoyable though sir,' Wiggy reacted to the praise with just the right amount of modesty. 'Nice to see such an all round air of sportsmanship enhancing the game.'

Once again Wiggy's answer brought a glance that could only be interpreted as 'very impressed.'

Felicity joined the conversation, saying, 'you're obviously a little above the average at this game, you played with an air of masterly assurance.' Her statement brought their eyes together, and both held each other's gaze as each brain frantically assessed the other. They were both aware of the magnetism that passed between them, like two unalike poles there was a very positive reaction.

'Oh, just grammar school team, and the town club,' Wiggy answered hastily, aware that he had paused a bit to long as he stared into those entrancing blue eyes.

The Captain stifled a grin. It was not the first time he had seen his beautiful daughter's effect on young naval personnel, albeit, up to this time, the young men on the other end of her gaze had been of junior officer status.

'Petty Officer Mitchell says you deliver a wicked off spin, and it's not just pure luck; would you care to open the bowling for us?' His words had the effect of rescuing Wiggy from his daughter's gaze.

'Aye aye sir,' he answered nautically, and then added in not quite such a seamanlike manner, 'be delighted to.'

'Jolly good Bennett,' the Captain smiled pleasantly, and then turning to his daughter said, 'come along Flic, let's go and impress the fielders for a moment.' With the smile lingering at the corners of his mouth, he nodded to the company present, and they strolled off to the next group.

'Looks like you impressed more than the Captain,' Geoff Mitchell said, smiling as he nudged Wiggy with his elbow. The Boss grinned as he noticed Wiggy colour up slightly. 'Looks as if you may be a part of someone else's party discussions tonight; Felicity, or Flic as her father likes to call her, is quite an ambassador for her father, she brings a breath of fresh air to all his functions, and she just cannot help being a bit flirtatious with young unmarried officers. This has the effect of putting them at ease amidst the essentially stuffy atmosphere of official functions.' He paused looking pointedly at Wiggy. 'That should serve to indicate to you her assessment of your future direction. Take heed young man, your style has been noted.'

The buzz of conversation hovering around the mingled teams was brought to an abrupt end by the umpire's pleasant statement, 'It's time for the Royals chaps, let's crack on.'

Cups and saucers and plates rattled as they were hurriedly emptied, and placed on the tables.

The navy team took up fielding positions and Wiggy confidently advised some of them where he wanted them. He placed his slips where he preferred to have them, in a slanted line to the right of the wicket keeper, who, in response shifted his stance slightly to peer over the off stump.

As a spin bowler he would be tempting the batsman to balls delivered to the off side to start with, and if the batsman appeared at ease with that, he would deliver a few down the middle to get the feel of his man.

Wiggy stood twenty yards back, at his run point, and when the umpire had finished with the batsman, and indicated start of bowling, he began his run up. The first ball was released with all the freshness and vigour pent up in his lithe frame. With unerring accuracy it touched ground on the off side, bounced slightly, and turned inwards slipping past the straight bat that had been accurately placed had the ball not been delivered with diverting spin. The unfortunate opening batsman was punished for not meeting the ball earlier, as the ball snicked the off to middle bail from its perch and landed in the outstretched hands of the amazed wicket keeper. For three seconds the whole field, players and spectators, stared open mouthed at the scene being played out before their eyes. The umpire indicated out, and everyone in the stands jumped to their feet and roared simultaneously. The fielders ran to the bowler en masse congratulating him physically with claps on the back, and arms around his shoulders, amid loud shouts of delight. Lieutenants, Sub Lieutenants, Chiefs and Petty Officers and other rates, all showing hands on appreciation, whilst to the rear Captain Godfrey Dunbar-Naismith shouted, 'Absolutely excellent young man.'

During all this commotion, a young marine Lieutenant strolled dejectedly back to the pavilion fully aware that he had been clean bowled by a young man destined to be going places. Three minutes later the third man was at the crease, and ready to take his first ball. He wisely played defensively for the next five balls, and breathed a sigh of relief as the bowling end changed.

The next two overs brought fifteen runs for the Royals, and the game continued to be played at a fast pace. The other bowler for the navy delivered at medium pace, and a higher bounce than was expected caught the batsman unawares. In the instant that he corrected his stroke the ball took the edge of the bat, and soared straight up in the air almost as if precession had created a ninety degree deflection. There, poised underneath the ball as it reached its apex, and began its descent were Wiggy's eagerly awaiting hands. The ball fell neatly into his cupped hands, and was immediately encircled in the steel-like grip of eight fingers and two locked thumbs. Wiggy yelled joyously, tossed the ball in the air again and caught it one-handed, as if to show that the first catch was no fluke. A roar of approval rose above the field, and once more Wiggy stood centre-field receiving the accolades of his team mates and the acclamations of the spectators. Ten minutes later another roar rose to the heavens as the fourth ball of Wiggy's fifth over was snicked into the outstretched gloved hand of a diving wicket keeper.

Wiggy still had two balls left of his over, so he stood patiently awaiting the next batsman, rubbing the ball down his trousers. Suddenly a roar came from the Royal Marines team as a tall very impressive looking fifth man strode purposefully from the pavilion. Colour Sergeant 'Rocky' Stone raised his bat and waved towards his supporters. Amidst calls of 'come on Rocky, let's show these Dabtoes how to play cricket,' and other polite encouragements (due to the mixed gender audience), Colour Sergeant Stone marched to the crease with well paced determination. He took guidance from the umpire for middle peg, and patted the ground aggressively to mark his spot. Declining to scan the field, he stood ready to receive his first ball.

Wiggy was far too intelligent to be impressed with physical posturing, but there was something about this huge marine that was absolutely natural. He was a trained killer; that was his job. He saved the lives of his men by training them to be just as efficient at the gory side of his job, as he was. They, in turn would emulate his purposeful extremes, and by so doing would preserve the right of all marines to consider themselves invincible. To the layman they are the ultimate in 'death or glory boys'. Amongst themselves, they are just marines doing a job that their harsh training equips them for, with no uncertainties, and absolutely no doubt about their invincibility.

Wiggy delivered his fifth; the huge marine, anticipating the length leapt forward and met the ball with the meat of the bat. The ball went soaring away for six causing a rapturous burst of applause from his team mates and the rest of the spectators in the stands. He acknowledged their appreciation with a wave of the bat, and, having got off the mark, attacked Wiggy's last ball of the over with similar vigour; it hit the ground and bounced over the boundary for a four. The marines amongst the crowd were ecstatic.

As the ball was returned to the other end, Wiggy took up his favoured fielding position at 'mid on', and pondered over the seemingly invincible marine. Luck could be discounted, sheer aggression could not. This man would have to be met with guile, he had a good eye, and went for the ball; his forward leaps were well timed and accurate, but his style was impulsive and certainly would not sustain a long innings. With this in mind Wiggy decided to change tactics for his sixth over if his worthy opponent was still facing his bowling.

The score had increased by four singles by the time he took the ball again, so he still had the same antagonist to deal with. As the ends changed, Geoff Mitchell turned to the Boss and voiced his opinion. 'He's going to have to change tactics, the bootneck's score stands at twenty now, he's knocking them all over the field,' he said matter of factly.

'The Captain doesn't look worried yet,' the Boss replied. 'I think he has it in mind to wait and see how young Bennett deals with the situation.'

As if to confirm the Boss' words, Wiggy was seen to have a word in the umpire's ear. The umpire nodded, and took a side pace to his left as Wiggy walked back, turned, and began his run. To everybody's amazement he bowled around the wicket, the ball lofted and then hit the ground three yards short of the crease on the leg stump side. The big marine attacked with his usual aggressive leap forward, but this time his bat only displaced air. The ball hit the ground and shot forward six inches above the crease, and felled the centre stump. Rocky Stone turned around with the momentum of his swing, his eyes bulging, and his face grimacing as he observed his exciting innings come to an end as the stump tumbled head over heels towards the wicket keeper, and the bails descended to the ground in time with the keeper's descent from his joyous leap in the air.

After a simultaneous gasp of amazement from the crowd, Colour Sergeant Joshua 'Rocky' Stone contained his chagrin, and amidst loud cheers from everyone he walked towards Wiggy, his hand raised to the shake position. Their hands met, and they shook firmly, neither one trying to make the sporting handshake a wrestling match.

'You're a clever Dabtoe, I salute your excellent ball,' Colour Sergeant Stone said sincerely, his rugged features and steely blue eyes verifying his statement. 'We'll have a beer tonight to celebrate your field craft.' He made the invitation as if congratulating a fellow marine for a well planned attack on an enemy position.

The crowd rose to applaud him as he marched off the field, with his bat at the 'slope arms' position as if toting a rifle. His fellow marines appreciated his humour, and shouted in unison, 'left, left, left right left,' and then clapped him heartily on the back as he marched towards the pavilion steps.

The crowd settled down slowly, but groups could be heard murmuring as they discussed the big marine's exciting innings. His sporting, if somewhat unskilled, attack on Wiggy's deliveries gave heart to his fellow marines. Their game continued in the same fast style. Whilst the privates amongst the marine team had a crack at everything, and added significantly to their score in ones and twos, a couple of Lieutenants with previous college training played a steadier game. By the time the final wicket fell, the Royals had scored 118 runs, a very good score, considering that Wiggy had decimated their earlier batsmen before his Captain had changed bowlers.

The showers were adequate at the United Services ground, but with HMS *Vernon* just across the road, and the Royal Marine barracks just up the road, the officers joined Captain Dunbar-Naismith at his quarters, whilst all the NCOs and other rates strolled up the road in chatting groups to the Royal Marine Barracks for a shower and brush up. Major Harold Baxter RM MM joined the Captain at his house in Vernon and used private facilities, while the other officers used adjoining quarters for their needs.

By 1900 hours that evening the Gymnasium at Royal Marine Barracks had been completely decorated with flags and bunting for the evening's entertainment, and gave a nautical effect as a backdrop to the trestle tables and chairs that had been set out for the evening meal. One table formed a 'T' at the end for high ranking officers and guests. The greater portion of the gymnasium was ringed by chairs, and became a rather decent dance floor due to its well polished parquet flooring. A local dance band had set their instruments up on the stage, and was in the process of tuning up together.

Later, with the minimum of formality out of the way all were seated and the meal began rather ordinarily with an excellent mulligatawny soup. Wiggy had a moment's difficulty containing his surprise when Felicity took the next seat to his left. He could not have known of course that this had come about because her father had whispered in the senior steward's ear, and his wishes had quite naturally been obeyed. Their eyes met, and once again that mutual electricity danced between their eyes, something that was noted by those sitting opposite.

'A thought has just occurred to me Wiggy,' she opened the conversation with a conspiratorially whisper. 'I don't know your real name. If I am to know you better, I must know your real name, not just a naval nom-de-plume.' She did not turn her head away after she had posed the question, and when Wiggy turned to answer her, their eyes were only inches apart.

'Donald...Wilfred...Bennett,' he replied, accentuating each word with exaggerated lucidity.

'And what does Daddy do?,' she continued the inquisition with husky determination, her eyes flicking down to his mouth, and then back up to meet his gaze.

'He is senior partner in a group of solicitors, namely 'Bennett, Thoroughgood and Morton of Worcester'.'

'Crikey, that sounds terribly important,' she teased, her face remaining close to his. 'Were you supposed to be another Bennett added to the business title? Was the future meant to be 'Bennett, Thoroughgood, Morton and Bennett'?'

He turned away from her enquiringly teasing eyes and took a sip from his wineglass. Replacing the glass on the coaster he turned to face her openly honest gaze again fully aware of the interest that emanated from them. She now had her wineglass poised, and those delightfully enticing blue eyes stayed locked on his as she tilted the glass and took a sip. The movement seemed heavily seductive to him, he knew that his own eyes, and in fact his whole facial expression betrayed the fact that this golden haired Goddess had completely entrapped him. He was rescued from that flirtatious gaze by a steward removing his soup plate, and another steward placing the main course in front of him. The conversation now reverted to light chat until the last course was finished, and the plates removed. Wine glasses were recharged, and the Captain took that opportunity to rise to his feet and introduce the senior guest, Commodore Douglas Fairchild DSM. This senior naval officer would be delivering the trophies into the hands of those individuals who were deemed worthy of recognition.

Since the match had ended the Boss had been soliciting comments from guests, spectators and team members. Apart from the obvious winners of trophies, two names were consistently mentioned as providing the excitement of the match. This allowed the Boss to prime the top table as to the general feelings of the majority of those present, it allowed them to ensure both teams were similarly honoured, thereby ensuring an evening of equanimity.

The Queen was toasted in line with tradition, but the solemnity of the toast quickly gave way to party chatter as the Commodore rose to his feet and moved to the trophy table. As pre-arranged the youngest member of the navy team collected the winner's trophy. Captain Godfrey Dunbar-Naismith collected the trophy for the highest scoring innings; then came the surprise of the evening. The Boss, acting as master of ceremonies introduced the winners of the last and final trophies, but first he imparted an important piece of news. 'This very year, 1957, against the West Indies, Colin Cowdrey and Peter May put together a fourth wicket partnership of 411 runs. All of you cricket enthusiasts will no doubt be aware that this is a heck of a record to date. I mention this because the young man I am about to name was fourth man for the navy team today. He brought a new thrill to this annual local derby by clean bowling two, catching one, and delivering another into the hands of the wicket keeper. Ladies and gentlemen, a young man with an assured sporting future in the Royal Navy: Ordinary Seaman Bennett.'

The gymnasium erupted into loud clapping and shouts of acclaim. The surprised look that flashed across Wiggy's face was quickly erased as he rose, and marched dutifully up to the trophy table and accepted a model of a cricketer on a marble plinth from the Commodore. 'A well deserved trophy Bennett, I hope to be there to witness your next visit to the crease,' he said as they shook hands lightly. Wiggy thanked the Commodore, and turning smartly to the right, positioned himself beside his Captain and Upper Yardsman John Lewis, a young man just four months younger than himself.

The Boss raised his right hand and the loud clapping gradually ceased.

'Someone else provided us with an exciting innings. A man who brought everyone in the stands and the pavilion to their feet with his fierce exhibition of attacking batting. Someone the navy has enjoyed battling with for the last three seasons. Ladies and gentlemen, Colour Sergeant Royal Marines Joshua Stone; better known as 'Rocky'.'

Colour Sergeant Stone's features cracked momentarily with a look of surprise. He quickly collected his wits and strode purposefully to the trophy table. For one instant everyone thought he had forgotten the procedure, and was about to salute. The right hand that had started its journey upwards travelled to a position ninety degrees to his body. The hand clasped the outstretched trophy and transferred it to his left hand, and then grasped the Commodore's hand in a barely perceptible shake. 'You certainly gave Bennett something to think about Colour Sergeant Stone, thank you for an entertaining innings this afternoon.'

'Thank you sir, I enjoyed the game sir.'

He turned right, body rigid, muscles taut, and with measured steps took up a position next to Wiggy.

The Commodore's speech was thankfully short and to the point but appreciative of the sportsmanship, and to navy standards, the skill of the opposing teams.

Everybody reacted to the Boss' prompt, and gave the Commodore a short but hearty burst of applause. Formalities over, the entertainment could now begin.

'Right Dabtoe,' Rocky Stone said with mock severity. 'We'll have that pint now.'

Felicity moved to join Wiggy as he followed the Colour Sergeant to the bar. He reacted by making a gesture of holding a glass to his lips, and wobbling his hand to indicate he was about to be bought a drink. Felicity pouted playfully, and with a toss of her head grabbed Upper Yardsman Lewis, and hauled him into the gathering procession circling the floor doing the 'Gay Gordon's'.

The Captain and his wife led the procession, closely followed by the Commodore and his wife, and Major Harold Baxter and his wife.

Wiggy and Colour Sergeant Stone would be forgiven their absence on the floor because it was unlikely that the festivities of the evening would give them another opportunity to congratulate each other with a mutual show of respect. During the ten minutes it took to consume the pint of Brickwood's best bitter Wiggy got to know Rocky Stone a little better, and as they plonked their glasses down on the bar simultaneously the Colour Sergeant said to him with a knowing grin, 'I think someone is waiting for a dance with you, off you go and enjoy yourself, that young lady works very hard to make these occasions a success.'

A square dance was just coming to an end, and it was immediately noted by all that the senior officers and their ladies, having done their duty, very gamely walked to their table a little out of puff. The remainder of the dance floor gave them a polite clap, and then stood waiting for whatever came next. The escape from the floor of the senior people gave the band the cue to provide some entertainment for the younger people present. The band paused politely until the senior officers and their wives were seated, and then bopped it up a bit with Bill Haley's 'Rock Around the Clock.' For an instant, Pompey Lil flashed into Wiggy's mind. The thought brought a grin to his face as he recalled Shiner's encounter with Cardiff Rose and Belfast Betty.

'Gotcha!'

Wiggy turned to meet the slightly flushed face of Felicity as her right hand grabbed his left shoulder possessively. 'Hope you can jive, and bop as good as you play cricket,' she grinned dragging him towards the floor.

He returned her grin, and seconds later their lithe young bodies were cavorting to a pretty good rendition of Bill Haley's classic song.

'Flic seems to be attracted to that young sailor,' her mother said, turning to face her husband. 'She has spent a fair portion of the evening socialising with him.'

'That young sailor,' her husband replied, his eyes following the young couple's agile performance on the dance floor, 'is quite a determined young man. Did you see how he went about his counter attack on Colour Sergeant Stone? His fast spin deliveries were being knocked everywhere by sheer aggressive batting. You could almost see his brain churning over while he fielded at mid on, and then he came back to bowl with a change of tactics and completely foxed the man with a beautifully pitched ball to the leg side.' The Captain smiled at his wife and confided, 'I intend to find out a little more about this young fellow, we cannot have such obvious talent within our grasp, and not oil the wheels a little to let the talent blossom.' The band stopped playing, halting the Captain's conversation.

Wiggy's collar; silk, and lanyard were awry from their exertions, so while they had a breather he straightened himself out. Felicity leaned towards him companionably, a hand on each of his forearms. Tilted slightly forward like that, her beautiful calves and well formed thighs, hugged by a snug fitting skirt, were accentuated, bringing appreciative glances from the young studs in the vicinity.

'Must shuffle around now,' she whispered in Wiggy's ear. 'I have to share myself around you know,' she grinned cheekily, and then added, 'see you later after I have danced with a few of the old fogies.'

She disappeared into the hands of a middle-aged navy Lieutenant as the band struck up with a quick step. Wiggy was grabbed by a determined wren two ringer with the words, 'come along young man, let's try a real dance.'

Slightly dazed by being commandeered so abruptly, Wiggy fluffed his first few steps as the Wren Lieutenant assumed the lead. He quickly corrected the situation and masterfully applied the conventional role of man leading.

'My word, you do dance well,' the mature lady complimented him, as she settled down to enjoy this dance with her now dominant partner. She turned out to be very light on her feet, and well practiced, and Wiggy began to enjoy the pure harmony of their steps. The lady too showed she was thoroughly enjoying this quickstep; perhaps she too had envisaged this dance as having the potential of yet another tiresome duty with an awkward young man not at all skilled in the somewhat higher social arts practiced in wardroom circles.

The quick step came to an end, and the band put down their instruments for a short intermission to enjoy some refreshments. With dancing no longer in progress, the dance floor erupted into a loud buzz of conversation as a long queue suddenly assembled at the bar.

Wiggy was just thanking the Wren Lieutenant for the excellent dance, when Felicity appeared at their side.

'Ah, Olivia,' she greeted the Lieutenant. 'How did you find my escort's performance on the dance floor? As good as his prowess on the cricket field?' Her tone bore a deliberately possessive inflection.

'Better if anything,' the lady replied, and then elaborated. 'A totally enjoyable few minutes. One gets so used to people who just march a dance with rigid arms as if they are still on the parade ground,' she went on, then added quietly with raised eyebrow, and quirky slant to her mouth 'and that includes some of high rank.'

Felicity grinned at the confidence the Lieutenant had shared and then asked, 'Are you free for badminton on Wednesday evening? HMS *Excellent* wives have invited us over, it will be an all female event, and I would like to have as many of the team as possible in attendance.'

'Nothing on my card for Wednesday,' the Lieutenant answered. 'Be delighted.' She paused, and then added, 'I like playing at Whaley, it's so nice to have the occasional game on well cared-for lawns, rather than the parquet flooring of a gym.'

'See you there then, 1600 hours,' Felicity said, wiggling the fingers of her right hand at the Lieutenant in the female gesture of 'cheerio for now.' She then hauled Wiggy off to a table close to Mummy and Daddy.

'What would you like to drink Donald?' she asked, as Wiggy held her seat out while she eased herself into it. A well mannered gesture not lost on her parents.

'Oh, I'll get them,' Wiggy replied, making as if to walk to the bar.

'No, no, sit down,' she said, smiling at his male attempt to do the right thing. 'The mess steward collects the orders for these tables, and we sign a chit. This one's on Daddy.'

'Is it okay if I have a pint of bitter?' he asked, at the same time noticing that all other beer glasses on this set of tables were half pint.

Felicity grinned at him and attracting the attention of the steward, ordered for both of them.

Immediately following the placement of glasses on tables, the Captain raised his glass and turned to face Wiggy and his daughter at the next table. 'Here's to your future successes, Bennett, whatever source they are gained from, sporting, and, or career.' His eyes gazed steadily at Wiggy as he spoke, they conveyed a look of conviction in his own ability to judge a man's character.

'Hear, hear,' a few voices called as they raised their glasses in Wiggy's direction.

'Why thank you sir!' Wiggy answered, not in the least flustered by the seniority of those showing their appreciation of his afternoon's sport. 'This has been a momentous day for me,' he continued sincerely, 'and this evening's festivities have been made most enjoyable by the presence of your daughter.'

More than one eyebrow rose a little at Wiggy's statement of fact, and the Captain returned the gaze with the same direct honesty.

'Tell me young man, what are your intentions; and your hopes for the near future?'

All eyes at the adjoining table remained on Wiggy. More than one of those of high rank waited to hear the answer this confident and unpretentious young man would give.

He glanced towards Felicity, and the sincere look he got in return showed she too would like to hear his view of his own future. He smiled at her before turning his gaze back to the Captain.

'For personal reasons sir,' he began, 'it is very important that I become a good Able Seaman.' A couple of coughs from his attentive audience created a pause. As if in reaction to the surprised coughs, he continued, 'having said that, I feel I owe you an explanation.' He paused again as if getting his mind clear. 'For as long as I can remember, there has been an old sepia photograph hanging above the mantelpiece of the parlour in the family home. The subject of this photograph is a very fierce looking Able Seaman in a straw hat. The picture is signed at the bottom, and although fading a little due to its age, it is completely legible. It says 'Able Seaman Wilfred Bennett, HMS *Drake*', and is dated 1875. Wilfred Bennett was my great Grandfather, and the photograph is all that remains to tell us of his existence, and his chosen life. All other effects were lost in a fire when my father was a young boy. I will also add that my great Grandfather died without seeing his grandson; my father. The photograph meant very little to me as a young boy, but as I gained knowledge in the history of our nation, I began to look at it with inspired interest, and it became very important to me to emulate this determined looking ancestor. To that end, I shall proceed to the rate of Able Seaman, and thereafter allow my career to lead me to whatever fate has in store.' Wiggy stopped speaking abruptly and cast his eyes around the faces at the adjacent tables. All had listened intently to his little speech, but none so intently as Felicity. She could not contain her rapture at his well spoken explanation of his initial desire in his young life.

'Oh Donald,' she cooed. 'That is a wonderful thing to do.' She turned to her father, her face still glowing with youthful awe. 'Don't you think so Daddy?'

The Captain coughed lightly into his left fist, he had been taken aback momentarily by his daughter's enraptured reaction to Wiggy's words.

'Very commendable young man,' he said turning to face Wiggy again. 'But I must say in all honesty; do not linger too long in honouring your stalwart forebear. The navy is in a state of flux; new technology is burgeoning upon us. The first Alternating Current warships are now commissioned; the Daring Class destroyers. The navy needs young men of your calibre to be future leaders in what will be known as Britain's new navy. Not all of us will have the aptitude to be engineers, technicians, and mechanics in this new navy; those of us with executive qualities however, should seek to become major statisticians in a navy that will quickly advance to push button warfare. Good seamen officers, up to date with the new order of things will be absolutely essential.' He paused, watching Wiggy's reaction to his words. He was not disappointed; Wiggy's eyes were bright with the enthusiasm of a young man who had joined the navy full of the heroics of Nelson, and the warfaring stories of Hornblower. All of this may have been the dreams of the young boy who was born Donald Wilfred Bennett, but the Captain's view of the future, and where useful young men should aim their desires, had inspired this resourceful young fellow with visions of the future and its bright prospects.

The Captain read the fire in Wiggy's eyes, and knew his judgement of this young sailor was correct when he added, 'you think hard on what I have said Bennett, and don't dilly dally too long.' He smiled, and continued, 'Although, having said that, I did admire the perspicacity of your spoken intentions, and your hopes for the future.'

The band struck up again, and a waltz drew people onto the floor.

'May we be excused Daddy?'

Captain Godfrey Dunbar-Naismith gazed at his beloved daughter. 'Of course you may Flic; enough of this shoptalk, off you go and enjoy the remainder of the evening.'

Felicity grabbed Wiggy possessively by the hand whilst politely thanking her father, and guided him away to the dance floor. Her mother spoke as she watched the couple come together in a slow seductive waltz. 'I really do think our daughter has found a young man she is truly interested in for the first time. If it is to be so, I do hope he gets his act together very quickly, and strives to achieve his true station in life.'

Her words carried all the hopes of a mother who only wanted the best for her daughter. She moved in well ordered circles where duty was the keyword to be considered at all times. She did not want her daughter to be the brunt of smutty behind-hand conversations, or accusations of impropriety with a person who wore the uniform of a lower order in the service to which she was not only bound by marriage, but also the expectations of the wives of her husband's senior and junior officers. She was as much a commander in her social group as her husband was as the CO of a major naval establishment.

'Don't worry my dear,' her husband reassured her, then added with an air of determination, 'Flic knows what she's doing. Even if her heart has been given its first really romantic nudge, if this is the young man for her, I assure you he will be a junior officer before anything more serious can be envisaged.'

He rose from his seat and held out his hand. 'I do think the pace of this dance is to my liking, will you join me dear?'

The Captain guided his wife onto the floor, and with total awareness of the fact that all eyes were assessing their abilities, began to move to the demands of the music. They smiled at each other, and settled into the rhythm of the waltz. The Commodore and his wife, followed by Major Baxter and his wife followed their lead, and soon the dance floor was full of everybody except bar staff, stewards, and young marines of the duty watch clearing up glasses and washing them in a curtained-off area of the bar. A few of these young helpers would be dragged onto the floor later by young females invited to the dance to balance up the genders a little. There is nothing like a service sports get-together to act as a great equaliser between other ranks; naval officers also are known to bend their tacit rule of no fraternisation with the lower deck at such events; the status quo however quickly returns to normal the following day.

After a thoroughly enjoyable evening the dance came to a close with everybody standing to attention paying proper marks of respect to the Queen, as the national anthem was played.

As the national anthem came to a close, Felicity hustled Wiggy through the double fire doors of the gym that acted as a main entrance. 'I have to go back to Vernon in Daddy's official car, it's the rules you know. What are you doing next Wednesday evening?' she asked hurriedly.

They had stopped in a shadowy area to the left of the doors, but she spoke in a half whisper.

Wiggy put his hands on her shoulders, and gazing at where her eyes would be, said gently, 'I start judo training Wednesday afternoon at RNB; afterwards we all go to the Home Club for a drink before returning to *Vanguard*, why do you ask?'

'I am free for the evening after Badminton at Whale Island; can you meet me at the 'Still and West' in old Portsmouth?'

Wiggy paused momentarily as this unexpected invitation was blurted out. 'Sure I can,' he answered, a little bemused. 'But I shall have to be in uniform, is that okay?'

'Oh, just be there you silly boy,' she said laughing. He couldn't see it due to the gloom, but her face changed as she added, 'I shall be waiting for you, so don't let me down.'

'As if I would,' he replied with an edge of surprised sincerity.

A group of people came through the doors led by the Captain; they were all chatting light heartedly in the manner of senior officers who had enjoyed a good evening's entertainment with their men.

'Must go,' Felicity stood on her toes and planted a hot hurried kiss on Wiggy's lips before he could answer. 'See you Wednesday.' Without a backward glance she was gone, appearing again in the light of the doorway.

'Ah, there you are Flic, jump in the back with Mammaw will you, I just want to wish that interesting young man a good night.'

'Here I am sir!' Wiggy's form appeared beside him.

'Now don't you forget what I told you Bennett; I shall be keeping an eye on your progress after this excellent day's sport and this evening's discussion.'

'I assure you sir; your words this evening have served to hasten me towards the ends you advise. Thank you for your interest sir.'

'Well done my boy, crack on and get done what must be done. I shall watch your career with interest.'

The Captain nodded 'good night' at Wiggy, and climbed into the front passenger seat of the official car supplied by the naval transport department for that evening. The Commodore and his wife were similarly cared for, and as the cortege of cars edged gently away, Wiggy waved at the intense face of Felicity as the cars disappeared into the darkness.

With his mind full of thoughts of the impossible, brightened now and then by a fleeting thought of 'what if it is possible that the gorgeous daughter of a senior officer actually seriously likes me,' he walked back into the gymnasium and gave a hand stacking chairs before joining his new mates in their barrack room, where spare beds had been arranged for Upper Yardsmen and below. He had plenty to think about that night before weariness closed his eyes. He drifted off to sleep, his gradual loss of consciousness holding desperately on to the vision of a blonde haired blue eyed goddess, who had altered the course of his life forever. A quirky grin flicked across his face as he muttered sleepily, 'Veni…Vidi…Vici,' then he was gone, his final thought an indication of where his dreams would take him.

5

BARROSA **TWO** *VIGO* **TWO**

The following Monday found all four young seaman gunners washing the already gleaming topcoat of X Turret. Shiner stood back to view his work, and as ever could not resist the urge to make a comment. 'Christ!' he blasphemed, gazing along the length of the turret to where Bogey was vigorously scrubbing, 'this soddin' gun's as big as a fuckin' council 'ouse, can yuh imagine scrubbing yer own drum until yuh could see yer face in it? The bloody neighbour's ud think yuh'd lost yer marbles!'

'Ah shurrup yuh moaning git,' Bogey laughed at his friend. 'If yuh'd picked sprouts on a frosty mornin', with yer fingers throbbin' with cold, yuh'd realise what a doddle jobs like these are; it's money fer old rope.'

'Aw shut yer face, yuh shit kickin', sheep shaggin' Shropshire git,' Shiner threw back with typical lower deck invective. Then quickly dipping his cloth in his bucket, hurled it at Bogey shouting, 'take that, hayseed!' His laugh as the cloth hit Bogey at the back of the neck, quickly disappeared as Bogey reacted before Shiner could dive for cover. He had crossed the twenty feet separating them, and grabbed Shiner by the scruff of the neck with amazing agility for a man of his size. Without hesitation he dipped the cloth in Shiner's bucket, and rammed it down the back of Shiner's shirt. The cold water brought howls of shock from Shiner that turned into frantic giggles as he tried to free himself from Bogey's vice like grip.

'Lemme go, yuh big git, ahhh; it's fuckin' cold Bogey, lemme go!'

The commotion brought Dusty and Wiggy round from the other side of the turret, they both howled with laughter as they witnessed the dampened Shiner struggling, and wriggling, trying to shake off his large shipmate. Bogey finally relented, and released him.

'Yuh basterd,' Shiner laughed, pulling the tail of his shirt out from his trousers, and letting the cloth flop down onto the deck. In a flash, he had picked the cloth up, dipped it in the bucket again, and hurled it at Bogey. At the very moment that the wet cloth wrapped itself round Bogey's face, the tannoy burst into life. 'Ordinary Seamen Bennett, Miller, Wright and Knight, report to the Regulating Office.'

The pipe ended the frivolity around X Turret instantly. The two jokers hurriedly squared off their number eight shirts, and still soaking wet, followed Wiggy and Dusty at a hurried pace to the Regulating Office.

'Here!' A Leading Regulator called loudly from the 'Drafting Section', as all four stepped respectfully through the door, each face carrying its own level of apprehension. No one ever walked into a Regulating Office with a smile. It was not unknown for the wearer of a polite smile to be ordered to 'wipe that fuckin' grin off yer face, NOW!'

'Yer draft chits are in,' the Leading Regulator said, and then noticing the appearance of Bogey and Shiner said, 'bloody ell, is it pissin' down like that up top?' Having made the statement his eyes went down to his desk. 'Wright A. and Knight R.' He looked up again, his eyes asking confirmation.

'Here,' they answered in unison.

The Leading Regulator handed two pieces of paper over the counter to Bogey saying, 'you both join HMS *Vigo* at HMS *Excellent* on Friday as Ship's Company. She's a day runner for the Gunnery School. Bennett D. and Miller P.,' he continued, and without waiting for a reply pushed two pieces of paper across the counter towards Wiggy. HMS *Barrosa*, 28th of October, but the pair of you join HMS *Excellent* for pre-commissioning training on Monday, your Divisional Officer has been informed.' With barely a pause, he continued giving them information. 'Wright and Knight; collect drafting routine cards here AM Thursday and complete your drafting routine. You will be at the gangway with your kit at 0900 hours Friday morning where you will catch the PAS boat to reserve fleet moorings at *Excellent*. Bennett and Miller, you collect drafting routine cards here AM Friday, and do your drafting routine immediately. You will be at the gangway with all kit at 0900 hours Monday where you will also catch the PAS boat to reserve fleet moorings. That's all, off you go, your Divisional Officer will call for you when he is ready.'

Slightly dazed, they left the Regulating Office, and walked aft to the gun deck again. Just as they got there the tannoy burst forth with the order 'Stand Easy'. They traipsed all the way back again, and joined the NAAFI queue where they all bought a goffer and a fresh cheese roll.

Like many of the others of the Ship's Company they sat down in the canteen flat with their backs against the bulkhead to enjoy their snack; as usual it was Shiner who opened up first.

'The Boss has fixed that you know. He mentioned he would try to get me aboard a day runner in the Home Fleet, and he did mention *Vigo*.'

'Me too,' Bogey broke in. 'I've got *Vigo* because of the rugby team…Christ, these sporting people have a hell of a lot of clout in this man's navy. I didn't think I was good enough, to tell you the truth.'

'Don't knock yourself Bogey,' Wiggy scolded. 'They would not have selected you if you were not what they wanted. Manning the fleet comes first with navy manpower, so you can be sure you would not have been selected, I think they may have you in mind for the navy team. Anyway, you'll probably get as much sea time in as those on China station, or the Med, you just won't get the foreign runs ashore.'

'Oh, thanks fer reminding me Wiggy. You are alright; yu'll be shaggin' yer way around the Med by Chrimbo.'

'Aren't you happy with the draft then?' Dusty asked, reacting to Bogey's bitter tone.

'Weeell, yes and no,' Bogey replied. 'On the one hand it's great to be selected for the command rugby team, and be in a position where I can get off duty for every game, and practice session, but on the other hand I joined this man's navy to get about a bit. It seems that all I shall be doing for the next year is poncing up the Solent, and enjoying the pleasures of Brickwood's Sunshine Ales rather than an exotic pint of San Miguel or something.'

'You can make another worthwhile use of this home fleet draft you know,' Wiggy came in again.

'Yeah, what's that then?'

'You have still to pass your Educational Test Leading Rate (ETLR). While you are attached to Whale Island why don't you go to night school, and get that done and dusted, I bet your new Divisional Officer will be pleased to arrange extra tuition whenever *Vigo* is not mooching around providing firing practice for pre-commissioning crews. Don't moan about it, be positive and use it to your own advantage.' Wiggy paused; nobody else broke in, sensing that he had something else to say.

'There is another thing, Bogey.'

'Whassat?' Bogey asked, looking puzzled.

'You can get your marriage arranged now without any doubts of where you are going to be.'

Bogey's face changed as Margaret and his son flashed into his mind. He reddened slightly as a pang of guilt streaked through his brain. 'Fuckin' 'ell!' he swore, reacting to the pang of guilt in the only way he knew how. ''Ere's me moanin' about an 'ome draft, when I already 'ave a good reason to need one.'

'OUT PIPES,' the tannoy ordered loudly.

They all sprang to their feet, hastily threw the paper bags in the waste bin, and proceeded back to work.

Bogey had cheered up a bit by the time they returned to their cleaning gear.

'Watyer doin' durin yer Crimble leave?' he asked Shiner.

Shiner looked back at him, a puzzled frown creasing his brow. 'Dunno yet,' he replied. 'I'll 'ave ter see 'ow things shape up between me and Beryl.'

Bogey slapped his forehead. 'Aw Christ,' he swore. 'Sorry mate, I'd forgot all about Beryl.'

'What the fuck are yer on about Bogey?'

'Well,' Bogey started, but then did not answer the question directly. 'It just occurred to me that Wiggy and Dusty will 'ave early leave and be in the Med for Chrimbo. That only leaves you tuh come ter me wedding,' he finally came to the point.

'Oh shit yeah! See what yer mean Boges me old mate.'

They both worked in silence for a few minutes.

'Tell yer what I'll do Boges,' Shiner said after a moment's thought. 'I'll tell Beryl within the next couple of dates. I can't expect 'er to want tuh come as well, anyway,' he paused. 'I dunno where this romance is goin' yet. She seems keen, and I reckon she's a bloody good-un. But I'll give it a couple of weeks before I tell 'er, yuh never know, by then she may not want tuh let me out uv 'er sight, she may be so besotted with me.' He grinned as he lightened the conversation up a bit.

'Well I 'ope yer can make it, cos I was goin' ter ask yuh tuh be best man.'

Shiner turned to his pal, a look of sheer surprise made his chin drop. 'Christ Boges,' he uttered through his surprise. 'Aven't yer got any decent mates ter do that job?'

'What the fuck d'yer mean by that yuh scrawny little basterd. Yuh've always been me best mate, who the fuck else d'yer think I'd ask ter do the soddin' job.'

Bogey's strong words made Shiner stare at his pal. The look of utter sincerity that accompanied the coarse statement served to assure him that Bogey had long thought of asking him to do the job when the time came.

'I just didn't expect ter be asked pal. That's the only reason I answered like I did. Christ Boges, it's not every day yer asked ter be somebody's best man yer know.'

Bogey looked directly at his shipmate and grinned as he saw the look of awkwardness in his face.

'Look, yuh little basterd,' he began with a broadening grin. 'If yer don't say yer goin' ter be me best man, I'll stuff this fuckin' cloth down yer neck again.' He waved the cloth threateningly at Shiner as he spoke.

Shiner reacted in like manner, and dropping to his knees, clasped his hands together, and with a look of theatrical submission pleaded, 'Oh no Boges, anything, but not the wet cloth again please.'

They had a good laugh together as Shiner rose to his feet.

'Yuh'll do it then will yer?'

'Course I will mate,' Shiner reacted, the air of mirth still clinging to his mouth.

Later that afternoon they were led to the divisional office by Petty Officer Hancock.

'Well men,' Lieutenant Forrester began. 'Your stay with us has been short but eventful. Each of you has made your individual mark, and raised interest in many quarters. Your work aboard this ship has been satisfactory, and it has been noted that your sporting abilities are regarded in higher offices as worthy of encouragement. This means that you, Wright, and you Knight, find yourself in reserve fleet for a while to see what the navy can do for you regarding your talents. You, Miller, and you, Bennett, are getting into the Med fleet aboard HMS *Barrosa*. You all know that four destroyers form the fourth destroyer squadron, with *Agincourt* as Captain 'D', and *Corunna* and *Alamein* making up the four. Wish I was coming with you, it's about time I was at sea again.'

He turned his head towards Wiggy, continuing, 'Bennett, keep up the cricket at every opportunity, and take heed of the advice of senior officers who have come into contact with you, one way and another. Miller, you will find people keeping their eye on your physical abilities.' He glanced down at a message pad on his table, then looked up and continued. 'A Royal Marine PTI, and a Naval Commando have seen fit to report your skills to the Commanding Officer of HMS *Excellent*. I have noted that fact on your gunnery history sheet and this flimsy will stay with your documents.' He paused, and looked at all of them in turn. 'I shall be seeing all of you again as I do my rounds of our part of ship, but I shall take this opportunity to say cheerio to you all, and wish you every success for the future.'

With those final words, he shook every man by the hand as they passed through the door. Petty Officer Hancock stayed in the office, having ordered, 'back to your jobs, report to Leading Seaman Wilson.'

They made their way back to 01 deck in complete silence, each deeply entrenched in his own thoughts.

'What's up with you lot; why the serious looks?'

None of them answered Leading Seaman Wilson for a moment, but then Wiggy spoke up in his own inimitable way. 'It's not a game any more hooky,' he opened up. 'The boyhood and youthful dreams of a swashbuckling life on the ocean wave have suddenly transformed into reality. The needs of Britain's senior service must come first.'

Leading Seaman Wilson stared at Wiggy for a moment as the statement sunk in. His long years as a Leading Seaman had taught him that the needs of the individual were as nothing compared to the requirements of the service. He wouldn't have used Wiggy's words to describe it though. He reacted with an order, but Wiggy's unusual statement still rang in his ears. 'Grab a broom each, and sweep down decks,' he indicated with a sweep of his arm.

He watched them as they swept the wind blown dust from shoreside that had gathered by the beadings underneath the guardrails. 'It's not a game any more,' he repeated Wiggy's words under his breath, then muttered bitterly, 'it sure isn't. Five fuckin' years waiting for my name to reach the top of the PO's roster is no fuckin' game!'

'Is that all now hooky?' Dusty asked, broom grasped lightly in left hand.

Leading Seaman Wilson came out of his trance. 'Nah, get the hose out and give the decks a quick wash down, there's five minutes yet till secure.'

Able Seaman Woods had his backside sticking out of the top part of ship locker. Shiner, always with an eye open for some devilment, was handling the hose while the others broom-washed the deck. He gave Dusty a nudge, and indicated the Able Seaman's backside, edging the hose towards it in devilish manner. Slinger Woods suddenly became aware of water splashing behind him. He glanced around and caught the look in Shiner's eyes. 'Don't even consider it Shiner,' he laughed. Shiner flicked the hose teasingly, and a stream of water swirled at Slinger's feet, then with a loud chortle Shiner moved the hose away as the laughing Able Seaman feinted to get him, with a pace forward. Minutes later the tannoy blared out 'Secure, hands to tea.'

Amidst loud banter, the Topmen made their way to the dining hall to grab a wet of tea, and a slab of cake.

They all sat down at the same table, their cheerful banter mingling with the idle chatter coming from other tables.

'Happy with yer draft chits?' Leading Seaman Wilson asked, his mouth bulging with slab cake.

Wiggy swallowed and replied, 'well at least myself and Dusty are away from major ports, and training establishments, which seem to be controlled by a surfeit of Jossmen and Crushers.'

'Lucky old you,' Bogey broke in wryly.

Leading Seaman Wilson looked at Bogey and asked, 'not happy with *Vigo* then?'

'Yeah, I am really. It's just that I 'ave this yearnin' for foreign shores, that's what I joined the navy for.'

'It's not all trips up the Solent to the firing range yuh know,' Wilson said reassuringly. 'When fleet exercises are in force, yuh get up to Scotland, and believe me, there are some bloody wild runs ashore up there. You get to France and Spain, then Atlantic exercises usually end up with a run ashore in Oporto and Lisbon in Portugal. Then La Pallice, La Rochelle, Bayonne, Biarritz in La Belle France. Remember also, as Ship's Company on the *Vigo*, you get the best messdeck, and all PCT Matelots are bunged up forrard.' He paused with a broad grin creasing his face. 'Well comparatively good messes, for a scabby old destroyer which has seen better days. All the gunnery rates doing PCTs are right up to the paintshop door in one and two messes, and just forrard and below them is the cable locker, then a big open space called the forepeak. Some old destroyers used to have the forepeak filled with concrete for ramming the enemy, and by Christ did that make them plough through the oggin rather than ride over it. Believe me you will soon find out if the navy is really for you when the weather gets a bit stroppy, some of those old buggers would pitch and roll on wet grass. So don't worry Bogey, you will get to live the complete life of a seagoing matelot.'

'Is she that bad at sea?' Shiner asked, grinning with his pals at the description of the seagoing capabilities of a World War Two destroyer.

'Destroyers are built to fight in all weathers,' Wilson replied. 'Sometimes they get knocked about pretty badly. Such things as guardrails and stanchions flattened, all boats converted to morning sticks, and splits in decks. In bad weather a destroyer can appear to spend more time covered by water than a submarine, they have a low profile you see. Anything force eight and above can put the upper scupper out of bounds, and lifelines rigged from forrard to aft.' He paused again, aware that his young messmates were hanging onto every word, so he added a bit of local knowledge. 'Yuh see that destroyer tied alongside North Wall, almost acting as a fender ship; 'er name's HMS *Savage*.' He watched the nods of heads on the other side of the table. 'Well she was broached a couple of years ago in a storm force ten. She was pushed over on 'er port side to seventy degrees. It is said that 'er main engines and gearboxes shifted, and that is why she stays alongside North Wall until they decide whether to drydock 'er or turn 'er into razor blades.'

The number of men arriving in the dining hall for tea increased. Those that had finished would be expected to leave and make room for others. 'Eat it and beat it' was the terminology applied to cafeteria messing. Leading Seaman Wilson led the Exodus. 'Shower time,' he said purposefully, gulping down his last mouthful of tea.

——— · ———

On Wednesday afternoon, Dusty arrived at the gymnasium in Royal Naval Barracks with an eager Wiggy close by his side. They were the first there, so Dusty had the opportunity to introduce Wiggy to all the judo fanatics as they arrived in ones and twos.

'This is Christine, and this is Jane,' he introduced the two Wrens, and just like any healthy young ladies would, they both gave Wiggy a thoroughly sensuous looking over, leaving no one in any doubt as to the unspoken thoughts meandering through their young minds.

Leading Seaman Jesse Rhodes, Naval Commando breezed in, and seeing Wiggy enjoying the centre ground said, 'Ah, nice to see you made it Wiggy, you weren't full of shit after all!'

Wiggy shook hands with the commando, and they shared a grin together at the blunt truth of the greeting. 'In this pastime,' Jesse clarified, 'everybody you meet in a pub is either a lapsed judo expert, or a wannabe judo expert. You are the only fellah to date, in fact, in my whole naval career to date, who has actually put his body where his mouth has been. Bloody great to see you are as good as your word.'

Sergeant Tommy Watkins came through the doors. 'What ho Jesse, hi Dusty…and who do we have here?'

'This is my pal Wiggy Bennett,' Dusty did the introductions. The Sergeant stared into Wiggy's eyes, and thrust his right hand out. 'I couldn't get to the match on Saturday; I was up the line on weekend. Everybody in RMB is talking about the young Dabtoe who put a hell of a show on with Rocky Stone. Old Joshua loves a fight, so I bet no one enjoyed it more than he did,' he said, pumping Wiggy's hand vigorously.

At the same moment a flurry of movement, and loud shouts of, 'hello there serge, hello there Rocky,' came from the varied ranks assembled.

The welcoming calls made the group Dusty was with swing round to face the door. Colour Sergeant Stone acknowledged the greetings from service personnel and civilians alike. 'Hi there all,' he returned their greetings with a broad grin.

Approaching Tommy Watkins, he clapped him on the back good naturedly by way of greeting, this was followed by a clasping of hands, which turned into more than a firm handshake as the two tensed up, testing each other. Their faces set in to a tight grin, made slightly hideous by the bulging face muscles barely an inch apart.

'Mind if I join you Tommy?' the big marine asked through pursed lips, still trying to maintain the grin.

'Pleasure, Rocky,' Tommy Watkins grinned back, his face getting a little red about the neck as he countered the wiry strength of his opponent.

They broke their grip simultaneously, almost as if they had rehearsed this greeting a thousand times, and they were both breathing a little heavily from the exertion of the half a minute it took to carry out their macho greeting. The Colour Sergeant caught sight of Wiggy, and his arms went akimbo as he placed his hands on his hips. 'Well I'll be darned, don't tell me you're a black belt judo as well?'

Wiggy grinned back at the big marine. They were about the same height, but the Sergeant was bulkier by about twenty pounds. Their hands met in a good natured clasp, and released just as quickly.

'Afraid not Colour Sergeant, this is my first try at this close contact sport, cricket has been my only sporting outlet to date.'

'Well, well, well, Dabtoe,' Joshua Stone said grinning. He turned to Tommy Watkins. 'Mind if I start this young fellow off learning the 'breakfalls'; we have something in common,' he said, turning back to face Wiggy. 'It is called perseverance.'

Tommy Watkins acknowledged the determined grin on his superior's clenched lips. 'He's all yours Josh,' then turning to Wiggy he added, 'you couldn't start with a better trainer: Black Belt, Third Dan, inter services heavyweight champion.'

It was not in Wiggy's nature to be overawed; he looked the big marine directly in the eyes and said pleasantly with the merest hint of mirth, 'Oh golly, does that mean I'm in for a good hiding?'

That simple statement cut through the macho atmosphere surrounding them all. Everybody, seeing the look on Wiggy's face as he spoke, broke into a short spasm of laughter. Joshua Stone laughed as loud as anyone, saying, 'You'll do me Dabtoe, that's just the attitude we want, to make a good judo man out of you, we'll start off with 'U Kemi', the art of falling.' He turned to his fellow marine, 'spare Judogis still in the same place.'

A nod from Tommy Watkins gave confirmation of the fact, and soon Wiggy was taking his first lesson on how to dress himself properly in a sloppy, baggy, coarse, white Judogi, tied around the waist with a red belt.

The Colour Sergeant started off by showing a movement in slow motion, then proceeded to see how Wiggy adapted to being grabbed roughly, and wrestled to the ground easily.

'It will all be basic stuff until we get you falling properly, but you're reacting very well so far, any aches and pains yet?'

'Not really,' Wiggy replied, blowing quite heavily. 'I never realised how strenuous it could be though, just rolling to the floor, and getting up again. By the way, when do we get to a point where the trainee gets to throw the instructor to the ground a few times?'

The Sergeant acknowledged Wiggy's grin. 'You'll get your turn when you've learnt to land properly,' he said, his words showing that he was breathing slightly heavier.

'God, this is only slow pace, and I'm blowing like an old buffalo already,' Wiggy said, hoping to prolong this short break in the action. 'I'm thoroughly knackered already.'

'That's because you're new at it, it's surprising how landing and getting up again saps your strength until you begin to familiarise. It helps at the beginning if you have someone to train with on a regular basis for twenty minutes or so. You can probably understand even at this stage, that a competitive bout only lasts three minutes or five minutes of actual judo contact. The energy that is used up is amazing. It takes a lot of practice to gain the strength and skill to be able to fight to win, and keep it up relentlessly for that length of time.'

Wiggy's fervent hope was recognised, the wily Sergeant noticed his pupil's slight distress and like any good instructor decided not to push Wiggy beyond his physical capabilities at his first training session.

'Your pal is pretty useful, isn't he?' Rocky said, watching Dusty and Jesse. 'Tommy will be eager to keep him in this group.'

'Not for long I'm afraid; both of us join HMS *Barrosa* after three weeks pre-commissioning training at HMS *Excellent*.'

Where's she bound for?'

'Med Fleet, Fourth Destroyer Squadron, how long for I don't know; but if the commission goes its full course it will be over a couple of years.'

'Mmmm,' Colour Sergeant Stone mused, and then after a short consideration said, 'you may spend a fair portion of your time in Gibraltar, and certainly up Sliema Creek, Malta. It's also quite likely that the shore base in Malta, HMS *Phoenicia* will be your home base. Both Gib and Malta have reasonable facilities for you to continue your judo training, and a word in the right ear will make sure that a couple of mats and a couple of judo suits find their way aboard the *Barrosa*. I'll find out who your club swinger's going to be and have a word with him.'

They continued watching the action taking place on the mats for a few more minutes, and Wiggy watched intently as Rocky explained some of the actions, keeping up a commentary accentuated by arm movements and body posturing. Later on, amongst all the chat in the shower room, Colour Sergeant Stone briefed Sergeant Tommy Watkins on his training session with Wiggy. 'Definitely worth our time and interest. We shall have to do something to help them keep this up. It's all down to them really, but I am as certain as I have ever been about anything, that these two Dabtoes are determined to find an action career that takes them away from ship-side cosmetics. We should try and grease the wheels a little; it will encourage them to keep their minds on their future. Who knows, we may be training future Special Boats Section specialists.'

'It may help if we have a word with the Boss at Pitt Street,' Tommy Watkins said. 'He may well know who has been drafted as Barrosa's club swinger; usually a Leading Hand on destroyers isn't it?'

'Are you all going to the Home Club afterwards?'

'Oh yeah!' Sergeant Watkins answered, grinning with serious affirmation.

'I'll pop round to Pitt Street then, before I join you, see if I can catch Geoff Mitchell or the Boss. If they haven't got the answer on the tip of their tongues, it will only take a quick phone call to Haslemere to find out.'

The Colour Sergeant dressed hurriedly and left RNB by the back gate before the remainder was gathered outside the gymnasium prior to walking the short distance to the Home Club.

Fifteen minutes later he appeared at the shoulder of Tommy Watkins, who was in the process of paying for the first round of beers. He had his hand deep in the kitty bag sorting out the right money.

'Mine's a pint of bitter,' Rocky said, with a broad smile.

Tommy Watkins grinned back at him, shaking the kitty bag under Rocky's nose.

Still wearing the grin, Rocky sorted out two florins from the change in his pocket and tossed them into the bag.

'Another bitter please,' Tommy asked the bartender, then, pints in hand, they joined the eagerly awaiting group of fellow judokas.

'A Leading Hand by the name of Stan Robinson is your PTI when *Barrosa* commissions.'

Wiggy and Dusty looked at each other, and then back to the big Marine. He noticed the question in their eyes.

'The Boss assured me that Robinson will be completely briefed about your special talents, and you will probably get to see him next Tuesday at Horsey Island Fire Fighting School. You probably haven't been told yet, but your Pre-Commissioning Training starts with two days fire fighting training, and ends with an exam on Wednesday evening.' He grinned at their puzzlement, and answered their unasked question. 'I just popped down to Pitt Street to get the gen from the Boss, we can't let you young fellahs lose interest once you're out of our sight, can we?' he added with a chuckle.

Jesse Rhodes suddenly twigged on to what this conversation was about. 'Don't worry Rocky,' he broke in. 'I'm based at Whaley at the moment, as you very well know. They can join me and a couple of my mates in the gym, I'm sure they'd like another couple of bodies to throw around.'

The conversation within the group stayed on the usual subject until 1600 hours, and was only broken up by a shout from the barman, 'The bus is in Unicorn Road if anybody wants a lift!'

A mass exodus occurred; Colour Sergeant Stone and Sergeant Watkins left together, followed by Jesse Rhodes; he would be walking through the dockyard to Excellent Steps for the short hop across to Whale Island moorings.

Christine and Jane walked out together; they only had a short walk to Wrens barracks opposite Royal Naval Barracks, abutting onto Lion Terrace. Dusty started to follow the two girls out, and then noticed that Wiggy had not made a move.

'Aren't you coming?'

'I'm meeting someone at 1800 hours; we are going for a bite to eat together.'

Dusty looked a bit stunned, so Wiggy enlightened him. 'I met someone at the cricket dance on Saturday night, and we hit it off together.'

'Oh!' Dusty replied, the frown that had set on his face changing to a grin. 'Best of luck mate, looks as if I will be spending blank week Wednesday night on board with Bogey; Shiner's off gallivanting with the swimming team in Aldershot.'

Christine pushed the door open saying, 'Are you coming Dusty?'

'Nah, you go on, I'll give you a ring tomorrow; not duty are yuh?'

'No!' she called back, and then added, 'see you in here at seven if you like.'

'Great!' Dusty gave her a thumbs-up sign; grinned broadly at her as with fluttering eyelids she gradually closed the door on herself.

A couple of minutes later, after saying cheerio to Wiggy he walked out, and, talk of the devil, bumped into Bogey, who was rushing in to catch them, having just clambered off the bus with the rest of a very thirsty rugby team. He looked at Dusty running for the bus, and his face dropped. 'Aw come on mate,' he moaned, panting slightly, his face still as red as a beetroot from his afternoon's exertions. 'Yuh can't leave me 'ere ter 'ave a pint on me own with thirty comparative strangers, come on pal be an oppo.'

Dusty laughed at his pal's dishevelled appearance and his red face. 'If fuckin' Hancock saw you like that, you'd be up ter yer nuts in the shit again.'

He turned and waved the bus driver to go on, as he jokily berated Bogey. 'Come on yuh scruffy basterd, Wiggy's still in there, so we'll let him get the beers in.'

Wiggy was just draining his glass as they walked in, and was obviously making ready to leave.

Bogey grinned at him, but with a question in his eyes

Wiggy put his hands up palms facing Bogey. 'Before you ask I have got a date this evening.'

'O 'ave yuh, yuh lucky git,' Bogey replied grinning, as he took a light punch at one of the raised hands. 'Best you get the fuckin' beers in then innit!'

Wiggy sighed resignedly, but good naturedly, and led them to the bar. Just as he had bought a pint for all of them, another pint appeared at Bogey's right hand, pushed there by the kitty holder of the rugby team. 'Cheers mate,' he said, turning and following his two shipmates to a table with a pint in each hand, and nary a flicker of conscience on his face.

Dusty looked at Bogey, and with a wry grin shook his head from side to side saying, 'Fuckin' 'ell Boges, yer like a bottomless barrel.'

Wiggy laughed and added, 'Yeah, and he'll be finished both of them before we're half way through ours.'

Bogey ignored the remarks and returned the banter good naturedly, by chastising Wiggy verbally for not mentioning his date until now.

'Look you two; my date tonight is a bit clandestine, I can't say too much about it.'

'Not married is she?' Dusty asked.

Before Wiggy could answer, Bogey broke in, 'what's clandestine mean?'

Wiggy glanced at him, clearly changed his mind about his reply, and just said, 'secret', before turning back to Dusty.

'Of course she's not married. It's just that we have to keep our meeting to ourselves for the time being. Look, bear with me for a while, all will be revealed in due course, I promise you. Anyway, how did the match go this afternoon?'

Wiggy changed the subject swiftly; well aware that his pals would not let sleeping dogs lie.

'RAMC Aldershot fifteen, Portsmouth Command twenty-two,' Bogey answered, and was about to bring the subject back to Wiggy's date.

'What!' Wiggy exclaimed hurriedly. 'You played a team of male nurses, and bed makers?'

His quick retort worked; Bogey looked a bit miffed as he replied, 'hardest basterds I've come up against yet, and no, they are not all sick berth attendants, a few of them were Doctors and Surgeons.'

'Oh, all right then Boges, I didn't mean to offend the afternoon's enemy, I'm just a bit surprised that varied ranks of scab lifters would enjoy such a hard body contact sport.'

'You'd better believe it, if their bedside manner is anything like their tackling, fuck goin' sick in that man's army,' Bogey said with conviction. 'Anyway,' he continued, 'you two don't look so bad after an afternoon's wrestling with other men.' He flicked his eyes upwards, and then, trying to be camp added, 'who won dears?'

Both Wiggy and Dusty grinned at his none too effectual impersonation of effeminacy. They also noticed that he had drained one of his pints, whilst they had only supped half of theirs.

Bogey looked at their glasses. 'Come on then, see the basterds off, it's my call,' he said, grabbing hold of his second full glass.

'Don't get me one Boges,' Wiggy said, taking this opportunity to rise from his chair. 'I will see you two later on tonight, keep my two cans of beer, I should be back before ten o'clock.'

With that, Wiggy drained his glass, grabbed his hat and his Burberry, and escaped into the cool evening air.

'Well old mate,' Dusty grinned at Bogey. 'There's only you and me left, if I grab Cardiff Rose...d'yer mind 'avin it away with Belfast Betty?'

Bogey looked at the expression on Dusty's face, and then gave a great roar of a laugh. 'Christ, for one moment there, I thought yuh were fuckin' serious.'

'You're a fussy basterd,' Dusty laughed back. 'Just because Belfast Betty's said to enjoy a bag of chips while someone's poking 'er fire.'

'Ha ha hah,' Bogey roared, not in the least bothered by the attention of the few old salts in the bar. 'You know what they say about Cardiff Rose, don't yer?' he shouted through his mirth. 'She's 'ad enough ter put a guardrail round the moon.'

Servicemen at the adjacent tables caught on to the source of the mirth, and laughed with them. One old three badgeman roared, 'Yeah! And I'm responsible for a couple of miles of that guardrail!'

That did it, the whole bar descended into roars of laughter, enhanced by the few beers consumed.

'Christ! No wonder they're so bloody fat if they get through that many chips a night,' another wag called out, then grinned happily at the response of his fellow drinkers.

'Fuckin' expensive chips at a pound a bag,' someone shouted, referring to the general charge for a short time with one of the loosely referred-to Pompey Ladies.

'Ah, but you do get a rebate,' someone shouted. 'Belfast Betty shares the chips with you.'

'Ooooh, does she?' A shrill voice called from the corner. 'Fuck 'avin' 'ot chips rammed up yer duckers as a sex aid.'

The level of mirth rose, then began to lapse as spontaneous attempts at witticisms became less obvious to the highly charged minds of the men of the senior service playing at silly sailors. The level of bonhomie at all the tables and along the bar meant that no one was a stranger anymore, so as the two pals downed their beers and made for the door, they left to the loud cheerios of all those who had shared a few minutes of mutual mirth.

They made their way down Queen Street, taking the Lion Terrace side from force of habit, as they passed the Main Gate of Royal Naval Barracks. Arriving back on board, they had supper first, then took off their number twos jacket, removed their shoes and slipped on flip flops. They had both showered after their sporting exertions that afternoon, so a quick sluice down before turning in could wait until later.

'You two fancy makin' up a four for a game of Nomination?'

Tug Wilson riffled the well worn pack of cards enticingly, and the two pals took seats at the messdeck table to make up a four.

'Cut for deal, ace high, high takes,' Tug said, slapping the cards on the table.

■ ・ ■

At that very moment, barely 300 yards away as the crow flies, Wiggy and Felicity were picking at a lovely meal at a table for two in the dining room of the 'Still and West' in Old Portsmouth. Wiggy was so hungry he would have liked nothing better than to devour the lamb cutlets with as much well mannered haste as a crumbling of discipline would allow. This however was a secondary priority when sitting across from a vision of female elegance, whose only interest was the words emitting romantically from a pair of lips she just could not take her eyes off. Being well mannered people, the act of forming words with a full mouth was not the done thing, so the short silences allowed for nothing more than a quick nibble, hastily swallowed, in order to keep the hushed conversation flowing.

'You would not have asked me to meet you here unless you are interested in me,' Wiggy said quietly, bringing the conversation to a more direct level, as his eyes held hers across the table.

Felicity paused for a moment, glanced down at her plate, and then meeting his enquiring gaze said in words of a similarly hushed manner, 'I am off to university at Winchester on Monday, so I proposed this date rather hurriedly the other night for that reason. Now that we have learnt that your ship is going to be the *Barrosa*, and we are now also sure of her destination, we have approximately a month to get to know each other a little better.' She paused, her gaze intensified. 'It is essential that we test our feelings…especially as it seems love may be involved,' she blurted out, holding her breath as she observed his reaction.

Wiggy could not stop the look of wonder that suddenly took hold of his features. He started to speak with his mouth half full, then caught himself, and swallowed hard. He touched his serviette to his lips, and still gripping it in his left hand held her gaze for a moment searching for the unspoken feelings behind the swiftly delivered word 'love'.

'Is that how you feel?' He put the serviette down and slid his hand across the table to cover hers. She immediately altered the position of her hand, and grasped his fingers between hers.

'I have never known this feeling before, I feel as if I have known you all my life but have only just realised you are here. Something inside me is encouraging me not to let this moment pass me by. Do you feel that too?'

Wiggy's heart seemed to lift, his pulse quickened, grasping his wine glass, he took a sip. The glass lingered at his lips as he swallowed. The rich, smooth Burgundy enhanced his feeling of pleasure, and then he found another desire rising, the chemicals of lust were stirring in his body. The physical receivers of these inner messages were preparing for action before his glass came to rest on the table again. He raised a lightly clenched hand to his mouth, and coughed gently into it, feeling his colour rising giving his cheeks a rosier appearance.

'Forgive me Felicity,' he almost whispered. 'Your declaration took me by surprise somewhat.'

She gazed at him, fascinated by the mutual honesty of his reply.

'You don't think it's unwise for a Captain's daughter to declare her feelings for a young sailor, do you? Surely!'

'Good Lord no!' he hastened to answer, and then added saucily, 'not in my case anyway.'

'Good, my dear Donald, I am very relieved to hear that, because you do not have the mien of an ordinary sailor. You have the qualities that are sought in a future naval officer, and that is what I see in you, you lovely man, and that is why I dared to be so blunt when describing my feelings.'

He listened, giving the impression that he was hanging onto every word she spoke. His face did flicker slightly as a reaction to the fork that gradually rose from her plate with a button mushroom pronged on the end. The fork hovered temptingly in front of his lips, so without hesitation he parted them just sufficiently, and accepted her gift. He noticed a hint of devilment make her eyes crease as she said, 'You have just accepted my gift of love, you are now mine forever.' She waved the fork playfully in front of his face, as she continued to gaze into his eyes.

He gazed back in return, the aura surrounding them charged with anticipation to the extent that his simple act of adding the remainder of the wine to each glass held an exquisite feeling of total togetherness, a union of their souls portraying the absoluteness of their inner conviction that they belonged together. She stared at his deliberately slow actions, fascinated by the seductive impression that such a simple action could produce.

He placed the bottle back on the table, and raised his glass to the level of her eyes; his voice was husky as he said, 'your love is not unrequited; it is received with the same fervour that made you speak up first.'

Fascinated by his choice of words, her right hand mirrored his as they both raised their glasses and drained them. The glasses came down to the table simultaneously, almost as if the bond between them both had twinned their sensibilities to the point of total equilibrium.

'Felicity,' he said gently. 'I love you! I love you madly! Please tell me, where do we go from here?' His simplistic question seemed out of place for the moment, but Wiggy's mind had looked ahead, a declaration of love was not a declaration of intent. Young love, purely by its nature of being hot and impulsive encourages the mind to pursue a course which is designed to end at but one conclusion: ultimately, the act of making love. Wiggy however, without realising it, was looking beyond that outcome. Would their love survive a two-year separation? Would Felicity meet someone at University? Would he fall for one of the Mediterranean beauties that he was bound to come into contact with during his tour of duty? None of these things had been considered by either of them seriously, but that simple question, 'where do we go from here?' proved precisely that a portion of his mind had not succumbed to the natural sensations of desire that the evening had brought forth. In his first real confrontation with the practical elements of love, he had unknowingly separated lust from lasting love.

Felicity answered him quietly and distinctly, with all the confidence of a young woman who has been brought up to be a dutiful daughter. 'Daddy is not an old stick in the mud,' she said confidently, knowing that this was part of the reasoning behind Wiggy's question. 'Mammaw can be an old fusspot, but she always pays heed to what my father feels important.'

Wiggy glanced at her enquiringly.

Felicity reacted by clarifying. 'Daddy knows I am a grown up girl. All my life to date, from the awkwardness of puberty, I have attended his functions, and Mammaw's little soirees with her crowd. They both know that I have learnt to be adept socially; organize my own little diversions like badminton, and the odd charity dance and occasional fete.' She paused, just long enough to give her next statement full effect. 'And both my parents know I am having dinner with you Donald!'

His mouth dropped open slightly; Felicity noticed the surprise on his face and continued. 'Do you know what Daddy said when

163

I approached him with my news? He said, "good for you Flic, have a great evening".'

'He really said that, did he? And there was me thinking our date was of a clandestine nature, when all the time it was approved by your parents,' he said, with a bemused smile creasing his face, then he added, his face breaking into a broad grin, 'I don't know whether to be disappointed or not, there was some excitement in having a highly secret date with you, you know.'

She giggled quietly, enjoying the genuine amusement showing in his face. Her female instincts read the true nature of the man through his smile. On the one hand, his determinedly gentlemanly stance on the cricket field assured her he had grit; and then, on the other hand she had seen how comfortable he was with her father and his senior guests at the cricket dance. He had an uncanny ability to be at ease with his peers, or with his superiors, he was surrounded by a distinctly unstuffy aura, which was most refreshing when considering the lowly position he had chosen to start his adult life.

He watched in silence for a moment, knowing that she was continually assessing him. Her hands had now grasped both of his in the centre of the table, and his eyes flicked up to her face as she said, 'Does it amaze you that a senior naval Captain should allow his only precious daughter to go out on a date with an Ordinary Seaman?'

'I don't know how I feel about that at the moment, naval training does not prepare you for a situation like this.' He met her gaze with equal candour as he went on, 'but what I do know most certainly is, this evening with you has given me a glance of my future. My future with you and my future in the navy.' He paused, and then hastened to add, 'I cannot have misread all the indications that have passed between us this evening in such a short time, therefore I feel I must do everything in my power to satisfy the needs of the seafaring nature of my job, and the private side of my life. I hope that doesn't sound too class related, but that has to be considered, it's all about balance in the final analysis.'

'I understand your words entirely,' she whispered back at him. 'The very fact that you have made that statement only goes to prove what Daddy sees in you.' She grinned impishly, 'Even dear old fluttery mammaw is quite taken with you, but of course she would never show it; even less, put her feelings into words.'

Wiggy glanced down at his watch, it was 2100 hours. They had only picked at the meal, and both had declined the dessert.

'Look Flic,'…he stopped abruptly, realising he had used her family nickname for her. They laughed spontaneously, as she replied graciously, 'It sounds even nicer coming from your lips,' then urged, 'go on Wiggs, what were you going to say?'

The familiarity in return brought another stifled laugh from them both.

'D'you know what!' he exclaimed, the effects of the laugh still creasing his face. 'I think I like Wiggs, it has a certain seductiveness to it when you say it.'

'Is that how people are going to know us then?' She laughed joyously, and then went on, 'Wiggs and Flic! Flic and Wiggs,' she practiced, showing her pleasure. 'It certainly sounds less fussy than Donald and Felicity, or Felicity and Donald, doesn't it?'

The air was charged with muted jollity as they enjoyed this burgeoning familiarity between themselves.

'Or Felicity and Wilfred, or Flic and Benny,' he added to the list, keen to keep this moment alive, as they groaned with mutual humour at his efforts.

'Look Flic,' he started again, but had to stop as she clapped a hand to her mouth to stifle a loud giggle.

'Go on Wiggs, spit it out,' she finally controlled herself enough to speak, but still giggling in a most attractive manner.

He sobered a little. 'Can we meet Saturday or Sunday?' His face changed gradually from the humour of the moment.

'Why not Saturday *and* Sunday,' she answered cheekily, that impish glint returning to her eyes.

'D'you mind coming to morning service on Sunday, it's always a good service, and the old sin bosun is a damned good sermoniser: you are C of E I presume?' she posed the question tentatively.

'Oh yes,' he replied, a bit taken aback by the easy way she slipped into a bit of lower deck terminology. Also, he had not expected to have been inveigled into a church visit quite so unexpectedly.

'Don't mind do you?' She had noticed his slightly stunned look.

'Good Lord no,' he assured her quickly. 'Just not expecting exactly that, at this moment.'

'Good! That's Sunday organised, now what about Saturday?'

He thought for a moment. 'What time is convenient for you?'

'Oh, seven o'clockish I suppose, just have to excuse myself from dinner with Mammaw and Daddy. They will have guests anyway, so it shouldn't be too hard.'

'What about here then Flic.'

'Just had a thought,' her face lit up with whatever revelation had occurred to her. 'Alma Cogan and Dicky Valentine are heading the bill at the Kings Theatre, would you like that?'

He grinned at her as she gazed at him expectantly. 'You are a one Flic, two surprises in as many minutes but, yes great, I would love a night at the theatre.'

She grinned that impish grin again. 'That's settled then, now get me back to Vernon before my feet grow out of these glass slippers, and the pumpkin ends up in the soup.'

He laughed genuinely at her naval humour, rising from his chair. 'My, what a girl! Can you phone a taxi while I settle up?'

Outside, they sealed the evening with their first passionate kiss, and then the taxi drew alongside forcing them to separate.

'Main Dockyard gate please,' Wiggy ordered the driver. 'Can you stop at Vernon first?'

The driver eased away without a word, and minutes later pulled up just before Vernon main gate.

They parted without any overt indication of their feelings for each other, and Felicity said, just before she pushed the door to, 'thanks for a lovely evening, my treat Saturday, it's only fair.'

With those words lingering in his thoughts he hardly noticed the taxi moving off, and seconds later pulling up at the front of the bus stops just outside the dockyard gate. He paid the driver, absently, giving him a small tip, and strolled through the gate, mind fully occupied with Felicity.

— · —

On the Thursday evening of that week, Shiner and Bogey started packing their kit after supper. As usual with the four pals it was a group effort, not out of necessity, but just mucking in together. It was payday, and most of the mess was ashore therefore it was no inconvenience to anyone to have kit spread all over the messdeck tables, ready to be stowed neatly into kitbags and cases. The remainder of that evening was whiled away playing nomination whist with short interludes to carry out post mortems whilst sucking on a can of beer. The beer ration they shared this evening had been increased by well-meaning messmates who had sold them their ration before proceeding ashore. This was a lower deck form of benevolence frowned upon by Lords of the Admiralty, but thoroughly endorsed by Bogey, a man to whom two cans of beer were a mere five minutes' distraction.

The following morning at 0900 hours, Dusty and Wiggy stood at the guardrails of 01 deck and waved cheerio to the other half of the foursome.

'See you on Monday!' Dusty yelled.

'Nah!' Bogey yelled back, 'see you in the home club at six!'

Wiggy gave a thumbs-up sign, confirming he had heard, above the roar of the boat's engines as it pulled away from the catamaran.

'Well!' Dusty said, as they watched the boat disappear around North Corner. 'I suppose we had better collect our cards, and say cheerio to all these nice people on this ship!'

'Talking of nice people, we had better see his highness Hancock first,' Wiggy said advisedly.

'Hope to Christ Barrosa is not blessed with one like him,' Dusty answered, a hint of foreboding putting an edge to his statement, as they strolled to the Top Part of Ship locker to face the stern gaze of Petty Officer Hancock. By teatime they had finished their drafting routine, the victualling office having reduced their meal card to those meals they were entitled to before boarding the boat for Whale Island.

They found two seats together in the dining hall, and sat down to enjoy a cheese wedge and an apple, their tea mugs brimming with dark pussers' tea.

'Miserable bugger innee?' Dusty opened up as they sat down.

'You have to mean Hancock.'

'I bloody well do!' Dusty continued, somewhat heatedly. 'He never made an effort to say anything to Shiner and Bogey; not a kiss my arse or goodbye. He looked straight past them, the ignorant basterd. If the DO can be good enough to wish his men well, why shouldn't his second in command offer similar good wishes?'

'I don't think niceties like wishing an Ordinary Seaman well are in the vocabulary of the average arse kicker of Petty Officer level. I should imagine we will get the same treatment on Monday morning, so don't you go expecting the red carpet treatment,' Wiggy answered, and then continued as Dusty remained silent, 'compared with Geoff Mitchell, and the two bootneck Sergeants we've met he's just lacking in leadership qualities. He probably knows that, so counteracts his disability by being a right arsehole. He's just another Petty Officer who got his rate because he waited the distance.'

Dusty mused on Wiggy's words, and the conversation continued as they finished tea and went forrard to their mess. Tug Wilson and Slinger Woods returned from the bathroom as they were stripping their hammocks to scrub them clean in the bathroom.

'Done yer drafting routine then 'av yer?' Slinger said as he finished towelling down before putting his underwear on.

'Yeah,' they answered together.

'Yuh'll be in bunks on Monday night then, yuh'll miss yer hammock yuh know.'

'What's the accommodation like then?' Wiggy asked.

'You will be put down the 'Indian Village' alongside reserve fleet moorings, pretty ropey down there, they're rough but clean. I think the navy leaves the village like that just to harden blokes up a bit before they get back in the fleet again.'

'Bullshit!' Tug Wilson broke in, and then gave his view. 'It's part of the original gunnery school, and they like to keep it like that, the blocks at the top of Whaley are the real accommodation, but they are reserved for gunnery classes.'

With those words ringing in their ears, the two pals wrapped their towels around their waists and left for the bathroom. They scrubbed hammock and mattress, and hung them in the drying room, this would mean that they joined Whale Island with one clean hammock, and one only used for three nights. Regulators were inclined to cast a critical eye on crabby hammocks and unscrubbed kit bags.

They had supper before rigging their clean hammocks, and then left them up ready for pipe down.

It was Friday night, many messmates had gone on long weekend leave, and many had proceeded ashore after supper, leaving only four in the mess. Tug Wilson and Slinger Woods decided to go ashore when they had finished their ration, so the two pals were left alone in the mess enjoying a game of cribbage.

'I have a date tomorrow,' Wiggy said conversationally.

'Same bird?'

'Yes, she's a lovely lady you know.'

'Quite taken with 'er then are yuh?' Dusty's eyes went back to the cards in his hand as he spoke.

Wiggy looked up at him. Dusty, aware of the movement, looked up again and met his eyes with an open gaze.

'She has become very special to me, and meeting her may have caused me to reassess my ideas for the future.'

'Bloody 'ell, that is serious!' Dusty chaffed good naturedly. 'Does that mean no more dreams of being a naval commando? No more heroic hopes. All dreams of leaping RNB, and taking Pompey harbour in one stride shelved in favour of a leg over and chips,' Dusty teased.

Wiggy smiled at the ribbing, and then chose that moment to state what would be widely known in the near future. 'She is the daughter of the Captain of HMS *Vernon.*'

Dusty's mouth dropped open, his raised eyebrows making his eyes bulge with astonishment at the blunt admission. His lack of verbal retort encouraged Wiggy to continue. 'Having spent Saturday night at the cricket dinner and dance with her parents and their guests, and then having another dinner date with her when she confided that the meeting was with her parents' consent, has made our association a bit more serious than a casual friendship.' He paused a moment taking in Dusty's wide eyed attention. 'I do believe, my respected friend that she and I are in love.' He saw Dusty's change of face. 'No, no, he continued, 'nothing like that, she is a really dutiful daughter, not hoighty toighty or anything, she works hard at her Dad's social commitments, and she is respected by everyone who comes into contact with her.'

'Where are yuh goin' tomorrow then?'

Wiggy looked at the unchanged look of incredulity in Dusty's face and said, 'She is buying tickets for the variety show at Kings Theatre, so I am meeting her there at seven.'

'What do I tell Boges and Shiner then, when I meet them at the home club?'

'Oh, I'll be there at six for a quick pint, I promised Bogey didn't I? Providing they are on time,' he added, emphasising the real importance of his intentions that evening.

Dusty gave his pal a quizzical grin. 'Do I tell about this hot date? Or am I under orders to keep it under wraps?'

Wiggy reacted to the question with his own lop sided grin. 'You can talk about me when I am gone,' he said, the grin broadening. 'Meeting Christine are you?' he asked, changing the subject whilst keeping the conversation alive.

The game of cribbage had been forgotten during Wiggy's revelation, and both sets of cards lay face down on the table. Dusty picked up his cards and feathered them out in his hand. Laying a seven of clubs he said, 'yeah, she'll be there, but I'm not letting it get serious yet.'

'Fifteen two,' Wiggy said, laying the eight of hearts down and moving his back peg.

'Twenty-four for three,' Dusty retaliated, laying down the nine of hearts.

'Thirty-one for two,' Wiggy shouted gleefully, slapping the seven of spades down.

The game continued until they had completed the second round of the crib board. Dusty pegged out with his first take of the last hand, so they stowed the cards and board in the mess locker, and then cracked another can of beer each. When it was finished, Dusty looked around the empty mess. 'Christ!' He blasphemed loudly. 'Like a fuckin' morgue in 'ere boyo, innit? Fancy a pint at the dockyard canteen?'

Wiggy looked at his pal's hopeful glance. 'Certainly, why not,' he replied grinning all over his face. 'What an excellent idea.' He looked thoughtful for a moment, and then added, 'we only have to put on our jacket and silk, it's number twos negative collars for the dockyard canteen.'

They made it in time to catch the 2030 hours PAS boat, and having given the Quartermaster their station cards, hopped aboard, patting their chests out of force of habit to ensure paybook was safely stowed. It was a pleasant evening, and the surrounding illumination always gave something to gaze at. The engine roared, and the launch surged through the murky harbour waters towards Welcome Jetty. They clasped the forrard handrail firmly, and turned their backs to the increased windage. Their collars blew up around their heads and necks, protecting them from the coolness caused by the forward motion of the craft.

Purchasing their first pint, they sat down watching a crowd of like minded sailors enjoying a game of darts.

'Fancy a game Wiggs?' Dusty asked, knowing full well his pal would not refuse. Since his induction into the navy he had learnt to throw a 'mean arrer', as Bogey would put it.

Wiggy nodded with a mouth full of ale, so Dusty, noticing that there was already a 'D' up, called to the chalker, 'put a 'T' up mate!'

'A 'T'?' Wiggy queried, frowning.

'Yeah, a 'T' for Taff, there's already a 'D' up there.'

'Oh of course! I keep forgetting about your Celtic origins, don't I?' Wiggy grinned, then changing the subject, asked, 'you're not in any way serious about Christine then?'

'What makes you ask?'

'You said you were not letting it get too serious, while we were playing crib; that's the only reason I ask.'

'Oh,' Dusty clicked on, 'she's a great girl; bubbly, full of fun, great to be with, and not at all clingy.'

'Does she drop 'em?'

Dusty looked at the broad grin on Wiggy's face, and took the question in the same vein it was asked. 'Not until she met this smooth talking basterd!' He laughed back, and then clarified with the truth, 'she's good fun; as I've already said. But I think she would want commitment before she kicked 'em off; her pal Jane is much the same. They just give the impression that they are fellah crazy, whereas in fact they are just normal young women who prefer the company of us sporty types. She's only latched onto me through the judo set, they both like being in with a crowd.'

'Your chalks mate!'

Dusty took the chalk, and later he and Wiggy won their first game. As ever in a dockyard canteen, a group of lads soon mould together, and by 2200 hours everybody around the board had enjoyed a very good evening. Amidst loud banter, and the bonhomie encouraged by a couple of pints of beer, the two pals drained their glasses, and shouted cheerios to sailors they would probably never bump into again; such was the communion of 'ships that pass in the night'.

— · —

At 1015 hours on Sunday 30th September 1957, Wiggy was chatting to Felicity and a couple of her friends outside the dockyard church when they were joined by the Reverend Ian Bartholomew. They shook hands, and after an introductory chat the Reverend approached Wiggy with a request that had been implanted purposefully by Captain Godfrey Dunbar-Naismith.

'Do you mind reading the first lesson Donald?' he asked.

Wiggy stood stunned for a couple of seconds, then, quickly gathering himself, he replied with a smile that replaced the surprised look, 'Why, certainly Reverend,' and then after a short pause added, 'may I choose the lesson?'

It was now the Reverend's turn to look slightly surprised. 'Why…er…certainly Donald,' he agreed, having stuttered a bit as he gathered himself. 'What is your preference?'

'Mathew six, verses five to twenty-one,' Wiggy stated without hesitation, his eyes telling the vicar that he had chosen the lesson with some religious knowledge.

'Ah!' the Chaplain smiled, and then quoted from verse seven, 'Use not vain repetitions like the heathens do.'

'Precisely sir,' Wiggy replied, smiling back at the knowledgeable minister.

'Will you excuse me? I must get my Sexton to prepare the page,' the Chaplain said, quickly disappearing through the church doors. The people who had been chatting, followed the lead of the Captain and his Wife, and followed after them in to the church.

Felicity sat in the front pews with her parents, and other officers and families. Wiggy, and the remainder of the congregation of all ranks, ratings, and gender, filled up the pews behind. Wiggy ensured he had an aisle seat in preparation for his reading of the first lesson.

The morning service got under way with a hearty rendering of, 'O God our help in ages past', and in typical naval fashion everyone gave of their best. The surrounding areas of the dockyard rang to the vocal efforts of the faithful, giving praise to the lord in cheerful voice.

When the time came, the Reverend Ian Bartholomew introduced Wiggy. 'The first lesson this morning will be read by Ordinary Seaman Donald Bennett of HMS *Vanguard*.'

Wiggy rose from his seat, and walked the short distance to the lectern. He looked down at the pages, and chapter six gazed back at him from the holy book. Looking up again, his eyes met the fully expectant looks of the congregation.

'Mathew six verses five to twenty-one,' he introduced the lesson. He paused for a moment, and then began to read from the holy book in a firm, sincere, and well paced tone of voice. 'And when thou prayest, thou shalt not be as the hypocrites are; for they love to pray standing in the synagogues and the corner of the street that they may be seen of men. Verily I say unto you. They have their reward.' He continued the reading, his eyes scanning from left to right until he came to verse twenty-one; then raising his head, he looked towards Felicity and in a clear voice said, 'for where your treasure is, there will your heart be also.' Their eyes locked for a second. 'Here endeth the first lesson.'

Every face in the congregation stared at this young man, and not one set of eyes saw an Ordinary Seaman, they saw a young man who doubtlessly was destined for greater things. Felicity could not drag her eyes away from him as he read, nor as he stepped down from the lectern. She even turned her head as he rounded the first set of pews; she knew the lesson had been read for her. He had chosen it in the blink of an eye when he had been approached, and he had chosen the last verse with purpose of mind. Her head full of wonder, her eyes came to the front again, and the remainder of the service continued in a haze of barely discerned hymns, prayers, and sermon.

On completion of the blessing, the congregation filed through the door shaking the Chaplain's hand in turns, and making a short personal statement of 'thanks for a nice service,' or, 'lovely sermon Reverend!'

'Where on earth did you gain such a command of the new testament?' Felicity whispered at Wiggy as they came together outside.

'Oh quite simple, church was a regular Sunday Morning event in our household. I myself was confirmed at twelve years of age. Christianity was a daily part of our existence; I must add though that I am perhaps not as fervent in my church going habits as my parents. Modern behavioural patterns have affected my religion to some degree, fire and brimstone preaching presents itself as a little over the top, to my way of thinking.'

Felicity listened to his forthright statement of fact, realising that his conversational answer came perfectly natural to him. He had no reservations concerning his faith; his style was simple and up- front: 'I am a Christian, take it or leave it!'

'You will have enjoyed the modern element of Reverend Bartholomew's sermon then?' Felicity asked, still unable to drag her eyes away from him.

He was aware of the intensity in her eyes, and held her gaze as he answered, 'the theme of his sermon was excellent for this day and age,' and then he quoted Proverbs Chapter one verse twenty-three; 'how long ye simple ones, will ye love simplicity, and the scorners delight in their scorning, and fools hate knowledge.' I believe your father's deeply felt thoughts on the matter. The navy must very quickly adjust its attitudes to this new age of electronics and atomic warfare. Anyone who abhors change, or who clings to simplistic tactics for an increasingly technological navy will be no use to anyone.'

'I could not have put it better myself young man.'

The voice of Felicity's father spoke beside him, and then continued, 'glad you liked the service, all of us were impressed by your choice of the lesson, weren't we Flic?'

'Oh, certainly Daddy,' she replied, colouring a little because she realised that her father had read the reason for Wiggy's choice correctly.

'Look Flic, bring this young man along for our usual after service Tiffin, you know your mammaw likes to be surrounded by chatty people after a good service.' He leaned a little closer to his daughter, and added with a whisper, 'the sin bosun is popping along also, so the more the merrier!'

Approximately thirty people, all of service definition of one kind or another gathered at the Captain's house in HMS *Vernon*. The large dining table in the huge dining room had been placed against a wall, and the Captain's Steward, with a couple of duty Wrens were putting the finishing touches to the buffet lunch. No alcohol was evident, but soft drinks were plentiful, and for those who preferred something warmer, tea and coffee was provided.

'Nice of your Dad to invite me,' Wiggy said, as they chose a corner to nibble and chat.

'Well, you did read the first lesson,' Felicity answered directly, and then elucidated. 'I have been aware all my life, that when Daddy does something, it is generally with some purpose in mind. I believe he has taken this opportunity to introduce you to the lighter side of what is called essential duties for those of commissioned status. You have begun the induction process my lad; so to speak.'

She had that impish smile curling the corner of her mouth, as she added, 'And now it's time to circulate, will you join me?' The impish grin turned to a coy smile.

They filled two coffee cups, and then began moving around the room chatting lightly to groups of twos and threes. No one was allowed to be reclusive or for that matter, exclusive at 'do's' like this, light hearted sociability was the order of the day.

Commodore Fairchild kept Wiggy and Felicity in his group for fifteen minutes, and before long, as the Commodore had intended, the conversation turned to the morning's service. 'The

Chaplain tells me you chose the lesson yourself, I must admit, it was short and to the point, was that for any specific reason?'

Wiggy and Felicity's eyes met for a moment, as the Commodore's question became clear. Once again Felicity coloured slightly, and dropped her gaze for a moment, wondering how Wiggy would get out of this one.

Without a flicker of self doubt, he answered sincerely, 'Mathew six is a favourite of my parents. All my life I have been familiar with my father's cautious approach to decision making, and quite often when he disappeared into his study, it would be for the purpose of quiet prayer, very often brought about by a difficult case his partnership was dealing with. He considered a quiet word with the almighty an essential part of his work.'

The forthright reply impressed the Commodore; his wife however, with typical feminine intuition had been watching Felicity. She knew without a doubt that this confident young sailor had won Felicity's heart.

'You didn't see yourself as a solicitor then Bennett?' The Commodore continued his chat.

Wiggy smiled pleasantly as he replied, 'I think my great grandfather's genes must have jumped a couple of generations. For as long as I can remember I had but one desire; and that was to join the Royal Navy. I'm afraid I never once in my life saw myself as anything other than a sailor, terrible disappointment for my parents; however, they have come to terms with my decision over the last year.'

His answer pleased the Commodore. It was refreshing to realise that the seafaring nation that gave birth to the world's historically most efficient sea power, could still inspire young men to throw in their lot for their country.

Other guests joined the Commodore's group, having the effect of freeing Wiggy and Felicity from the centre of conversation. They moved on and found lighter discussion with some Midshipmen who were gathered around a young Lieutenant who was serving on HMS *Ceylon* which, during the latter end of the Suez war, had assisted the paratroop attack on Gamil airfield with naval gunfire support. He was relating to his enthralled audience how the *Ceylon* had been ordered into the fray when the

Prime Minister of New Zealand had withdrawn HMNZS *Royalist* from the operation.

'The ship's company of the *Royalist*,' he was saying, 'were totally disgusted at being withdrawn, and were not afraid of presenting their views to the New Zealand navy board.'

All eyes turned to Felicity, effectively stopping the story as she and Wiggy approached.

'How do you do, my name is Christopher Tompkins,' the Lieutenant greeted them, extending his hand towards Felicity; and then, a little less assuredly towards Wiggy.

'How do you do sir,' Wiggy took his turn with a smile. They then both shook hands with the three Midshipmen. The ease with which this Ordinary Seaman presented himself took them all aback; his educated delivery was definitely out of context with his uniform to their ingrained view.

'I couldn't help catching the tail end of your conversation sir,' Wiggy said, and then went on, 'I don't think that news reached us at the time.'

'Oh, we met the *Royalist* in Gibraltar during a refuelling stop. They felt, quite naturally I think, that we had stolen their moment of glory; never seen so many long faces on a ship.'

'I believe my old training ship HMS *Ocean* was out there as well,' Wiggy added to the conversation, more as a statement of fact than a question.

'Yes, she was,' the Lieutenant replied. 'Her and the *Theseus* were acting as Helicopter Carriers, and also carried Commando units. In fact, with the *Eagle*, *Bulwark*, and *Albion* out there as well, a lot of our flat tops got a fair bit of seatime in.'

'What was your job aboard the *Ceylon* Christopher?' Felicity asked, filling a short pause in the conversation.

'Deputy Communications Officer. Da-dit-da and all that you know, doesn't sound very exciting does it, but by jove, the signal traffic at the time kept all us Comms types on our toes for the duration of hostilities.'

'Nice to have met you all,' Felicity said, smiling sweetly at each in turn. 'Must be off now, come along Donald, time we said hello to the si...,' she caught herself just in time, 'the Chaplain,' she finished, acknowledging her near faux pas, with a girlish giggle.

'Cheerio,' Wiggy said, smiling at the group. 'Nice to have met you.'

The Lieutenant and the Midshipmen gazed thoughtfully at the retiring couple very aware that Felicity had her hand on Wiggy's elbow, as if steering him towards the Reverend Bartholomew.

'What an unusual fellow!' one Midshipman exclaimed to his companions.

'You don't suppose he's one of us in fancy dress do you?' a second Midshipman answered, unable to come to terms molding personality with uniform.

'It's a changing navy,' the Lieutenant broke in. 'We have become accustomed to suitable senior rates being elevated to Wardroom status in the gunnery world, and other non-substantive jobs. I think now we may see many educated lower deckers becoming subbies in the near future as the navy realises that to keep the right people they must give advancement in keeping with people's abilities.'

'Quite right sir!' the third Midshipman chipped in somewhat seriously. 'Most embarrassing to be in charge of an able fellow whose education appears superior to one's own.'

'Profoundly put!' the Lieutenant answered, grinning at his subordinate.

'Ah hello again Felicity; and you Donald,' the Chaplain greeted them in that prominently cheerful way that clerics seem to adopt. 'We were just talking about your choice of lesson; you have excellent knowledge of the New Testament,' he added.

'He has pretty good knowledge of the Old Testament also!' The Captain joined the conversation. He turned to the Chaplain and continued, 'your sermon based on Proverbs twenty-three raised a complimentary comment from young Bennett here; he considered your views most poignant for our day and age.' He paused, looking around his audience. 'He referred, I believe, to those amongst us who would cling to our historic conservatism. Well tried as it may be, I wonder if we should become a little less doctrinaire; it is so easy to stifle a bright young mind.' He paused again, glancing round his circle of listeners, and then added, with a quirky smile, 'mind you, we must beware an excess of egalitarianism; we are, after all, a fighting service, and chain of command is vital to our well being.'

The Captain's enlightened approach appealed to Wiggy, this other world that he found himself accepted into was a far cry from the everyday world that he worked in, so much so that the Captain's statement, 'It's so easy to stifle a bright young mind,' brought Petty Officer Hancock to mind. The Captain's word 'doctrinaire', and trained ape, flashed through his mind simultaneously.

The conversation continued with the discussion of the future for the senior service. Wiggy listened attentively, knowing full well that he was privileged to be in such surroundings, particularly when such high powered comments were being made at conversational level. When the light lunch finished, he was left with plenty to think about. The navy he would be associated with was in the hands of some far seeing people at this moment, and this served to assure him he must 'pull his finger out' and get on with his future; but, for the time being he had a fire fighting course to contend with, followed by live firings aboard HMS *Vigo*, his first time in an enclosed turret.

By 1400 hours everyone had snacked and had a darned good chat with everybody else. Guests were beginning to make their ways to private cars, and the Captain's Steward was quietly advising his staff from the duty watch what to do, and where to take things. All this was happening in an unhurried yet purposeful manner as Felicity guided Wiggy to a spot where they could talk more or less privately for a while.

The nebulosity of their future together began at this moment. No future meetings could be arranged due to the uncertainty of their future commitments. Felicity already had her digs in Winchester, and Wiggy had her address safely stowed in his paybook wallet.

'I will get in touch with you when I get home on Friday evening,' she said, a hint of sadness evident in her face. 'I shall be home every weekend because I have duties to perform here also.' She paused, her eyes holding his. He was surprised to see that they had filled, and appeared to swim as she searched his face. There were far too many people around for any overt show of affection, so Wiggy grasped her hand for a moment, and then, with far more assuredness than he felt, said, 'see you Saturday afternoon, if I'm not duty, or at sea.' With that, he gave her hand another squeeze, and ramming on his hat broke away from her and headed for the main gate of HMS *Vernon*.

Back aboard *Vanguard*, he and Dusty packed their kits in an empty messdeck, having collected their daily beer ration from the NAAFI.

'Seeing Christine tonight?' Wiggy asked.

'Nah, I've arranged to meet 'er on Wednesday at judo, we had a good night at the Home Club last night, so decided to leave it until Wednesday. 'Ow did your church parade go?'

'Very pleasant, buffet lunch at Vernon afterwards and a good chat with everyone. A Lieutenant off the Cruiser *Ceylon* was there, quite proud of his part in the Suez affair.'

'What did 'e do then?'

'HMS *Ceylon* provided naval gunfire support when the commandos took Gamil airfield; and guess what!'

Dusty shook his head from side to side, silently indicating that he had absolutely no idea as to what Wiggy's revelation would be.

'HMS *Ocean* took part in the offensive. She must have come straight from those duties to sea training duties.'

'Bloody 'ell!' Dusty swore; 'we only missed it by a couple of months then.'

'Looks that way,' Wiggy answered, grinning widely at Dusty's expression of losing out. 'I'll tell you something else we never heard,' he added, his face taking on a conspiratorial look.

'Wassat?' Dusty asked, reacting quickly.

'The Yankee fleet actually shadowed the British and the French fleets, even to the extent of illuminating our ships; that's how worried they were about our two countries having a go outside of NATO command. They were terrified we would stir up a Russian reaction, and create something more on a global level. Bit of a fiasco it turns out as the truth becomes evident.'

'Bloody politics again,' Dusty retorted, and then added as he crunched up his empty can between his clenched palms, 'it's a bloody job tuh know oo's scratchin oo's back, innit boyo. There's the Yanks, supposedly our buddies, and because we took the ball out tuh play with somebody else, they get a shitty on about it.'

Wiggy grinned at Dusty's simplistic view. 'Oh don't worry about it, we will all be big buddies again as the political flak subsides,' he assured his friend.

Nine hundred hours on Monday morning, the 1st of October 1957, found the two Ordinary Seamen piling their kit into one compact heap on the pontoon alongside reserve fleet. A convenient four wheeled handcart was strategically placed on the short tarmac section that led to the road running past the rear of the drill shed area of Whale Island.

Having hauled their kit the quarter of a mile to the Regulating Office, they completed a short loan draft joining routine to collect bedding, and visit the victualling office and the pay office.

Thirty minutes later, they hauled the fully loaded handcart back to the Indian Village.

The parade ground sounded like something from Babel as they circumnavigated it. Several classes of Quarters Armourers, Gunners Armourers, and Fire Control were spread around the large gravel patch practicing rifle drill. The loose furniture around the rifles was creating a loud thwack, as bare hands slapped polished wood carrying out the separate movements of 'slope arms', 'present arms', and 'order arms'. In one corner of the parade ground a class dressed in number two uniform were practicing marching with 'arms reversed', stopping every now and then to practice the order, 'rest on your arms reversed'. Someone of importance had died, and this group would be escort for the coffin, and then provide a funeral guard.

They deposited their kits in the Nissen hut allocated, and noticed that all other beds had kit laying upon them. They changed into number eight working dress, put on their boots, and slung their gas mask bag over a shoulder. After stowing the handcart back in its place they doubled up to the Regulating Office; here they were ordered to report to the dining hall at 1130 hours for early dinner, and then muster at 1230 hours for transport to Horsey Island Fire Fighting School.

'This is a Two Gallon Gas and Water Fire Extinguisher,' the Petty Officer Mechanical Engineer shouted at the eighteen men facing him in three orderly ranks. 'First, let us look at the component parts of this Extinguisher. This is the screwed head of the cylinder, and as you can see it has got a piercer, which, when forced down by this plunger pierces the top of the gas canister. The gas now escapes creating pressure in the water cylinder, pushing the water out through this rubber hose.' He paused for breath, and then faced them with a gas canister in each hand. He shook the gas canister in his right hand vigorously up and down. 'D'yuh hear that? That rattle indicates that this canister is not charged, it is empty, therefore it is useless,' he emphasised loudly. 'Whereas this canister,' he shook the one in his left hand, 'does not rattle; therefore we can assume that this canister is fully charged.' He placed the charged canister into the full water cylinder, screwed the top back on, and flicked the protective knob over the plunger. 'The rubber hose,' he continued, waving it at his attentive audience, 'is fitted with a two way, 'jet / spray' nozzle.' He operated the two way slide at the nozzle as he spoke. 'Always remember, the jagged edge on this side of the slide stands for jet, the smooth edge on the other side stands for spray. What would you use on a ship's normal voltage electrical fire? You!' He pointed at a sailor in the front rank.

'Spray!' the young sailor shouted confidently.

'And what if the fire is in the WT office or the Operations Room? Anybody,' he shouted, gazing along the ranks for an answer. No one answered quickly enough. 'Come on you shower of numb nuts, what would we use on a High Tension voltage Electrical fire? Come on,' he urged. 'You've all done basic fire fighting; one of you must recall the long name.'

Wiggy had not wished to be a 'flip to the front', but now felt obliged to answer.

'Carbon Tetrachloride,' he said loudly from his position of right hand marker front rank. The Petty Officer's eyes swung towards Wiggy. He strolled across, and placed himself squarely in front of his attentive pupil. 'What's your name?' he asked.

'Ordinary Seaman Bennett sir.'

'Well, Ordinary Seaman Bennett, as you so clearly remember the name, perhaps you can enlighten us as to HOW this magic compound eliminates fires in a High Tension situation?'

'It reacts to the heat, producing a dense vapour which smothers the fumes,' Wiggy answered, staring over the left shoulder of his instructor so as not to appear insubordinate with a direct stare. 'So why do we use this, and not water?' the Petty Officer persisted.

'Water is a conductor of Electricity sir.'

'This,' he shouted, 'is a Carbon Tetrachloride extinguisher.' The Petty Officer continued his instruction on First Aid Fire Fighting equipment, finishing off his oral instruction with a lecture on the use of the Two Gallon Gas and Foam extinguisher; from then until 1700 hours, the whole group practiced on real fires.

Very soon all the trainees were covered in grime and sweating profusely; even covered from head to toe in protective clothing; it did not stop the oily smoke creeping under Anti Flash gear. By Wednesday they would be covered in oilskins as well as overalls and Anti Flash gear, the sweat of today's efforts would reach bucket-like volumes as the day wore on.

The transport arrived, and sixty men clambered aboard three lorries, to be transported back to Whale Island for a much needed shower and supper.

'Before you go,' an instructor shouted. 'Tomorrow morning, make sure you have pen or pencil with you. The first part of the day will be theoretical, and we don't provide 'hand outs' on every part of the subjects you will be taught, so you will have some writing to do; the paper will be provided.'

With those words ringing in their ears, the Bedford trucks drew away, and rattled their way to Hilsea, then the drive became smoother as they drove up Twyford Avenue, turning right for the 'Causeway' into Whale Island.

That evening a large reunion party got under way in the junior rates bar. Bogey and Shiner met up with their two pals, and all of them joined the remainder of their class from HMS *Raleigh*, and other acquaintances from their time aboard HMS *Ocean*. Everyone they socialised with that evening was a gunnery rate on Pre-Commissioning Training for the Fourth Destroyer Squadron.

■— ▪ —■

The Royal Air Force Britannia turbo prop passenger aircraft landed on the short runway that was carved between the nation of Spain on one side, and the British possession of Gibraltar on the other side. The Royal Air Force Policeman glanced at Able Seaman Smith, and said sternly, 'When we have collected your kit, I hand you over to the navy. They will be waiting for us outside the airport. Do you give me your word; you will be on your best behaviour until then?'

'I ain't causin' any trouble mate, my beef ain't with you, or the navy; it's some of the smart arse pricks they seem to be takin' in just lately,' Smith answered sourly.

'That's your problem pal,' the Snowdrop retorted. 'Mine is delivering you back to your own kind.'

They descended from the aircraft, and after Smith had all his kit on a trolley the Snowdrop handed him over to two navy Crushers, with all the relevant paperwork.

'As 'ee be'aved 'imself?' a huge Leading Patrolman asked; his eyes boring into Smith's.

'No problem at all,' the RAF Policeman replied, and then added with a grin, 'just seems to be carrying a big lump of wood on both shoulders.'

''Ee won't 'ave them fer long!'

'Fuckin' 'ell, Frankenstein!' Smith muttered under his breath, noticing the hooded eyes, and bushy eyebrows, and the scar that ran from the left ear to the corner of the mouth that was definitely caused by a blade.

'In yer get Smith,' the Leading Patrolman ordered, towering over his charge as he opened the back doors of the Bedford utility van.

Fifteen minutes later the van passed through the gates of HMS *Rooke*, and drew to a stop outside the Regulating Office.

Smith hauled his kit out of the back, and placed it by the door. He was then escorted into the building and told to stand by the wall while the two Regulators entered the Master at Arms' office.

Minutes later the door opened again. 'In yer go Smith,' Frankenstein ordered as he and his colleague came out.

Able Seaman Smith braced himself, and then stepped smartly into the office, closing the door behind him. He stood smartly to attention in front of the desk, staring at the wall over the top of the Master at Arms' head. The Master Regulator was perusing some documents in front of him.

'So you have a down on Ordinary Seamen do you?' The Master at Arms looked up as he spoke.

Smith brought his eyes down, a little surprised at the question. 'No Master!' he exclaimed, and then explained, 'just 'ad a tangle wiv one 'oo was a bit too big fer 'is boots.'

The Master at Arms gave the man in front of him a good looking over, noticing that Smith looked quite smart in his civilian clothing.

'More than a tangle Smith, in fact my colleagues in the UK accuse you of an unwarranted attack in the last instance, and that is why you find yourself here on my 'Stone Frigate'. He paused, and looked down at the papers in front of him. 'We are all going to be watching you. If an incident like this,' he waved the papers at Smith, 'occurs on my patch, be assured, there will be witnesses who can be brought forward to testify against you.' He tossed Smith's paybook, and an envelope containing personal effects down at the front of the desk. 'Get out of here now!' he ordered tersely; 'I do not want to see your face in here again. Do your joining routine, settle in your messdeck, and report for work on completion.'

'Aye aye Master at Arms,' Smith replied, picked up his belongings and made for the door, a bit dazed at the speed with which he had been dispensed.

'C'mere Smith,' a voice called loudly at him from behind the Regulating Office counters, and then tossed his joining routine papers on top of it. 'Get your kit into your allocated messdeck, and then get into the dress of the day and complete your joining routine. You should have finished in time to report back to me before hands to dinner is piped.'

Smith hauled his kit to his new messdeck, found his locker and bed, and then changed into number eight working dress. Picking up his joining card, he chose to start at the pay office, followed by the victualling office. Happy, now that he could be paid and fed, he completed the remainder of his joining routine carrying his bedding and Anti Flash gear back to his messdeck. It was passing through his mind that no one in his divisional office had queried his unexpected arrival. 'Just in time!' His divisional Petty Officer had said. 'Whatever Drafty's reason is for sending you, he must be psychic. One of our RP2s has just broken his right arm coming off a bloody scooter. It'll be a few weeks before he can keep a watch again. You've got the Dogs Middle, and Forenoon at Europa point.'

Able Seaman Smith returned the completed documents, his confidence growing all the time. No one, that is, except the regulating branch, seemed to be aware of his situation. His own branch had treated him with the respect afforded a highly trained Radar Plot Operator second class.

'So I'm not for the old heave ho,' he muttered to himself. 'I've got meself a fuckin' good job agin.'

The surliness of the Regulating Petty Officer meant nothing now, he was safe; he had a good job, and providing he kept his nose clean, he would have no problems.

'I've just been informed you're straight into watch keeping at the point,' the Petty Officer grunted. 'That means you are free until 1530 hours when the transport leaves from outside this office.'

As an experienced operator Smith quickly fell into the routine of his new job. The Petty Officer Radar Plot in charge of his watch soon began to look on his new watchkeeper as a most reliable addition to his shift. Smith, for his own part, decided to change his appearance; he requested to discontinue shaving, and within two weeks of the request being signed by the First Lieutenant of HMS *Rooke*, he was sporting the beginnings of a full set.

By the time Dusty Miller had finished his most important Fire Fighting training to date, his arch enemy Able Seaman Smith had taken on a new outward appearance. The daily improving blond beard, with a hint of ginger here and there, and a definite auburn tint by the ears, looked quite impressive. It also made him look ten years older than the one good conduct badge he had sported for the last twelve months indicated. His transformation of character was almost complete, all that was missing now was a base shore-sides where he could exercise a little more freedom of movement, and blend into the anonymity of civilian life.

During the time it took Dusty Miller and Wiggy Bennett to complete Pre-Commissioning training, and HMS *Barrosa* had done her Commissioning Ceremony, followed by 'work up' and war games at Portland Bill, Able Seaman Smith and two fellow Radar Plot Operators had rented a flat between themselves at the rear of the Universal Bar. The flat was situated in a side street which was overlooked by the Arizona Night club. Smith's new life was near complete, but one more event which he had no control over added to his new lifestyle. The Radar Plot Operator who had broken his arm returned to full duties, and took over his old job. Smith, by general consent of his superiors was now put 'daywork' at the Radar Base. This made him 'Special Duties', and the only thing that could disturb this idyllic existence (for a sailor) was he could be called out to fill any shift slot in an emergency, or, he could be called upon to fill a billet in a ship serving in the Mediterranean, should the need arise. Other than this, every night was his own; and every weekend from Saturday 1200 hours. Very soon he had befriended one of the chorus girls in the Arizona Nightclub; the mutual benefits of this association were obvious: she had a bed close to her work, and he had a lover who appreciated free digs.

6

PREPARATION FOR 'BISCAY'

On the 12th of November 1957, the Fourth Destroyer Squadron breathed a sigh of relief and steamed joyfully out of Portland Harbour. Work up and War Games were completed. The staff at Portland was satisfied that all ships could begin their commissions with an element of safety, and could give a proficient account of themselves if called upon to do so. Total efficiency would develop as Captain 'D' kept himself and his three commanders on their toes with continual exercises, and 'General Quarters' every evening during the 'dog watches'. General Quarters on the whole, although done with a lot of shouted orders, could be a time of great humour. Ordinary sailors would be given a chance to be Physical Training Instructors for instance. This brought the comedian out in most men, and needless to say, being seafaring men some quite crude examples of simulated self abuse would be turned into a fitness programme.

The anchor would be hauled up, using a huge deck tackle; hard work, but an essential act of seamanship to be learned. Seaboat drills were perfected, a jury mast was rigged, and awnings used as sails. 'Point Ship' used a third anchor at the stern, and although the Kedge Anchor would not be dropped, preparing for this evolution was a big job. Replenishment at sea, Liquids and Stores, RAS (L) or RAS(S) would be carried out with an RFA vessel to perfect this very essential manoeuvre for Captain and officers to practice station keeping 120 feet or closer to the supplying vessel.

That's Life in a Blue Suit

Royal navy ships rarely go from A to B in a straight line, particularly Destroyers and Frigates. Every hour of every day is utilised to the full, particularly at the beginning of a commission.

Contact with the American Sixth Fleet is a darn good reason to show off. The Commanders of the four ships of the squadron gave the yanks a treat. Approaching in 'Line Astern' at twenty-five knots, the whole squadron, at a flag signal from Captain 'D', would angle to port a couple of degrees, then streak across the sterns of the American ships at close quarters, and then resume line astern formation on the other side. The thrill of this manoeuvre has to be seen to be fully appreciated. Nothing looks as effective as a Battle Class Destroyer in the hands of a capable commander, and four of them acting in absolute harmony is a thrill to remember forever.

Two days out from Portland Harbour an emergency occurred aboard HMS *Barrosa*. A young sailor reported sick, and appendicitis was suspected. With only an SBA on board it became essential that *Barrosa* got within helicopter range of Gibraltar. Any of the ports along the western coasts of Spain and Portugal could have been asked for assistance, but as the lad was only suffering an abdominal pain that could be an appendix pain, it was decided to head for Gibraltar at full speed.

The second boiler was connected, and very soon *Barrosa* was streaking across a reasonably calm sea at its top speed of thirty-five knots. She hurtled through the light swell of the Eastern Atlantic with a wake fifteen feet high, an awesome sight, and a most exhilarating experience for those new to the job.

Dusty was First Dogwatchman, and had been detailed for wheelhouse duties. As helmsman he would assist the Quartermaster and the Bosun's Mate of the watch by operating either the port or the starboard engine telegraph and revolution counter.

Because of the emergency situation the Coxswain, a Chief Petty Officer was on the wheel, and when he was satisfied with the handling of the ship at full speed, he would ask the Captain's permission to allow other wheelhouse personnel to take the wheel, starting with the Chief Quarter Master who was a Petty Officer.

Dusty took over the starboard telegraph when he relieved the helmsman of the afternoon watch. Both telegraphs showed full ahead, with maximum revolutions set.

Steering the ship at this speed required minimum wheel movements to keep the gyro compass steering repeater bang on course. Great concentration was essential however; at this speed a slight overuse or correction could send the ship heeling over to port or starboard, taking some time to get her steady once again.

The watch was divided into four half hour stints generally, but quite naturally it was only fair to give everybody a chance on the wheel, and Dusty was not left out.

'Permission for Ordinary Seaman Miller to take the wheel sir,' the Chief Quartermaster spoke into the microphone. There was a pause from the conning position on the bridge.

The officer of the watch turned to Captain Ploughright saying, 'It's Ordinary Seaman Miller's trick on the wheel sir, do I allow it?'

The Captain thought for a second, glancing at the sea to starboard, and then answered, 'yes, let's give the young fellow a go. Tell the Coxswain to keep a close eye on him.'

'Aye aye sir,' the officer of the watch replied. 'Very good,' he said into the conning microphone.

'Ordinary Seaman Miller on the wheel sir,' Dusty began his takeover speech. 'Steering by gyro; course to steer 180 degrees, both engine telegraphs showing full ahead, 300 revolutions set sir.'

'Very good Miller,' the Officer of the Watch replied, and then added. 'Keep an eye on him Coxswain.'

The Captain kept his eye on the conning position rudder indicator; it showed him just how much wheel Dusty was using to keep her dead on 180 degrees. He occasionally glanced at the bridge gyro repeater, both instruments told him just how well Dusty was coping with his first really responsible ship-board task since joining the navy. After five minutes it became obvious to everyone that Dusty was reacting to any slip of the compass tape to port or starboard instantly, and with just enough wheel to correct the movement; he had learnt how to anticipate when his action had produced the desired effect, by bringing the wheel amidships ready for any counter action before it occurred. This is a habit learnt very quickly when paying full attention to the movement of the ship, and knowing when to counteract that movement. Dusty's time on the wheel during work up, and sea watches now proved its worth.

At 1800 hours when the watches changed, the Coxswain swung the microphone over to himself saying, 'Bridge, wheelhouse, Coxswain speaking sir.'

'Yes Coxswain,' came the reply.

'With your permission sir, I will leave the wheelhouse in the capable hands of the Chief Quartermaster, and take over again for the middle watch.'

There was a pause as the Officer of the Watch glanced towards the Captain.

The Captain nodded his assent adding, 'he will have to be on the wheel when we enter harbour, so it's good sense that he and the Chief Quartermaster go watch and watch about.'

Having been relieved, Dusty went down to weather deck level, coming out onto the upper deck through the port side screen door by the galley. He grabbed a lifeline and walked aft the length of the deck to the stern superstructure. The vibration below decks was horrendous, but with typical lower deck stoicism everything except conversation went on as normal. The terrific vibration set up by the screws at full revolutions was conducted up through the hull via the 'A' brackets. To the layman sleep would seem impossible, but to the hardened destroyerman, having done a day's work, then kept a night shift, the desire for sleep overcame any hardship. The youngsters in the mess followed the lead of their elders; to be heard complaining was out of the question. The example set by these stalwarts was essential; messdeck routines, and the demands of a fleet destroyer could not be affected by a few discomforts below decks; hence supper was eaten holding onto the plate with one hand, and shovelling food down with the other. Everyone chipped in and helped the cooks of the day, and trays were returned clean, to the galley along the upper deck with one hand for the navy and one hand for oneself. By 2000 hours hammocks were being slung, and bodies were soon swinging gently to the movement of the ship, and another sound soon added to the constant vibration as loud snores, started from the young and inexperienced, joined those of the veterans, as each man's distinctive melody mingled with the ambient noise below decks.

By 0500 hours on Thursday the 15th of November, the *Barrosa* was rounding Cape St Vincent, (Cabo de Sao Vicente) about fifteen sea miles off the port beam, and three hours later with Cadiz not far to port she reduced speed to fifteen knots whilst a Wessex Whirwind helicopter hoisted the young man into its interior, and with a wave from its crew sped away to Gibraltar. Later that afternoon *Barrosa* entered harbour, and by 1600 hours had reverted to harbour routine.

'Fancy a run ashore tonight Wiggs?' Dusty asked.

'Damned good idea my man, the whole NATO fleet will be here at the weekend, so a quiet pint tonight is an excellent idea.'

They had tea, and then joined the crush in the bathroom; an hour later, they strolled meaningfully out of the dockyard gate.

First stop was the United Services Club, which catered to the immediate needs of thirsty servicemen before they hit the main street of Gibraltar with its many popular bars, many of which provided floor shows and food.

Next came the Trocadero, then the Café Suizo, or the squeezo as it was called by the Royal Navy. After that, a short stagger across the road and one was drinking in the Universal Bar. Here they were soon rubbing shoulders with soldiers from the Black Watch, a battalion of Fusiliers and the RAF; all of whom formed part of the Garrison that was the Gibraltar of the fifties in the aftermath of the Suez War, and the struggles of EOKA in Cyprus striving to become an independent state.

'Hey, I like it in here,' Dusty said, gazing at a delightful lady performing a Spanish dance on the wide stage.

'Bit bloody noisy though, don't you think?' Wiggy said.

'Pardon!' Dusty answered, cocking an ear and grinning.

The clattering of the castanets rose to a crescendo, and suddenly the lovely lady finished her stint with a loud stomping of feet.

'Thank God for that!' Wiggy said, joining everybody else clapping the young lady off the stage.

'It might be noisy, but the wine's cheap,' Dusty said, raising a half full glass off the table and taking a gulp. 'Works out at about a tanner a half pint glass,' he went on, staring down into the dark red liquid.

'A bit rough though, don't you think? I'm going to treat this stuff with respect; I've heard these Spanish wines have a habit of creeping up on you, and blowing your bloody head off.'

'Nah, there's a couple of old boys at the back stomping about like mad in a big vat of it, this is straight from peasants' feet to the bar,' Dusty joshed his pal, draining his glass of the last gulp.

'You watch it pal,' Wiggy grinned back at him. 'I'm not toting you back aboard across my shoulders.'

'Yeah but it's cheaper than the beer at sixpence a tot innit boyo, the beer in 'ere is a bob a bottle.'

The badinage continued, further emphasising Wiggy's statement concerning the strength of the Spanish rough red, but it was noticeable that the next time Dusty went back to the bar he returned with two bottles of beer.

'The club's open upstairs, fancy a change of scenery?' Wiggy asked, as Dusty plonked the two bottles on the table.

'Ang on, I was just goin' to shove some money in the Juke Box, they've got that new one of Connie Francis on there.'

Dusty sat down again just as the strains of 'Who's sorry now' added to the noise of drinking servicemen.

'You sentimental old git,' Wiggy laughed at him, adding, 'Is that what a week away from Christine does to you?'

'Nah, she's my favourite singer,' Dusty replied. 'These bloody pongos 'ave put Elvis's Hound Dog on three times in the last 'alf hour, and I'm just a bit cheesed off with 'earin' it.'

Wiggy laughed aloud at his pal's exasperation which was of course fuelled by the strong wine. 'Come on,' he urged, 'let's see this off and go upstairs for a good floor show, it's only a couple of bob to get in.'

It was not long before they were sitting down at a nicely clothed table with beautiful Flamenco dancers flitting around the tables flirting with their male admirers. They were just doing their job and exhorting the mainly male audience to buy them drinks, the commission from which boosted their low income.

'Just goin' for a slash Wiggs,' Dusty said, easing himself around the table.

He ambled down the stairs, and accidentally brushed into a bearded figure coming up the stairs.

'Sorry mate!' he apologised.

'Just watch where yer goin'!' was the reply he got for his apology, as the grumpy figure continued up the stairs.

Dusty paused for a moment, turning his head around. His face creased in a questioning frown. 'Nah! Can't be,' he muttered to himself as a picture of Able Seaman Smith flashed through his mind.

By the time he returned to the table the band was in full swing, and six Flamenco dancers were strutting their stuff, stomping their feet and clacking their castanets with great vigour. The noise was tremendous; no conversation could proceed until the lead dancer had finished her exciting sequences of movements. She had been joined by a male dancer whose speed and agility were phenomenal, greatly encouraged by his audience of British servicemen shouting, 'go on Felipe, give it some!'

The act came to an end, and the band went straight from Flamenco to the song 'Granada'. A member of the band had stood up to add the vocals to this powerful song with a rich tenor voice. The band played a little quieter around the singer as he accompanied himself on a rhythm guitar played in the style of Manitas de Platas (Hands of Silver), probably the most famous Gypsy guitarist of that time. Felipe and his partner were accompanying the singer whirling to the music with faultless timing. As the song came to an end they sprang nimbly off the stage and whirled amongst the audience accepting the plaudits graciously.

The show was still going strong at midnight, when Dusty and Wiggy rose from their seats, drained their glasses, and wobbled down the stairs. The course they steered ambling back to the dockyard resembled their squadron at sea; they were not proceeding to their destination in a straight line. Their wandering footsteps however, quickly took on a less diversionary nature as the shape of HMS *Barrosa* loomed in their sights. Without a word, they stopped, adjusted their hats, and straightened up as well as they were able to, and then, with a great pretence of sobriety clambered up the gangway, saluted, and collected their station cards off a grinning Quartermaster. The duty Petty Officer gave them a hard glance, and then turned away to face forrard, grinning also, as the two wobbly sailors quietly made their way aft to their messdeck. Soundlessly, the two pals reached the deck of ten mess on the port side aft, undressed with great attention to detail, as only the inebriated can, and then swung into their hammocks which some thoughtful messmate had slung and unlashed for them.

━━ ∙ ━━

On Saturday morning, amongst much piping and ceremonial, the NATO fleet started entering harbour. Berthing priorities meant that *Barrosa* had to slip her berthing hawsers and move off the jetty to allow *Corunna* to go inboard of her. *Alamein* came in first and berthed alongside the wall, and then *Corunna* to the stern of her. Captain 'D' aboard *Agincourt* berthed alongside *Alamein*, and then *Barrosa* moved in to go alongside *Corunna*. Unfortunately for Commander Plowright he got his angle wrong when coming alongside, and the tripping palm of his port anchor lifted a plate along the starboard break of the forecastle of HMS *Corunna*. Anyone in the Officers' toilet at the time could have had his bottom wiped with the fluke of a close stowing anchor.

Captain 'D' immediately ordered *Barrosa* to sea, and much to the chagrin of the lower deck, spent the remainder of the day entering harbour and practicing coming alongside the Coaling Jetty on the breakwater to Gibraltar Harbour. Quite naturally this was not a popular way to spend a Saturday afternoon in harbour.

Meanwhile streams of sailors of many nationalities were walking purposefully towards the main dockyard gate. A few effeminate men of different sexual persuasion were hanging around the toilet block on the corner before the United Services Club. But as was customary these curious gentlemen were ignored, the fun further into town being much more to a thirsty sailor's liking.

Conveniently, both Dusty and Wiggy were in the second part of starboard watch, and were duty this Saturday. The pair of them ended up as 'duty hands', and this meant that they could be called out for any jobs that did not require the whole of the duty part of the watch. Fire and emergency parties were exercised as soon as they had secured alongside HMS *Corunna*. Commander Plowright descended the gangway in full dress as soon as it was secured, and made his way smartly to HMS *Alamein*, and thence aboard *Agincourt* to meet his squadron Commander, no doubt to discuss his unfortunate misjudgement, before going on to other important details.

By 1830 hours all four ships' crews who were not duty were ashore joining a huge throng of approximately 8000 other thirsty sailors filling the main street from the Queens cinema at the dockyard end to Smokey Joes café closer to the Spanish border end. The meeting of all these nationalities in one long corridor poured thousands of pounds of foreign currencies into the coffers of hundreds of shopkeepers, bar and restaurant owners, and any other entrepreneur who gathered to extract the easy money flowing from sailors' pockets into bottomless tills. Some units of the American Fleet were in, so quite naturally for Gibraltar, all prices were hiked up to what could be successfully extracted from friendly, if somewhat gullible American sailors.

The day ashore started off much as usual, and by 1900 hours the usual badinage between English speaking navies began to turn to something of a more competitive nature. Odd little spates were prevented from getting out of hand by more sensible shipmates.

Up until this time, only a couple of policemen could be observed paying attention to traffic duties, but also keeping a weather eye open for likely trouble spots. Not a Crusher or a Redcap was in sight anywhere. This did not mean that they were not about; they just did not make their presence too obvious. More often than not, the sight of a blue patrol van passing slowly along the road was sufficient to quell any aggressive behaviour that began to rear its ugly head as the intake of a few drinks began to take effect.

As the night wore on the inevitable happened. Suddenly, a British sailor and an American sailor fell through the doors of the

Trocadero raining blows on each other in a determined manner. Attempts to stop the brawl by shipmates were to no avail, and only served to make things worse. Within minutes ten sailors of different nationalities had joined the melee of writhing bodies, and soon the fight was spreading up the street yards at a time. Minutes later it reached the Café squeezo, and then the Universal bar. Shopkeepers and other proprietors along this popular strip began closing their doors, and as a bar emptied so the doors were clanged shut.

'Duty hands gangway,' the Quartermaster of HMS *Barrosa* piped, and his words were echoing around the British ships mingled with similar calls from surrounding ships of the NATO fleet.

'Here, grab these,' the Quartermaster said, handing a white belt with trenching tool helve attached, white gaiters and a wrist band with 'Naval Patrol' emblazoned on it to Dusty and Wiggy.

They grabbed the tools of the patrolman, and with the duty hands of the rest of the Fourth Destroyer Squadron clambered into the back of a lorry on the jetty. A crusher in the back of the lorry briefed them all, as the lorry rattled its way out of the dockyard.

They sped towards HMS *Rooke*, and suddenly the driver screeched to a stop outside the power station opposite the naval base. They poured out of the lorry and fell in three ranks in front of a Regulating Petty Officer who gave them a quick looking over and then led them at the double up to the town square, and the main street. With helves still in belts, they immediately started picking up sailors, and dragging them from the fray bundled them onto the lorry which had reversed up the side road to the square. An American sailor, leaning against the wall of the Café Suizo had his hands cupped over his right eye screaming in pain and fear.

'You!' the Regulating Petty Officer yelled, grabbing Dusty. 'Give me a hand with this one.'

They took hold of the sailor on each side, and steered him towards a utility van. As they helped him into the van his hands came away from his face exposing the gruesome sight of his eye hanging on his cheek; someone had gouged it out. The utility van eased away from the scene, and made its way to BMH Gibraltar as quickly as was possible.

In amongst the writhing sailors, American Shore Patrolmen were wielding their batons to good effect, whacking men on the shoulders, or giving them a dig in the ribs if they did not react quickly enough to a lawful order. Other men could be seen hopping around comically after being rapped sharply on the shins. Not one British patrolman had drawn his helve, but they were having a similar effect on grappling men by using strong arm tactics in twos and threes if a verbal warning was ignored. Wiggy grabbed hold of one lad, who immediately stopped fighting seeing a shipmate in front of him. Wiggy led him to the truck and gave him a shove up the step of the backboard. Returning to the fray, he grabbed the waving arm of another British sailor who was sporting a buckled and definitely broken, nose. The sailor's other arm was held by a sailor with a cap badge that boasted HMAS *Bonaventure*. This Australian Carrier was a familiar sight; it always joined one fleet or another for major exercises. Between them they wrestled the struggling sailor into the truck. The Crusher taking charge inside quickly made him obey the order, 'sit down and stop acting the cunt!'

Soon, due to the efforts of the regular patrolmen, backed up by duty personnel of ships, the big fight began to break up. Across from the Café Suizo, hidden in the shadows of a side road, a bearded figure had watched the proceedings with some envy. Hidden in the alcove of a small bar, nothing would have pleased Able Seaman Smith more than to be involved in this Saturday night brawl that had evolved into a running street fight of mass proportions. As the fight began to break up and numbers in the street began to thin out, Smith gasped in disbelief as his eyes fell on two familiar figures escorting a bloodied young sailor to a truck that was now full enough to return to the dockyard. After shoving the lad inside, Dusty and Wiggy returned to the street, and it was at this time that Smith caught a full look at their faces, leaving him in no doubt as to the identity of the two young sailors out there in the street.

'Right, c'mere you two!' The Regulating Petty Officer ordered from the doorway of the Café Suizo. 'You stand 'ere', he ordered Wiggy. 'And you come with me,' he ordered Dusty, and then, having placed Dusty at the corner of the side street opposite, the Petty Officer went on his way positioning other duty patrolmen in strategic positions along the street. Smith could not believe his eyes as he peered from the darkness of the stairwell leading down to a small bar that had closed its doors as the army of scrapping, writhing, wrestling sailors approached. Standing not five feet from him, with his back to him, was the cause of the festering hate that filled his belly since that night in Billy Manning's funfair. From his position he could see Wiggy turn around as the proprietor of the Café Suizo opened his doors again. He instantly realised that everyone's attention was focused on that side of the street again. Before he could stop himself, he had taken two steps forward and thrown an arm around Dusty's throat. With superhuman strength he pulled Dusty to the alcove, swung him round and savagely kneed him in the groin. As Dusty reacted to the blow, and bent forward, his hands automatically reaching down to protect his most sensitive area, Smith's knee came up again, and this time connected with the left side of Dusty's jaw. His head snapped back, his brain switched off, and he was aware of falling backwards, tumbling down steps, but unable to help himself. His body crashed against the door at the bottom, and instantly a figure standing over him was kicking him savagely around the head and body. He tried to move his hands to protect his vulnerable parts but his body would not move as the blows of a shoe bruised his abdomen and chest, occasionally catching him on the head. Suddenly, the beating stopped, and outlined in the dim light was a retreating figure, the contours of his face broken up by hair. This was all Dusty registered as his mind verged on complete unconsciousness.

Smith dashed across the road, and in less than a minute was sitting on the edge of his bed in his own room of the flat gasping for breath. Slowly the reactions to his exertions of the last three minutes subsided and he flopped back on the bed his arms outstretched, and chest still heaving. A staccato 'ha-ha' burst from his lips. 'Gotcher yuh barsterd!

He continued breathing heavily, and as the tension in his body slowly decreased he repeated his vengeful statement, 'gotcher yuh Welsh twat!' The fact that his terrible hatred had suddenly emerged and led him into a cowardly attack streaked through his mind. He swept the moment of conscience away swiftly, grunting, ''e fuckin' well 'ad it comin' to 'im!' He felt a load had been lifted from his shoulders as his mind sought ways of denying the ingress of conscience. The circle had turned, he had become the vanquisher. Having twice been on the losing end, he now felt vindicated by the chance that fate had granted him, and he had accepted without hesitation.

Back out on the street Wiggy glanced across to where Dusty had been standing, before the door had opened behind him, distracting his attention. People were starting to enter the bars again now that the short alcohol inflamed battle had ceased. 'Dusty!' he shouted, knowing that his shipmate would not move away from the position he had been ordered to guard. He moved a few paces left, the better to see up the side street. He shouted again, and would have liked to run across the road for a better look, but that would have meant leaving his post.

'What's the matter?' the Regulating Petty Officer shouted, running up to Wiggy.

'You put my shipmate over there,' he indicated with a finger, 'I turned to answer the proprietor as he opened the door, and when I turned around again my oppo had disappeared.'

'Come on then, let's 'ave a look!'

They crossed the street together, and peered up the dimly lit alley. The odd sailor or two was walking down from the Wintergardens bar a little further up, but there was no sign of Dusty.

A groan made them swing around to the unlit entrance in the wall. They peered down into the well at the bottom of the steps as a figure stirred and groaned again. They walked cautiously down the steps, and between them dragged Dusty back up to the road, and then into the better lighting of main street.

'Jesus Christ!' Wiggy swore, as he stared at the battered face of his pal.

'Oh bloody hell!' The Regulating Petty Officer gasped, as he saw Dusty's blood-saturated white front. 'Hold him there,' he said, and then dashed across the road to a patrol van.

The huge patrolman who had met Smith at the Airport ran across to Dusty, his colleague hot on his heels. They quickly loaded Dusty onto the back seats, and without a word rushed him off to BMH as quickly as traffic would allow. Wiggy and the Regulating Petty Officer gazed after the retreating van, lost for words. The Petty Officer finally found his voice, and swore, 'how the fuckin hell did that happen? We'd cleared the street, and everything had settled down!'

Wiggy glanced at his leader, noticing the worry etched in his face. 'He did not get that way by falling down those steps,' he spoke his mind. 'Somebody has given him a severe kicking, and whoever did it took him from behind, that's for sure, Dusty is a dab hand at judo, he would never allow anybody to get close enough to deliver such a beating.'

'Some sly basterd must have been lying in wait then,' the Regulating Petty Officer replied. 'He saw his chance to get a patrolman and took it, the dirty bushwhacking basterd.'

It took ten minutes for the patrol van to wend its way to the military hospital. By the time the van drew to a halt at the main entrance doors Dusty was sitting up, now fully aware of his pain racked body. The Crushers helped him out of the van, and supporting him from each side, helped him into the treatment room.

'Fuckin' hell, was it that bad down there tonight?' the duty medical orderly asked incredulously, staring at Dusty sympathetically; and then added more conversationally, 'first a Yank with an eye out, and now you me old mate. Help me get him up here,' he said, turning to the patrolmen.

A QUARANCS nurse came into the treatment room closely followed by a medical officer. They quickly assessed the damage as Dusty was helped to undress.

'Mind if I ask him a couple of questions sir,' Frankenstein asked.

'Yes go ahead,' the Doctor replied, not breaking from his inspection of Dusty's injuries.

'Did yuh get a look at 'oo did this to yer mate?' the huge patrolman asked, and then took in fully the victim's terribly knocked about upper face and eyes. 'Christ!' He swore angrily, a savage glint in his eyes. 'This wasn't done with fists; this is the result of a savage kicking.'

'He got me from behind,' Dusty answered the Leading Patrolman's angry statement. 'And before I could retaliate he'd kicked ten barrels of shit out of me. It didn't help being thrown down those steps either,' he added, raising a hand to rub a lump on the back of his head. The nursing sister, immediately alerted to another wound, grasped his hand gently, and raised it from his head. She peered at the blood matted hair, seeing an open wound beneath it. 'This needs stitching,' she said firmly, holding the matted hair apart for the doctor to have a look.

The Doctor, Sister and Medical orderly continued with their ministrations causing Dusty to flinch as the first stitch went in, but then he gritted his teeth stoically while they continued to patch him up.

'Can you remember seein' anythin' of 'im?' the Patrolman persisted. 'Did 'ee 'ave a cap on? What uniform was 'ee wearin'? Anythin' that may 'elp us grab this git.'

'He wasn't wearin' uniform,' Dusty replied, holding on to a dim outline of his assailant hurrying from the scene of his crime. 'He was in civvies, and 'ad a beard of some sort.'

'Ow big was 'ee then d'yuh reckon; tall, short, thin, fat?'

'About same size as me; five foot eight, 170 poundsish,' Dusty replied, wishing now he had seen more of his bushwhacker.

'Okay then mate, that gives us a bit ter be goin' on with. You get better, and we'll see if we can get this basterd.' The big patrolman glanced apologetically at the Sister as he swore.

The two of them ambled out of the hospital, clambered into their Utility Van and drove back to Main Street. All had returned to normal, so they parked in the side street leading to 'Irish town', and the second patrolman had a quiet smoke whilst they discussed Dusty's injuries.

'Get the pad out Fred,' Frankenstein said. 'Best we start the report now, while it's still fresh in our 'eads.'

At 0900 hours next morning, belligerent sailors of the previous evening who had reacted against the advice of shore patrol ratings, and their regulating branch directors were transported from whatever cells they had been placed in, back to their ships in the dockyard. Charge sheets for disorderly behaviour, and conduct unbecoming, plus resisting arrest would be completed quickly and sent to Commanding Officers of all ships concerned. Most of the British combatants would find themselves doing fourteen days number nines; so for the next two weeks the only rest they would get would be between the hours of 2230 and 0500. That rest could be severely curtailed by essential night watches at sea. Minimum punishment would be seven days pay and stoppage of leave, and the really bad lads would find themselves facing a cleared lower deck while their Commanding Officers read out a warrant. These men could find themselves serving up to ninety days detention, and proven wounding could attract two years in Colchester military prison, and then dismissal from the service.

— · —

Master at Arms Leonard Jackson sat listening to his duty Regulating Petty Officer of the night before. When the Petty Officer had finished, the Leading Patrolmen Frankenstein, and his colleague Fred presented their report. Later that day a medical report from BMH would arrive, and when all the known data was collated, a full report would be sent to the Provost's Office of the Gibraltar Garrison. Civilian authorities would also be involved in conjunction with the Governor's staff, but for the time being Master at Arms Jackson would continue to investigate using the facts already known. The Royal Naval Investigation Branch (RNSIB), and their civilian counterparts were already collecting evidence from the scene of the attack.

Master at Arms Jackson peered once more at the reports presented by his staff. 'Ordinary Seaman Miller,' he read out loud. 'Off HMS *Barrosa*.' He scanned the paper silently for a moment. 'Yuh know this bit about civilian clothes and a beard worries me,' he spoke, out loud, his face reflecting his thoughts. 'None of the sailors ashore off the ships would be in civvies, except senior rates of course.' He pondered for a while. 'All servicemen based on the rock can wear civvies off duty, which doesn't thin it down much.' He rose from his chair, 'not much we can do today,' he muttered, opening his office door.

He walked out of the Regulating Office, and said to his two waiting patrolmen, 'Not much we can do today, Sunday, you sod off and enjoy your twenty-four off, I'll see you again tomorrow afternoon.' He closed his door again, and returning to his seat, pondered over the reports once more. Everything he read pointed unquestionably to a cowardly attack from the rear by someone in civilian attire, who sported a full set. Leaving the two reports scattered on his blotter, he rose from his chair and opened the top drawer of his filing cabinet. Finding the file he was looking for, he sat down again and began browsing through the papers. The first paper was headed:

FROM: PROVOST PORTSMOUTH.

TO: MAA L. JACKSON. HMS *ROOKE*.

He read the contents of the paper again, and then peered at the passport sized head and shoulders photograph clipped to the papers. 'Hmm, no beard there,' he muttered to himself. He read through the papers again, but no other name appeared in the text, just 'REF A/B R. SMITH RP2' followed by his official number. His mind could not let go of the flash of memory that made him extract this file. Gazing once more at the outline of Smith's face staring back at him, realisation suddenly hit him. He reached for his diary, and flicked back the pages; reading swiftly through the requests, and the defaulters of each page. In a few minutes he came up with the evidence that his retentive mind had made him search for. His finger stabbed down on the name; Smith, and there written underneath the name was:

'REQUEST TO DISCONTINUE SHAVING.'

'Right!' he muttered to himself, 'that's where we start our enquiries tomorrow.'

Happy, now, that he had somewhere to start his enquiries, he cleared his desk, had a final look around, locked up, and returned to his married quarters. Once again it had been impossible for him to have a short weekend at home with his family

At the same time as the Master at Arms of HMS *Rooke* had carried out his immediate duties concerning the previous night's street battle, Wiggy and the LSBA of HMS *Barrosa* had reacted to a call from BMH saying Dusty was well enough to return to his ship. The Medical Officer recommended seven days light duties until his heavily bruised ribs, midriff, and groin ceased to be painful.

Dusty walked out of the Utility Van with a stoop, and his legs wide apart. The tenderness of his testicles made him wince as one leg shuffled after another. The bumpy, narrow roads of Gibraltar allowed him little relief, and climbing the ship's gangway increased the pain his body was suffering a hundredfold. The Quartermaster and his Bosun's Mate helped him from the top step to deck level, while Wiggy and the LSBA steadied him from behind. From there he was steered to a cot in the sick bay, being in no condition to hoist his body up into a hammock.

At 1100 hours on Monday morning Dusty had two surprise visitors.

'Ow are yuh doin' mate?' Frankenstein grinned at him. 'Me and Fred 'ere thought we'd come and see 'ow yer are, we're off duty until 1200 hours. We 'ave ter see the Master at Arms at 1330 this avo so we thought we'd let 'im know 'ow yer are.' He paused a second, and then added the real reason for his visit. 'Is there anything else yuh can tell us? 'Ave yer remembered anything that might 'elp us a bit more?'

Dusty's face broke into a painful grin as he tried to put on a brave face. He had just spent the last half hour talking to his Captain, who had visited him, not as an act of duty, more an act of compassion, but it still involved the pain of speaking with sore ribs seeming to creak at every breath. At this moment the last thing he needed was a lengthy discussion.

'Must be something about me that attracts punch-ups, this is the third time in as many months that some basterd's 'ad a go at me.'

'Were yuh on duty the other two times?' Fred asked, opening his mouth for the first time.

'Nah, once on the *Vanguard*; and the same bloke 'ad a go at me ashore.'

'What was 'is name?'

Dusty thought for a moment before answering. 'An Able Seaman by the name of Smith, why do you ask?' he added with a puzzled look.

'Oh, we 'ave tuh ask,' Fred answered...'Everybody, including the RNSIB is onto this one, and as it's a navy problem initially we 'ave ter be seen tuh be doin' our job.'

Five minutes later Dusty was glad to see the back of them; well meaning as they were, their minds were concerned with answers, rather than discomfort.

Wiggy came in carrying a tray with his oppo's dinner on it. (Oppos did this sort of thing if a buddy was incapacitated.)

'Christ I've bin bloody chopsin all mornin',' Dusty complained, and then looking at his pal grinned, 'you wouldn't care to chew that for me first, would yuh boyo?'

They both laughed, and Dusty winced as pain punished him for his moment of mirth.

'Would you like me to hang on for a while?' Wiggy asked, realising that his pal probably preferred silence for a while.

'You sod off and 'ave yer dinner, I'm goin' tuh give my jaws a rest as soon as I've demolished this.'

The LSBA rose from his desk. He had been working quietly whilst Dusty had received his visitors.

'I think you could do with a rest mate,' he said, checking the stitches on the back of Dusty's head as he spoke. 'Unless it's somebody important, no more visitors today young man, I'm off to dinner now, you enjoy that, and I'll return the tray when I get back.'

Later, at 1330 hours, Frankenstein and his colleague Fred sat in the Master at Arms' office and related what had passed between Ordinary Seaman Miller and themselves.

'Seems a guy by the name of Smith 'ad a go at 'im a couple of times while 'ee was on the *Vanguard*,' Fred said.

The Master at Arms threw a sheaf of papers onto his desk in front of them. 'That man's name is Smith; do you recall picking him up from the airport a couple of months ago, this very day, the 19th September 1957?'

'Yeah, I remember 'im, cocky, surly basterd, but he soon clammed up when 'ee saw my mate 'ere.'

'Well,' Master at Arms Jackson continued. 'He works up at Europa Point now, so I want the pair of you to go up there now, and ask him where he was on Saturday night. Don't let him be vague; you want to know his exact whereabouts from 2100 hours until midnight. If he was in a bar, who was he with? Verify exactly time and position and get names, don't be frightened of leaning on him a bit. Make him think this could be a manslaughter enquiry if it helps to open him up, but don't tell him Miller's exact condition until you can see where he's coming from. Finally, phone me up here immediately if he comes up with an alibi and I'll get CID and RNSIB onto it right away.'

One hour later Able Seaman Smith was confronted by the two Crushers.

'Christ! Frankenstein again,' flashed through Smith's mind as he gazed into the irregular battle hardened features of Leading Patrolman Charlie Ward, alias 'Sharkey' to his peers.

They took Smith out to the Utility Van and sat him in the back. They clambered in after him and sat on the wooden bench seat opposite, glaring directly into his eyes.

'We are investigating an attack on Saturday night that could turn into a charge of manslaughter or murder,' Fred opened up, watching for a reaction.

Smith struggled for composure, but asked unblinkingly, 'what's that got to do with me?'

'We don't know yet, but we do want ter know where yuh were between the hours of 2100 and midnight on Saturday.'

Smith glanced at Frankenstein, holding the hard stare for a moment, and then turning to Fred answered with the same steely glare, 'I wuz in the Arizona Club wiv me bird; why?'

Fred ignored the question, and held Smith's confident gaze. 'Where can we find your bird? What's 'er name?' He asked, his stern features not flickering.

''Er name's Gonzuella, and she lives in the flats opposite the Arizona,' Smith answered confidently now he was telling the truth.

'What's the number on the door?'

'It ain't got a number, it's got a name!' Smith retorted, now not in the least worried by the line of questioning.

'What's the name then Smith?' Fred growled, leaning closer.

'Los Tres Caballeros,' Smith replied, once more shifting his gaze to Frankenstein, and holding his savage eyes confidently.

'Right Smith!' Frankenstein opened his mouth for the first time; really annoyed by Smith's cocky answers. 'A young OD by the name of Miller took a savage kicking Saturday night, and is at this moment laid up in a pretty bad way. The basterd 'oo did 'im over was in civvies and 'ad a beard, and d'yer know what?' He leaned closer to Smith. 'Your name came into the frame; funny that innit? Yuh was on the *Vanguard* with 'im, and yuh 'ad a go at 'im twice, then lo and be-old 'ee gets done in Gib and you are supposedly not many yards away in the bloody Arizona with yer Spanish lady. If it was you asshole,' his voice dropped to a threatening whisper. 'Me and my mate Fred 'ere will be the ones ter bring yer in, and we'll be 'opin like 'ell that yuh resist arrest.' He grinned evilly showing the gapped and crooked teeth that accentuated the scar running from the corner of his mouth to his ear.

'We won't be able ter kick yore 'ead in, but we can inflict some awful pain without it showin'.'

Smith's mind was racing, as he stared back into those awfully savage eyes. He knew that one sign of weakness would give him away; one flicker of doubt and this terrible interrogator would know it.

'Fred!' Leading Patrolman Sharkey Ward said to his colleague. 'You go and phone the Jaunty, and I'll stay 'ere with this twat. See if 'ee wants ter talk a little bit more.'

Fred glanced at his partner, and climbed from the van. Turning round and shoving his head inside again he said with a hint of worry in his voice, 'If yuh hit 'im, make sure it's where it can't be seen.'

Smith didn't know it, but this was all part of the act, to leave him believing that such a thing could happen.

The statement had the desired effect, but not in the way Frankenstein would have preferred.

'Yuh can belt me if yer like, but it still won't alter the fact that I wuz in the Arizona wiv me bird, and she is goin' ter back me up on that,' Smith said, holding the big Patrolman's eyes as he spoke. 'Yu'll just 'ave ter look somewhere else fer yore bully boy, cos it ain't this jack shit, and yuh can't prove otherwise.'

'Yer a confident basterd Smith,' Frankenstein retorted. 'But yu'll go down for this one, yore the guy we're lookin' for, and by

Christ I'm goin' ter 'ave yuh for it. That young lad didn't 'ave a chance, otherwise the tables would 'ave bin turned. If there's one thing I 'ate in this life more than a coward, it's a coward who comes from be-ind,' he fingered his long scar meaningfully as he spoke those words.

Fred returned, breaking the tension in the van. 'Right that's got the Jossman going, 'ee's phonin' the cops straight away, and they'll be there in a couple of minutes.' He turned to Smith saying tersely, 'you can fuck off inside and get on with yer work, if we need yuh, we know where yuh are.'

Able Seaman Smith jumped out of the van, and walked back into the Radar Operations Room. 'Okay mate,' he said to an operator who had been placed at his set. He scanned the screen, his mind absorbing everything instinctively. His mind went back to that Saturday night recalling how he had slipped out of the Arizona at 2200 hours when Gonzuella had taken the stage for her twenty minute stint. He had watched the ruckus on main street whilst hiding in the shadows, and could not believe his luck when he was given the chance to avenge himself. The sudden sighting of Miller, followed by him being placed in a position where he was vulnerable to an attack from the rear had been a chance he was unable to resist. Gonzuella had not seen him leave, of that he was absolutely sure. She had not seen his return, because when she returned to their table, she hugged and kissed him, the excitement of her act making her demonstrative in the way only Spanish women can be. She had no idea he had left his seat in the corner alcove. She was his rock solid alibi, and his present confidence in that alibi gave him the hardness to stare those two diligent patrolmen in the eye and brazen it out.

Leading Patrolman Charlie Ward, alias Sharkey, alias Frankenstein, did not smoke. His partner Fred did smoke, so most of their conversations were held outside the van. Sharkey was leaning against the side of the van upwind of his colleague and their conversation had reached the point of absolute certainty of Smith's guilt. ''Ee's the basterd we're after, I'm dead certain of it, there's too much coincidence 'ere for it not ter be 'im, and ain't 'ee just the 'ardest faced basterd yuh've ever seen?' Sharkey said, watching the smoke from Fred's cigarette rise aimlessly into the still air.

Before Fred could reply, a Petty Officer appeared in the doorway to the station.

'Jossman on the phone for you Fred,' he shouted.

Fred rushed up the steps, and disappeared inside. He reappeared about three minutes later shaking his head as he looked down towards his colleague. 'Come on Sharkey!' he said loudly, 'let's bugger off, she's given 'im a water tight alibi.'

Leading Patrolman Ward frowned deeply, the creases on his face distorting further the previous reshaping that had taken place. 'Shit!' he exclaimed angrily. 'I wuz lookin forward to takin' that bushwackin' basterd in.'

'All is not lost me old mate,' Fred consoled his partner. 'She was bound to say that faced by a copper in uniform, and a deadly serious RNSIB man.'

'What? D'yuh think she may 'ave lied?'

'Nah, I'm not suggesting she may 'ave told a porkie, but the easiest way of not involving 'erself was to say that Smith did not leave 'er side all night. She gets up and is lost in 'er act, and I reckon that is when Smith sneaked out and ran into 'is old enemy.'

'Best we 'ave a run ashore in civvies sometime, and take in the show then innit mate,' Leading Patrolman Ward answered his partner's logic. 'Both you and I know,' he continued, 'to all intents and purposes the only thing that'll crack this is a witness to the attack. No such eye witness is available, and the lad isself cannot shed further light on it, but a quiet chat wiv this Spanish dancer, peraps buy 'er a couple of sticky greens, may shed further light on the evening's events.'

'Yer on my mate!' Fred answered, nodding his head eagerly as if to emphasise his agreement. He started the van, and said as they began the journey back to HMS Rooke, 'well at least there's three of us who are certain that Smith is our man, so I reckon the Jossman will let us stay on this one, what d'yuh reckon?'

'I 'ope 'ee does, because one hint of dissent between Smith and 'is girl friend and we'll be all over 'im like a bad rash.'

Fred grinned at his colleague's expression, and they continued the short journey in silence.

— • —

That same Monday most of the ships that had met off Cape Finisterre, and exercised together before giving their crews a weekend break in Gibraltar, left harbour and went about the business of their own governments. The Fourth Destroyer Squadron, after a couple of weeks working up, and then a week on passage, stayed in harbour for a further week, carrying out an assisted maintenance period. They would meet up with their NATO allies again sometime in February for 'Exercise Biscay'.

Before joining the squadron in Malta, HMS *Barrosa* had a week's 'Guard Boat Gibraltar' duty to fulfil. This duty kept everyone on their toes around the clock keeping tabs on all vessels entering and leaving the area from a point approximately thirty-six degrees north, eight degrees west. Cruising around that grid she could dash off and investigate any ship, whether for intelligence purposes or just plain curiosity, whether it had come out of the Mediterranean or up the west coast of Africa. British Destroyers were great at surprising sleepy 'Trampers' at night. They would suddenly appear alongside a sloppily commanded vessel loud hailer blaring, and demanding to know why the Aldis Lantern signal had not been acknowledged. Invariably this was a shock to a sleepy Bridge watch, not paying proper attention to their duties.

There was always a Russian spy trawler to contend with,; the antennae bristling from the superstructure gave full credence to the knowledge that all radio message traffic was being intercepted. *Barrosa's* Guard Boat duty orders would be no secret, and therefore well known to the trawler Captain and his officers. By the late fifties, the cat and mouse game had in some cases taken on a light hearted nature. It was not unknown for a British destroyer and a Russian trawler to steam alongside each other at a distance of sixty feet whilst the commanders of each vessel exchanged a bottle of Scotch for a bottle of Vodka by heaving line transfer. This was a game between Captains of course, but everyone on the British Destroyer joined in the well meaning intention of this gesture between Commanders, and very often the British crew would fabricate some ingenious device and position it behind the Bridge of the Destroyer, just to give the Russians something to stare at and take photographs of.

On Tuesday the 17th of December 1957 HMS *Barrosa* sailed into Gibraltar harbour again; refuelled at 'Coaling Jetty', then broke free of land, and sailed east across the Mediterranean. Two nights in Messina gave those so inclined plenty of time to sate their particular desires, and get sloshed on the local Italian wines. State brothels were still tolerated by the government, and the peoples of Italy. This tolerance would cease on the 28th of January 1958, but for the time being there was no shortage of clients.

Wiggy and Dusty, although healthy young men in all respects and needs of testosterone charged youth, declined the invitation to visit such a house, preferring a nice bottle of Chianti, and thoughts of present romances. At least their letters to Felicity and Christine could contain the untarnished truth. Not so two of their messmates, who made a beeline for the first house offering release. They arrived back at the bar fully sated, but full of a horror story they had witnessed after their desperately needed tryst with two middle aged Italian working ladies.

'Cor fuckin' 'ell!' Spud Murphy groaned, his face screwed up with genuine disgust. 'When we'd finished, all these old birds were 'avin' a good laugh and a chat wiv us. All of a sudden this big, and I mean big, old dear lifted up 'er dress, dropped 'er kecks, and waved 'er arse at us. Aw, Jesus Christ!' The disgust on his face changed to mock horror, 'honest to God 'er whole arse and legs were covered in large scabs, some of them oozing pus. It must 'ave been second degree syph', aw shit man it was fuckin' awful. If ever I pay for it agin, I'm goin' to inspect it fully, and even then wear overalls.'

The laughs of his audience, enjoying his explicit description, did nothing to erase the look of horror, mingled with humorous undertones. If his run ashore oppo had not said, laughingly, 'Aw fer fuck's sake shit in it Spud,' no doubt the story would have continued, and young imaginations would have run riot with gory mirth about all the dangers inherent with unprotected sex in such situations as these.

Wiggy could not stop himself asking, 'did you wear a Johnny, Spud?'

'Yeah, thank fuck!' Spud replied, nodding his head vigorously. 'When I saw that arse, I raised my 'ead and said a silent prayer to 'ooever it was 'oo ordered the Quartermaster always to 'ave a box of johnnies on the gangway. I wouldn't even dream of goin' bareback now that I've seen that.' He looked around the amused faces, all of whom were silently encouraging his overdone act of horror.

'Imagine gazin' inter the eye of yer old trouser python every mornin' wonderin' if it's goin ter ooze pus, or 'ave developed red roses round its fore. Aw shit man, it doesn't bear thinking about!'

The last sentence brought another round of guffaws, and then Buck Taylor started singing in low tones:

'Red roses round my fore,
Make me chase arsehole more,
I'm rotten to the core,
From sleepin' with an whore...'

He stopped singing, and ducked as Spud threw a playful flat handed blow at his head.

'Okay yuh funny git, I get the message,' Spud laughed, 'no need ter rub it in.'

They all joined together in a good laugh at Buck Taylor's partial rendition of an old naval canteen song. Nobody laughed louder than Spud Murphy, but at the back of his mind he felt relieved that the God who protects drunks and sailors had given him the good sense to protect himself in the wild and often hedonistic life that is enjoyed by sailors the world over when shore-sides.

Three days later HMS *Barrosa* entered Sliema Creek, Malta. The other three ships of the squadron were moored bow to stern in a line down the Creek. A mooring space had been left between *Agincourt* and *Corunna* for squadron second in command Commander Plowright, Captain of HMS *Barrosa*. A small harbour tug stood by ready to assist if needed in the restricted area to manoeuvre in. *Barrosa* paid marks of respect to all vessels as she passed, and then began her 180 degree swing around, but first the Seaboat carrying the buoy jumpers had to be lowered and slipped into the water.

William G. Thomas

Declining assistance from the Tug; and with Captain 'D' watching from the open bridge of the *Agincourt*, Commander Plowright completed his half circle, and then eased the bow of his ship up to the buoy. As soon as the engines were stopped two buoy jumpers leapt aboard the slippery buoy, connected up the hawser, and then leapt back into the boat. The stern hawser was connected in a similar fashion; now all that was left to do was the heavy work. Half a shackle of anchor cable was separated, and put aside to be hauled aft. The buoy jumpers leapt aboard the forrard buoy again and secured the anchor cable to the buoy with a 'ship to buoy shackle'. When the half shackle of cable was manhandled to the Quarterdeck, the cable would be attached to the buoy and the ship in similar manner and the hawser would be removed. Now all that remained to be done was for the 'Men under Punishment' to clamber down the forrard length of cable in a 'Bosun's Chair' and paint it white, not a pleasant task because when the job was finished it was hard to tell the difference between the man under punishment and the cable. The stern section could be painted from the Seaboat, so was not so arduous. Now with all these tasks completed the ship would be safe from high winds in this restricted mooring space, and if Captain 'D' was satisfied with the outward appearance of the ship, the crew could revert to harbour routine immediately.

Later that evening, all men not on duty bathed, and got 'tarted' up in their Number one suits in great good humour, and soon many of them were having their first experience of being transported ashore in a Maltese fishing boat propelled from the stern by a usually cheerful fellow waggling a sculling oar from side to side. These Dgaisha owners provided the major mode of liberty transportation within the harbours at this time.

Many lads proceeding ashore had never visited Malta before, but their eyes had glowed and their ears had twitched as older hands had exaggerated the wonders of 'Straight Street', otherwise infamously known as 'The Gut' to every British serviceman. Many revellers would be gently conned whilst testing the doubtful delights of The Gut, and many youngsters would break their cherry before they had gone beyond the first bar. Most would be drunk as Lords, and flat broke before they

214

even reached the halfway point. It is true to say that the further one passes along The Gut, the more mentally disoriented, and vulnerable one becomes. A wag has described this wondrously boozy and sex orientated street in terms of waste proceeding to the Sigmoid area of the bowel: 'they gobbles yer up like fresh fruit at the beginning, and then as yer pass further along The Gut they sucks all the goodness out uv yer, and shits yer out at the uver end, as useless as a heap of shit.'

By 2nd January all would have forgotten their thick heads, and got stuck into further training routines. The Seaman branch carried out 'Landing Party' training, and had to learn to form up as an 'Internal Security Platoon', not quite as professional as the Army, but the Gunnery Officer and the Gunnery Instructor of HMS *Barrosa* had the Platoon knocked into shape quite quickly.

All Seamen would spend two weeks training with the Royal Marines; this was mainly to ensure that men were fit enough to handle an obstacle course, and be proficient in the handling and use of the four types of arms carried aboard, namely the Bren Gun, Lee Enfield Rifle, the Lanchester Sub Machine Gun, and the Hand Grenade. After ten days of training the average Dabtoe was 100% fitter. Even sailors who had been in sedentary jobs since their last bout of serious training began to find the course exciting as their muscles acclimatised to excess use.

Having a run ashore after a day of purposeful training was not on most men's agenda; by the time they had done their Dhobying and tomorrow's kit had been prepared, most men were ready for the sack, and a good night's sleep. The run ashore with the Royal Marine Staff at a bar local to the training area on completion was a jolly affair verging on a full SODS Opera.

By this time, most of the lads in the squadron new to Malta had all become seasoned veterans, and watched their pockets a little better. Complaints of being overcharged were generally laughed at, so one soon learnt to stick to the well tried nightspots. These were usually houses of booze and entertainment which catered to the British Military taste for ribald nights ashore, and knew that without these guys they would not have a business, so prices were always set at that which a serviceman could afford, with very little differential between any of the major places of entertainment.

Quite naturally such a volume of young men bent on enjoying themselves attracts a large police presence. The policing of The Gut was the responsibility of the Maltese Government, and of course units of Military Police were always somewhere nearby in case of trouble. The worst thing any British Serviceman could do would be to present himself in an argumentative, or even self righteous manner if accosted by the local police. For very little reason they would whip the lad away to the local police station, and lock him up for the night. Should the lad be foolish enough to struggle even in the mildest way that appeared to be resisting arrest, these policemen, led by a man of prodigious size with a nickname that was a metaphor (but we shall know him as Titan) would immediately set about subduing the poor unfortunate. More than a few have returned to their ship or base wearing the signs of a severe drubbing that was purported to have been gained whilst resisting arrest, or starting a fight in the police station whilst under questioning.

— · —

Having been fully involved in the last two weeks' training at the Commando Training Base, Dusty and Wiggy were now fully paid up members of a bunch of messmates who gelled together as only trained men can. With everything aboard returning to normal, and the daily grind of keeping the squadron shipshape, runs ashore became a matter of a release from drudgery, and so it was that one evening the two oppos and a few of their messmates were enjoying a ribald night in the infamous 'Cotton Club' on Straight Street. A bunch of lads from 101 Commando were having a great evening hurling light insults at two ladies of indiscernible North African nationality, who had spent a lifetime entertaining young men who were far from home, and had nothing better to do with a few hours of their time.

The lads from the Barrosa found a table that six of them could fit around comfortably, and Wiggy opted to buy the first round. He returned with a tray full of beer and glasses, and after everyone had got a drink in front of them they began to take in their surroundings, and soon realised what all the mirth was about. 'Are those two birds about to do what I think they're about to do?' Wiggy asked.

His statement made Dusty look towards the heavy table that the two women were contorting their bellies on. Before he could say anything Buck Taylor piped in, 'Yuh can bet yer life on it, they do it ter drag the punters in, and they don't give a shite what anyone thinks.'

'It's the same as the old donkey shows in Tangiers, but they can't get a donkey on that table so they use the glass and the bottle,' Spud Murphy said knowledgeably, and then turning to Wiggy added, 'yer about to get a surprise, nobody'll mind if yer disgusted, that's what it's all about.'

The show moved on and very soon the beer bottle and the glass became very useful props for this type of pornographic exhibitionism. The height of the entertainment, and the final act, brought the house down when the beer bottle was used, base first, and the glass was swallowed rim first. The most sickening part of the show however on this particular evening was provided by a drunken three badge sailor. He grabbed the much abused glass, poured his beer in it, and downed it in one long gulp. Not a face in the bar was devoid of one expression of disgust or another. Wiggy, unable to contain his disgust rose to his feet and screamed, 'you dirty basterd,' and made as if to lunge at the disgusting exhibitionist. Dusty, totally surprised by his pal's seething anger, just managed to grab hold of Wiggy before he layed into this vile being. The remainder of the lads at the table forced Wiggy back into his seat and held him there, but Wiggy was not to be silenced. 'You're a disgrace to our uniform,' he yelled across the floor, his face contorted with hatred.

Everyone else was also hurling abuse across the floor. They didn't mind encouraging the women to greater efforts with their stage props, but when one of their own kind foolishly carried out a personal act as they came to the last motion of their finale it was a step too far. The drunken slob thought the boos and hisses and the disgusted looks were for the floor show, and were all part of the act; but one incensed Commando rose from his seat, and before his chums could stop him, he had given the disgusting creature a sharp blow to the body with the heel of his hand. The sozzled sailor was sent staggering back into a table tipping its liquid contents all over the occupants.

It was then that all hell broke loose, the Commandos at the overturned table reacted with typical indignation, causing the drunken slob to throw a punch at one of them, and this was an act of supreme foolishness. One Commando grabbed the arm throwing the punch, and using the man's own forward motion threw him to the floor, and so a right old ding dong got under way.

Out in the street whistles started blowing, and in seconds six Maltese Policemen led by the bullying Titan started laying into the fringe members of the disturbance with their truncheons and boots. The Commando who had jarred the matelot with the heel of his hand caught a savage blow to the forehead as he started to give a good account of himself. He crumpled into a khaki heap on the road, where he was trampled upon as the fracas continued. Two of his pals fought their way to him, and dragged him to one side. ''Ee's not fuckin' breathin!' one of them shouted to his pal; this Commando in turn felt the pulse at the wrist, and then the neck. Feeling no pulse he started pounding his pal's chest with crossed palms. A Redcap patrol Land Rover screeched to a stop beside them, and ignoring the melee they picked up the Commando and eased his inert body into the back of the Land Rover. As they jumped back in the front of the vehicle, the downed Commando's two pals jumped into the back and continued resuscitation as the Land Rover rushed away.

In the few minutes it took for all this to happen Dusty and his messmates were still struggling to contain the anger that was oozing from every pore of Wiggy's frame, until finally, with the obnoxious sailor removed, and the bar nearly empty Wiggy's anger began to subside.

'Jesus Christ Wiggs,' Dusty said. 'Where did all that come from?'

Wiggy looked at his pals a little sheepishly now. 'I don't know,' he replied honestly. 'The sight of someone in the same uniform as me doing such a disgusting thing just inflamed me. Anyway,' he grinned, 'I've gone off the Cotton Club now and

I've only had half a pint here, fancy a move somewhere where we can get a peaceful pint?'

Two hours later the duty MO at Bigi Military Hospital confronted the two Commandos that had struggled to save their friend with the sad news that a brain haemorrhage had robbed them of a good pal and a brave comrade. The following night 101 Commando, led by a Captain gave those concerned a lesson in tactics when they stormed The Gut in force, enclaving all civilian uniformed authority within their own police stations, in fear of getting a dose of their own medicine.

The natural outcome of this dreadful event was that The Gut was put out of bounds to all service personal until further notice, and by the 21st of January, when the Fourth Destroyer Squadron slipped and proceeded to sea, the 'accidental death' of the Commando was old news.

Captain 'D' led his other pristine ships to sea in line astern, and his eagerness to get his squadron back in fighting fettle again showed itself when the alarm sirens on all four ships, and the cry 'Alarm Aircraft' sent all ships' companies scurrying to action stations. Seconds later a prearranged Shackleton appeared on the horizon towing a drogue, this gave all main 4.5 inch Mark Four twin mountings on each ship in turn, a chance to blast away a few rounds of ammunition at a range of approximately 5000 yards. A second pass at reduced range allowed all the AA Bofor mountings to have a go at peppering the drogue.

After a few passes, both to port and to starboard the Shackleton tired of the game and headed back to base. Suddenly, at a flag order from Captain 'D' all four ships turned ninety degrees to starboard and raced at full speed to a surface encounter with a tug towing a framework with a radar reflector attached. At ten sea miles distance, with all safety elements checked for the tug's crew, all four ships main armament opened up on the towed framework using 'Direct Action' surface ammunition, so each ship had fired a broadside of four fifty-four pound shells, and the tug's crew would assist on board Director Radar and several bridge crew to check for fall of shot. After that first broadside all ships swung to starboard and steamed in line astern for some time before swinging 180 degrees to port and then allowing each ship in turn to hammer away at the target at a reduced range.

Dusty and Wiggy had not reached a level of gunnery expertise where they could be part of the turret's crew. They were both in the gunbay, which was part of the rotating structure, feeding shells and cordite into hoists on both sides, which would be fed into each loading tray and rammed by the guns crew left and right gun. By 1630 hours that day the Fourth Destroyer Squadron had expended its practice allowance for that month, and all the young Seaman Gunners Quarters ratings had spent the longest time to date in conditions of sustained gunfire. They would soon acclimatise to the claustrophobic conditions, with machinery hurtling backwards and forwards, guns banging loudly, barrels and breach rings recoiling; the acrid stench of cordite not fully blown up the barrel by the 'Air Blast' mechanism, operated by the opening breach.

Finally, all men of a guns crew joined together under the leadership of the Captain of the Gun and joined in the 'Sponging Out' routine. When this was completed rubber tampions were placed over the muzzle of each gun barrel to prevent ingress of seawater, the proper screw expansion tampions would be fitted as soon as ships entered harbour. The rubber tampions saved valuable minutes in action situations because they did not have to be removed before opening fire. After clearing up decks the ship secured from Action Stations, leaving the First Dogwatchmen to keep the ship alive.

At daybreak the following day, the 'Morning Watchmen' prepared for light jackstay transfer with the stores ship RFA *Retainer*. No stores would be passed to the four ships of the squadron, but last night's film would be exchanged, and the chance for fresh bread would not be refused.

Captain 'D' went alongside first, his executive second in command taking charge, and when happy with his station keeping, the jackstay transfer went ahead, his own ship supplying the gear. When completely rigged the crew of the *Retainer* hooked on the test weight, and it was passed backwards and forwards safely.

The exercise completed, *Agincourt* increased revolutions and moved off to starboard 500 feet to watch his other ships' commanders carry out the evolution.

As Squadron second in command, Commander Plowright took *Barrosa* alongside, and thirty minutes later had completed the evolution. Breathing a sigh of relief he increased revolutions and moved off in a wide circle falling in astern of HMS *Agincourt*. All eyes now turned to *Corunna*. She in turn carried out a faultless light jackstay transfer, until it came time to separate. From a distance it had not been easy to discern what had been the problem, but an enquiry later resulted in the Chief Quartermaster of HMS *Corunna* getting a severe reprimand. As a result of not paying sufficient attention, he allowed the *Corunna* to drift slightly towards *Retainer*. A sharp, 'watch your helm!' from the Bridge, made him over react using too much wheel. The ship heeled over to port, as it veered to starboard, and the jackstay hurtled through its leading block dragging twenty men with it. They all managed to let go but the force of the initial pull on the rope had smashed the leading man into a guardrail stanchion, shattering his pelvis. The unfortunate sailor was rushed away to sick bay where the SBA immediately gave him a shot of morphine to stop his screaming.

Corunna continued to bring the evolution to a close, and circled around to take station behind *Barrosa*, as *Alamein* moved forward. While all this was going on the LSBA had advised his Captain that the Medical Officer off HMS *Agincourt* would have to be brought across to assess professionally the extent of the damage to the sailor's pelvic bone. The message was passed to Captain 'D' by Aldis Lantern.

Both *Agincourt* and *Corunna* broke station and lay off a few hundred feet, and the squadron MO was transferred to *Corunna* by Seaboat. This unfortunate incident gave the young crew of the Whaler their first chance to try out their rowing technique in a long Mediterranean swell. Meanwhile HMS *Barrosa* remained on station 500 feet off *Alamein*'s starboard side, having been ordered to act as Captain 'D' for the remainder of the exercise.

In the meantime serious decisions had to be made. Within half an hour *Corunna* was making for Malta at high speed, and just over an hour later she had travelled the twenty-five nautical sea miles, and had Grand Harbour in sight. A helicopter was already visible and minutes later the injured man was transferred. An hour and a quarter later *Corunna* was back with her squadron.

The squadron now intact again, they surged forward at speed to apprehend RFA *Tidereach* to refill their FFO tanks (Furnace Fuel Oil). RFA *Tidereach* was quickly captured and submitted to her captor's demands. She refuelled two ships at one time, one off the starboard beam and one off the port beam; she could have refuelled all four had it been wartime, but today two at a time would be sufficient, for manpower reasons. The only mishap of the exercise was when *Alamein*'s stokers disconnected the hoseline with a bit of blow-through pressure still in it; the result was that all standing in the vicinity and all the starboard superstructure were severely speckled with the tar like quality of FFO. Accidents like this happen now and then, but one hour later the offending liquid had been scrubbed off; now the scrubbers could concentrate on cleaning themselves up.

Later that evening the watch on deck rigged darkened ship screens over all access doors and all messdecks dropped their deadlights over the scuttles.

Some time later as night exercises continued, the navigation lights were switched off, every ship was now invisible, leaving the ship unseen to the naked eye, and only detectable by radar.

As part of the exercise Captains now turned in, leaving the safety of the ships in the hands of Bridge Officers of the watch. They would wake the Captain when anything occurred, trivial or otherwise, and keep him informed. He would get very little rest, on call all of the night hours, but such are the duties of 'God'.

Below decks all flats and passages were bathed in an eerie red glow, allowing all below decks proceeding on watch to acclimatise to night vision. The situation would continue as the squadron practiced continually for its part in Exercise Biscay. For the present, somewhere out there, thirty nautical miles off Malta, a British submarine lurked, and the squadron had to find it and sink it before it attacked them. The serious game of practicing for war goes on, destroyers giving the taxpayers an excellent return for their money.

RFA ships *Retainer* and *Tidereach* now played the part of a convoy, with the four Destroyers of the squadron sniffing around them for possible submarine attack. The whole idea of the exercise was to give sonar operations rooms' crews a chance to pick up an underwater contact, and hold it within the sonar beam. Squid Bombs of course, were not used, but a pre-primed grenade dropped over the side by the Gunners Party member of the watch effectively said to the Sub Commander, 'Gotcha,' and just before midnight that Thursday 24th January 1958 HMS *Alamein* was the last of the squadron to achieve that goal. The submarine could now return to Malta with RFA *Retainer*, whilst *Tidereach* remained with the squadron.

— · —

Meanwhile, the Naval Drafting Commander had reacted to the request for another Radar Plot Operator second class to be drafted to HMS *Corunna*, by reminding Gibraltar that they already had one RP2 surplus to requirements for just such an emergency. At midday on Wednesday 23rd January 1958 the Tilly driver bringing the afternoon watch to Europa Point handed an official message to Able Seaman Smith. The message ordered in straight forward terms, 'report to Regulating Office immediately.'

Able Seaman Smith steeled himself as he read the terse message, but only a faint hardening of the eyes betrayed his immediate thoughts. Thus it was he walked into the Regulating Office of HMS *Rooke* ready to be questioned again about the events of 1st December 1957. He reported directly to the Regulating Petty Officer at the first desk just inside the door. The RPO glanced at the message sheet, then said firmly, 'drafting section, over there,' indicating further up the office with his thumb. The RPO at the drafting section glanced up at Smith, and said bluntly, 'back here at 1330 hours, get yer dinner, pack a steaming kit, and be ready to fly to Malta, yer joining HMS *Corunna*!'

Able Seaman Smith walked out of the Regulating Office in a daze. He stopped at the rum bar in the dining hall, downed his tot, and joined the small queue for dinner. He ate his meal deep in thought, his head full of all sorts of difficulties he would not have time to sort out. One of his two flat mates spied him sitting alone at the table. 'Penny for um, yuh miserable lookin' git,' he said jocularly plonking his plate on the table.

'Just got a fuckin' draft,' Smith moaned, and then added, 'Will yer tell Gonzuella I've been fucked off tuh Malta at short notice, and I don't know why or how long I'll be gone.'

'Christ, that's a bit sudden innit, why are they sendin' yer so sudden like?'

'Dunno, something must 'ave appened on the *Corunna*; that's the barsterd they're sending me to.'

Dave Unwin was thoughtful for a moment, but then his reply showed where his thoughts lay. 'Is she goin ter pay yore share of the rent?'

Smith thought for a moment, swallowed, and then placing his eating irons on his plate, said, 'ang on a mo, I'll get yer my share of next month's rent.' He rose from the table, dropped his plates at the scullery counter and then proceeded to his messdeck. Unlocking his kit locker he removed four Gibraltese pound notes from his wallet, and locked everything up again.

''Ere!' he said, pushing the folded notes into his flatmate's top pocket. 'That'll keep yer 'appy for next month, if I'm not back by then Gonzuella will 'ave ter chip in for March,' he glanced at his watch. 'Gotter fuck off nah, pack a steamin' kit, and get ready tuh fly tuh Malta.'

'Best of luck mate…see yer when yer gets back,' Dave Unwin said to the retreating figure of his pal.

The old Dakota roared and rattled as it struggled along the short runway, its wings appearing to flap as it reached take-off speed. Just as it seemed it was about to test the depth of water in Algeciras bay, it clawed its way into the sky. The facial expressions of its passengers showed that jaws were still clamped tight, minds concentrating on not letting the sphincter muscle relax momentarily. The tension of the flight still remained with the passengers as they walked the short distance across the tarmac to the Terminal Building of RAF Luqa Malta. Their dazed expressions, tinged with grins of relief, betrayed their inner fears as they produced their documents.

A Leading Aircraftsman glanced at Able Seaman Smith's papers, and passed them on to a Flight Sergeant. The Sergeant looked at the documents, and then riffled through a pile of documents on his desk; finally he said, 'we're billeting you here until 0500 hours Friday morning; you will then board a chopper which will take you to HMS *Corunna*.' He read in silence for a moment, and then added, 'no shore leave I'm afraid, you'll have to use the NAAFI here if you want a couple of pints.' He turned to the LAC. 'Show him where to get bedding, and set him up until Friday.'

At 0500 hours on the dot on Friday morning, the helicopter rose into the air and took a north easterly course for ten minutes having had *Corunna* in sight since crossing the coastline. The pilot came up the starboard side of HMS *Corunna* and adjusted his air speed accordingly. After a minute, satisfied with his station keeping he moved over the *Corunna*'s Fxle, and Smith was lowered to the deck in a faultless operation. As Smith was hurried away from the drop zone, a bag of mail was hooked onto the hoist, and the helicopter moved off to starboard. The crew waved cheerfully, and set off back to their base in Malta. Two hours later the *Corunna* took up position line astern of HMS *Barrosa*, and the squadron, led by Captain 'D' headed for the straits of Messina on passage for Naples, and a weekend's run ashore for the ships of the squadron. Their passage took them past Stromboli, which was huffing and puffing co-operatively for those with an eye for a good photograph.

The squadron did not hurry through the Tyrrhenian Sea and at 0800 hours on Saturday morning the Officer of the Watch used the tannoy system to inform the Ship's Company that Mount Vesuvius could be seen off the starboard bow. Capri had been passed during the hours of darkness so was of little interest. Some time later the squadron entered harbour with plenty of naval pomp and ceremony, proper marks of respect being passed between all navies gathering in Naples for the run up to 'Exercise Biscay'.

All four ships of the squadron had to berth stern to the jetty, and this was achieved by dropping an anchor and then going astern until up against a large fender pontoon. Once in this position berthing hawsers could be used as required, and when all was secure the ships reverted to Saturday routine.

All Command Officers had to attend a NATO conference to discuss 'Biscay' followed by a social evening hosted by the Italian Navy. Their crews would find other entertainment in a dockside area of Napoli that had not fully recovered from the effects of the Second World War. Young lads still pestered passers by in uniform to buy their sisters for a set period of time amongst the dereliction that still pervaded in this city of great historical importance. Even sailors, who supposedly have little resistance to invitations for a 'good time' draw the line somewhere, and passed through this area in favour of other entertainment. This proved a little expensive, but everyone found an Italian wine to their taste which fitted disposable income. It came as no surprise when Ships' Companies returned aboard a little worse for wear, but amiable; superior eyes turned the other way, allowing tipsy sailors to collect station cards and get below quietly.

Noisy and boisterous revelers were told to 'pipe down', or else! Belligerence of any sort was dealt with systematically next morning, ending up with the appropriate leave restrictions.

On Monday morning Commander Plowright led *Corunna* and *Alamein* out to sea again. Captain 'D' would remain in Naples as part of Exercise Biscay planning team. He would find time to brief his Squadron Commanders in Gibraltar where they would carry out a self maintenance period previous to the major exercise. For the time being *Barrosa*, *Corunna*, and *Alamein* would spend a few days in La Spezia, and Genoa, showing the flag.

Early on Tuesday morning, having held a stationary contact on their radar screens for a considerable time, the squadron approached the contact. Daylight showed a heavy swell, with curling rollers occasionally washing down the Fxle, and there, wallowing helplessly in the swell was a Coaster of some 500 tons. *Corunna* and *Alamein* laid off 500 feet astern of the Coaster whilst Commander Plowright took the Barrosa abeam of its starboard side at 300 feet.

'Ahoy there!' he yelled through the ship's loud hailer. Nothing happened until the third call, and just before he was about to replace the microphone, the bridge door opened on the Coaster, and two figures came out onto the bridge wing. The port lookout on Barrosa's bridge let out a loud laugh as he peered through his binoculars. The Officer of the Watch and the Signalman echoed the laugh as they saw the funny side of the facial expressions shown by the two men on the bridge wing opposite. The sight of the Destroyer, bristling with weapons, supported by another two astern of them gave them good cause to be startled. Commander Plowright allowed himself a momentary grin, and then placing the microphone to his mouth again, shouted, 'where is your captain?'

'They don't understand you sir,' the Officer of the Watch said, keeping his binoculars trained on the two.

'CAPITANO!' Commander Plowright tried again.

This time they both shook their heads vigorously from side to side, and one shouted back, 'no Capitano!'

'Look up forrard of her sir... by the bullring,' the Officer of the Watch said, indicating with a finger. 'That's a parted towing hawser if I'm not mistaken.'

'You're right Timothy,' Commander Plowright answered, and then added thoughtfully, 'wonder if they knew they were adrift. Anybody speak Italian?' he asked, his eyes sweeping the crowd of faces on the bridge.

'Leading Writer Knowles does sir, his mother is of Italian extraction,' the Supply Officer said.

'Get him up here will you!'

The Officer of the Watch picked up the ship's broadcast microphone. 'D'you hear there, Officer of the Watch speaking. Leading Writer Knowles bridge; at the double.'

Two minutes later Leading Writer Knowles presented himself to the Captain.

'You speak Italian I've been advised, Leading Hand, do you think you could get those two chaps over there to tell us what the hell they are doing adrift out here?'

'I'll do my best sir,' he answered, taking the proffered loudspeaker microphone.

For two minutes the Leading Hand chose his words carefully, and then listened intently as one of the Italians shouted back with the aid of a voice tube. Finally he turned to his Captain with a grin saying, 'they are as surprised to find themselves adrift this morning as you are sir.' The grin faded as he went on, 'Apparently they were being towed from Civitavechia to Napoli for major engine repairs that can only be done with screw and propshaft removed. When they fell asleep last night they had a Tug in front of them; they have no idea when the towline parted.'

'Thanks Leading Hand,' Commander Plowright said, and then turning to his First Lieutenant, continued, 'it's obvious they have no radio.' He paused a moment staring at the swell. 'Do you think two men could haul in a towing hawser, if we attempted to take them in tow?'

'Not a snowball's chance in hell sir, in my opinion,' Lieutenant Commander Dyson replied, and added, 'with this swell we can't get men aboard her; even if we stream the Inflatable Liferaft, I doubt if they have a jumping ladder, or even a scrambling net. Bit too dodgy to try and transfer men, I would think so sir.'

'My thoughts also Number One, I think it would be far wiser to try and find her Tug.' The Captain turned back to Leading Writer Knowles. 'Tell them we are going to find their Tug, will you,' and then turning away shouted, 'Yeoman!'

He turned to his Petty Officer Signalman saying, 'make to *Corunna* and *Alamein*: Coaster lost its tow, I will remain here, you return to Naples and search for Tug.'

'Bit lax of them don't you think sir?' Lieutenant Commander Dyson said, as his Captain's attention returned to the Coaster. 'It's normal to keep a towing watch either end of the line. They seem to be devoid of even the most basic requirements a towed vessel should carry.'

'Probably a private job Number One; what is it from Civitavechia to Naples, 180…200 miles? They probably thought it was a short tow, so cut corners to cut expenses. I bet those two men on there are Dockyard Mateys, and not experienced seafarers,' he paused thoughtfully. 'D'you suppose they have enough food and water aboard, Number One?'

'Good point sir,' Lieutenant Commander Dyson answered, and then turning to Leading Writer Knowles said, 'Find out what food they have.'

They watched Knowles pass the question, then saw the spokesman make a shrugging gesture with his hands half raised.

'No mangare,' they saw his lips form the words.

Commander Plowright turned to his Supply Officer. 'Freddy,' he called, almost as if on impulse. 'Get your SPOV (Supply Petty Officer Victualling) to put a couple of loaves of bread, and a large tin of corned beef together,' and then turning back to his First Lieutenant ordered, 'Tell Petty Officer McHenry to break out the distance line from the light jackstay rig, I may need a bit more room than a heaving line can give me.'

'How do you intend to do this sir? This swell leaves little room for close manoeuvring.'

'I will approach her bow to, and wallow beam to the swell just as she is. You pop up to the bullring with Petty Officer McHenry, and make sure he has his best heaving line thrower with him. Leading Writer Knowles; tell those men to get up forrard on the Fxle, we are going to pass food and water…right guns,' he continued, turning to his Gunnery Officer. 'I will take the con, you keep telling me estimated distance as I approach.' Without pause seemingly, he then passed the necessary orders to the wheelhouse.

The *Barrosa* came to life, slicing through the heavy swell cleanly, her 3300 tons rising, and falling with a bump as bows met the next roller. The heaving line transfer crew took shelter behind 'A' Turret as the Fxle became awash, and then, as the ship came beam-to the weather moved up the Fxle as Commander Plowright edged his way forward slowly towards the Coaster. The heaving line thrower quickly threw a lashing around the Tripod and himself, and then leaned into the comfort of his safety harness. Holding the coils of the heaving line divided between two hands, he double checked that the messenger line was attached, and waited for his chance to cast his line at the Coaster. The First Lieutenant, Petty Officer McHenry, and the Communications rating with headset and lead, clung to the starboard guardrail stanchions peering intently ahead as the ship's bow got closer and closer. Both ships now rose and fell in unison...fifty feet...forty feet, and then the ship shuddered, as Commander Plowright put his engines astern. Forward motion stopped at thirty feet from the Coaster. The heaving line thrower leaned back into his safety line and hurled the coils in his right hand at the small ship just as both vessels descended into the trough of a wave together. The Monkey's Fist knot dropped onto the deck of the Coaster and both Italians pounced on it, hauling the line in swiftly hand over hand. The canvas bag tied onto the forty feet marker of the distance line was quickly opened and emptied of its contents, and then without hesitation Petty Officer McHenry and the heaving line thrower started hauling the line back. The Communications rating kept the bridge informed all the time, even though every action took place in full view of everyone on the open bridge.

'Half astern both engines,' Commander Plowright ordered, backing his ship off. Minutes later he brought her round to starboard, waving back to the two men on the Coaster who had waved at their pusser's grey benefactor as it pulled away. The ship layed off about 500 feet and kept station off the Coaster's starboard quarter, and as the day wore on the sea began to flatten out. This was a great relief to everyone; nothing is more uncomfortable than wallowing beam-on in a heavy swell. Thirty-five and forty degree rolls are the norm, and the odd tilt to forty-five degrees has people walking on the bulkheads.

At 1400 hours that afternoon, the Operations Room reported three contacts twenty-two miles to the southeast steering a course of 315 degrees. Plain voice radio contact had been made with the *Corunna*, who confirmed that they had met the Tug retracing its course. Commander Plowright's relief at the success of his fellow Commanders was short lived: the Officer of the Watch attracted his attention holding out a sound powered telephone towards him saying, 'TAS Officer sir, he wants to speak to you privately.'

Commander Plowright frowned as he took the phone. 'Yes Terry, Captain here, what's the problem?'

'I'm using the phone sir because I don't want to use bridge communications. Something strange is going on out there, and I can't be sure of my facts. Our hydrophones are picking up screw noises now and then from the position of the Coaster. The sound is obviously not being made by the Coaster, so I need your permission to verify what it is we are listening to. If there is something down there, our first ping will tell him he's rumbled.'

'Don't use sonar until I ask for it!' Commander Plowright answered hurriedly and perhaps a little sharply. 'Give me time to get the second boiler connected.' He replaced his handset, his mind racing. His immediate thoughts were, 'It can't be one of ours; if it was a Yank he would have made contact. The Italians, the French,' he mused. 'No, they wouldn't put a sub in such a position, and so close to an ally.' He turned to the Bridge Messenger. 'Bennett, tell Petty Officer G I Martin to report to me on the bridge.'

Ordinary Seaman Bennett jumped to obey his Captain, and three minutes later Petty Officer Gunnery Instructor Martin was receiving his Captain's orders. 'How long will it take to prime four grenades G I?' he asked, noticing the momentary look of surprise that flitted across the Gunnery Instructor's face. 'I need them as quickly as is safely possible.'

'Fifteen minutes sir, I'll sign the Integrity log while I'm here. Any idea where the Gunner is sir?'

The Captain thought for a second. 'Sub Lieutenant Dodds had the middle watch last night so he will probably be turned in. You crack on; I'll get the Bridge Messenger to inform him of what's going on. I will also get the Gunner's Mate of the watch to meet you port side of the mast. Off you go G I!'

The Officer of the Watch of the afternoon had a puzzled expression on his face which the Captain noticed. 'Sorry Graham, I had to get things moving quickly. I think there's a Sub using that Coaster as a cover, keeping tabs on the squadron. It can only be a Russian, so in approximately fifteen minutes we are going to give him a cold war surprise. I am going to start pinging him, and drop some grenades just to let him know we are on to him. You get through to number two boiler room and tell the POME to connect all sprayers as I'll need full power very shortly.'

'The Gunner has been informed sir,' Ordinary Seaman Bennett reported back.

'Right Bennett, keeping you busy aren't I? Now I want you to pop down to the Engineer's Office, and ask him to come to the bridge.'

The Navigating Officer caught his Captain's eye. 'Shades of convoy duty during the Second World War, this Pilot; that was a favorite trick of Jerry U Boat Commanders. This daring chappie is going to show us how he reacts to discovery before very long, it will be interesting to see if he dives, or makes a run for it,' he said, grinning as he anticipated turning the tables on this resourceful Russian Submarine Commander.

At 1420 hours, with second boiler at full pressure, and the Gunners Party rating of the watch fully briefed and prepared, Commander Plowright hit the button to sound 'Action Stations'. The alarm klaxons sounded throughout the ship as men grabbed their respirators with Anti Flash Gear attached, quickly buckled on lifebelt pouches, and hurried to their action stations. Two minutes later all departments had reported 'closed up'.

Commander Plowright picked up the microphone to the Sonar Control Room. 'Okay TASO, let it rip!' he ordered loudly, his face showing the excitement of anticipation.

A loud PINGGGG pressed through the water at 5000 feet per second, bounced off the hull of the Submarine, and returned to sender. At that same moment Commander Plowright signalled Petty Officer Martin.

The Gunnery Instructor leaned over the bridge screen and ordered the Gunner's Mate of the watch to start dropping grenades.

'He's off sir,' the TASO yelled excitedly from the Sonar Control Room. 'He's turning to port; you will have to go round the bows of the Coaster to pick him up again.'

'Crafty devil,' Commander Plowright said under his breath, and then ordered, 'Half ahead both engines.'

The ship surged forward as the twin screws bit into the water. 'Yeoman!' the Captain yelled, 'make to *Corunna* and *Alamein*: have contact with Russian Sub, break off and follow.'

The Yeoman was already flashing the two ships, now some ten miles distant, as his Captain ordered, 'port twenty… midships…starboard twenty…midships…steer 300.'

The ship levelled off. 'Contact bearing red three zero,' came from the SCR.

'Steer by asdics,' Commander Plowright ordered the wheelhouse, his eyes moving across to the conning position asdics repeater.

'Contact increasing speed sir, fifteen knots,' came from the SCR as the Doppler effect of the returning echo indicated an increase in speed. 'Range 1000 yards, and increasing...Range 1200 yards,' the running commentary went on.

'Revolutions two six zero,' the Captain ordered the wheelhouse, glancing at his navigator. 'The blighter's doing twenty knots and increasing, what sort of bloody submarine is this?'

'Contact increasing speed to thirty knots, range 2000 yards,' the excited operator sang up from the SCR.

'Full speed ahead both engines,' Commander Plowright ordered.

The automatic response to his order went unheeded as the excited voice from the SCR yelled, 'contact speed thirty-five knots...range 2000 yards.' And then seconds later, 'contact speed forty knots...2500 yards...losing contact.'

'Keep trying SCR,' Commander Plowright replied, his voice reflecting his amazement at an action he had just played the leading part in. If the submarine had turned to fight, his whole training as a Fleet Destroyer Captain was tuned to that eventuality. What could he do with a potential enemy that had just shown him a clean pair of heels?

'We have just been made redundant in the field of underwater warfare Pilot, there can be no doubt about what just happened, we are at full speed, and could not keep contact. How the hell do I explain that to Admiralty?' He leant on the binnacle, his eyes gazing over the front bridge screen unseeingly. 'Yeoman,' he called. 'Make to *Corunna* and *Alamein*: "lost contact, break off search".' And then added to himself, 'no sense in chasing an impossibility.'

He knew that not far away the Commander of the Submarine would be at periscope depth watching the squadron intently, and would just perform a disappearing act whenever approached.

'Bring her back to normal speed Pilot, and secure from action stations,' he ordered, and then added, turning to his First Lieutenant, 'I think it would be a good idea to stream the Bathythermograph before I signal Admiralty...then we can assure them that sea temperatures were not distorting our sonar beam. See to it Number One, I am going to concoct a message to Admiralty with the PO Telegraphist.'

One hour later, the delicate rocket shaped Bathythermograph was reeled inboard. The smoked glass slide which held a record of water temperature and depth in graph form was removed, and the Bathythermograph was rinsed down with fresh water, dried, and carefully replaced in its container. The slide would be sent to the London Nautical Research Establishment, and all its details logged and used for chart making. In this incidence water temperature was the important factor so that Commander Plowright could assure his superiors in Admiralty that severely differing temperatures could not be a reason for misjudging the assumed Russian Submarine's speed. His own report on the incident could be stated quite simply. He had reacted to a sonar contact; he had held the contact for two sea miles and then lost contact due to the unusually high speed, taking it out of range of his sonar.

'Just add, speed in excess of forty knots PO, and send in code,' he added.

The Boffins in Admiralty would now add this surprising snippet to all the other information that came their way in the continual cold war game of spy and counterspy. Not much escaped the vigilance of those concerned on either side, but this exciting event would create a new flurry of activity amongst those whose job it was to gather the intelligence that led to a better understanding of the other side's technology. The only difference between wartime and peacetime service in this cold war atmosphere was that nobody was throwing bricks at each other. The seatime component of this 'cold war' was very often equal to that of wartime. Men were still lost at sea in the continual exercises that kept them prepared for the eventuality of a third World War.

Having done everything he possibly could do under the circumstances, Commander Plowright ordered his squadron to lie to the weather side of the Coaster to provide a 'lee' while the Tug came closer to its lost charge. The rollers that had made the earlier part of the day most uncomfortable were now down to three or four feet high, and were further reduced by having been under the keels of the Fourth Destroyer Squadron. The Tug Skipper unhesitatingly put his well padded prow up to the Coaster's midships section, and two of his crew leapt aboard the Coaster. He then saved them all a lot of work by easing his boat up to the bows of the Coaster where the four men only had to haul in the eye of the towline through the bullring and secure it inboard.

Three ships' companies watched all this going on, and in the manner of all sailors having reached a certain state of high efficiency in their own sphere, were not short of criticism. To a man though, they all applauded the Tug Skipper and his crew for the daring way they replaced the tow. They raised a 'hurrah' as the two men who leapt aboard the Coaster, jumped back aboard the Tug after the towline was secured. Thirty minutes later the *Barrosa* led the *Corunna* and the *Alamein* past the Tug in line astern as the hands on their decks raised a rousing cheer for the Tug's Crew and its charge following faithfully 200 metres behind. Once more the world's greatest navy had done its job policing the seas of the world, and helping where it could. No doubt the two dockyard men aboard the Coaster would never find an answer to why their benefactor had suddenly dashed off for a short distance. They were probably even more astonished when *Corunna* and *Alamein* approached the area at 30 knots, chasing after their temporary Squadron Commander whose ship could only be distinguished by the height of its wake.

— ∎ —

At 0900 hours on 30th January 1958, the three destroyers berthed alongside the harbour wall of La Spezia. As the gangway leading aboard HMS *Barrosa* was finally secured, the figure of a man appeared from the back of the crowd of onlookers, and walked confidently towards the gangway. He was smartly dressed in grey pinstripe suit, and a slightly darker Trilby sat atop his head. Over his left forearm he carried a neatly folded Macintosh, and suspended from his right hand was an officious looking briefcase. He took long strides up the gangway and introduced himself to Sub Lieutenant Dodds. Without hesitation the Second Officer of the Day took the man personally to the Captain's cabin. Having been thanked by his Captain, Sub Lieutenant Dodds returned to the gangway. A great bustle of work was in progress as four hands from each part of ship hauled fresh provisions aboard watched by the Stores Petty Officer Victualling, and the Ship's Chandler who had provided the stores, previously ordered by Lieutenant Fred Darwin (alias the ape man), the Supply Officer.

Forrard and aft, parts of ship hands were doubling up berthing hawsers, and the 'side party' was already over the side on a paint stage tidying up the 'pennant numbers'. Later they would carry out the relatively unpleasant task of touching up that part of the hull just above the water line with 'boot topping', an extremely thick tar-like black paint. The decks of all three ships were alive with men carrying out specific tasks, gradually improving the appearance of the ships from the shoreside view first. Local dignitaries would be arriving during the day, keeping all three Commanders very busy; first though was the official discussion about the very fast assumed Russian Submarine.

By 1000 hours the smartly dressed courier had concluded his business aboard HMS *Barrosa* and departed the ship. Safely tucked away in his attaché case was the all-important glass slide which would prove sea temperatures at Submarine depth in the area in which the chase took place. Accompanying it was a full report on the incident written personally by Commander Plowright.

An official car pulled alongside the gangway, and the courier climbed in the back. The car immediately glided away en route to Genoa airport; and by 1500 hours that day the contents of the official brown envelope were being studied by the intelligence service in their dreary Victorian Offices in London.

Commander Plowright ordered a 'make and mend' for all three ships that day, so except for the duty part of the watch, and those disinclined, the majority of the Ship's Company could proceed ashore after tot and dinner. Few however, would be rushing to catch the first liberty boat.

Dusty and Wiggy had the middle watch (2359-0400 hours) that morning, so they were entitled to the afternoon off anyway. They now had three days free of duty watches, and their next duty would be in Genoa on Saturday. Not being entitled to a tot, the pals had dinner, and decided to forego their thrice weekly stint of judo practice on 'B' gundeck. Their sport required a certain amount of space to frolic around in, and it was hard for determined goofers to ignore the spectacle of two young men pitting their wits against each other in such a physical manner. Very often the increasing crowd of spectators hampered their efforts, so this encouraged them to train at such times when the majority of the crew was having tea. This was also a better time for Stan Robinson; he had more space to instruct and advise.

The dockyard area of La Spezia was right on the edge of town, so very quickly the two pals were walking up a main thoroughfare leading to the centre of the town. The buildings close to the docks were centuries old, and had only been converted to shops and bars over the last fifty years. The odd gantry pivot above windows on the first and second floors indicated that the previous use of the buildings had been as warehouses.

They tried a bottle of beer in the first bar they came to, and were pleasantly surprised by its coolness and flavour. It was locally brewed, and judging by the number of crates stacked up against the back wall, was very popular amongst the men who worked in and around the port. The ceiling and walls were festooned with all sorts of fishing paraphernalia, and a moderately sized Swordfish held centre position on one wall, fully encased in a glass showcase, the base of which had been decorated to resemble a stony seabed. The few locals at the bar at this time of day were all eating fish snacks with a salad garnish of one sort or another, and the room furthest away from the road was occupied by people in smart Italian suits, suggesting that they were the local business elite. One thing stood out that levelled off the obvious class difference; they were all drinking the same house wine supplied to each dining table as an integral part of the meal.

No one displayed the slightest interest in the lads as they entered the bar, their uniforms being a regular sight in this part of the world. Seamen in uniform are, generally speaking, good spenders when they get ashore, and were well looked after in the hope that they would stay in that first bar. It was a bit early in the day for the two pals to turn this into a full blown social occasion, so they enjoyed this one beer each and then, placing the empty bottles and the two glasses on the bar, showed off by saying in Italian, 'gratzias, arrivaderci senor.' The barman grinned at their accents, and replied in thickly accented English, 'you are welcome.'

They spent the afternoon window shopping, a pastime not generally considered the first priority of sailors off a ship new in port. Uppermost in their minds at this moment was a suitable gift for their girlfriends. Wiggy probably had the hardest task; what do you buy for a Captain's daughter that she did not already have? The answer to that one was of course look for something with a definite local influence. Finally, after two hours of ambling from display to display they found a shop that specialised in local silk goods. The head scarves were totally beautiful; depicting many old Roman events. One of Vesuvius erupting looked particularly attractive, but then some embroidered squares caught their eyes. After much deliberation they both left the shop, each with a small gift wrapped parcel. Wiggy had taken a fancy to an old Roman bath scene, depicting female slaves, beauties of that era, bathing semi nude, but very tastefully done.

Dusty had opted for a well embroidered picture of La Spezia's old harbour, revived with ancient knowledge of fishing tackle and seafarers' dress. The gifts had cost them £2-10 shillings each in Italian Lira, the equivalent of half a week's wage. Expensive, but then the quality of the gift left the recipient in no doubt as to where the thoughts of the buyer were at that moment. It also indicated the depth of respect felt for the lucky girl.

'Phew, I'm glad that bit's over,' Wiggy sighed as they left the silk shop. 'I was beginning to despair of being able to find something suitable.'

'Flippin' hard work buyin' rabbits, innit boyo,' Dusty replied, using the common naval expression for describing gifts bought for loved ones.

Wiggy glanced at his watch. 'Best we make it back aboard if we want supper before tonight's excursion.'

Three hours later, bathed and fed, they were sitting in a bar popular to seafarers on the edge of the town. The bar consisted of one large room, not over furnished, but with robust tables and chairs generously spaced out. Their messmates Spud Murphy and Buck Taylor had joined them for an evening ashore, and this bar was notorious as a male bastion for good sing songs later on in the evening. Dusty glanced up as a gang of sailors off HMS *Corunna* spread themselves around a table across the other side of the room. His eyes casually took in the blond bearded sailor who took a seat with his back to him.

The bar was quickly filling with sailors from all three British ships. Old oppos meeting each other were taking the mickey out of each other, having not been in contact for some time; soon the bar was alive with the banter, jokes, and general jollity enjoyed by the British Navy whenever ships come together in harbour. There was a competitive element to all this as well, and what energy is not expended on an inter ship football match, or dockside tug of war is usually saved for the 'piss up' later in the evening.

The bar staff were hard at work keeping an ever increasing supply of beer going across the bar. One sturdy Italian fellow had a full time job clearing empty bottles off tables, and it became apparent that neither the staff nor the few locals were in the least bit bothered by the large influx of foreign sailors.

A little later, the first raucous song started up, sung with fast lyrics by a well-oiled veteran of many a SODS opera. Others around the loudly chattering gathering joined in spasmodically as they remembered the odd word or two.

> '*She's a big girl fat girl, twice the size er me,*
> *Airs on er belly like the branches on a tree*
> *She can run, jump, fuck, fight,*
> *Wheel a barrer push a bike*
> *That's my girl Salome...*'

On it went in fast time, most confusing for those trying to discern the words, but all the seasoned salts in the gathering held firm to the pace of the dirty song, and did not give an inch when it came to the foulest of the lyrics.

'I've never heard that one before, have you Dusty?' Wiggy said loudly.

'You'll soon get tuh know em,' Buck Taylor jumped in, as loud cheers enhanced by alcohol followed the end of the song. 'But there aren't many matelots 'oo knows 'em all the way froo, just a few old piss 'eads 'oo's life revolves around do's like this,' he enlightened the young sailors, shouting loudly to be heard over the next dirty ditty getting an airing.

> *'One night in gay paree,*
> *I paid five francs to see*
> *A tattooed French ladee*
> *Tattooed from 'ead to knee'*

This old war song had been suitably adjusted to fit the style of the Royal Navy.

> *'And tattooed on 'er jaw*
> *Was a British man-O-war...,'*

the singer continued, with the chorus of voices around him not adding very tunefully to the outcome.

Wiggy glanced at the locals as this old war song continued reverberating around the large room. They showed not an iota of disgust in the din surrounding them, and not one had deserted his bar stool. In fact, in some cases they were actually paying attention to the rough songsters. It was then that Wiggy noticed that there was not one woman in the bar. 'No flipping wonder!' he thought to himself as a sailor off HMS *Corunna* jumped up on a table and started singing:

> *'This old 'at er mine*
> *It's seen some fuckin time,*
> *And the outside as seen some stormy wevver*
> *I toss this 'at aside*
> *And wiv it goes me pride,*
> *Thank the Lord I didn't join forever.'*

At this point he threw his hat at a pal sitting at the table, and before he could continue, a chorus of voices shouted from across the room:

>   'Sit down yuh cunt
>   Sit down yuh cunt
>   Sit down yuh cunt sit down'

He looked across at them, laughing. It all had to be taken in good part, so he made to sit down. This brought the laughing invitation:

>   'Sing, Sing, or show your ring'

He made as if to drop his pants, and was greeted by the roar:

>   'We don't want tuh see yer ring
>   So sing you basterd sing'

The whole room played out this act, and the singer of 'This Old Hat' continued with his rendition getting a loud cheer for playing along with the crowd. Seemingly hours later, he came to the final part of the act; discarding his underpants. It was at this stage that a sailor holding a sheet of paper rammed it between the singer's buttocks. A second sailor set fire to the paper using his already prepared cigarette lighter. The song now became 'The Dance of the Flaming Arseholes' as the performer leapt around the table with the flames from the paper just beginning to lick his buttocks and genitalia. The flames were doused by another sailor using the performer's own beer. The bar erupted into thunderous applause as the performer took his bows turning in a circle to the four main cardinal points of the compass. More beer was tossed at his posterior as he completed each turn of the circle, much to the delight of the locals, who had obviously witnessed this spectacle before, and thoroughly enjoyed the antics of the Royal Navy at play, letting its hair down. The show died down for a while as the proprietor and his staff worked hard replenishing all the empty glasses. The sturdy glass and bottle collector had suddenly acquired a mop and bucket and was good naturedly mopping up the beer which had become an essential part of the act; sailors were helpfully lifting their feet as he mopped underneath the tables, and then deftly screwed the mop head into the cone of the bucket.

The performer of 'The Dance of the Flaming Arseholes', having shown all his pals the singed hairs of his buttocks, began to get dressed. The pal who had held his clothes handed him each item in turn, suitably screwing up his nose with a great impression of the effete male camping it up. This brought howls of laughter from the floor, which developed into a raucous round of applause as the performer finally plonked his hat on his head, and with a grin spreading from ear to ear, bowed elaborately to his audience; but he had not quite finished his act. With a haughty expression on his face, he swept an arm in a half circle and sang:

> *'You working class*
> *Can kiss my ass*
> *I've got the Buffer's job at last'*

He paused for a mere second then went on:

> *'The Buffers job is fuckin' grim*
> *I think I'll wrap the basterd in'*

Still holding the floor, this experienced SODS Opera performer finished his act when with a doleful expression he moved straight into:

> *'Pack my bag, pack my grip*
> *I'm not goin' on next trip*
> *Bye Bye Blackbird*
> *No more getting up on Sunday mornins*
> *No more scrubbing decks and furlin' awnins*
> *Blackbird bye bye'*

The whole room, to a man, joined in this popular old shanty, with some using their own ship's name instead of 'Blackbird'.

Dusty was clapping and shouting as loud as anyone as this man's act finally closed. He could not help but notice that the blond bearded figure rose from the same table as the performer, and headed for the toilet door at the rear of the room. As the door opened, the brighter light shining from the other side caused Dusty to turn his full gaze towards the door. It was at that instant that the bearded sailor was silhouetted in the bright light. Dusty gasped as his mind suddenly flashed back to the severe kicking he had been subjected to by a cowardly bushwhacker; there framed in the light of the doorway was the very same configuration he had seen when his attacker ran up the steps from where he lay severely beaten, and barely conscious. Uncontrollable anger surged through him for an instant, and his immediate instinct was to hurtle through that door and confront his attacker head on.

'What on earth's the matter Dusty?' Wiggy asked. He was sitting in such a way that Dusty was fully visible to him as he watched the last performer and his pals.

His words had an instant effect on Dusty, who turned to his pal saying, 'did yer see that bearded guy who just went out for a slash?'

'Yes I did notice him walking across.'

'Well I'm a hundred percent certain that he is the basterd who kicked shit out uv me in Gibraltar.'

So saying, Dusty rose from his seat. 'You stay here Wiggs; I'm goin tuh 'ave a look at this basterd, see if I know 'im from somewhere.'

Spud Murphy and Buck Taylor turned round as Dusty got up from his seat.

'What's up Dusty?' Spud asked.

'Nowt,' Dusty answered, 'just goin' for a slash.'

He walked into the toilet, unzipping his fly as he approached the urinal. He glanced sideways as he came alongside the bearded sailor. The bearded one returned the glance, and both faces turned to stone as they recognised each other.

'It was you yuh basterd!' Dusty blurted out as he recognised the features of his enemy under the covering of hair.

Smith reacted instantly, as Dusty's words hit him. With his penis still out, he stepped back, and at the same instant threw a fist at Dusty's head. Dusty reacted instantly, grabbing the right arm at the wrist, and twisting viciously. Smith's body arched forward helplessly as the effect of the twist made him bend from the waist. Dusty immediately applied both thumbs to Smith's hand, and put the pressure on. Smith was rendered harmless, he tried to correct his body position and in so doing fell through the door into the back yard with Dusty still forcing that arm into an unnatural position. Dusty drew his right foot back, his intention being to kick this vicious aggressor in the head. A split second flash of decency changed the blow to an incapacitating blow into the area of Smith's solar plexus. Smith gasped and fell forward on to his face just as Dusty let the arm go. He propped himself up on his arms, palms downwards. Dusty reacted by placing a foot on each of the backs of the hands, and leaning forward grabbed each of Smith's ears in a closed fist. He twisted the ears backwards as he raised Smith's head; Smith groaned with pain, still gasping for air.

'Every fuckin' regulator, every MP, and every fuckin' policeman in Gib would just love to be first tuh get their 'ands on you, yuh bushwhackin basterd,' Dusty spat the words into Smith's face. 'But I got yuh first, yuh evil twat, and this is my revenge. Leave it 'ere, or I let the law take its course, d'yuh 'ear me?' he hissed, screwing further back on Smith's ears.

'Okay, okay, that's it,' Smith gasped. 'That's an end to it, I swear!'

Dusty gazed into the pain-racked eyes, and believed what he saw. He let Smith go, squared off his number one suit meaningfully, and strolled back out to the bar.

Able Seaman Smith stayed panting on his hands and knees. It took him a couple of minutes before he could rise to his feet. His first instinct was to square off his clothing as he staggered back to the urinal. A washbasin in the corner had a cracked mirror above it, and as he gazed at his own reflection he realised immediately, that apart from very red ears, he appeared to be unmarked. His right arm however was very painful, so too was his stomach, but his breathing was returning to normal. The fact that his face was unmarked gave power to his rate of recovery, and within minutes he was prepared to return to his table. He took a final look at himself, and made his way back into the bar.

'Fuckin' 'ell smudger!' a shipmate said loudly upon seeing his return. 'Yuh look fuckin' awful, what's up wiv yer?'

'Ah, it's that last glass of Vermouth I 'ad on top uv the beer, I knew I shouldn't 'ave mixed it,' Smith replied, easing his pain-racked body into his chair.

'Better out than in then,' the shipmate declared philosophically, assuming that Smith had gone to the toilet to call for 'Hughie' (be sick).

Wiggy watched Smith return painfully to his chair. 'You got him then, did you?' he said, turning to look at his pal expectantly.

'I think it's sorted out for now, but d'yuh recognise him,' Dusty replied, meeting Wiggy's direct stare.

'I haven't a clue, never seen him before!'

'Remember Able Seaman Smith?'

Wiggy thought for a moment, and then enlightenment lit up his face. 'You mean that arsehole that had two goes at you on the *Vanguard*? The same one who invited me to give him oral sex?'

Dusty's face broke into a broad grin as he said, 'the very same; but how the hell he came to be in Gib, and now on the *Corunna* is beyond me.'

Spud Murphy turned round in his chair. 'What the 'ell are you two gabbin abaht?' he asked, adding with a grin, 'shut yer gobs and enjoy the fun, otherwise yuh'll never pass yer AB's exam.' Buck Taylor grinned at his shipmate's assessment of the two's lack of interest in the entertainment.

A good tenor voice attracted everyone's attention to the table in the middle of the room. He was giving an old army song, very slightly converted here and there to suit a Royal Naval SODS opera artiste's style, a tuneful airing.

> 'Now the brothels of Egypt
> Were famed and renowned
> The harlots quite fair in the sphere
> But the fairest a Greek
> Was owned by a Sheikh
> One Abdul the Bulbul Emir
>
> Now a traveling Brothel
> It came to the town
> It was owned by a Russian from far
> He issued a challenge to all who could fuck
> From Ivan Stravinsky Skavar'

The song, although tuneful, and well sung, went on for several verses, once again joined patchily as others remembered an odd line or two. The singer was obviously the only matelot present who had made the dirty ditty his 'party piece'; but if it was not for guys like him, an old traditional style of seamanlike entertainment would disappear, and with it would go another bit of that comradely style that has always been part of the British Service Man's psyche. Everybody did join in the one part that always stood out in this SODS song, and that was the lines:

> *'Old Abdul the fool*
> *Left the flange of his tool*
> *Up Ivan Stravinsky Skavar'*

No sooner had these lines been shown full appreciation, and vociferously sung by all servicemen present, than the next one started; but suddenly the whole room fell into the silence of anticipation as they realised what the next act was going to be. The LSBA off HMS *Corunna* stood atop a table; both hands perched on his hips, his lips pursed in an effeminate pout. 'Shuttup you lot!' he lisped gaining howls of delighted cat calls before a sort of silence was afforded him.

'This is the story of Ella Cindra, and the three Sisty Uglers,' he began. Absolute silence descended on the floor, as slightly sozzled sailors with mouths wide agape listened intently to the remainder of this cleverly told tale. Only a few sailors ever managed to learn it all the way through from memory, and this guy had it off to a 'T'. It was made funnier because the LSBA was well practiced at camping it up, and he was obviously very popular amongst his shipmates. He got the loudest applause of the evening, and amidst howls of laughter collapsed off the table into the waiting arms of his oppos, whilst blowing kisses in such a comic fashion as can only be achieved by someone well practiced in camped up fun.

His efforts were a bit of an anti climax, as silence settled on the floor for the first time; but not for long, an Italian stepped forward not wishing the fun to end, and was greeted by a roar.

He took full advantage of his sudden limelight, and treated everyone to a beautifully rendered 'O Sole Mio'. The rich Italian Tenor voice filled the room, and even hardened old three badgemen listened with polite attention. He received a roar of applause for his efforts, and was immediately followed by a Leading Stoker singing the popular rugby song, 'Swing low, sweet chariot, coming for to carry me home.' Everybody joined in this because it is an action song; everyone's arms and hands enacting the movements that are a major addition to the lyrics, and are most suggestive and definitely rude.

The Italians lining the bar liked this one, and their comical attempts to emulate the actions of their guests were funnier than the practiced actions of the navy singers. They received a good laugh for their attempts which pleased them very much. Suddenly a uniformed figure appeared in the doorway dressed in the patrol rig of an Italian naval officer. His mixed band of Italian and British sailors stepped into the bar behind him. The Officer nodded politely to the bartender; this was the signal to stop serving. Everyone seated, and all those at the bar knew the implications of this visit, but no one moaned, or became stroppy about the entry of official authority; any one of them could be doing the same job tomorrow night. The bar began to empty slowly as obedient revellers downed the last dregs from their glasses. Those so inclined finished off the night with a quickie in one of the nearby state brothels, while those who were married or disinclined for other reasons, squared themselves off, and wobbled their way back aboard their respective ships.

Spud Murphy and Buck Taylor had opted to sample the delights of the local working ladies, which left Dusty and Wiggy alone to discuss the evening's battle without eavesdroppers.

'Are you going to report it to the Coxswain?' Wiggy asked, as they made their way towards the dock area.

'Nah, I'm going to leave it,' Dusty replied in a manner that suggested he had given the matter some thought. 'I know now that I am more than a match for him, he'll never catch me unawares again. It's somethin' personal now, nothing to do with justice; or even revenge. I'm his enemy and ee's my enemy, and that's okay with me, I 'ave no problem with the fact that ee is the way ee is…and another thing,' he added seriously. ''Ee must do 'is job all right, and ee seems tuh have a lot of mates, that means it's just me ee can't stand the sight of.'

'I get your point,' Wiggy replied, and then added a cautionary note, 'he won't let it stop here, mark my words, this is a personal thing with him. He may have given you the assurance tonight that this evening's action has brought the matter to a close; but think on my friend, the score now is three to one in your favour. Do you honestly think a man with his obsession will be happy with that fact nagging at his barbaric brain constantly?'

'I'm still going to keep it my business,' Dusty answered determinedly. 'If the authorities; either military or civilian in Gib come up with the facts, well, there is nothing I can do but allow the law to take its course. Any basterd guilty of an attack from be-ind deserves what they get, but I am not goin tuh shop 'im, it's personal, I can 'andle anything ee throws at me.'

The sight of the ship ahead of them brought the discussion to a close. Each man, however, nursed his own thoughts on the matter. Wiggy could not help but mull over Dusty's decision, his upbringing and natural sense of justice told him that Smith must be brought to trial for the attack on his friend in Gibraltar, no matter the fact that Dusty regarded it as his own personal battle. Civilised society demanded that people guilty of such crimes against the individual should be brought to justice, and justice should be seen to be done. The attack on his friend began to worry him more than he had at first realised, he lay in his hammock that night torn between two realities and two loyalties. It frightened him somewhat that his duty to the service had a greater bearing on his thoughts than his loyalty to the intentions of his best friend. Finally he nodded off, but he was far from coming to terms with his divided feelings.

At 0810 hours next morning both the Ordinary Seamen found themselves in the queue to the paintshop hatch. Here, they would exchange their station cards for a pot and one of pusser's grey paint, thereafter they would spend the forenoon touching up the surfaces of the superstructure aft.

Suddenly, at 0900 hours the tannoy blared out, 'd'yuh hear there, the Captain will speak to the ship's company at stand easy this forenoon.'

The call brought Wiggy out of his trance-like recollection of the previous night's thoughts, and just further aft, Dusty frowned, and muttered to himself, 'wonder what the hell's that about?'

By 1030 hours that forenoon all buzzes and assumptions that had swept around the ship during the last hour had been swept aside by the Captain's news.

'D'you hear there, Captain speaking. I have just received a signal from Captain 'D' in Naples concerning Exercise Biscay. The signal reads, "due to recent events, Exercise Biscay is to be reviewed and replanned. The exercise is therefore cancelled until further notice. All ships will be forwarded their new orders as a result of this decision".' He paused for a moment. '*Barrosa*'s new orders are sent with this signal. We will leave harbour at 1500 hours today and proceed to Icelandic waters, where we will carry out three weeks' Fisheries Protection duties. That is all.'

The reaction on every face in every messdeck was one of astonishment; it was almost as if a minute's silence had been ordered. Finally a hubbub of surprised conversation broke out, only interrupted by the ship's tannoy ordering, 'Out pipes, hands turn to by parts of ship!'

The shock news broke Wiggy's previous train of thought. He had been on the verge of reporting his feelings to his Divisional Officer, but now the Captain's speech had put a completely different light on the matter. He could delay his decision, and give it more thought. For the next month at least, *Corunna* and *Barrosa* would be separated by the Mediterranean, the North Sea, and the North Atlantic, hence Able Seaman Smith and Dusty would be equally far apart.

After dinner, part of ship hands singled up berthing hawsers, and prepared to put to sea. By 1500 hours she was free of land, and with all parts of ship hands lined up smartly in number two uniforms, she passed out of La Spezia harbour, all marks of respect having been made on passing HMS *Corunna* and *Alamein*, and units of the Italian Navy. Clear of harbour, hands stood down from harbour stations, and cleared away for sea. All spick and span, the Fleet Destroyer tested the waves as the Captain ordered fifteen knots, and the prow of this handsome ship vigorously challenged the element for which she was built. The following evening the *Barrosa* refuelled at sea from RFA *Tidereach*, this was quicker than entering Gibraltar to refuel. Her first stop after rounding the northwest tip of Spain would be Plymouth.

Upon entering harbour Commander Plowright was ordered to the C-in-C's offices and did not return until the evening. In the meantime his crew had stored ship and took on enough Arctic Clothing for all upper deck personnel.

During his visit to C-in-C's offices, a Civil Servant from Whitehall had kept him in conference for most of the day; all of which was related to the assumed Russian Submarine he had contacted and chased, only to be outrun. The outcome of learning at first hand every detail of Commander Plowright's actions would assist NATO planners in arranging the replanned exercise in such a manner as to make it an enticing event for the assumed Russian Submarine, possibly trapping him into showing his full turn of speed. NATO had enough Anti Submarine Frigates, and other ships fitted with attack sonar to cover a huge area of the Atlantic. What was needed was a big enough bait to get the Submarine into the central area of the exercise where she could observe NATO tactics in a convoy situation. Not an easy event to plan for, but nevertheless, with only the teasing knowledge provided by Commander Plowright, an exciting job for navy tacticians.

The British Navy of the time was continually searching for a sonar outfit with greater range, depth, width of beam, and resolution. This exercise would give the Boffins an ideal opportunity to test their latest invention, by placing the Sonar Trials Ship in amongst the rest of the NATO fleet taking part in Exercise Biscay.

Commander Plowright's first words to his First Lieutenant upon returning aboard at 1800 hours were, 'All ready to slip and proceed Number One?'

'Immediately sir, Special Sea Dutymen are at their stations.'

HMS *Barrosa* slipped silently out of Plymouth Harbour, just her silhouette visible in the dusk of the evening sky. Her Captain left the Eddystone Lighthouse to port, and set course for Lizard Point, and thence around Land's End. The following day found the ship to the west of Northern Ireland, and the Navigating Officer planning his course and speed to pass through the 'Little Minch', around the north of Skye, and be in Gairloch by 0900 hours on Wednesday 7th February 1958.

The climate change had become very noticeable for the crew with upper deck duties to perform. The winter temperatures in the Mediterranean had been at normal body comfort level for naval summer clothing, none tropical. This sudden drop to British winter level now had all upper deck personnel heavily dressed in winter clothing. The sight of snow capped mountains to the east, and the light winds from the north increased by the ship's fifteen knots brought the temperature down even further as it whistled over Loch Gairloch. Bronzed bodies that had been working without shirts just a few days ago were now clad in four layers of clothing topped by Arctic ear muffed caps.

Along with fresh milk, fresh bread, and vegetables, a new Lieutenant was seen to join the ship. The two gold rings on each cuff were interspaced with a ring of red. This meant that the ship's medical orderly, LSBA Stanley Norton, now had back up. Surgeon Lieutenant Geoffrey Middlecote had just been lumbered with his first responsible sea job. If things went beyond scab lifting and lancing boils to the urgent need of skillful use of a scalpel, he would have to attend to the emergency at first hand. His responsibilities did not stop at shipboard accidents, there would probably be fifty or more trawlers on the fishing grounds at any one time, and this was a huge responsibility for a young two ringer Surgeon.

The Captain gave shore leave to all but the duty part of the watch that evening. Those who could go ashore, but did not wish to do so, did a sub for those who were duty but would like to go ashore. One boiler was kept ready; and the kettle on the boil ready for next morning.

At 0915 hours Thursday morning, HMS *Barrosa* steamed steadily out of Gairloch and into the Minch, soon leaving the Western Isles far behind. She rounded the north of Scotland and set course to leave the Faroes to port as she steamed towards her patrol station off the disputed fishing grounds of Iceland. The politics of this matter were in the hands of politicians. Protection duties meant just that, and *Barrosa* would be at the sharp end for the next three weeks.

As HMS *Barrosa* neared her patrol station, HMS *Broadsword*, the present protection vessel did not stand on ceremony; she would pass within a hundred feet of HMS *Barrosa* determinedly steaming away from Iceland. As the two ships approached each other, the crew of the *Broadsword* lined her starboard guardrails, and as their Captain paid first marks of respect to the more senior Captain of HMS *Barrosa*, his crew raised a rousing cheer for the men relieving them. Their cheers were met by a barrage of old potatoes, laughingly hurled at them by the crew of the *Barrosa*, after their Captain had returned the salute. HMS *Barrosa* had officially taken over her duties at 0900 hours on Saturday 10th February 1958.

The first item on the agenda was for Commander Plowright to introduce himself to all the Skippers of Trawlers on station. A Trawler fully loaded and ready for home asked him to drop his Whaler and stand by to receive a parting gift. Thirty minutes later the Whaler returned; the oarsmen knee deep in Icelandic Cod. It took fifteen minutes to empty the boat, and a further two hours for the Boat Party to scrub it clean after it was hoisted back on its davits. The fishy gift fed all the ship's company for dinner, with enough left over to run a fish bar for nine o'clockers that evening. Such was the first day of HMS *Barrosa*'s 'Fish Patrol'.

7

'BISCAY' REPLANNED

Harold Macmillan was Prime Minister of Great Britain at the time, and Dwight D. Eisenhower was President of the United States of America. America was the major power of the North Atlantic Treaty of 1959 when countries like Britain, Canada, France, Holland, Belgium and Luxembourg became founder members. A great block of European countries had come together, now including West Germany, to form a defensive treaty against possible aggression towards any of them by a force outside of NATO. The one country considered likely of making an incursion against any of them was Communist Russia; and the so called 'Cold War' was expanding considerably as each side vied to increase their technological superiority over the other. The high danger point of this huge arms race, mainly between Russia and the United States of America came in the early sixties when Nikita Kruchev tried to get one over President Kennedy by placing missiles on the Island of Cuba, fully backed of course by Fidel Castro. Thankfully, after much brinkmanship, the leaders of the two major powers came to their senses and worked out an agreement that saved the world at that moment from a nuclear holocaust. During more recent times (1956) the British and French forces acted against President Nasser over his nationalisation of the Suez Canal. This did not please the United States of America at all, fearing the reaction of Soviet Russia. A major spate like this did have some effect on the members of what would become to be known as NATO, but when it came to the major issue of defence, the United States and Great Britain in particular, were in general, unified in their stance against an increasingly technologically advanced Soviet Russia.

The NATO Navies of the late fifties were becoming increasingly aware of being tailed by so called Russian Trawlers. Anywhere that a considerable number of NATO ships gathered attracted the attention of these interlopers bristling with antennae of all shapes and sizes. Many times, Russian warships gave cause for concern by manoeuvring too close to a NATO fleet intentionally trying to disrupt the exercise. This was a dangerous game to play; it only takes one gun pointed with possible aggressive intent, to start a battle.

The re-scheduling of Exercise Biscay was politicised as the inability of all the nations within the NATO fold to provide sufficient ships to carry out such a wide ranging exercise. It was widely seen as the most ambitious gathering of navies since the 'D Day' landings; therefore planning time had to be extended. Some media outlets of the western world carried the headline: 'NATO NAVIES CANCEL EXERCISE DUE TO LACK OF SHIPS,' all encouraged by their respective governments to make such a headline front page news. There was some truth in the statement, but unknown to anyone outside the NATO planning board. The bait being considered was a fleet of Merchant Vessels, fifty in number, to provide a central point of interest. The very act of getting that number of ships all going in the same direction at approximately the same time to make up a convoy was a major feat of cooperation between the Merchant Services and their military counterparts, hence the choice of area was of major importance.

The area of the Atlantic to the west of Portugal would not take Merchant Vessels plying that trade route too far out of their scheduled shipping lane, and no doubt the fleet owners would be enticed with a little logistical assistance where necessary. A small price to pay, to ensure that all military forces had enough scope to practice for the eventuality of having to protect the NATO countries' trade routes, in reality.

By Monday 12th February 1958, the NATO planners were hard at work re-appraising Exercise Biscay. The Sonar Boffins were quickly at work experimenting with a new type of Sonar that was a brilliant idea, if the concept could be made to work in reality. They had come up with the idea of a Sonar emitter and receiver that could work at keel level but could be lowered to a depth of 500 feet if so desired. They named this device 'Changeable Depth Sonar Buoy.' The ship on whose stern this was fitted could operate amongst any fleet of ships at sea, and not look in the least out of place. Its only drawback was manoeuvrability when the CDSB was streamed.

— ▪ —

By 1100 hours that Monday a gale force six and increasing was blowing off the south west coast of Iceland. Suddenly a call for help crackled over the airwaves asking for medical assistance. Two miles to the north east of *Barrosa* the *Tartan Lady* out of Aberdeen had a crewman with three fingers of his right hand totally severed. The accident had occurred whilst hauling coal from bunker to boiler front by winch. The ship had rolled suddenly, throwing the man into the moving parts of lifting cable and block.

'Too rough to use a boat Number One,' Commander Plowright shouted his opinion at his First Lieutenant. 'We shall have to use a Naval Inflatable Liferaft; see to it Number one, will you.'

'Aye aye sir,' was the instant reply.

With no time to lose, and with the Chief Boatswain's Mate and the First Lieutenant watching, Petty Officer Neville Milligan, and the Able Seaman who would crew the Liferaft were preparing it to enter the water. It was an operation with inherent dangers due to the movement of the ship reacting to the increasingly bad weather. Every now and then a particularly aggressive wave would drench them all in freezing seawater. For that reason everyone on deck wore lifejackets partly inflated, and a line secured men actually involved with the operation to the superstructure hand rail.

By the time Commander Plowright eased his ship within a hundred feet of the *Tartan Lady*, the Able Seaman had squeezed himself through the rubber neck of a diving suit, and with the metal neck ring securing the tight fitting rubber helmet to the suit, he was to all intents and purposes watertight, and water resistant but bloody cold. All ropework was laid out and ready and Petty Officer G I Martin had assumed control of the Coston Gun line Rifle. He blew hard on his whistle, and the receiving crew took cover. He fired without hesitation, and the line soared across and draped itself over the wheelhouse of the Trawler. The Skipper, who had ducked down behind his door, rose to his feet and grabbed the line, passing it to one of his crewmen without a word. The Trawler crew quickly hauled in the line, and then the messenger line attached to it. The First Lieutenant of the *Barrosa* now took charge with the aid of a hand held loud hailer. The Liferaft was dropped into the water, and as it rose on a wave, the crewman jumped in. The Trawler crew hauled the Liferaft over to their ship whilst *Barrosa*'s crew paid out on the inhaul. The Trawlermen quickly eased their injured shipmate in the raft, where he was grabbed by the Able Seaman and secured to the inside by a lifeline, and all this with the Liferaft rising and falling a distance of seven to ten feet, as each wave swept beneath it. By the time their man was securely in the raft the trawlermen had coiled up *Barrosa*'s ropework and tossed it into the Liferaft, their Skipper could now give *Barrosa* a bit more sea room by easing gently away. The Quarterdeckmen hauled in the raft with great difficulty, but being as gentle as they could, brought the injured man aboard. He was immediately taken through the after superstructure screen door, and into the sickbay, his hand covered in a plastic bag that was awash with his blood. They stayed and helped undress the man and lay him out on the operating table, and then left Surgeon Lieutenant Middlecote and his assistant to repair what was left of the man's right hand.

Dusty Miller and Wiggy Bennett, both of them manning the inhaul, looked on with respect as the stoical Trawlerman was brought aboard and steered through the door into the superstructure. The blood filled bag covering the man's right hand brought on memories of how they had jumped to and obeyed orders when presented with their first evidence of the result of a naval accident. In this case fortunately, there were no broken and charred bodies to deal with.

'Brave basterd innee!' Dusty commented

Wiggy's reply was a bit more circumspect, as he observed the tight set of the man's jaw. 'They are a breed apart, the dangers they have to put up with surpass that even of Coal Miners.'

'Oy you two!' The young mens' eyes darted back to Petty Officer Milligan. 'Get that bloody messenger line back on its reel.' They quickly forgot about the brave Duncan McLeish, and hurried forrard with the messenger line for the light jackstay gear, to put it 'back on its reel'.

A sudden loud yell made everyone look up from their given task just in time to see Spud Murphy disappear over the side in reaction to a heavy lurch to port. He was replacing the guardrail stanchion that had been dropped to facilitate the easy handling of the Inflatable Liferaft. Even though he had a safety line around his well covered body, and his life jacket on, he still got a dunking in a stroppy sea cold enough to kill a man in two minutes. Everybody dropped what they were doing, and rushed to help the safety number straining for all he was worth to help his shipmate. Spud was quickly hauled inboard again, and the panic was over. Once again, strict observance of safety measures had saved a man's life.

'Get him down the messdeck, and out of that foul weather clothing,' Lieutenant Commander Dyson ordered; then turning to Wiggy said, 'Bennett, go to the victualling office and tell the SPOV that a tot of neaters is required in ten mess.'

Ten minutes later, a very surprised Spud Murphy downed a neat tot of pusser's bubbly. He shuddered slightly, and then smacked his lips with relish as the smooth dark liquid reached bottom. 'What time's hands to bathe tomorrow?' he asked with a sly grin, giving everyone a laugh; including the First Lieutenant.

The weather worsened as the day proceeded, and very soon a force nine gale was howling through the rigging, gradually increasing to storm force ten.

The storm blew itself out during the night, and even though the Trawlers had sought shelter in the lee of the land, not many fishermen slept that night. *Barrosa* put more distance between herself and land, and rode out the storm until morning, by which time it had abated to force eight.

As the weather got better the Trawlers wasted no time getting back to work, and soon all were trawling their nets, some regardless of the imposed limit line.

Two Icelandic Gunboats were keeping an eye on everything, but as yet made no move to approach Trawlers which were obviously taunting them by fishing the disputed line.

Petty Officer Telegraphist Howard appeared on the bridge, and approached the Officer of the Watch. 'Can I speak to the Captain Sir?' he asked.

'One moment PO, I'll see,' he said, bending down to the voicepipe to the Captain's cabin.

'Bridge here sir; Petty Officer Howard would like a word.'

'Put him on Timothy,' the Captain replied.

Petty Officer Howard stepped up to the voicepipe. 'Petty Officer Howard speaking sir, I've just received the following from the Skipper of the *Tartan Lady*,' he paused for a second looking down at his clipboard. 'Can you send your Whaler over whilst we are in close proximity? Have rather special gift for you and your crew.'

'Thank you PO, send back, "will review the situation, and comply with your request when able to do so".'

Petty Officer Howard retreated from the bridge giving his oppo, the Yeoman of Signals, a wink as he passed him.

Five minutes later Commander Plowright appeared on his bridge. Lookouts suddenly appeared more attentive seeing his arrival, and the Yeoman of Signals stood like a statue, hands clasped behind his back.

'Lovely day it's turned out to be Timothy,' the Captain greeted his Officer of the Watch, and then glanced across to Midshipman Blenkinsopp bent over the chart table, barely recognisable as a human being in his layers of clothing topped by a hooded duffle coat, pegged all the way from knees to chin.

'How far are we off the *Tartan Lady* Blenkinsopp?' he asked, looking down at the pile of clothing just below him.

'Er…about a mile I would judge sir,' the Midshipman replied, not in the least prepared for the question.

'Tell me exactly how far *Tartan Lady* is away from us Blenkinsopp,' the Captain ordered tartly. 'I don't like hurried estimations of proximity when we have the necessary aids to give us exact range.'

The Gunnery Officer grinned as he trained his glasses on the *Tartan Lady*.

Midshipman Blenkinsopp thrust his face into the cowl covering the small circular radar screen. 'Tartan Lady is at 1000 yards sir, relative bearing red four zero,' he said, turning to look upwards at his Captain.

'That's better Blenkinsopp, your initial estimation was twice that distance, be more precise in future.'

'Aye aye sir,' the chastened Midshipman replied, his blushing cheeks hidden by the cowl of his duffle coat.

Commander Plowright raised his binoculars and scanned 360 degrees. He allowed his gaze to remain on the Gunboats for some time, and then followed the line of a couple of Trawlers. 'Ops room, bridge,' he called, and then waited, poised for the response. 'Those two Trawlers, are they over the imposed line?'

'It's touch and go sir,' the radar operator replied. 'According to our plot, they are dead on the line, a bit of brinkmanship going on sir.'

'Thank you Jones,' Commander Plowright replied, recognising the voice of the forenoon watchman in his Ops Room.

'Get us to within 200 feet of *Tartan Lady* Timothy; I don't want the Whaler in the water for too long.'

He watched the ship reacting to the commands of the Officer of the Watch, and then looked down to speak to the Midshipman. 'Blenkinsopp!'

The Midshipman turned at the sound of his name, his face showing tension under the hooded cowl.

'While the wheelhouse is busy getting us close to *Tartan Lady*, pipe the Seaboat away, and second part of the watch to muster starboard side of the funnel.'

'Aye aye sir,' Midshipman Blenkinsopp replied, hurriedly collecting his thoughts to remember all the words of this routine pipe. He did not possess a Bosun's Call; both of these were in the wheelhouse with the Quartermaster of the Watch and his Bosun's Mate.

'D'yuh here there,' he started, not at all confidently. 'Away Seaboats Crew! Second part of port watch muster starboard side of the funnel.' His voice grew in confidence as he realised he was getting it right. Commander Plowright stifled a grin, and raised his glasses to hide a flicker of amusement.

A scurry of activity broke loose on the boat deck starboard side of the funnel. The Seaboat's crew scrambled into the twenty-seven foot Whaler, and under the orders of Petty Officer McHenry, the lowerers slipped the gripes, and then obeyed the order, 'turns for lowering.' The boat was lowered to within three foot of the water, and at the order, 'slip' the disengaging gear was released and the boat dropped onto the crest of a wave as accurately judged by Petty Officer McHenry. The 'Boat Rope' now towed the boat forward in the water at ship's speed, and the Coxswain put his rudder to port to swing the boat away from the ship's side. At this stage the bowman cast off the boat rope, and the Seaboat now reacted to the actions of five straining oarsmen.

The Seaboat was gone for thirty minutes, while all pairs of eyes free to goof followed the passage of the boat to the Trawler and back. Not a pair of eyes failed to goggle as every man who watched gasped with astonishment as they set eyes on the special gift passed down into the Whaler. Its wet, dark body was laid along the thwarts between curious oarsmen, and then, with shouts of encouragement from the Trawler's crew, the Coxswain of the Seaboat ordered his port oarsmen to 'bear off.' With enough gap now to get his oars into the water the Coxswain ordered, 'stand by', quickly followed by, 'give way together.'

Ten minutes later he brought the Seaboat underneath the Torpedo Derrick starboard side of the *Barrosa*, and the huge sea creature was hoisted inboard tail uppermost. The huge halibut was judged to be 250 lbs in weight, and was suspended from the superstructure overhang by the Torpedo tubes. With its nose touching the deck it was measured to be seven feet long, and there it hung long enough for everyone to get a chance to see a sight that they had never considered possible.

The Seaboat was hoisted in by hands from all parts of ship and departments off watch, and as soon as the keel left the water Commander Plowright had his ship under way, and then handed the 'con' to his Officer of the Watch. Ten minutes later, the

Leading Seaman RP2 of the afternoon watch advised the Officer, 'Two Trawlers inside the limit, sir'.

'Very good Leading Seaman Starkey, I will inform the Captain,' the TASO answered.

'Captain sir.'

'Yes Terry,' Commander Plowright replied, having first cleared his mouth of food.

'Sorry to disturb your lunch sir, but Ops Room have just reported that two of our Trawlers are definitely the wrong side of the imposed line.'

'We had better be ready for trouble then. Set us an intercept course, but retain your present eight knots. I'll be with you in a few minutes when I have finished my lunch.' Commander Plowright felt the ship reacting to his orders, and finished his lunch unhurriedly. He downed a glass of his favourite red wine and said, 'thank you Johnson,' to his Steward. Still savouring the wine he donned his scarf, huge duffle coat, and arctic mittens.

Well wrapped up as he was, he still felt the bitter air on exposed parts of his face as he stepped out onto his bridge.

'Bridge, this Ops,' the bridge speaker sang out.

'Bridge,' the Officer of the Watch answered.

'We are just on the limit line now sir; the two Trawlers are the ones at red nine zero,' Leading Seaman Starkey informed him.

'Thank you Starkey,' the TASO replied, and then took the few steps to the port side of the bridge screen and joined his Captain, the Yeoman of Signals, a bunting tosser, and the port lookout, each looking long and hard at the two Trawlers.

'Third contact coming from landward, three miles, speed approximately twenty-five knots,' advised Leading Seaman Starkey.

'Very good,' Sub Lieutenant Dodds answered from his place at the binnacle as Second Officer of the Watch.

'Sub,' the Captain called to Dodds, not taking his eyes off the fast approaching Gunboat.

'Yes sir,' the Second Officer of the Watch replied.

'Tell the Wheelhouse to pipe Special Sea Dutymen to their stations, close all red and blue openings.'

'Aye aye sir,' Sub Lieutenant Dodds replied, quickly passing the Captain's orders to the wheelhouse.

The Bosun's Call blasted into the wheelhouse microphone, followed by, 'Special Sea Dutymen to your stations. Close all red and blue openings. Damage control party muster in the canteen flat.'

The ship was not steaming into a fight with a belligerent opponent; it was steaming towards an expected tussle with a craft from a non-belligerent country. The dispute was Iceland's attempts to expand her fishing limits, thereby preventing Britain's use of historically important fishing grounds. Bumps and scrapes were bound to happen as the fishery protection vessel defended her charges with the minimum amount of force required to prevent their arrest; subsequent impounding, and confiscation of fishing tackle. Thousands of pounds of private money was at stake here, as well as the feeding of a nation. The British Navy was in no way hesitant when it came to the rescue of a British Trawler.

The Trawlers *Blythe Spirit* and *Andy Capp*, both North Easterners, were already hauling in their nets, and heading for the line, but not quite fast enough. The Icelandic Gunboat was hurtling through the sea trying to reach *Blythe Spirit* while she was hampered by a trailing net. It was touch and go, but the Trawler's net appeared climbing its derrick leg just in time to be swung inboard. *Andy Capp*, already in safety had her nets inboard and opened with fish spewing all over the deck. Her crew, not giving a damn for the Gunboat's intentions immediately got stuck into the job of gutting and sorting. Both Skippers now had to show their skills, by veering and turning, whilst urging every ounce of speed out of their ancient coal burners.

The Gunboat streaked across the stern of *Blythe Spirit* having been an instant too late to damage her nets. The Trawler's crew all stuck a finger skywards showing total contempt for the Gunboat's crew, and the Skipper's damaging intention. The Gunboat's crew ignored the insult, slowed down, and came round in a circle to try and grapple the Trawler. By that time the Skipper of Blythe Spirit had showed the Gunboat its stern, and began to weave from port to starboard as he ran at full speed from his tormentor. The Trawlermen on deck opened the net and fish spewed everywhere. Totally ignoring the Gunboat they got on with their work as if she was not there, while their Skipper gamely made diverting sweeps from side to side. *Barrosa* caught up astern, and shouldered the Gunboat to one side. It immediately increased speed, and tried to grapple the Fxle screen of *Blythe Spirit*. The Trawler Skipper counteracted by swinging to starboard, hauling the grappling line through the burning gloves of the cursing Gunboat's crew before they had a chance to secure it. *Barrosa* surged forward to once again come between pursuer and pursued. The Trawler now veered sharply to port bringing her under the Fxle of her protector; a wise and intended move because he had now presented the Gunboat with only the starboard side of his vessel. For two hours the chase continued until twenty miles had passed beneath the keels of the four ships. Finally the Gunboat broke off the chase, emitting a loud raspberry from its squeaky electric horn. *Barrosa* had the last word with a long blast from a real steam foghorn.

HMS *Barrosa* remained with the two Trawlers until the Gunboat was just a speck on the horizon, and then, with a sudden burst of speed she veered to starboard, waved goodbye to the Trawlers, and set off to tail the Gunboat over the limit line. *Blythe Spirit* and *Andy Capp* held their course to pass the Faroes, and onwards to their home port, their holds fully laden. They would no doubt have a tale or two to tell about the actions of a determined Destroyer crew, and an equally determined Icelandic Gunboat.

■ ▪ ■

On Friday 1st March 1958, the Chief Petty Officer's mess of HMS *Barrosa* set the questions for the last inter-ships quiz. The Chief Engine Room Artificer, who was also Mess President sat in *Barrosa*'s Radio Shack, for an hour broadcast, and then repeated all the questions of the quiz. He then asked if all ships had answered the questions. It took a further fifteen minutes to give the answers over the air, and then a further half hour for all ships to relay their score to the *Barrosa*'s Radio Shack. All this was done on trust, and everybody knew it.

Northern Lights out of Aberdeen won the last quiz, and was rewarded with two crates of beer. The Chief ERA said 'Phew' meaningfully, and went off the air, leaving the Captain to have a final word to all the Trawlermen, the air waves then became alive with all the retaliatory bonhomie that these popular events seem to encourage. It was still going on an hour later as each Trawler Skipper said his piece.

At 0900 hours on Sunday 3rd March 1958 a speck appeared on the southern horizon. The Ops Room were waiting for the Officer of the Watch to confirm he had sighted the Destroyer HMS *Aisne* visually. An hour later, all hands not on watch gathered on *Barrosa*'s upper deck. HMS *Aisne* steamed slowly past in a Northerly direction as the ship's company of Barrosa gave her a rousing cheer. This cheer was met by the traditional barrage of old potatoes, and loud laughs from the ship's company of the *Aisne*. The laughs issuing from the southerly bound vessel were tinged with perhaps a little hint of relief at having safely completed their turn of duty off Iceland.

During 'stand easy' that morning Commander Plowright spoke to his ship's company over the tannoy. 'D'yuh hear there, Captain speaking,' he began. 'First of all let me say well done to everyone for an excellently performed patrol. It was not always easy, as Able Seaman Murphy will confirm. I believe he asked for a repeat performance providing a tot was part of the deal again.' Roars of laughter echoed from the messdecks, there was something specifically significant about a Captain seeing the funny side of an event.

'We have been ordered into harbour for one week's assisted maintenance.' Another roar of approval rippled through the ship. 'We shall enter Rosyth Dockyard on Tuesday morning, where I shall try to give each watch in turn a bit of time off.' Loud cheers again. 'That's all for now, well done everyone.'

The Captain's few words had the desired effect, everyone felt a bit uplifted, a bit bouncier, more ready to laugh; a certain rise in cheeriness pervaded the lower deck. The night's film, always preceded by a Tom and Jerry cartoon was received with loud shouts of 'good old Fred,' as Fred Quimby's name flashed up on the screen. 'Good old Fred,' was followed by 'fuck Fred,' and then 'after you with Fred,' followed by howls of maniacally silly sailor laughter. Such was film routine at 2015 hours nightly at sea. (With apologies to that marvellous cartoonist Fred Quimby. Such is the price of fame.) A chance to shrug off the rigours of the day with a bit of communal Tom Foolery.

The general euphoria felt by everyone began to disappear during the latter part of the morning watch. Gale force seas forecast for the Faroes area gradually developed from force nine to hurricane force with gusts of 100 miles an hour, forcing Commander Plowright to bring his ship round into the weather. The upper deck was out of bounds, and emergency rations were broke out as the galley remained shut down. The ship was being battered by forty foot waves with the odd one reaching sixty foot in height, towering over the open bridge with awesome intent. The tops of the waves were whipped by the powerful wind, and the spindrift off the tops was like ice drops as it hit the ship, removing paint as efficiently as an industrial shot blast.

Commander Plowright remained on his bridge for fifteen hours, until the storm gradually began to blow itself out. At 1900 hours that day he caught the first glimpse of his Fxle deck, and gasped at what his eyes told him, giving him cause to wonder what state the rest of his command was in. For the moment, all he could see forrard was guard rails flattened to the deck. He turned to his first Lieutenant who had also not had any rest. 'As soon as possible get the Chief Boatswain's Mate to raise a damage report on upper deck fittings, and the Engineer had better get his Chief ERA to do likewise for his department.'

At that moment, Surgeon Lieutenant Middlecote appeared on the bridge with his LSBA.

'My word,' he said. 'That was a rough one sir,' and then added his opinion of the stern of the ship. 'All is well aft sir, but I suspect everyone is somewhat relieved to be joined up with the forrard part of the ship again.'

Commander Plowright allowed himself a grin. It was easy to see that this young officer was not a Destroyerman. Ship's Company living aft was used to being isolated in rough weather, but there were always the catwalks that joined the gun platforms from forrard to aft, and it had to be really rough to reduce the effectiveness of lifelines as a means of travelling from aft to forrard and vice versa.

'What's it like midships along the waist?' Commander Plowright asked.

LSBA Norton answered, having first glanced at his boss. 'We don't have a Dinghy and a Skimming Dish any more, they are reduced to matchsticks I'm afraid sir. We haven't seen the starboard side yet.'

'Good Lord, that bad is it!' the Captain replied, looking to his right as he noticed his First Lieutenant walking to the rear of the flagdeck.

'The Whaler's badly damaged as well sir; a big one must have landed on it. It's totally splayed amidships.' Without a glance forrard to his Captain, he walked to the port side of the flagdeck and looked aft. 'The cutter's okay sir, no damage visible.'

Commander Plowright became thoughtful for a moment, and then made a decision. 'Have the watch on deck turn the Cutter out, it will have to serve as the Seaboat if an emergency occurs.'

Everyone turned as the Supply Officer joined the group.

'Hello Freddy, everything all right in your department?' the Captain asked.

'Oh there's bound to be a batten or two broken in store rooms. There's not much that can be jostled around in the cool room, or the fridge space, they are a bit run down after three weeks at sea. We will do checks now that the Butcher and his Tanky can open up hatches to get tomorrow's stores up.'

'That will suffice Freddy, anything else for the moment?'

'Yes sir,' Freddy the ape man Darwin said politely. 'The ship's company has not had a hot meal today sir, rum was issued forrard and aft, but we had to keep the galley battened down all day.' He looked expectantly at his captain.

'Most certainly Freddy, thanks for reminding me; a damn good 'pot mess' I suggest, always popular with the men.'

'Very good sir, I shall see to it immediately.'

The Supply Officer left the bridge, and by 2130 hours of the first watch everyone was tucking in to a soup plate full of meaty stew and a thick wedge of bread. Those on watch had not been forgotten, messmates went round with 'Fannies' of steaming stew and wedges of bread. Hygiene may have been a bit lax, but needs must when the devil drives. An hour later everyone was treated to a thick mug of 'KI' usually reserved for middle watchmen only but after such a day, a thick nourishing mug of chocolate mixed with custard powder was well deserved by all on board.

The Navigating Officer had to revise his speed to keep to Estimated Time of Arrival (ETA), and Commander Plowright was not going to let a storm get in the way of his time keeping, so the *Barrosa* was soon ploughing through a still choppy sea at a determined twenty knots. Storm damage was still being assessed, but a list of immediate defects had been signalled ahead, and all debris not washed overboard would be kept for dockyard assessment. The navy was big on accountability, and the tax payers money had to be carefully administered.

Trawlers were constantly passing on their way to the fishing grounds, so the ensign was dipped several times a day as marks of respect were passed between seafarers. Men working on the upper deck gave a friendly wave to each other, and even Commander Plowright was seen to raise his hat in acknowledgement. So it was in good spirits that HMS *Barrosa* entered Rosyth Dockyard, and berthed at 0900 hours on the dot, as the Navigator had planned.

The cheerful, efficient berthing procedure carried out by an experienced crew was catching, Dockyard Mateys streamed on board, reacting in similar fashion to the polite and friendly reception of *Barrosa*'s Ship's Company. Within an hour Windy Hammers were clattering loudly and chips of old paintwork were being blown into corners everywhere. Dockyard welders soon struck an arc and repairs to damaged structure got under way enthusiastically. Damaged guard rail stanchions were deposited ashore and were quickly on their way to the engineering shed to be refurbished.

A huge split above the galley, and running the length of the main air intakes was fitted with a strengthening plate and welded from above and below. This split had been caused by a huge wave that *Barrosa* had hung on the crest of just long enough to expose her propellers astern, and at the same time, her keel forrard; the damage gave a whole new meaning to the shipboard term 'the break of the Fxle.'

At 1200 hours a roar went through the ship as the pipe 'hands to dinner' was followed by 'make and mend to both parts of starboard watch.' Not surprisingly there was no mad rush to get ashore. Most men of the starboard watch had tot and dinner, and then climbed into number two uniform and made for the Dockyard Canteen for a couple of pints of 'heavy', returning aboard to get their heads down until supper time. Older hands had their hammocks slung by the time the port watch turned to after dinner.

By this time in the commission, it was generally considered that Wiggy Bennett was a definite candidate for Wardroom Status. His first job aboard was 'Side Party' in harbour, and Quarterdeck part of ship for all other shipboard tasks. Three monthly job changes were imminent, and lists of job changes were already promulgated on the ship's notice board. Wiggy had been assigned the job of Navigator's Yeoman, a job generally reserved for a Radar Plot Operator second class, but for the next three months it would be Wiggy keeping the charts in order and generally learning to be the Pilot's second dickey, so to speak. His pal Dusty's job changed from 'Boat Party' to the Fxle part of ship. Having spent the first few months learning to be a proficient bowman of the motor cutter, which was a watch keeping job in harbour, he would now become proficient in the use of 'Anchors and Cables', a far larger subject than is generally considered. Job changes came into force on the Monday, so when *Barrosa* put to sea again on the Wednesday, both pals would have changed messes on the Sunday previous; Dusty to five mess, and Wiggy to two mess right up forrard to the paintshop hatch. Dusty was a little further aft, just down the ladder from the canteen flat.

The news on Tuesday afternoon that HMS *Barrosa* would have to call in Portsmouth to pick up a new Skimming Dish, and replenish her main armament shells and cordite, sent men scurrying for the shoreside telephone. First in the queue was Wiggy, who managed to raise Felicity on a pre-arranged number at 1700 hours that evening. The delighted chatter that went on for five minutes had the effect of making the remainder of the queue a bit disgruntled.

'Come on Wiggs!' Spud Murphy grumbled, 'there's ten of us aht 'ere.'

'Must go Flic,' Wiggy laughed. 'I am about to get pounced on by ten lusty sailors.'

Her laugh made a pleasant end to the impromptu telephone call as Spud grabbed the receiver from him having impatiently held the door open in preparation to dive in.

'Gissit!' he hissed, and then waved the phone under Wiggy's nose as he affectedly wiggled his hips while attempting to wriggle into the small space. Wiggy gave him a playful shove into the kiosk and pushed the door to heavily; leaning on it with both hands. Meanwhile the rest of the queue started harrying Spud to 'get on with it, yuh dozy basterd!'

Dusty strolled across and joined the queue. 'Did yuh get through?' he asked his pal.

'Yes, great line, no bother at all,' Wiggy replied without altering his pace as he headed for the gangway. He saluted, and then turned aft, as if going to ten mess, and then, realising his error, grinned at the Bosun's Mate, and headed forrard to his new mess.

Thirty minutes later Dusty poked his head into the forrard messdeck. 'Guess what,' he said as he spotted his pal, and then without waiting for a reply blurted out, 'she's 'ad tuh go on advanced Easter leave, and I know she's not on the phone at home.'

'Oh bloody hard shit old buddy!' Wiggy answered with uncharacteristically rude candour, and then tried to make a joke of the problem. 'Never mind, that means you can have that long awaited tryst with Cardiff Rose and Belfast Betty.'

'Ahggg, God ferbid!' Dusty reacted. 'I'd like tuh piss through it again.'

They both had a laugh together, and then Wiggy took his two cans of beer out of his locker. 'Your mess,' he indicated through the mess door.

'Yeah, why not, we're both free until clear up messdecks and flats for rounds.'

By the time *Barrosa* swept down the Firth of Forth the next day, not only were all her Ordinary Seamen and her Junior Seamen in new jobs, but the ship literally shone in her repainted glory; all thanks to the work of Rosyth Dockyard, and some maintenance help from the local Fleet Maintenance Unit. Her head bit into the crisp force six that was blowing across the estuary as she turned south, and headed down the North Sea. Commander Plowright was in no hurry; 'C-in-C nav home Portsmouth' had advised him to enter harbour at 0900 hours on Friday morning, and give his Ship's Company extended long weekend leave until the following Tuesday morning. That meant that everyone who wanted to could get home to visit wives and children, or Mums and Dads before rushing off to sea again. All northern members of the Ship's Company had been afforded the same privilege whilst in Rosyth. A bit of hard luck for midlanders due to travelling time, but even they got a couple of full days at home.

As HMS *Barrosa* slewed to a stern sea, making life a bit hard for the helmsman, the cold wind blowing from the Arctic seas was in great contrast to the somewhat warmer temperatures enjoyed in Vigo, northern Spain. HMS *Corunna* had left Vigo, having been ordered to sail to Portsmouth where she would have her starboard 'A' bracket inspected for suspected damage. Heavier than normal vibrations at the stern had forced the Captain of the *Corunna* into Vigo where ship's divers had confirmed that all was not well where the prop shaft passed through the bearing. A ship's construction engineer was sent out from England, and he confirmed that docking was essential to assess the defect accurately. This confirmation set wheels in motion at Admiralty, and it was soon decided to get her to Portsmouth to the only drydock available at that moment. HMS *Protector* had just finished refit prior to going back into service as Antarctic Survey Vessel, and Falklands guard ship.

The lower deck of HMS *Corunna* was not at all displeased with this outcome. They had been on their way to relieve HMS *Barrosa* as fishery protection vessel; now however, they could look forward to at least a month in Portsmouth, meaning that if their patrol duties had been terminally cancelled, they had escaped the bitter cold of Arctic seas. If not terminally cancelled, at least the job would be done in far more clement weather. Not so the Ship's Company of HMS *Aisne*, the sudden discovery that they were ordered to Iceland in lieu of HMS *Corunna* was cause for a good old drip below decks.

By the time the first long-weekenders were leaving the *Barrosa* at 1215 hours, HMS *Corunna*, assisted by a harbour Tug, was tying up alongside North Corner Jetty. She had limped home on one screw, so her relieved crew were also ready to appreciate long weekend leave for non-duty hands, but men required for duty would get their turn. The Dockyard took charge of HMS *Corunna*, and by the following Monday morning she was fully prepared for docking. In the meantime, non-duty members of her crew did exactly the same as *Barrosa*'s crew; enjoyed the delights of Portsmouth nightlife.

Wiggy was off with Felicity, who had picked him up outside Unicorn Gate in a taxi. He jumped in the back seat beside her and gasped as he set eyes on her. She was a vision, dressed smartly against the cool March air with one of those fluffy hats that come down over the ears, but let the hair hang down. He looked into her gorgeous moist, dazzling pools of pure sapphire, and words were not necessary. Their lips met as the driver pulled away, too busy with traffic to notice the couple so much in love in the back seat, as he drove them to the 'Still and West' for lunch.

Dusty phoned up HMS *Vigo* to see if his old pals Shiner and Bogey were free to meet him that night. Shiner was meeting Beryl in the Isle of Wight for the weekend, but Bogey was glad to be able to have a run ashore with his oppo again, so they arranged to meet in the Home Club.

Bogey burst into the Home Club, where Dusty had his pint waiting for him at the bar. A few surrounding drinkers glanced casually their way as they met with robust handshakes and clasps on the shoulder. Had they have hugged the eyes would have remained on them a moment longer, minds making instant opinions. As it was the onlookers saw two old shipmates meeting for a drink together after a few months on different ships.

'Did yer get tied up?' Dusty asked, the pleasure of their meeting lingering on his face.

'Course I did; Sunday the 20th of December, straight after mornin' service.'

'Did Shiner do best man for yuh?'

'Sure ee did.'

'Are yer sisters still intact?' Dusty said, nudging him, grinning widely.

Bogey laughed one of his loud guffaws. 'Course they are, ee was the perfect gent. Yooed 'ardly know the new Shiner, Beryl's turned 'im into a respectable sailor.' He grinned broadly as he added, 'If there is such a beast.'

They chewed the fat together whilst seeing off a couple of pints, and then decided to move onto another pub where a bit of life might be stirring on this Friday night. The Albany and the Lennox were so full, people were drinking in the entrance lobby. The Sussex Hotel was bursting at the seams in both bars, so they tried up the side road.

The Railway Cellars was a Scrumpy house quite popular with Darts and Domino players, and there was some room at the bar.

'Fancy a pint of rough Scrumpy?' Bogey asked.

'Nah, 'aven't touched it since the last five bob run we 'ad at Torpoint when we left *Raleigh*.'

'Don't think I 'ave either,' Bogey replied, and then ordered two pints of Brickwood's best bitter.

Bogey's size always caused a few heads to turn when he entered a bar; and so it was tonight. A group of lads sitting at a corner table glanced his way. One pair of eyes however, remained on the big sailor and his lighter oppo. The eyes belonged to a blond, bewhiskered young man dressed in civvies.

'Well fuck my old boot!' the blond one muttered, just loud enough to be heard by his mates. His eyes remained on Dusty Miller, the old hatred surging through him as his face took on a surly scowl. 'You too! Ordinary Seaman fuckin' Miller,' he said through gritted teeth. He turned inwards to face his mates again, and one of his shipmates instantly recognised the aggressive stare.

'Hey Smudge!' he chided in a low voice. 'No fuckin' trouble! D'yuh 'ear me. Whatever's upset yuh ferget it, we 'aven't come 'ere fer a punch up.'

All eyes at the table were now taking a closer look at Dusty and Bogey. They knew by Bogey's size that it would take at least three of them to control him if his back was against the wall. They also judged Dusty quite rightly as a 'hard little bastard'.

'C'mon Smudge ferget it,' another civilian clad sailor piped in, adding meaningfully, 'I'm not goin' roly poly in me best clobber, so if yuh start anyfin yer on yer own shipmate.'

Smith gazed into the eyes of all his pals at the table in turn. 'This doesn't concern any of yuh, but d'yuh see the smaller of the two guys?'

A few of his oppos nodded as they gazed at Bogey and Dusty enjoying a joke, and totally unaware of the presence of the aggressive Able Seaman Smith.

'Well so far it's three-one tuh 'im,' Smith continued bitterly. 'Not one of the scraps 'as bin a straight stand up fight. Twice ee's used a judo or wrestling 'old on me, and once ee got me wiv a sucker punch, when I thought I 'ad 'im. Nah you lads, me and that git 'ave gotter settle it, but this time it'll be wiv a level start for boff of us.' He failed to mention his bushwhacking attack from behind in Gibraltar, the one meeting where he came off best. 'You lot stay put, this ain't yore fight,' he reminded them, rising determinedly to his feet.

Pushing his chair back under the table, he straightened up, turned around, and started walking the four paces to where Dusty and Bogey were still involved in animated bar chat. The walking caught Dusty's eye as he glanced past Bogey. His facial expression changed from appreciative laugh to narrow eyed scowl as he recognised the approaching figure. Bogey saw the look and turned around.

'Fuck off Smith!' he bristled savagely, and then added with equal vehemence, 'or I'll finish this one off!'

Smith stopped two paces away. 'Tell yer big oppo this ain't about 'im,' he gritted, holding Dusty's hard gaze. 'You and me 'ave got ter settle this eyeball tuh eyeball; no first advantage either side.' His hard gaze met Dusty's just as firmly.

'Yuh said it was finished last time we met,' Dusty scowled back at him.

'Yeah, but if yuh remember rightly, yuh 'ad me in an unarmed combat 'old; 'ardly a fair fight that, is it?'

Bogey took a step forward menacingly, his intention clear to everyone by his stance. He was about to hurl Smith through the window of the bar.

'NOT IN 'ERE!' the Landlord yelled. 'Any fisticuffs can be settled over the road in the railway car park; plenty uv fuckin' room there!'

The whole room was now aware that a battle was in the offing. Some younger drinkers looked at the trio expectantly, but the older drinkers just glanced across and then returned to their Darts and Dominoes.

'Ow's abaht it then OD?' Smith's eyes glared, but his voice was a mere whisper of menace. 'Just you and me; no kickin', no fuckin' judo, let's just see oo's really best when it comes tuh a straight knuckling session; a fully trained AB or a fuckin' jumped up OD wiv ideas beyond 'is station.'

Smith's tantalising statement infuriated Dusty.

'Yer on!' he gritted through tight lips, 'but just one other thing,' he added.

'Wassat!' Smith sneered back, wrongly sensing a possible get out clause in Dusty's reply.

'I want my mate Bogey 'ere, tuh keep an eye on things. One of your pals too, I've got no fuckin' reason tuh take yuh at your word.'

Smith shrugged acquiescently, and then turning to his oppos gave a 'come here' signal with a jerk of his head.

One of the men at the table rose to his feet, and walked over, his face creased with apprehension.

'Arfer,' Smith said, slapping his hand on his oppo's shoulder. 'Yer just goin tuh watch a fair fight, and make sure this twat fights fair!' He indicated Dusty disparagingly with a jerk of his thumb.

The bar had fallen into total silence watching this declaration of war unfolding before them. They watched the four men troop out of the bar, and no sooner had the door closed behind them, the general hubbub of conversation started again. Nobody made a move to follow the group outside.

Able Seaman Smith led the way into the car park, zig zagging between parked cars until he found a dimly lit space. He indicated this was the chosen battleground by taking off jacket and tie, and handing them to his mate Arthur. Rolling up his sleeves, he stood poised, watching as Dusty removed cap, silk, lanyard, and jacket. He then pushed up the sleeves of his seaman's jersey, and finally removed his blue collar, draping them all over Bogey's extended right arm as he removed each item; only then did he turn to face his aggressor, fists raised, with right fist leading.

'Ah, a cack 'anded cunt,' Smith sneered, referring to Dusty's Southpaw stance, and then flicked out the first jab of the fight. His left fist went over Dusty's right lead, and was warded off. Smith then leapt swiftly aside as Dusty's left fist hurtled into the space he had dodged from.

'Nice try OD!' Smith said scornfully.

He should have kept his mouth shut and concentrated on his defence because Dusty quickly corrected his balance and threw a straight right which took Smith on his left eyebrow. The punch split the skin above the eye, and sent him reeling backwards falling heavily on his buttocks. Dusty held off while Smith regained his feet, his left forearm going across his eyes in an attempt to clear the stream of blood that was beginning to cloud the eye. That was the end of Smith's chatty fight. He gathered himself, dancing lightly on his feet for a moment, and then, pursing his lips determinedly, he moved forward feinting with his left, and then slammed a right into Dusty's midriff. Dusty took the blow, and danced backwards gasping slightly. He spent the next twenty seconds warding off a flurry of blows that only connected with his shoulders and forearms. Smith's arms began to tire, and he backed off, still dancing lightly on his feet. Dusty moved forward confidently as Smith raised his guard and warded off two straight right jabs and then retaliated with a straight right that took Dusty full on the nose. He danced backwards absorbing the sharp pain, and blinking off the rush of tears clouding his eyes. He covered up, protecting his head from a flurry of blows that started to numb his forearms. His eyes misty with teardrops, he dodged and weaved, keeping his broken nose well covered. His eyes began to clear a little and the sight of Smith confidently raining blows on him from every angle as if he had the fight won stirred his blood again. He saw a gap in Smith's flailing attack, and automatically his arm tensed and threw a blow into the gap. He felt the sudden jar surge up his arm as his fist connected with

Smith's mouth, mashing the lips against the teeth, and loosening the upper frontal ones. Those teeth would have been lost had Smith not reacted instinctively at the last moment; but still too late to prevent severe damage to his mouth. Smith reacted by lunging forward and clasping Dusty round the shoulders, hanging on in the hope of regaining strength and vision again. Dusty went along with the move, just as eager to regain his breath, and to regain some stamina. His nose hurt like hell; he was also aware that his eyes were puffed up impairing his vision somewhat. They clung to each other swaying from side to side, their feet moving as if in some combatative waltz as they both gasped painfully for air.

'Ave you two 'ad enough?' a concerned Arthur yelled at them, his words making Bogey aware. 'Ave you 'ad enough Smith?' he joined Arthur, knowing full well that Dusty would not be first to concede. As if in reply the two protagonists pushed away from each other and started flailing their arms at each other again. There was no coordination in their punches now; it was pure grit that made them both carry on this battle. This was the final scene of an act that had started with skill and determination, but had now descended into a stubborn refusal to quit on either half. They were both tired to the point of staggering blindly into each other. Both had taken damaging punches, but both were oblivious to the pain, and both were aware that their strength was waning fast. With leaden arms, lungs bursting, and eyes glazed, their heads drooping on each other's shoulder, but still swinging ineffective blows at each other's midriffs, they sank to their knees.

'C'mon lads yuh've 'ad enough, c'mon now yuh've 'ad a bloody good fight, let's call it a day!' Bogey shouted, on the verge of becoming emotional as an effect of watching the brave battlers. 'C'mon the pair of yuh, there's nothing left to fight for, if yuh 'aven't proved the point now yuh never will do.'

The two figures on their knees sank to the ground and lay there gasping; only the sound of a police siren, wailing eerily in the distance registered in their weary minds. They still had their arms draped over each other's shoulders, and Smith was trying to say something. The words finally emerged from his painfully damaged lips with a great effort.

'Fffuckin' good fight!' His lips dribbled as the words came out with great difficulty.

'Is that it then Smudger?' Dusty's head swayed as he tried to focus on his opponent. Neither of them realised that this was the first act of familiarity that either of them had ever conceded.

'That's it!' Smith answered with as much meaning as his injured mouth would allow, and then surprisingly, his right hand crept forward and grasped Dusty's right wrist. 'Sorted!' he said, as Dusty turned his hand and retaliated to his grip.

'Sorted!' Dusty replied, knowing instinctively in his partially disoriented state, that the cycle of unnecessary aggression had come to an end.

They staggered to their feet assisted by their pals, suddenly becoming aware that the siren sounded louder. Trailing clothes they stumbled from the shadowy rays of incandescent light, and took cover under a half demolished brick archway where they struggled to put their clothes back on, assisted by two pals who were both very relieved to see the battle finished. A bloody, and for Smith's temperament, a seemingly proper end to an obsession that he could only shake off in this manner; it was over as sure as if a peace treaty had been signed.

The old Wolsley Police Car came screaming into the parking ground, its siren wailing balefully as it roared up and down the rows of parked cars. Finally having sped round the whole car park, and finding absolutely nothing, it screeched to a halt at the entrance, switched off its siren, and disappeared into the light traffic of Commercial Road. At the same time, four men appeared from under a brick archway, half demolished in the never ending modernisation of Central Portsmouth.

Bogey and Dusty had thrown on their Burberrys and turned the collar up. In Dusty's case it was as much to hide his battered appearance as keep out the chill March wind. Smudge Smith and Arthur donned their three-quarter-length Italian style raincoats and the four of them made it across the road to the public toilets on the Guildhall side of Portsmouth Town station Railway Bridge.

'Wot time's yer leave expire Dusty?' Smith asked, whilst gazing at the mashed lips and lumpy eyebrows reflecting back at him from the mirror above a wash basin.

'1200 hours; I'm duty tomorrow, so I've got a sort of short weekend.'

Smith turned and looked at him. 'Christ,' he blasphemed. 'We look as bad as each uvver, why don't you do the same as me, and get a bed for the night at Aggies.'

Bogey looked at his pal's reflection in the mirror. 'That's a fuckin' good idea Dusty, it'll give yer a chance to clean up properly, and look a bit better before yuh get aboard.'

Dusty nodded, seeing the sense in the suggestion. 'I think I'll go for five bobs worth of that,' he replied, and then winced as the movement of his lips tugged at his nose.

'See yuh Sunday then!' Bogey said as he left Dusty at the main entrance to Agnes Weston's.

'Twelve o'clock, Home Club,' Dusty confirmed.

The old boy at the reception desk gave Dusty a close look. 'By jove young man, you have been in the wars,' he said in a kindly manner.

'Aw just a Friday night dust up,' Dusty played it down. 'I'll be awright in the mornin' when I've 'ad a bath, and a good kip.'

Smudge Smith and his oppo displayed their tickets, and the old receptionist handed them their keys. 'Good Lord, you too!' Must have been quite a Friday night out there tonight,' the old boy said, his attitude confirming that he knew Able Seaman Smith very well. 'One of your better fights I presume,' he added, a quizzical grin lifting the corners of his mouth.

'The best granddad,' Smith confirmed, heading for the stairs before the old boy held him in conversation.

Dusty found the small room, and taking the towel and soap spent thirty minutes having a good old soak. The pain of his nose barely allowed him to touch it,;due to the buckled cartilage, he had to dab it gingerly to remove the last traces of blood. His eyes were puffy and bloodshot, and his vision was reduced due to the bottom lids of his eyes being pushed up by the bluish sacks beneath them. Noticing the dried blood on the front of his jersey, he dabbed a corner of the towel in the water, and rubbed at it laboriously until satisfied that he had removed the crusted drips.

Returning to his room, he hung his uniform up, and placed his paybook wallet and loose change alongside the Gideon Bible on the bedside cabinet. Reaching up to pull the light cord, he noticed a brass nameplate which boasted the name 'David Whitfield'.

'Well bugger me!' he muttered, 'I'll have tuh tell me Mum that I've slept in the same bed as 'er favourite singer.' He grinned, and then winced at the pain it caused him; but it did not stop him uttering the thought that caused the grin, 'but not at the same time.'

The following morning after a deep and undisturbed sleep, his eyes looked a lot better. Feeling almost cheerful, as if a milestone had been lifted from his back, he filled the washbowl with cold water and rinsed his face cautiously. Dressing himself, he made sure that each piece of uniform was reasonable in appearance. When he had finished, he stared at himself in the mirror, and bared his teeth as an afterthought. 'Ugh!' he exclaimed, with as much disgust as his wounded face would allow. He picked up the towel again, put his finger in a corner of it, wetted the corner, and then rubbed his teeth vigorously. After a minute he gazed at his teeth again, and apparently satisfied rinsed the corner of the towel and replaced it. 'Cheerio David,' he muttered as he went through the door. 'Nice to have shared your bed.'

A matronly old lady accepted his key, giving him a disapproving glance as she took in the contours of his face.

'I fell out of bed love,' he said, trying to appear nonchalant; but his attempt at light heartedness fell on deaf ears. The disapproval changed to a scowling, 'don't be flippant with me young man!'

A bit stung by the matronly old lady's remark, he strolled across the road to 'Jack's Tattoo Parlour', and ordered a cup of tea and a bacon sandwich at the snack bar next door. No one commented on his somewhat battered appearance, disorganised faces were not an unusual sight in the City of Portsmouth at weekends. He enjoyed the sandwich, stoically ignoring the pain that chewing caused him. When he had finished the sandwich he drained his tea mug, and began the walk up to Unicorn gate, ignoring the curious glances thrown at him by the dockyard constabulary as he strolled purposefully through its portals. He made his way to North Wall, his pace getting smarter as his ship came into view. As he neared the gangway he could not help but notice that the Aircraft Carrier HMS *Warrior* loomed over the

Barrosa to all intents and purposes looking like a huge guardian protecting its charge. He saluted as he stepped off the gangway, getting a hard stare from the Quartermaster as he collected his station card.

Everyone in the mess was at 'Stand Easy', so all his messmates together had a first hand view of their battle scarred messmate. For a moment there was total silence as everyone took in his appearance.

'Fuckin' 'ell Miller! What ran into you?'

It was the Leading Hand of the mess, and Killick of the Fxle part of ship who had spoken out.

'Ah, just a long standin' difference sorted out,' Dusty replied. 'Nothin' tuh fuss about, all sorted and finished.'

'Oo the fuck was that then?' Leading Seaman Wilkinson pursued the point.

'Oh I 'ad a difference with a bloke on *Vanguard* last September Hooky,' Dusty replied, still trying to be non-committal and then seeing that the next question was poised on his inquisitor's lips added, 'we just bumped into each other last night, and before yuh knew it we 'ad a set to. It's all done now, we're the best of oppos now that we 'ave cleared the air.'

C'mere, let's 'ave a look at that nose,' the Leading Hand ordered, rising from the messdeck table.

With the rest of his messmates looking on silently, Dusty obeyed his messdeck leader, and stood calmly while Leading Seaman Wilkinson assessed the damage to his nose. 'It's broken young feller, yuh'll 'ave tuh go and see the doc, can't ignore that!'

Dusty looked startled. 'Ah come off it Hooky, it's only a scrap I've 'ad, no need for a lot of fuss.'

'Self inflicted injury Miller! Done ashore! Not in the line of duty. If I ignored your state, I would not be doin' my job...and I could lose my hook for that, so you get into yer number eights and get up the sick bay at out pipes.' He gave Dusty a stern look, and added, 'that's a direct order.'

'Righto Hooky,' Dusty reacted to the stern warning, and obediently changed into number eight working dress, and proceeded to the sick bay. 'Out Pipes' blasted over the tannoy as he knocked at the sick bay door.

'Come in,' a voice called.

Dusty opened the door, and walked in to the clinical ambience of the sick bay. LSBA Norton looked up from his desk, about to say, 'yes, what can I do for you?' One look at Dusty, and the question died on his lips.

'Jesus Christ Miller, what happened to you?' he asked, rising from his seat looking concerned. 'This is the second time in three months, who in the hell did this to you?' He did not wait for an answer, but immediately inspected Dusty's nose. He felt the lump of cartilage, trying to be as gentle as possible. 'We can do something about that straight away,' he said determinedly as he placed the meaty part of each palm of his hands either side of Dusty's nose.

Dusty cringed inwardly, in anticipation of the pain that was about to descend upon him again. The LSBA squeezed, pulled downwards, and then gave a slight twist to his hands. There was an audible click, followed by a sharp 'aagh' from Dusty. His eyes welled with tears instantly as his nose clicked back into place. LSBA Norton dabbed the teardrops thoughtfully with cotton wool, and then proceeded to give first aid to the nicks and bruises covering the remainder of Dusty's face.

'Right, lie back there Miller,' the LSBA indicated the adjustable head of the sick bay cot. 'I'm going to clear your nose.' So saying, he started probing Dusty's nostrils with moistened cotton wool swabs. Within minutes he had carefully cleared all the congealed blood and mucous from the damaged organ, and Dusty was beginning to breathe normally.

'Is that better Miller?'

'Ah, that's great doc, I can breathe properly again,' Dusty replied, an edge of gratitude in his voice.

'Right let's have a look at those eyes next.'

He pulled the bottom lid of each eye down gently in turn, and with the thumb of his other hand raised the eyebrow. He gazed carefully into each eye in turn, 'no surface damage there,' he said matter of factly. 'Any headache? Dizziness, or a sensation of feeling sick?'

'Nah, it was only the nose that was bothering me doc, and you seem tuh 'ave put that right.'

LSBA Norton fussed around for a few moments, putting things away, and clearing away the bloodstained cotton wool. He looked around fastidiously, and then, satisfied his sick bay was absolutely clean, sat down at his desk.

'I have to put a note in your medical documents that I administered first aid for fight damage to the face, which occurred ashore.' He looked up at Dusty before continuing. 'Your Divisional Officer, and hence the Captain, will be informed of your condition. You will be called to your Divisional Officer's cabin, and asked to explain how the damage to your person came about. What happened to you was more than a pub brawl, no matter how much you try to play it down, I know you have been involved in a determined fight, I also assume that your opponent is suffering similar damage.'

He paused momentarily. 'Not a man on this ship is unaware of your capabilities, including myself. When a shipmate has the reputation of being a 'hard basterd' but not easily provoked, questions have to be asked. My advice is tell the truth, don't damage your good name by protecting an assailant out of misplaced loyalty. You see everyone knows that you are not the sort who goes looking for trouble. They will also realise that your appearance comes about by a sustained defence of your person. Be prepared for some close questioning, and don't protect someone for what may seem to you "honourable reasons".'

The LSBA finished his gently delivered advice, searching Dusty's face for some indication that his words had got through.

'I can only say it was a fair fight,' Dusty answered, and then without hesitating added, perhaps a little foolishly considering his protective stance, 'we even had two seconds to ensure it was totally fair.'

The LSBA made a mental note of that last statement. 'Okay Miller off you go, but don't forget my advice if you are called to give an account of your appearance.'

'Thanks doc, I'll remember that,' Dusty answered as he opened the sick bay door. LSBA Norton however, sensed little conviction in the reply.

Dusty made his way back to five mess suffering a few remarks from well meaning shipmates. He replied with a nod, or a wave of the hand, and once with a middle finger pointed skywards. Reaching the messdeck he put half a teaspoon of 'Limers' in a mug and added water. It was 1145 hours, and the mess was empty; very soon it would become a hive of activity and conversation as the rum arrived, and trays of food were shared around amongst a clatter of cutlery, plates and aluminium trays. For the time being though, only the noises from above and the hull and fire pump accompanied his thoughts. The complete turnaround in Able Seaman Smith's attitude was uppermost in his mind. He could not force the vision of sincerity in Smith's face out of his mind. Instinctively he knew that his bitterest enemy had become a friend, but the psychology of the matter was beyond his knowledge, so he did not dwell on the matter.

Wiggy came rushing up the gangway at 1155 hours, having just hurriedly vacated a cab. He had thrust some money at the driver who, taking a quick cursory check shouted, 'cheers mate' and stuffed the money in his bag. Obviously the tip was to his liking.

'Yuh wanna see the state of your oppo,' the Quartermaster said as he handed him his station card. ''Ee got a right bloody beltin' last night.'

Wiggy said nothing but hurried forrard. He slid down the ladder into five mess, his eyes making contact with Dusty as he reached the bottom. They gazed silently at each other for a matter of seconds. The horror on Wiggy's face startled Dusty into speaking first. 'Nah, it's not as bad as that Wiggs, this time it's all settled; and Bogey can verify that,' he added, seeing no change in Wiggy's concerned frown.

A foot on the top of the ladder made Wiggy step aside. The rum bosun came down, and nodding said, 'hi Wiggs,' grabbed the rum fanny and galloped up the ladder again. Leading Seaman Wilkinson landed at the bottom of the ladder.

'I'll see you later,' Wiggy said, putting a foot on the bottom rung. It was no place for a private conversation at tot time.

'Second part of starboard watch muster starboard side of the waist,' the tannoy sang out at 1305 hours.

The duty watch was mustered and set to work on essential tasks. A fire exercise would complete the afternoon's work, and then the duty watch would stand down, only being called out for tasks as they were required. Most events would be handled by the duty hands.

After the fire exercise, Petty Officer McHenry approached Dusty, telling him that his Divisional Officer wanted to see him in his cabin.

'Come in,' Lieutenant Branscombe shouted as Petty Officer McHenry knocked on his cabin door.

'Ordinary Seaman Miller to see you sir.'

The cabin was small, so Petty Officer McHenry stood in the passageway leaning through the door.

'Sit down Miller,' Lieutenant Branscombe said, indicating his bunk seat.

'You were involved in a nasty fight last night I am reliably informed, requiring first aid this morning. Is there anything we should know about, anything vindictive on someone's part, are you the victim of some form of vendetta?'

Dusty's face took on a startled expression as the last word was spoken. To him, the word was only known from novels he had read, and more associated with the Mediterranean races than the peoples of the British Isles. To hear the word used to describe this particular incident had connotations of murderous intent; this was not at all how he had envisaged his differences with Able Seaman Smith.

Lieutenant Branscombe noticed the change in expression and pursued the point. 'Let me put it more succinctly Miller; is someone out to get you?'

The emphasis on the 'is' jolted Dusty's mind into action, the lieutenant had spoken in the present tense. 'No sir!' he answered emphatically. 'No one is out to get me. When I was on the *Vanguard* I 'ad a difference with a messmate, we bumped into each other in the Railway Cellars last night, and we sorted it out man to man. No one else was involved in the scrap, just me and the other guy. We've cleared the air, and now it's all over.' He paused for a moment. Lieutenant Branscombe said nothing, but his eyes were judging the veracity of Dusty's words.

'We even shook hands and cleaned up together sir,' Dusty added truthfully.

Lieutenant Branscombe held Dusty's open gaze. 'You say you were the only ones involved in the fight, yet I am informed that there were two men acting as 'seconds'.

'Yes sir, a pal of 'is and a pal of mine. They were not involved; they just looked on to ensure it was a fair fight.'

The Officer looked searchingly at Dusty, tapping his pencil on the desk absently. Dusty's honest reply, without giving anything away impressed him. He could read the depth of his young gunnery rate's loyalty and could not help but admire him for it.

'Very well Miller, that is how I shall explain it to the Captain.' He turned to Petty Officer McHenry. 'Is he able to carry out his duties correctly?'

'Nothing out of the ordinary sir; as ever he showed willing and capable during the fire exercise.'

The Lieutenant began tapping the desk again, and suddenly came to a decision. 'That will be all Miller,' he said abruptly, bringing his enquiry to an end.

Dusty breathed a sigh of relief as he walked the few paces from the cabin flat to the canteen flat, and then down the ladder to five mess. Wiggy was there, sitting at the forrard messdeck table waiting for him. One of the mess had given him a mug of tea, but he had not joined the remainder of those on board at the after messdeck table.

'Hi Wiggs me old mate,' Dusty clapped his pal on the shoulder, adding, 'ang on a mo while I get a cuppa.' He filled his mug, and walked back, plonking himself down beside his pal.

'Did yuh 'ave a good night out?' he asked.

'Better than yours by all appearances,' Wiggy replied, his face showing the strength of his displeasure at seeing his best oppo's iodine mottled face, and sore looking nose. 'Is this due to another meeting with Smith?'

'Aw give us a break Wiggs, I've done nothing but answer fuckin' questions since I came back aboard this morning. First Hooky Wilkinson, then the doc, and I've just come from the DO's cabin after a grillin' by him; now yuh want me tuh go over it all again.'

'If I had done what I should have done in La Spezia, you would not be looking like you do now,' Wiggy went on, ignoring

Dusty's protestations. 'This is not going to end until that barbarian faces the music for bushwhacking you in Gibraltar.'

'Well yer wrong Wiggs, ee even got me into the home club last night. Anyway if yuh don't believe me, ask Bogey. Believe it or not 'im and a bloke called Arthur overlooked the fight to make sure it was fair. Now you know that if everythin' was not right, or if Smith 'ad tried the dirty, Bogey would 'ave torn 'im ter pieces with 'is bare 'ands. As it was, the fight turned out a bloody good draw, and we shook 'ands on the outcome while we were still on our bloody knees. It's over Wiggs, yuh wouldn't recognise the bloke now ee's got whatever it was ee hated about me off his chest.'

Wiggy stared at his pal, disbelief etched in his furrowed brow. He could not believe that his pal was defending the man who had very nearly kicked him to death in Gibraltar. In his forthright, upstanding, and definitely brave outlook on life Wiggy could just not see the fighting dog, battle to the last breath, makeup that some men are imbued with. He could just not understand that a bitterness unresolved is like a canker gnawing at a battler's very soul. It was impossible for him to believe that such evil intent would not raise its ugly head should another similar occurrence happen involving any other guy like Dusty who rubbed Smith up the wrong way.

━━ · ━━

At that very moment, NATO planners decided upon a date on which to commence 'Exercise Biscay'. Commander in Chiefs of all NATO Navies would have their fleets come together in the Atlantic at 0800 hours on the first of April, where they would form a protective shield for a convoy of fifty merchant vessels heading for the supposedly beleaguered Azores. NATO planners had chosen the Azores, not merely out of nostalgic recollection of the last World War, but for the reality that it was an essential fuelling point for western fleets operating in that area of the Atlantic.

The Azores are a colony of Portugal, and during the war Britain had to invoke an old treaty dating back to 1373, because of the neutrality of Portugal at the onset of the war, and her balanced attitude of supplying both belligerents at that time from her vast colonial resources. Dr Antonio de Oliveira Salazar, as a Fascist Dictator had formed a relationship with Nazi Germany due to his support of Franco, the Fascist Dictator of Spain. Portugal still remains Britain's longest standing ally, its neutrality during the Second World War was a matter of expediency due to the might of Nazi Germany. During the First World War Portugal had been one of the first to send 50,000 troops to the front line to back up British and French forces. All of this was well known by the NATO planners, most of whom were veterans of the last war, and it was their duty to ensure that the western world was fully capable of defending itself against any country that was foolish enough to attempt military dominance over any member of a well established organisation. The importance of Portugal and its colonial interests would be of great importance if any belligerent country forced the world into a state of collective war frenzy.

— ∎ —

Simultaneously, on that Saturday morning the two undercover regulators came to hear of a big fight the previous night, involving four navy men. It was in the interests of 'good order and naval discipline' that this fight was investigated; it sounded a bit heavier than the run of the mill weekend punch-ups in Pompey. They could be quickly dealt with, without involving civilian authorities; also, no reports had come in from ships of badly knocked about crewmen, this was mainly because Captains usually dealt with their own domestic problems, and only reported such incidents if the situation warranted it.

A few phone calls ascertained that the police station to the rear of the Guildhall had received a phone call from a private resident at 2100 hours on Friday night, informing them that at that very moment he was watching the fight of the century through his bedroom window. His reason for reporting the fight was 'I am worried that someone returning for their car might get bashed up.'

The two undercover regulators quickly judged that the Railway Cellars was a good place to start their enquiries, so at 1400 hours they strolled into the pub, and ordered two bitter shandies.

'Allo you two,' the Landlord greeted them. 'I 'aven't seen yuh for a while, dockyard keeping yuh busy then?'

'No more than usual,' the undercover man paying for the drinks answered, and then added casually, 'I hear you had a big fight across the road last night me 'andsome.'

'Yeah, I 'ad ter speak out tuh stop it 'appenin' in 'ere; big lad off the *Vigo* looked as if ee was go-in ter 'eave a bloke in civvies out uv the winder, anyway they all fucked off tuh sort it out over the road.'

'Pissy arsed matelots on the Scrumpy eh?' the second regulator asked.

'Nah, that wuz the funny thing abaht it, the lad off the *Barrosa*, and the big lad off the *Vigo* were 'avin a laugh and a chat tergevver like old shipmates. This geezer in civvies oo was drinkin over there in the corner comes over to 'em and says somefin, and the whole bar thought we wuz in fer a right old ding dong, so I 'ad tuh put a stop tuh it sharpish like.'

'Suppose the civvies were matelots out of uniform were they then, got changed into civvies at Aggies?' the first undercover regulator asked conversationally.

'Oh, they wuz definitely matelots out of uniform, and they didn't all troop out tuhgevver. Most of them stayed at that table,' he indicated with a thumb. 'Just two of 'em went aht wiv the two geezers in uniform.'

The two undercover regulators left it at that as the Landlord moved away to serve a customer. They finished their shandies, shouted 'cheerio,' and walked out.

With just that short conversation in the pub, they had enough material to complete their investigation; but for now, their next stop would be Agnes Weston's Royal Sailors Rest.

The ease with which people spoke to them reflected their past. They were both born and bred Portsmouth men, and the way they spoke about naval personnel gave the impression that they were dockyard workers. In other words, they were both ideal candidates for the job they had become so good at.

'Tell you what!' Nobby Clark said to his oppo Jimmy Green. 'You call in at Aggies, and I'll pop into the dockyard and see what I can find out on the *Barrosa*.'

'Okay, good idea Nobby, see you in RNB for tea at four, okay.'

Nobby Clark replied with a thumbs-up sign as he continued up Unicorn Road.

Climbing the gangway, he flashed his ID at the Quartermaster. 'Can I speak to your Coxswain please, or your duty PO if the Coxswain's on weekend.'

The Quartermaster piped, 'Petty Officer McHenry gangway.' Two minutes later a frowning Petty Officer appeared from the after superstructure. He shook hands with the regulator who only asked him to confirm if one of the ship's company had returned aboard showing signs of having been in a fight. Petty Officer McHenry did his duty and answered in the affirmative.

'Sorry I'm in civvies,' Nobby Clark said, noticing the Petty Officer's querying glance. 'I've just come on duty, and they lumbered me with this one. What's the lad's name by the way?'

'Ordinary Seaman Miller,' Petty Officer McHenry answered, and then added, 'he's duty today, nothing wrong with him but a busted nose and a few cuts and bruises. Just an impromptu fist fight apparently; his DO has made a point of seeing him, and was satisfied with his explanation.'

'Thanks, that should clear this one up,' Nobby Clark said, extending his right hand.

He left the ship quite certain that he had tracked down the whereabouts of one of Friday night's battlers. His oppo Jimmy Green, in the meantime, had shown his ID card to the old receptionist in Agnes Weston's as a matter of habit. Without glancing at his ID the old boy said warmly, 'hello there Jimmy, we haven't seen you for ages.'

'Hello George,' Jimmy answered returning the smile, and clasping the proffered hand. 'I am just making a few enquiries about a punch up last night; it seems the sailor was in civvies.'

'Ah yes,' George's eyes flashed with recollection. 'One of our regular customers; he hasn't visited us for a few months,' he rambled on flicking back a page in his book. 'Ah! Here it is. Able

Seaman Smith, he's on the *Corunna* now according to the book. He's paid us for three nights, and will leave at 0700 hours Monday morning.' He turned round to the key rack. 'His key's up there, so he will be out and about somewhere in town. He's a lively bloke you know; but never in the time I have known him has he returned here incapable, and,' he added with emphasis, 'he's never pissed the bed!'

'Thanks George,' Jimmy answered, grinning at the old boy's sincerity.

By 1800 hours that day, the undercover regulators had placed their report on the incident with the duty Regulating Petty Officer at Naval Regulating Headquarters. By 0900 hours on Monday morning a copy of the report was placed on the desk in the office of the Naval Provost at C-in-C Nav Home in Portsmouth Dockyard. One hour later, the Commanding Officers of Her Majesty's Ships *Vigo*, *Barrosa*, and *Corunna* received orders that Ordinary Seaman Knight. R, Ordinary Seaman Miller. P, Able Seaman Smith. R, and Able Seaman Henderson. A, must report to Patrol Headquarters Portsmouth by 1100 hours that morning to answer civilian charges.

The four sailors were taken by Provost Vehicle to the Police Station where they were questioned by an Inspector individually. Ordinary Seaman Knight; and Able Seaman Henderson were dismissed without charge immediately. Able Seaman Smith and Ordinary Seaman Miller were bound over to their Commanding Officers to await charges reduced to 'Disturbing the Peace'. The upright citizen who had reported the fight, and who had watched it from start to finish explained what he had witnessed blow by blow, and was not frightened to admit that to all intents and purposes it was an honourable fight, and had involved no one except those present.

Back on board HMS *Barrosa* that afternoon, Wiggy was in high dudgeon at the injustice heaped on his pal's shoulders. This was the straw that broke the Camel's back. With great determination, and unknown to anyone aboard he started writing an itemised report on the whole affair.

Three days out from Portsmouth, HMS *Barrosa* reached a pre-ordered position well out into the Atlantic to the West of

Cape St Vincent. She had joined the remainder of the squadron, with the exception of HMS *Corunna*, forming a defence line with ten Destroyers and Frigates of other NATO Navies. Each ship had an area to patrol, and were spaced at maximum effective radar range from each other. Any inquisitive surface intruder would have to take a 500 mile sweep out into the Atlantic to escape detection; even then, far-seeing units of the RAF would find them. The Danish, Dutch, and Norwegian Navies had tight control of the North Sea, sweeping out to the North West of Scotland. The British Home Fleet was sniffing along the English Channel, and way out to the West of Ireland, linking up with units of the Scandinavian Navies.

The RFA's *Tidereach* and *Retainer* serviced the line of ships stretching out from Cape St Vincent, steaming the line replenishing each grey ghost they encountered twenty-four hours a day.

The *Tidereach*, carrying 15,000 tons of Furnace Fuel Oil could keep the whole line serviced for the whole two weeks at patrol speed, but bursts of twenty-five knots and above soon drained the tanks of these hunters, so the Royal Fleet Auxiliary Service had to keep other supply vessels on standby constantly.

The Patrol duties continued for three days as Merchant ships mustered along the Northern coast of Spain from San Sebastian to Santander. All these Merchant vessels were now under the command of the C-in-C NATO Fleet, and had to obey NATO Command orders. The British Cruisers *Birmingham*, *Kenya*, *Jamaica*, *Bermuda* and *Sheffield*, would each lead ten Merchant ships in a huge square formation out of the Bay of Biscay, and out into the Atlantic. These five Cruisers would be expected to have their ten trailing Merchant ships well to the West of Cape Finisterre by 2200 hours on 2nd April. The real job of protecting such a widely separated group of ships could then begin in earnest for all smaller ships with Anti Submarine capabilities.

At night all the ships would be darkened, relying totally on Radar as the all-seeing-eye above the waves, and the alertness of lookouts seeking shadowy shapes against the sky line; an almost impossible task requiring total concentration. Sonar operators would be carrying out continuous sweeps in the hopes of bouncing a ping off some underwater interloper, which in this case would be selected NATO Submarines designated the task of being the enemy in this major Naval Exercise.

Every ship commander was hoping that somewhere out there was a very advanced underwater attack vessel that would give them a chance to be the first Anti Submarine surface vessel to make contact. Jolly Jack, on the whole would not be aware of their Commanding Officers' prime ambition during this huge exercise; but TAS Officers and TAS senior rates would be burning with the desire to be the first Sonar Ops Room crew to make contact with this presumed Russian opponent.

The three destroyers of the Fourth Destroyer Squadron, and their ten allied vessels swept slowly Northwards as the 1st April approached. The Scandinavian Navies swept southwards and joined up with the British Home Fleet, and spread westwards, line abreast across the Atlantic. By the time the five British Cruisers had their charges in orderly convoy to the West of Cape Finisterre, they were surrounded by a ring of steel the size of which had not been seen since the last World War, and a lot of sea room was necessary for all ships' Captains to get used to Station Keeping in a situation that only a few of them had been a part of before.

Dawn broke on the Wednesday with an air attack by Meteors and Vampire jets of the Royal Air Force. A squadron of Sea Vixens off HMS *Eagle* was also the enemy for this dawn attack. When they had finished roaring overhead being tracked by every Gun Directors crew, and hence every Guns Crew, all ships gunnery rates were given a chance to show their skill when an RAF *Shackleton* droned overhead towing a drogue. It took a long sweep around the convoy giving every warship a chance to demolish the drogue. Normally a bit of 'aim off' would be applied to gun control transmitters and receivers so as not to unnecessarily damage the drogue, but for this important exercise every guns crew were allowed to go for it. Two hours later the crew of *Barrosa*'s Multiple Bofors Anti Aircraft Mounting was delightedly painting the shape of a drogue onto their gun casing having reduced the drogue to shreds. First blood to the Fourth Destroyer Squadron got a 'well done *Barrosa*,' signalled from *Agincourt*.

Suddenly the euphoria aboard *Barrosa* was forgotten as HMS *Alamein* made contact with a Submarine. From the front of the southern line of warships she swung inwards, steering by Asdics as she maintained contact with an underwater target keeping a steady eight knots towards the centre of the convoy. An American Destroyer quickly appeared off *Alamein*'s port beam, speedily followed by another off her starboard beam, all three maintaining contact. The Gunners party Able Seaman of the watch aboard *Alamein* obeyed his Captain's order, and informed the Submarine Commander by hand grenade that he was nobbled, and his attack had failed. Two hours later three Submarines were on the surface at the rear of the convoy, all of them sunk attempting to get at a Merchantman.

First contact was a major part of the exercise. Any Submarine penetrating the ring of Anti-Submarine Vessels and getting close to the convoy would surface when safe to do so, and make his success known. It was a dangerous game they played down there, so safety was of paramount importance. If any Submarine was caught, the Sub Commander was very limited in the extent of diversionary tactics he could employ.

Later that day, to hearty congratulations from Captain 'D', HMS *Corunna* took station astern of Barrosa in the ring of steel protecting the convoy.

'Yeoman,' Commander Plowright called. 'Make to *Corunna*: "nice of you to make up a four again!"'

The Yeoman grinned as he jotted down the message; he was a man who had learnt to enjoy the dry humour of Naval Captains.

Lieutenant Ross, the Navigating Officer appeared by his Captain's side. 'The Glass has been dropping all day sir,' he advised.

Commander Plowright looked at the Barometric Pressure column in the Ship's Log. 'Looks like we're in for a blow Pilot, some rain with it as well,' he said, glancing skywards out of force of habit.

Far to the west, inky looking cloud definitely foretold rain, but overhead, and to the east the lighter, sharper edged clouds indicated possible windy conditions. By the time the Middle Watchmen mustered at 1150 hours that night his forecast proved right with a blustery force eight blowing, making all ships'

Commanders double lookouts; Captains of vessels would get very little sleep this night.

By morning the weather front had passed over, but Navigating Officers and their Captains did not hold their breath. This area of the Atlantic between the 'Variables of Cancer' and the 'Westerlys' suffers constant depressions, and very windy conditions, just below Latitude forty degrees north.

The convoy continued to plough along at ten knots, and some of the Merchant ship Captains were beginning to get frustrated by the caution of NATO command. They had expected to see action on a near wartime footing, having been taken so far from their normal sea-lanes. The Admiral of the Fleet aboard the USS *Saratoga* was well aware of the frustration of a few of his less patient Merchant Ship Captains, and continued to re-assure them of the vital need for their presence; but truthfully, not one of the Merchant captains was privy to any planning going on aboard the mighty *Saratoga*. All they were required to do was plod along behind their leading cruiser, and leave everything else to the NATO navies.

By Sunday 7th April, the weather was still variable, and did not drop below force six. Suddenly a dull boom echoed over the turbulent sea from the south western end of the convoy. Every pair of hands that held binoculars swung towards the dull sound just in time to see a pall of black smoke and gushing steam appear above HMS *Alamein*. The Yeoman of Signals aboard *Barrosa* yelled out 'Flag D sir,' whilst keeping his binoculars on *Alamein*'s flagdeck. 'Flag F just hoisted sir; she is manoeuvring with difficulty and requires assistance.'

Almost immediately the two American Destroyers closest to the *Alamein* came alongside her port and starboard beam at 200 feet. *Alamein* was under way again, but without her forrard boiler room. Some minutes later it became clear what had happened aboard, as signals were passed to USS *Saratoga*, and to Captain 'D' of the Fourth Destroyer Squadron.

The Forrard boiler had blown completely; most of the blast of superheated steam had passed upwards and outwards. The blackened faces of the boiler room crew as they scrambled out of the airlock chased by a cloud of soot and brick dust showed how closely they had come to annihilation. The POME of the watch was last out of the airlock, and without hesitation checked his men, breathing a loud sigh of relief to find them all present. He slammed the airlock lid shut and the vacated boiler room was immediately steam drenched to avert the danger of a fire with fuel oil still dribbling from inserted burners.

With black smoke whirling above her, showing that her second boiler had a good fire under it *Alamein* got to work again, and the two American Destroyers veered away and took up their positions in the ring of steel again, their Captains waving an appreciative acknowledgement of the determination of the *Alamein*'s Captain to bring his ship back up to battle readiness regardless of the partial disablement of his ship. One hour later, after a direct order from the Fleet Commander and his Captain 'D', the Captain of HMS *Alamein* grudgingly swung his ship away from the convoy and made course for Gibraltar, never to rejoin her three sister ships again.

The weather eased a little below force six that Sunday night, allowing the C-in-C NATO Fleet to start Submarine attacks again. HMS *Barrosa* found herself on the inner ring of defence, with *Agincourt* to the southeast, and *Corunna* a mile to the northeast, in the outer ring of defence against Submarine attack. All ships had now reverted from three watches to the four watch system, the main attention being on Anti Submarine Warfare.

At 2355 hours that night, the second part of starboard watch on HMS *Barrosa* mustered in the galley flat for the middle watch. Dusty Miller found himself detailed off for the second two hours of Lifebuoy Sentry from 0200 hours until 0400 hours. This meant that he could while away the first two hours of the middle watch keeping himself busy doing one of the favoured pastimes generally reserved for watch on deck hours. He declined making up a four for cards, and sat among the older Able Seamen doing their knitting, fancy ropework, or rug or mat making, and opened his Seamanship Manual volume two 1951. He and Wiggy would be sitting an oral exam prior to getting their Able Seaman's rate in early May. They were both well aware of the fact that a man could be a brilliant able bodied sailor, but if you could not answer the questions in the book, you could kiss goodbye to any advancement until you were competent in theoretical knowledge as well as your skill of hand as a sailor. Both of them had achieved maximum early advancement upon leaving training with above average marks.

At 0155 hours Dusty closed his book, drained his mug of KI, and readied himself to relieve Wiggy as Lifebuoy Ghost. He went through the port screen door onto the weather deck, and ignoring the wind howling through the radial davits and stays of the motor cutter grabbed a lifeline and staggered his way towards the Quarterdeck.

■■ · ■■

At that very moment, Able Seaman Smith aboard the *Corunna*, unable to sleep due to the change of watch systems, strolled out onto the upper deck to have a smoke in the fresh air. The corner provided by the break of the Fxle where it joined the weather deck port side, had a nice angled corner sheltered from the weather. A man could stand under the bow of the motor cutter, just where the guardrail was shackled to the metal rise, and have a quiet smoke whilst gazing out on a stroppy sea. He was just finishing his smoke when the ship suddenly heeled over increasing speed as she did so.

'Another fuckin' sub,' he muttered, reaching out for the guardrail to retain his balance.

■■ · ■■

'Off you go Wiggs, it's my turn on the arse end now,' Dusty called jovially to his pal.

Wiggy nodded his appreciation, 'And you're bloody welcome to it,' he shouted back. 'See you for breakfast later.'

Dusty rang the Bridge, and carried out alarm tests in accordance with the rules, and then settled down to the two hours of vigilance that was ahead of him. The ship had not been fully darkened, but all unnecessary lights had been extinguished, and all deadlights were down. The odd wave or two leapt over the Quarterdeck to disappear down the scuppers just as quickly. The wind was blustery but warm, but that did not bother Dusty, tucked into the starboard corner of the superstructure where it joined the Quarterdeck. Clad as he was in seaboot stockings, number eights with seaman's jersey, and his half inflated lifejacket hanging loosely over that, he felt quite warm. Gazing around him he could only see the white tops of the nearest waves passing sternwards, and the white path made by the wake as the stern rose and fell. The rumble of the two propellers below him reminded him of his time in ten mess; before his part of ship change to Fxleman. His thoughts turned to Christine, and a pang of regret flashed through his brain as he recalled his feelings upon finding she was on advanced Easter leave.

'Hope she liked the prezzy I left 'er,' he muttered out loud, remembering the look on Jane's face as he left it with her. 'Wonder why no bugger's trapped 'er?' he mused out loud. 'Nice girl, likes a bit of fun…doesn't drop 'em for just any old sailor,' he grinned.

The ship heeled over violently, causing him to look over the starboard quarter. ''Ere we go,' he muttered. 'Another fuckin' sub!' His face suddenly paled, and for a second he was rooted to the spot. 'Jesus H Christ!' he blasphemed as his limbs unfroze and burst into action.

Five minutes earlier, the UC2 sonar operator carrying out regular sweeps with his sonar aboard HMS *Corunna* picked up an echo coming towards his ship from starboard. He held the contact immediately, and reported it to the Bridge. Seconds later he shouted incredulously, 'It's passing under us at twenty knots!'

'Port thirty!' the Officer of the Watch yelled down the conning microphone, and before the reply reached him, he ordered frantically, 'steer by asdics!'

The Quartermaster carried out his orders hastily, using the wheel to steady the ship as it overreacted to rudder and weather. Meanwhile the Officer of the Watch had gabbled down the voicepipe to his Captain's sea cabin that they were chasing the phantom Russian Submarine.

'Closing on ship dead ahead sir,' the port lookout shouted loudly.

The Officer of the Watch reacted by struggling to gaze into his radar screen.

'Closing rapidly sir…dead ahead,' the lookout screamed.

—— · ——

Lieutenant Brown, the TASO, was Officer of the Watch aboard *Barrosa*, and was carrying out a sweep to starboard with his binoculars. He saw the *Corunna* bearing down on his ship just as the starboard lookout screamed, 'ship bearing green four five sir!'

'HARD APORT!' the TASO yelled down to the wheelhouse.

The ship reacted instantly to the frantically applied wheel, and heeled over as the stern swung to starboard.

Dusty started moving just as the bow of HMS *Corunna* loomed over him. She rammed HMS *Barrosa* on the starboard stern quarter sending *Barrosa* heeling over sixty degrees to port. The last thing Dusty heard before his head met with a guardrail stanchion as he was thrown into the sea over the port side was the strangled squealing of buckling metal, and the loud popping of rivets as *Corunna*'s bow was pushed backwards right up to the paintshop hatch. As *Corunna* fell back away from the horrendously damaged stern part of HMS *Barrosa*, her cable deck fell over the enormous gap completely covering it, held in place by the anchor cables, as the bullring became immersed in water.

—— · ——

The Captain of HMS *Corunna* was hurled roughly to the deck as he struggled to reach his bridge.

—— · ——

Commander Plowright was thrown to the deck of his sea cabin as he vacated his bunk.

Every one below decks on *Barrosa* was rudely awakened to the certain fact that this was the end. All messes on the port side were suddenly deluged by the movement of tables, seat cushions and benches, the contents of lockers and cupboards, and a mass of bodies as everything that could not stay put in a sixty degree roll came to rest up the ship's side of the port hull.

— · —

As the *Corunna* heeled over force of habit made Able Seaman Smith feel for the pudding at his midriff that was his lifebelt. Minutes later he felt a huge shudder, and the front end of the ship seemed to lift unnaturally. He suddenly found himself thrown into the water so abruptly that he was not aware of a glancing blow to the head as he was thrown beneath the keel of the Motor Cutter. His arms automatically took on a swimming motion, and as his head began to clear he realised that he must open the pouch and get his lifejacket over his head. Treading water, he pulled the neck hole over his head, and inserted the nozzle between his lips. He had not noticed it in his panic to stay afloat, but the wind and the waves had swept him away from his ship. Her movement astern on both engines took her further away, but noticing that his lamp worked brought a sigh of relief from his lips. Patting the place where his whistle should be, he found that it was not there, so he continued inflating his lifejacket until he felt the comforting tightness around his neck. Something bumped him. 'Oh Christ – Shark!' he gasped out loud, and then terror took charge as he began flailing the water wildly with both arms. Twice his hand struck something, and then his light showed him a tangled mass of hair bobbing in the water. His terror subsided as he grasped the hair and pulled the head closer. His lips parted, still showing the effects of the fight. The gasp that issued from his lips this time was not brought on by sheer terror, but astonishment. 'Jesus Christ! It's you, Dusty Miller,' he choked. His surprised statement made him swallow a mouthful of Atlantic Ocean, but even though coughing and spluttering, he hauled Dusty's head up to the ring of his lifejacket. Unable to discern if this was a dead man he held, he shook Dusty, and then tried to angle his ear to Dusty's mouth. A slight groan emitted from the unconscious body, so he scrabbled desperately at the front of Dusty's lifejacket searching for the whistle slot. He found it, pulled the whistle free, and started blowing frantically.

Two things happened at this moment which were of distinct advantage to both men in the water. HMS *Birmingham* had been ordered to leave her position and race to the assistance of the Fourth Destroyer Squadron. She arrived on the scene sweeping the immediate area with her twenty-one inch searchlight. No one knew at this precise moment if there had been any casualties, but the ships' companies of both the *Barossa* and the *Corunna* were being mustered at Emergency Stations, and the Chief Shipwright of *Barossa* already had a team of Stokers shoring up the stern bulkhead in the watchkeeper's mess aft. Carley Floats had been slipped overboard by both damaged vessels in preparation for abandoning ship, and all boats were made ready. The watch on deck was turning out the Cutter, and the crew was aboard ready to be dropped into a force six sea. Everybody was so frantically busy preparing for the worst that not an iota of fear was shown by any man. Wiggy Bennett, having been involved in slipping the Carley Floats reported back to Petty Officer McHenry and asked, 'Has anybody seen Dusty? He was lifebuoy ghost.'

Petty Officer McHenry paled suddenly. 'Wilky!' He shouted at his Leading Hand, who was still mustering Fxlemen. 'Ave yuh seen Ordinary Seaman Miller?'

'No I 'aven't, and ee isn't amongst this lot 'ere. Knowin 'im ee's probably still at 'is post.'

■ ▪ ■

At that moment a keen lookout aboard the *Birmingham* shouted, 'green three zero, bodies in the water.'

The burning carbon rods in the searchlight lit up the scene like a mini sun, and minutes later a brave swimmer on a line took Dusty away from Able Seaman Smith and he was hauled quickly aboard HMS *Birmingham*. The seamen on deck immediately started resuscitation.

Able Seaman Smith was hauled inboard, and stood watching intently as a Leading Hand continued trying to resuscitate his old enemy. Now, all he could see in front of him was a fellow sailor, who like himself had suddenly fallen victim to one of the hazards of the sea when ships are acting in close proximity to one another. Looking at Dusty lying there inert, he suddenly yelled frantically, 'NAH! Ee…can't…go…that…fuckin'…way!'

One of the hands on deck touched his right arm. 'Come on mate,' he said gently, beginning to steer Smith away from the scene.

Able Seaman Smith shrugged off the kindly arm roughly. 'TRY THAT NEW SYSTEM,' he yelled, now almost incoherent. 'STOP FUCKIN' ABAHT WIV 'IS ARMS; GIVE 'IM THE KISS OF LIFE!' He shook off the arms that grasped at him, and lunged forward. Everybody gasped as he pinched Dusty's nose between thumb and forefinger, put the other hand under his neck, and clamped his lips on Dusty's mouth. He breathed into Dusty, and then paused looking sideways at his chest. He breathed in to him again…and then again. 'Come on yuh cunt, breave yuh barsterd breave.' He gave a few more blows, and suddenly Dusty's chest quivered and water oozed from the sides of his mouth. Strong arms grasped Able Seaman Smith and lifted him to his feet. 'Come on mate,' a firm voice said. 'Let the doc 'ave a go now.'

The Medical Officer of HMS *Birmingham* leant over Dusty's inert form, probing with his stethoscope, and two SBAs stood ready with a stretcher.

'Get him to the sick bay immediately,' the Doctor said tersely, and then turning to Smith said, 'well done young man, your determined intervention worked, he has a good heartbeat, now let's concentrate on getting the rest of the water out of his lungs.'

Able Seaman Smith stared after the retreating Medical Officer, his face alight with relief. 'Thank fuck fer that,' he said his eyes closing as his head tilted backwards slightly; almost as if giving thanks he whispered, 'yuh were on my side fer once!'

The Medical Officer stopped suddenly, and turned back to face Smith once again. 'What's your name?' he asked bluntly.

'Able Seaman Smith sir.'

'And your ship?'

'HMS *Corunna*.'

The Medical Officer pulled a notebook out of the top pocket of his white coat, and jotted the details down. He paused for a moment to call back one of the seaman not actually involved with the stretcher party, and then turned back to Smith.

'What's your friends' name?'

'Ordinary Seaman Miller sir; and ee's off the *Barrosa*.'

The Medical Officer looked puzzled for a second, and was about to ask the obvious question; but then he continued writing and, tearing the sheet off his notebook, passed it to the seaman saying, 'get up to the bridge with this, and tell the Captain both men are alive, but Ordinary Seaman Miller requires further attention.'

The Seaman dashed away, and Able Seaman Smith followed the Officer through the screen door.

'Tell me Smith,' the Medical Officer finally asked. 'How do you, off *Corunna*, find yourself rescuing a man off the *Barrosa*?'

Able Seaman Smith shrugged his shoulders as he answered truthfully, 'we just bumped into each uver out there sir.'

'How very fortunate for Miller, he would not have survived without what appears to be a divine intervention.'

A puzzled expression flicked across Smith's features as the Doctor's words sank in; but he kept his puzzlement to himself and followed the Medical Officer to the Sick Bay.

8

ROUGH PASSAGE TO GIBRALTAR

With four men handling the stretcher, the still partially concussed Ordinary Seaman was aware of being lifted and manhandled from the upper deck of HMS *Birmingham*. Getting four men and a stretcher through the screen door from the upper deck into the superstructure was awkward. The roll of the ship was affecting the balance of the stretcher bearers, as they tried to keep their charge steady. They passed through a series of bulkhead doors, and all the time Dusty was aware of clips being banged over, and then closed again after the group had passed through. They paused, and he felt the sensation of being raised and then lowered again, the straps were released and then gentle hands began to work on him. He spluttered as the remainder of the water began to dribble through his lips.

'Good job he was fully knocked out,' he heard an educated voice say, and then add, 'otherwise he could have taken in a lot more water.'

'Bad crack on the head sir,' another voice joined in.

Dusty felt fingers working gently on the back of his head as the blood matted hair was drawn to one side. He felt the wet swab cleaning the surface of his scalp.

'Old scar tissue here sir,' the second voice spoke again. 'This crack on the head has elongated another wound.'

'Is ee goin' ter be okay?' He recognised the voice of Able Seaman Smith.

'He will pull through alright,' the educated voice stated firmly, and then ordered, 'one of you chaps take this sailor to a bathroom so that he can get cleaned up and into something dry.'

The voice of the Medical Officer took on a different tone as he turned back to Able Seaman Smith. 'You probably saved your friend's life with your prompt action young man, you push off now there's a fine fellow, it's our turn to do our best for him. You have a bath and a mug of tea, we'll let you know when you can see your friend again.'

Dusty felt a firm hand rest on his shoulder as he turned and said to Dusty, 'see yuh mate, yuh do as yer told, yer lookin' an 'undred percent better awready.'

— · —

As the drama was being played out in the sick bay of HMS *Birmingham*, command decisions were being made as a result of the horrendous ramming of HMS *Barrosa*. The Fleet Destroyer had sustained severe stern damage resulting in a thirty degree list to port. This was partially affected by the Chief Stoker transferring liquids from the starboard side to relieve some of the pressure on the shoring up aft, which had been achieved by the Chief Shipwright and his damage control party.

Daylight came, and showed the full extent of the damage sustained by both Destroyers. *Corunna* could not proceed forward through the water due to the massive bow damage; she could however manoeuvre steaming astern. HMS *Barrosa* had a Tiller Flat that was a tangled mass of metal on the starboard side. She could steer by main engines though; fortunately the ramming action had not reached the starboard propeller; its 'A' bracket and bearing were also untouched.

HMS *Birmingham* and HMS *Agincourt* were ordered by C-in-C Fleet to escort the two severely damaged vessels into Gibraltar Harbour some 500 sea miles east by south. By 1000 hours that day the strange sight of a severely listing *Barrosa* leading an astern steaming *Corunna* on an easterly course was gazed upon by each ship of the NATO Fleet as they steamed past the damaged vessels, sirens screaming loud encouragement, and all hands on decks roaring their farewell in typical seamanlike manner.

The escort vessels took up position port and starboard side of the stricken destroyers as the mighty *Saratoga* veered away having voiced her farewell. Exercise Biscay would continue, but without any representative ship of the Fourth Destroyer Squadron. Somewhere out there a Russian Submarine Commander was probably gazing at the scene, perhaps not wholly aware that he was responsible for the awesome sight that met his eyes.

With the NATO Fleet disappearing astern, the Commanders of the two destroyers concentrated on steaming a course of 102 degrees as best they could. Commander Plowright had all his bridge watchkeeping officers around him as he put rarely used knowledge practiced during work-up to the test; the exercise however was rarely used to the extent that was called for at present. All Seaman Officers were about to gain an intense experience that would stay with them forever. Engine Room watchkeepers would be kept on their toes adjusting engine revolutions to the starboard engine only.

The force six gale had not abated, so at this stage of the passage to Gibraltar *Barrosa* was veering widely around a course of 102 degrees. *Corunna*, astern of her, was coping somewhat better even though steaming astern.

Stationed either side of their charges, HMS *Birmingham* to port, and HMS *Agincourt* to starboard, shepherded the two Destroyers from a distance. A flashing Aldis Lantern from the Bridge of the Cruiser stirred *Barrosa*'s Signalman of the Watch into action. Minutes later the Yeoman of Signals approached his Captain with the message sheet.

'Take the con number one,' Commander Plowright ordered, turning to his First Lieutenant. He stepped from the Binnacle and took the proffered message sheet from his Yeoman of Signals. His features showed a momentary sign of relief, followed a moment later by a hint of surprise that flickered in his eyes. 'Thank you Yeoman,' he said simply. 'Reply, "welcome news; thank your medical staff for their efforts".'

With the message sheet still in his hand he turned to the Bridge Messenger. 'Ordinary Seaman Groves,' he beckoned as he called the young sailor's name. 'Pop down to the Fxle and tell Petty Officer McHenry that I would like a word with Ordinary Seaman Bennett.'

305

Minutes later Wiggy Bennett stood respectfully in front of his Commanding Officer.

'At ease Bennett; I thought you might like to see this follow on to the signal from *Birmingham* earlier, before I announce the good news to the ship's company.'

Wiggy cast his tired eyes over the message sheet. His features left his Captain in no doubt as to the intense relief he felt at learning that his best friend had fully recovered. 'Absolutely excellent news sir, but the signal earlier this morning said nothing about Able Seaman Smith off the *Corunna* being his rescuer. I find that a little confusing; how on earth does a man off the *Corunna*, particularly this man, become the rescuer of a man off the *Barossa*?'

'My thoughts exactly,' the Captain replied. 'No doubt the full truth will come to light as soon as we enter Gibraltar, and it will probably coincide with Smith's arrest for his past crimes against your shipmate. Turn up for the books eh, Bennett. Bound to confuse the outcome of the whole affair.' Commander Plowright looked directly into the eyes of his young subordinate and said seriously, 'Do not let this outcome divert your thoughts. The report that you initiated on past actions concerning Able Seaman Smith showed great awareness of where your duties lie. The fact has been noted, and when you are called to substantiate the contents of your report you must do so with the same sense of purpose as when the report was presented to me.' Commander Plowright paused momentarily, and his frown changed to a light smile. 'Enjoy your make and mend today; you look in need of a good kip.'

'Thank you sir,' Wiggy said simply.

'Off you go then Bennett.'

'How are you finding it number one?' Commander Plowright asked his First Lieutenant, returning to the conning platform.

'I believe I have the measure of it sir,' the First Lieutenant replied light heartedly. 'At least I haven't gone round in a complete circle.'

A brief burst of short laughs met his remark, its delivery having the effect of relieving the tension among the junior officers around the Binnacle. Their turn would come, and the

First Lieutenant had set the mood. Just like him, they would not be perfect at conning the ship without the rudder, until they had practiced the art of anticipation.

Commander Plowright grinned through his tiredness. 'I will leave you with it Number One; I think I had better address the Ship's Company before the buzz mongers have a chance to practice their inventiveness.'

He had made no preparatory notes, so his speech would be short and to the point at this stage. He knew no more about the future of his command than the crew he was about to speak to. Gripping the rubber microphone in his right hand, he moved away from the officers surrounding the Binnacle, the spring coiled cable allowed him to walk to the starboard Bridge Screen, and rest his elbow atop of it. Staring sternwards at the winding pattern of the ship's wake, he thought for a few moments. Finally he brought the microphone up to his face and clicked the encased button.

'D'ye hear there, Captain speaking,' he started firmly, and then paused shortly knowing that below decks the crew would be collecting round the nearest ship's broadcast speaker. 'Firstly, I would like to inform you that Ordinary Seaman Miller has responded well to treatment, and is making a complete recovery.'

A loud cheer echoed through the ship as the men reacted to the good news.

'Apparently he was saved from drowning by an Able Seaman Smith off HMS *Corunna*, exactly how this came about we don't know, but no doubt the truth will come to light when we arrive at Gibraltar.' He paused for a moment collecting his thoughts. 'I have no doubt that as soon as we enter harbour we shall be straight into dry dock, and we shall all find ourselves in dockside accommodation, beyond that I cannot hazard a guess as to what the future may hold for us as a ship's company, although I sincerely hope that we shall be quickly repaired and allowed to complete this commission. As far as the dramatic events of the early hours of this morning are concerned I commend every one of you for the fearless way you reacted to a dire emergency. In particular, the damage control party did all that could be expected of them, and that is why we are staggering towards Gibraltar in our own ship rather than as survivors on another ship. Well done all of you, I am proud to be your Captain.' He paused again and then ended his speech with a strong, 'That is all,' in the traditional manner of all ships' commanders.

Commander Plowright knew his speech had pleased his men, jolly jack is never backward when voicing approval, and likewise, never short of suitable adjectives when not approving. The roars that escaped from screen doors and hatches told him he had been well received. His tired and lined face reflected his inner pleasure at the response of his men. Turning towards the conning platform once more he replaced the microphone, and became aware of the Supply Officer Lieutenant Darwin hovering as if to catch his attention at an appropriate moment.

'Can I help you Freddy?' he asked, noticing the worried expression his Supply Officer carried.

Lieutenant Darwin looked relieved that his Captain had afforded him some attention amongst all his other pressures.

'It's the rum room sir; as a result of the ramming it is flooded to the deckhead. I have only enough rum in the Victualling Office for the Senior Rates. Do you think we could ask Captain 'D' to help out?'

'Good Lord! Yes certainly!' Commander Plowright reacted loudly, turning towards the Flag deck as he spoke.

'Yoeman,' he called loudly.

The Yeoman of Signals hurried across and stood obediently in front of his Captain.

'How much do you want for three days' issues Freddy?' Commander Plowright asked.

Lieutenant Darwin had come prepared. '660 tots sir; that is ten gallons, two and 4/8ths pints. We have one gallon in the office so ten gallons will suffice,' he answered.

'Did you get that Yeoman?' Commander Plowright asked.

'Yes sir,' the Yeoman replied.

'Then make to *Agincourt*, "Rum Room pranged, can you help with ten gallons of Nelson's Blood to see us through to Gibraltar".'

Fifteen minutes later the Executive Officer of HMS *Agincourt* brought the Destroyer to within a hundred feet of the *Barossa* and the two ships steamed line abreast for a while practicing station keeping. When happy with the situation *Agincourt*'s Executive Officer edged a little closer, and the Coston Gun Line heralded the start of a hurriedly but efficiently carried out Heaving Line transfer. Five passes of two one-gallon rum jars later, and the lines were retrieved by the *Agincourt*. The Executive Officer immediately veered his ship away, no doubt very relieved that the transfer had been achieved without problem whilst he was under the watchful eye of Captain 'D'. No doubt several rum rats below decks on the *Barossa* breathed their own sigh of relief. Their God Dionysus had served his followers well this day, even though they were not aware of his mythical existence.

Poseidon however had no such feelings for earthly beings that traversed his domain. As 1400 hours approached that afternoon the glass dropped, and the wind rose sharply to force eight with gusts of sixty knots. HMS *Barossa*'s reaction was to yaw heavily as she corkscrewed to the effects of a stern sea. The thirty degree list to port became forty-five degrees as the stern rose to fifteen foot plus waves, and then lurched back as each successive wave passed the break of the Fxle.

Commander Plowright had been on his Bridge for twelve hours. His Steward had kept him supplied with food and drink which he had eaten without ceremony whilst staying on the job. On completion of the heaving line transfer he had ordered his First Lieutenant to get turned in. 'One of us must be on the Bridge at all times,' he had added.

Half a sea mile astern, HMS *Corunna* had a dire problem. The force eight gale driving at them from the west was lifting the drooping bow section with the action of each wave, and then letting it clang back against the Paintshop bulkhead dangerously. If this was allowed to continue it was possible that the Paintshop bulkhead could be breeched allowing the sea to engulf another section of the ship, namely, one and two messdeck.

Captain 'D' reacted to his junior commander's worried signal by bringing his ship close enough to get a first hand view of what was happening at the fore end of the *Corunna*. He stared at the awesome sight through his binoculars allowing an idea to formulate in his mind. Not wishing to delay entry into Gibraltar by heaving to and weathering the storm, he reached a decision that although dangerous to carry out, would facilitate the continuance of the passage if totally successful.

'I'm off down the WT Office to speak to *Corunna*,' he informed his Executive Officer. 'I think I may have a way to keep her moving.'

Thirty minutes later *Corunna* had swung her bow round to face east. Using her engines to good effect she kept the main force of the weather away from her damaged bow. HMS *Birmingham* put herself across the stern of *Corunna* at a safe distance, whilst Captain 'D' laid off her starboard side where he could watch his idea take form.

A Ship's Diver appeared on the Fxle of HMS *Corunna* fully dressed in a rubber suit but minus air bottles and flippers. All men of the Fxle part of ship were on deck, and a berthing hawser was laid out along what remained of the cable deck, and sternwards to the break of the Fxle. All attention now turned to the Ship's Diver. The brave Leading Seaman had volunteered to climb down the hanging bow to the Bullring, where he could pass a heaving line through the Bullring and bend it onto another one being suspended from what remained of the deck above. With a safety line around his waist, and three seamen backing it up, he descended the hanging bow using the guardrail stanchions like rungs of a ladder. He had to pause frequently to steady himself due to the movement of the ship, as the waves sweeping underneath caused her to rise and fall. This was causing the bow section to rise, and then clang back into place dangerously. The point at which the overhang was still attached just in front of the Capstans was beginning to show cracks where the motion of the sea raising and lowering the overhang gave it a hinge-like effect.

The diver reached the Bullring, while the three Seamen up above only allowed him enough slack to carry out his task. He waited for a wave to pass beneath and then quickly passed the end of his heaving line through the Bullring. He paused again, holding on with both hands. Then, as the ship descended again into a trough he bent the two heaving lines together. With both hands now free he adjusted his position at the bottom of the overhang, and began the climb back again. Suddenly the bow section reared upwards reacting to a thirty foot wave passing underneath making him cling on tenaciously. The suddenness of the action left the diver with two choices: hang on and possibly be crushed to death as the overhang fell into place again, or make a jump for it. He sensibly chose the latter, and heaved himself into the trough of the passing wave. Four more Fxlemen made a grab for the safety line, and he was quickly and unceremoniously hauled up the ship's side and onto the deck before the next wave could sweep him back into danger. Then, as if it was an everyday event, the seven sailors cast down the safety line, leaving the diver to release himself from the Bowline Knot, while they turned their attention to the berthing hawser.

The berthing hawser was hauled through the Bullring, and as soon as all the slack was taken up three turns were thrown around the port Capstan Barrel. The Chief Stoker reacted to the orders of the Fxle Officer and turned his 'T' handle to start the Capstan. The overhanging bow grated and screeched as the torn metal was forced to mate together by the berthing hawser. The Fxle Officer yelled 'vast heaving' and the men backing up the hawser immediately belayed it to the port Bollards. With no further ado *Corunna* completed a 180 degree turn to point her stern eastwards again, and proceed stern first towards Gibraltar once more.

Captain 'D' signalled HMS *Corunna*, commending her crew for an excellently performed action, adding that a citation for meritorious service should be added to the diver's papers.

— ∙ —

The westerly did not abate as the four vessels continued their passage east by south at a sedate eight knots. Three days after the ramming, the damaged Destroyers and their escorts were met in the Gulf of Cadiz by the duty guard boat and two seagoing tugs. Relieved of her duty, HMS *Agincourt* signalled farewell and headed back to the NATO Fleet to take up her duties once more.

Both the *Barrosa* and the *Corunna* entered Gibraltar Harbour firmly strapped to a Tugboat. *Barrosa* was immediately shunted into a drydock which had been made ready for her. *Corunna* meanwhile was ignominiously berthed to the Coaling Jetty breakwater, well away from prying eyes until her future was decided. Before the day was out, HMS *Barrosa* was sitting high and dry on the blocks with water cascading from her damaged compartments aft.

The whole of Gibraltar had turned out to gape at the damaged Destroyers; the road above the harbour was crammed with gaping onlookers waiting to see a sight that had not been witnessed in Gibraltar since World War Two. The shocking news of the near loss of the two Destroyers was front page news in Great Britain, and the Ministry of Defence quickly reassured the British nation that no sailors had lost their lives.

HMS *Birmingham* berthed alongside the Tower, and as soon as the gangway had been rigged four Naval Regulators walked smartly aboard, saluted, and introduced themselves to the Officer of the Day. Twenty minutes later they descended the Gangway with Able Seaman Smith handcuffed between two of the Patrolmen. They climbed through the side door of a Utility Van, and sped away out of the Dockyard towards HMS *Rooke*.

Looking particularly diminutive seated between the huge figure of Frankenstein, and his colleague Fred, Able Seaman Smith sat in silent contemplation.

'So I was right then? You are a bushwhackin basterd,' Frankenstein broke the silence. 'Bit of a weird git though aren't yuh. Christmas sees yer kickin' shit out uv a bloke, and Spring sees yer savin' the same bloke's life at sea in filthy bloody weather. That's a turn up for the books innit?'

'We 'ad sorted it all out in Portsmuff,' Smith answered morosely. 'Now yu just leave it be, and let me take wots comin tuh me.'

Frankenstein looked sideways at his prisoner. He had accosted many a stroppy matelot in his years as a crusher, and was used to all sorts of reactions from the guilty. This man beside him was not the same man who had met him eyeball to eyeball unflinchingly, even though as guilty as hell. This was a man who had got rid of whatever demon had been driving his previous unwarranted aggression.

'Well, Able Seaman Smith, in the light of wot 'as since 'appened, let me give you a bit of sound advice. At the moment the powers that be will be fully occupied organisin' a court martial for the poor unfortunate sod, and 'is poor unfortunate Skipper responsible for what 'appened out there. They don't 'ave any choice, they 'ave got ter face a court martial.' He paused for a second. Smith's blank expression however had not changed, so he went on, 'but you Able Seaman Smith are likely to be given a choice. You may be given the chance to opt for court martial, and 'ope for the best, or you can do yourself a favour by opting to take your Commanding Officer's punishment; namely the Commanding Officer of HMS *Rooke*. The Navy will probably be well pleased that they don't 'ave to convene two courts, and you'll probably end up in DQ's Pompey for ninety days, and not get 'eaved out uv the mob. Yuh see word's got round that yuh like bein' a sailor, and yore good at yer job. So, yuh stubborn arseole, are yuh goin' tuh take my advice?' He stared hard at Smith looking for a reaction. Smith did not return his hard gaze; he just gave a nod of his head and uttered the word, 'yeah!'

9

RETRIBUTION DILUTED

Ordinary Seaman Dusty Miller stood by the Quartermaster's desk on HMS *Birmingham* shaking hands with the dozen or so men who had played a part in his recovery. He descended the gangway, gave one final wave, and hatless, wearing only the washed and ironed clothes he had been hauled out of the water in, headed in the direction of his own ship. With his lifejacket rolled up in its pouch, and hanging under his left arm suspended on its belt, he probably presented an unusual sight to the uninitiated. At that precise moment, he was probably only one of two men who had good cause to be grateful to the designer of this particular style of life saver, which, although only partially inflated, had kept his unconscious body afloat until fate delivered him into the fearful arms of Able Seaman Smith.

As he approached his own ship, a sudden blast from HMS *Birmingham*'s siren made him turn around. She was preparing to rush back out into the Atlantic and rejoin Exercise Biscay, having released her charges safely on to dry land.

His attention now turned to the tug that was positioned in the entrance to the dry dock behind the broken stern of HMS *Barrosa*. The gangway was suspended on a crane hook already swinging over to allow the army of Dockyard Mateys aboard to prepare the ship inboard. A Tin Hat Diver was also being made ready to descend to the bottom of the dry dock to relay important information to the docking team leader.

Dusty held back while the streams of Dockyard Mateys hurried aboard. He looked up towards the Bridge, but everyone was too intent upon their duties to notice him. He wasn't completely ignored though; the Quartermaster, Bosun's Mate, and the seamen securing the gangway all greeted him warmly as he came aboard.

'Yer in the rattle!' one wag shouted, grinning broadly, and then added, 'absent wivaht leave, and goin' 'ands ter bave wivaht permission!'

'Bollocks!' Dusty retorted with a loud laugh, greatly cheered by this typical welcome. They all watched him walk forrard and through the screen door alongside the Fxle ladder.

'There goes one lucky basterd if ever I saw one!' the Quartermaster murmured, watching Dusty disappear from view.

'There's a buzz goin' round that the AB off the *Corunna* oo jumped in and saved 'im was the same guy oo kicked 'is 'ead in at crimbo,' the Bosun's mate said.

'Yeah,' the Quartermaster nodded. 'That makes 'im even more of a jam stranglin' git at arf two in the mornin'.'

Dusty strode forrard along the Burma Way grinning broadly in reply to shipmates as they greeted him. He knocked at the door to the Coxswain's office.

'Come in,' a voice shouted.

Dusty opened the door and walked in, closing it behind him. 'Reporting back for duty Swain,' he said, standing respectfully at the edge of the desk, his hand outstretched holding a buff envelope.

The Coxswain rose to his feet, face beaming. He extended his right hand, and they shook hands briefly. 'Glad to see you back Miller.' He looked at the bandage around Dusty's head. 'Take another knock to the head did you?'

'Yeah, twenty stitches in an L shape, I cracked me 'ead on a stanchion as I went over the side.'

'How's the guy off the *Corunna* who jumped in and kept you afloat?'

'Able Seaman Smith was collected by the regulating branch from HMS *Rooke* just before the sick bay released me.'

'It is the same Able Seaman Smith then is it?'

'Yeah, I'm afraid so, and he was honest enough to tell me that he was thrown in the water when *Corunna* hit us. He said he thought I was a shark when we bumped into each other, but one thing for sure, I owe him my life. I 'ope they take that into account when they charge 'im for that attack.'

The Coxswain looked at Dusty closely as the young sailor voiced his gratitude for an act of fate. He was silent for a second before he replied.

'It's out of our hands Miller, but I can assure you that justice will be done. Yourself and Ordinary Seaman Bennett will have your say, and no doubt mitigating circumstances will be taken into consideration. The navy however will want to assess Smith's mental state, so nothing will be done until a trick cyclist explores the reason for his obvious aggressive nature.' He paused again, noticing the effect his statement had on Dusty. 'You pop off to your mess now but be ready to see your Divisional Officer and the Captain at short notice. The ship is in Dockyard hands now so the Captain will have time to clear up other outstanding duties.'

'Thanks Swain,' Dusty said, turning and opening the door to leave. He closed it gently behind him as he stepped out of the office into the canteen flat. Three paces to starboard and he descended the ladder into five mess.

He took a bunch of keys out of his pocket and opened his locker. After a moment's fumbling around in his personal drawer he extracted his paybook wallet and removed a ten shilling note. He had noticed a local trader selling cheese rolls to the canteen manager as he came aboard; he was famished, so intended to be first in the queue when stand easy was piped in a few minutes.

'Stand Easy,' the tannoy blared, and Dusty was up the ladder, and had two cheese rolls in his hand just as a queue started to form behind him.

'Hi Dusty,' a chorus of voices called. 'Christ, not yer 'ead again!' The speaker this time was his old messmate Buck Taylor, his wide eyes and gaping mouth showing his surprise at Dusty's appearance.

'Hi Buck, great tuh be able tuh see yer,' Dusty acknowledged his shipmate. They shook hands firmly, and suddenly everyone was queuing up to wish him well.

At that moment a tall imposing figure rounded the corner of the Burma Way as it ended at the Coxswain's office door. Dusty grinned at his best pal, and the hubbub in the canteen flat subsided as the two oppos grabbed each other by the shoulders and let out whoops of male pleasure. They wrestled with each other for a moment, and then stood back hands clasped, left hands clasping each other's forearm. Wiggy broke the silence. 'You are just back in time to convince the DO that you are capable of becoming an Able Seaman.' He accentuated the two words heavily to suggest it was the ultimate. He grinned adding, 'believe it or not annual swimming tests are promulgated for next week, so you old chum are guilty of anticipating an order, and getting your swim in two weeks early.'

A few titters greeted Wiggy's ironic delivery, but he was leading his chum forrard. 'Join me for tea dear oppo,' he joshed. 'Convince me of the doubtful pleasures of taking an early morning swim.'

Dusty laughed at his pal's dryness and held out a cheese roll. 'Want one of these Wiggs?'

'No bloody fear!' Wiggy retorted. 'You look as if you need both of 'em. I shall be satisfied with a jam butty out of tea issues.'

Grinning broadly they passed through the door into one and two messes. Dusty picked an empty space on a bunk seat whilst Wiggy filled two mugs with tea. They chatted lightly for the remainder of stand easy, and decided that rather than go ashore tonight, they would enjoy a couple of cans on board.

The remainder of the day was taken up by the docking procedure. The *Barrosa* was gradually disappearing below ground level as the water gushed from the dock under pump pressure. The diver informed his controllers when the ship's keel was just short of the keel blocks, and then the dockyard rang to the sound of sledge hammers on wood from the Dockyard Mateys responsible for hammering in the wedges for each support strut which would ensure that the ship sat fairly and squarely on the keel blocks, perfectly balanced. A short while later *Barrosa* was free of the element she was built to survive in, and for the first time since her last docking prior to recommissioning her ship's bottom could be scraped and repainted, when repair work was finished. Down below in the dock bottom, the dockyard workers were scrambling around getting their share of the shoal of fish that had been trapped when the dock gate was positioned.

Early the next morning Dusty was called to see his Divisional Officer..., ...and then the Captain.

Neither officer broached the subject of Able Seaman Smith, fully aware that that man's problems would be top of the agenda very shortly. The Captain still showed the strain of the last few days, and that, added to the normal pressures of command during a major exercise probably meant that he looked forward to a couple of days of normal routine while the dockyard swarmed all over his ship.

During the afternoon the lower deck moved into dockyard accommodation. Officers were billeted ashore, but routines would remain unchanged with a room provided for the duty officer on the dockside. The huge barn-like structure that provided messing for junior rates was not divided into departmental messdecks. Room dividers and curtains separated the branches from each other so that individual routines particular to that branch did not affect anyone else. One huge bathroom and toilets area at the end of the building served something like 230 men. Consequently, between the hours of 1600 and 1800 there was two hours of comedy and theatricals, as never less than thirty buck naked sailors cavorted around doing their dhobying and showering. A bit different to the morning crush, when attitudes tended to be a bit grumpier.

A row of tables up the centre of the two aisles of the block served as a dining room for the three main meals of the day, and as recreation spaces during non-working hours. Evenly spaced around the massive building were the main broadcast speakers, interspersed by the most essential Ship's Radio Equipment speakers. The SRE room was the domain of anyone who fancied themselves as a DJ, and was a source of entertainment when the day's work had finished. The Galley was at the opposite end to the bathrooms, and worked the Cafeteria style of messing.

Tot time was run as a rum bar; another unpopular measure, it took the midday social occasion out of tot time. Beer issue was individual, but at least you could take your two cans back to your mess and enjoy them.

By the time the annual swimming tests took place at HMS *Rooke* end of the Harbour, the Ship's Company had settled into the routine of being in dockyard hands. Both Dusty and Wiggy convinced Lieutenant Branscombe that they were at that stage in their careers where they had earned the right to reach the exalted stage of Able Bodied Seamen. Although the outcome of the day's tests were a foregone conclusion in both of their cases, they still had to prove both practically, and theoretically capable in all aspects of seamanship. The main worry of the day had been signals. Sending and receiving Morse code by Aldis Lantern and by Semaphore had to be learnt in their spare time, as it was not generally the job of a Seaman on a day to day basis.

The day ended with a congratulatory comment from their Divisional Officer, and a smile from Petty Officer McHenry; he, if anyone, had ensured that their day proceeded smoothly, and it was he who posed the questions on Anchors and Cables in the presence of Lieutenant Branscombe, the last test of the day.

The celebration that night ended with a hasty gallop through the dockyard to beat the 0100 hours leave expiry time. Sub Lieutenant Dodds and Midshipman Blenkinsopp turned away grinning broadly as the two pals collected their station cards, the result of the night's celebration was quite clear in their fumbly actions, but they had not reached the stage of drunkenness at which the Navy has to apply corrective measures. Their day had ended in a pleasant glow, and no problems.

In a few days' time they would be standing in front of Commander Plowright's table, and walk away Able Seamen. Before that however, they had to spend an afternoon in the presence of the Coxswain filling in a witness statement each, taking care to only write down the actual events that took place that Christmas evening four months ago.

— · —

Following his removal from the Cruiser *Birmingham*, and his journey under escort to HMS *Rooke*, Able Seaman Smith was put in cells, and the relentless pursuit of the facts in the name of naval justice began. The charge would be 'wounding' in conjunction with the list of serious offences as laid down in Queens Regulations and Admiralty Instructions – investigation of offences chapter three, paragraph 0315. 1a of this paragraph states that in practice he could be sent for trial by court martial, other than at his own option. So even for this offence he could opt for Commanding Officer's punishment. Circumstances that occurred later would only be taken into account if the Commander of HMS *Rooke* felt so inclined when considering punishment, should Able Seaman Smith opt for 'Commanding Officer's punishment'.

As the senior officer at the base in which Able Seaman Smith was a member of the ship's company, he had already received investigative reports from the RNSIB, and the Garrison Provost, but the most relevant reports, when complete, would come from his own regulating staff. The civilian authorities had had little involvement in this affair, so it had already been agreed that this was purely a matter for the navy to sort out. With all prosecution evidence, and all witnesses present in Gibraltar at that moment, the only consideration left was the accused. Before being formally charged, only things pertaining to him had to be diligently prepared, and the first consideration could be initiated immediately.

Master at Arms Leonard Jackson appeared at the bars of Smith's cell as the doors were clanged shut, and locked. Without hesitation he called for Able Seaman Smith's attention.

'I am here to inform you,' he started, and then glanced down at his papers, 'that Queens Regulations and Admiralty Instructions investigation of offences section five, Paragraphs 0355 one and two requires you to undergo a medical examination. You have no choice in this matter, so I suggest you get yourself in the right frame of mind to undergo this doctor's examination, and to answer all his questions with good manners and proper respect. He is a naval doctor specialising in psychiatrics, and he will visit you in this cell. Have you anything to say on this matter?'

'Nothin' at all Master,' Smith replied simply.

The Master at Arms exited the cell block, returned to his office and set the wheels in motion for the psychiatrist to be available to him the following morning at 1000 hours. He kept the phone in his hand and dialed another three-digit number.

'Ah, Chief Steward,' he said pleasantly. 'Can you provide lunch, tea and biccies etc for a doctor I have visiting tomorrow?' He listened for a moment, and then said, 'I don't know, beyond tomorrow, but if he does require a few more meetings with his patient you will be the first to know obviously. The First Lieutenant, as Wardroom Mess Officer will fill you in with all the details, is that okay? Cheers.'

Having considered the physical needs of a most important member of the investigation team, Master at Arms Jackson turned to a pile of witness statement forms 266A. He started applying names to the first sheet of each thin bundle. Those intended for duty personnel on the night in question were placed to one side, while the remainder was placed in individual envelopes with the witness' name applied to the envelope. The ones intended for Ordinary Seamen Miller and Bennett were also marked, 'Coxswain, HMS *Barrosa*'. When all the papers were complete, he took a final glance down his list of witnesses, double checked the envelopes, and placed them alongside his local pile. 'Leading Patrolman Ward,' he called through his open door.

Frankenstein's huge form lumbered into his office. 'Yes Master at Arms,' he presented himself politely.

'You and Fred can crack on with your witness forms now,' he ordered, his tone less formal. 'You know the routine, oh, and give RPO Woolston a nudge, I'd like his done ASAP.'

Master at Arms Jackson placed the remainder of the envelopes in his filing cabinet; they would be delivered to their destination by a member of his staff. Tomorrow morning he would meet Captain Justin Tipton-Barnsworth DFC, and brief him on progress to date; in the meantime a watchkeeping roster had to be organised of Able Seaman Smith's peers from the duty watch of the day, all of whom would be responsible to the duty regulator for everything pertaining to Smith's stay in cells. Not a popular job amongst the lower deck, being nanny to someone you barely knew, but whose immediate needs had to be attended to when required. No fraternisation was allowed, but even the hardest of sentries was human, and invariably some chat took place when the duty regulator was not in the office next door.

— · —

The next morning at 0900 hours, a car from BMH entered HMS *Rooke*, and a rather regal looking gentleman with three gold rings, interspaced with red rings on each cuff of his jacket, alighted from the car. He was greeted with proper ceremony by the Executive Officer, and the Officer of the Day, and then ushered through into the presence of the Commanding Officer of HMS *Rooke*. After the usual pleasantries, all except the Officer of the Day sat down to coffee. Master at Arms Jackson was invited to brief the doctor on the situation to date, but only the prisoner's actual offence on the night was discussed, using only the reports of the regulating staff that had been present.

'I have read the medical report on the state of Ordinary Seaman Miller and am aware of the treatment he received at BMH,' the doctor assured those present. 'What I have not seen is a report initiated by a young fellow called Ordinary Seaman Bennett. I wish to read that report, it may give me some insight as to the state of mind of Able Seaman Smith before and after the assault on Ordinary Seaman Miller. Do you think a copy could be arranged for me?'

'I have one in my office sir,' the Master at Arms offered respectfully. 'I shall have it ready for you when you come over to interview Able Seaman Smith.'

'Thank you Master at Arms,' the doctor replied, his politeness a little extreme in its delivery.

At 0930 hours Master at Arms Jackson excused himself, and returned to the Regulating Office. 'Right!' he said loudly to his staff. 'Let's get a decent table and two decent chairs into Smith's cell. See to it Ward,' he ordered.

Leading Patrolman Ward in turn, ordered the Regulating Office runner, and the watchkeeping sailor to assist him, and they hurriedly obeyed the Master at Arms' order.

'Wot's this then?' Able Seaman Smith asked, curious at the sudden activity.

'Yore about ter be talked to by a high ranking 'Trick Cyclist' so just you be on yer best be-aviour,' Frankenstein answered Smith's puzzled frown.

Master at Arms Jackson entered the cell just as his patrolman spoke.

'That's enough chatter in here Leading Patrolman Ward, I will do any talking that is necessary.'

'Sorry Master,' the huge regulator answered sheepishly, giving his two helpers the waving thumb sign to vacate the cell.

'Right Able Seaman Smith,' the Master at Arms said sternly. 'In a few minutes a very senior doctor will be entering this cell to talk to you. How long he will decide to be with you I don't know, but no matter how long it is I want you to answer all his questions politely and truthfully; and don't think you can pull the wool over this gentleman's eyes, he is extremely experienced in his work. Have you got that Able Seaman Smith?' The Master at Arms glowered at his prisoner, as if ramming home his point.

'I'll be no bother Master,' Smith said resignedly, earning a less stern look from his jailer.

At 1000 hours exactly Master at Arms Jackson brought Doctor Addison Boswell Commander RN into Smith's cell and introduced him by his full title.

'Thank you Master at Arms,' the doctor said, and then asked without further ado, 'can you ensure that we are not disturbed during the time I am with Able Seaman Smith.'

'Certainly sir, and anything you need, we are only next door.'

The psychiatrist sat down, and opening his briefcase took out a sheaf of papers and a pen.

Settling into his chair he glanced up at Smith and said, 'Just a few personal details first.'

He wrote down all Smith's personal details at the top of the page in the area provided, and then opened what he preferred to call 'a conversation.'

'Rotherhithe I see,' he said, and looked up smiling. 'Quite a reputation as a hard place to grow up in, did you find it so?'

Smith was somewhat taken aback by the opening question, and the easy way in which it was asked. After a moment's hesitation he replied cautiously, 'yuh 'ad ter be able tuh look after yerself.'

'Did you find that you had to be able "to look after yourself"?' He quoted Smith's own words.

'All uv the time sir, especially Saturday nights.'

'Saturday nights were inclined to be a bit rough then, were they?'

'Usually a gang fight, but now and then a personal score 'ad tuh be settled.'

'Did you have many personal scores to settle?'

'Yuh 'ad tuh 'old yer end up wiv someone at least once a week.'

'What sort of thing would you have to "hold your end up" for?'

'Aw, anyfin, someone bumps into yuh; someone ogles yer bird, or makes a pass at 'er; someone gives yer a dirty look, anyfin that gits up yer nose.'

'Were these one to one confrontations? Stand up fights say, as a matter of honour?'

'Nah, sometimes yu'ed just sail into some git to 'ave 'im before ee got yu.'

'So the general atmosphere on a Saturday night was get your enemy in any way, before he got you?'

'That's the way it is sir. If yer easy meat yuh git pounced on, and yuh can't go anywhere wivaht gittin nutted. If yuh git stuck in, a lot uv blokes think twice before 'avin' a go at yer.'

'How old were you when you first fought as part of a gang?'

The question surprised Smith, and it showed in his facial expression. He gave the appearance of thinking hard for a few moments. Finally he answered apologetically, 'I'm not bein' awkward sir, but I can't remember when it started, it was always the same, before I started school I suppose.'

The doctor paused and wrote quickly for a few moments before pondering his next line of questioning.

'I see you joined the navy in early 1953.'

'Yes sir, I've been in abaht five years nah.'

'What made you join the navy for nine years?'

'It was somfin I always wanted, didn't fancy bein' a Pongo.'

Doctor Boswell stifled a grin with the back of his hand, and leant over the desk as if easing his position. 'Did you have any difficulties at the recruiting office, educational, or other?'

'Nah sir, I sailed through the exam…got everyfin right.'

'What did your local gang think of you leaving them in favour of the navy?'

'Aw, they wuz great, navy geezers were always poplar round our end. They muck in yuh see, no airs and graces, always go wiv the flow.'

'Did you pass your ETLR in training?'

'Sailed through that too, I wuz always good at me schoolin' see, geography and geometry wuz two of me favourites. I wuz told that was why I wuz selected fer Radar Plot Ratin', I could picture the erf in me 'ead, and writin' backwards wuz no problem.'

Doctor Boswell had to hide another grin. This simplistic and bluntly honest style that Smith had about him was beginning to appeal to him. He paused in his 'conversation' to make some thoughtful notes on the third sheet of paper. As he finished, a loud ship's broadcast bellowed out, 'Secure, Hands to dinner!' It then clicked off, leaving silence again.

'That will do for now Smith,' Doctor Boswell said, a faint smile on his features. 'I shall return at 1330 hours.' So saying, the tall elegant psychiatrist walked from the cell, closing the door behind him. 'Be back at half one,' he said to all in general, as he passed through the Regulating Office.

The seaman watchkeeper pushed the door open, and then waltzed in sideways carrying a full tray of food, and cutlery items. 'I'll bring yuh a mug of tea in a minute mate,' he said, plonking the tray down on the table.

'A fuckin' tot ud be more like it,' Smith retorted dryly.

'Yeah, and my arse would be in the next cell to yuh in the blink of an eye,' the watchkeeper replied tersely.

The Master at Arms rose quickly out of his seat as he observed the Doctor passing through the Regulating Office, and caught him as he passed through the door. 'Just thought I would ask sir; do you require any recording equipment?'

'Not at this stage Master, but when I do need it, I shall bring my own. I am just getting to know the fellow at the moment.'

'Aye aye sir,' the Master at Arms answered, and left it at that.

On the second day of his 'conversation' with Able Seaman Smith, Doctor Boswell brought his recording equipment, and set it up on the table. All he had to ask the regulating staff for was an electrical extension lead to reach into the cell.

'Don't let this bother you Smith, all this lot is to your advantage. If you require, I can play back anything that you would like to elaborate on, in that way we can end up with a clear picture. I should remind you at this stage of the proceedings that I am a serving officer in the Royal Navy, and my first loyalties must be to that service. Doing my duty must be my first priority, but having said that; I must also present a totally honest and unbiased opinion of your state of mind as a whole, not just the night in question. Have I explained that sufficiently well?'

'I fully understand sir, and all this gear doesn't bovver me,' Able Seaman Smith answered, giving the impression he was eager to press on with the 'conversation'.

The Doctor continued for another three days, and then retired to his office at BMH to begin the lengthy job of presenting a professional assessment of his patient. One week later, Captain Tipton-Barnsworth was presented with the full details of the Doctor's extensive work. Able Seaman Smith by that time was billeted in cells at Military Headquarters Gibraltar, awaiting arraignment at his Commanding Officer's table.

━━ ・ ━━

On Monday 22nd April 1958, Master at Arms Leonard Jackson presented himself at his Commander's office at 0900 hours. Whilst waiting for his boss to start his day, the Captain's Steward brought in a tray bearing all the essentials for morning tea.

'Help yourself please Master,' the Steward made his usual Monday morning offer.

'Thanks,' was the casual reply.

'Good morning Master at Arms,' Captain Justin Tipton-Barnsworth greeted his senior lower decker, as he placed a large file on his desk.

'The psychiatrist's report,' he said conversationally. 'And by the looks of it we have a lot of reading to do. I have asked for a navy legal advisor to join us, just to get our end perfectly in order. Whomever it is will go through this report with me, I have to be absolutely sure of my position should Able Seaman Smith opt for Commanding Officer's punishment. Wounding is a most serious offence, and even in the light of the man's brave action in saving the life of Ordinary Seaman Miller, I cannot allow that to cloud the issue, even though I must consider the act as a possibly mitigating factor.' The Captain paused for a few seconds. The Master at Arms waited silently.

'When I have sorted things out with the aid of the legal advisor,' the Captain began again, 'I shall have this report sent to you immediately. In the meantime having had a glance at the first page, I would suggest that you get your witness' statements together, and we can possibly get Smith to my table next Monday. Do you agree with that as a tentative date at this moment?'

'Ideal sir, if we can get it all sorted out by Friday 1600 hours, witnesses can be advised to be in *Rooke* here by first thing Monday morning.'

'Very good then Master at Arms, is there anything else I should know while we are here?'

'No sir, just a few requestmen for your Tuesday table.'

'Thank you Master at Arms, that will be all for now.'

— · —

At 0900 hours on Monday 29th April 1958 a row of smartly turned out ratings stood quietly in line awaiting the presence of Captain Tipton-Barnsworth at his table. A sudden bustle outside the door preceded the entrance of this eminent senior naval officer.

'Defaulter and witnesses hoe,' Master at Arms Jackson shouted.

When everyone had settled down, he stood the line at ease.

'Able Seaman Smith,' he called loudly.

Smith marched smartly to the table, and stood to attention in front of his Commanding Officer.

'Off caps,' the Master at Arms shouted, and then proceeded immediately to read out the charge.

'Able Seaman Smith sir, was guilty of conduct to the prejudice of good order and naval discipline in that on the night of Saturday the 31st of November 1957 at approximately 2200 hours he did attack Ordinary Seaman Miller of HMS *Barossa* causing wounding requiring treatment at BMH Gibraltar. This is an offence under the Naval Discipline Act, and is listed in Queens Regulations and Admiralty Instructions investigation of offences chapter three, paragraph 0315 as a serious offence.'

The Captain paused a moment after the Master at Arms finished the long statement of fact. He looked sternly at Able Seaman Smith. 'How do you plead to this charge; guilty, or not guilty?'

'Guilty sir,' Smith replied, his own face holding a suitably serious expression.

'In the light of evidence brought against you, do you opt for trial by court martial, or are you willing to accept my punishment?'

'I will accept Commanding Officer's punishment sir,' Smith replied without hesitation.

'Very well Able Seaman Smith. Have you read and signed all investigation reports, and witness statements, including Doctor Boswell's report?'

'I 'ave sir.'

'Have you received counselling from your Divisional Officer and a legal advisor?'

'I 'ave talked wiv my DO sir, but 'ave no need of a legal advisor.'

The Captain turned to an officer at his side. 'Lieutenant Prescott, do you have anything to add?'

'Yes sir, I have had a long discussion with Able Seaman Smith, and like Commander Boswell I find Smith truly contrite, and regretful of his actions on the 31st of November. As to his previous conduct over his five years of service, he has never broke good conduct, and all his past assessments have been "VG Satisfactory". His skill, and knowledge of his job is good, and he has favourable reports from all his previous Divisional Officers. I will, however, quote part of one past report: "this man has proved capable of looking for action whilst off duty ashore". His removal from HMS *Vanguard* is noted as being for service reasons, and of course forms part of the build up to this case. That's all sir.'

'Thank you Lieutenant Prescott.'

The Captain spoke once again to Able Seaman Smith. 'Would you like to question any part of the witness reports in relation to this charge?'

'No sir, everyfin is 'ow it 'appened.'

'Very well then Able Seaman Smith,' the Captain started his punishment speech. 'In the light of the seriousness of the charge of wounding, I have no option but to sentence you to a period of confinement in Detention Quarters, Portsmouth. In considering the length of your confinement I have taken your brave actions, performed regardless of self after a serious collision at sea into account. As an act of mitigation I have not used the full powers of punishment afforded me, but have reduced your sentence to sixty days' detention.'

A pause at the end of the Captain's decision signified the end of proceedings.

'Sixty days' detention, warrant to be read 1030 hours Wednesday the 1st of May 1958,' the Master at Arms said loudly, and then continued, 'on caps, left turn, quick march.'

Leading Patrolman Ward and his oppo Fred fell in beside Smith as he marched towards the double doors. Smith's words could be heard by all at the table before the doors closed behind the three of them. ''Ee didn't 'eave me aht, did ee? I'm still in the mob, ain't I?'

Even at that most serious moment, officers behind the Captain's table could be seen stifling amusement, and hiding grins behind hurriedly raised hands. The Captain glanced downwards and was heard to utter 'ahem.' The Master at Arms coughed. Dusty Miller breathed a sigh of relief. Wiggy Bennett's face stayed fixedly unmoved.

'Witnesses carry on,' the Master at Arms ordered.

As the doors were closed by the Royal Marine sentry, the Captain turned to his senior lower decker. 'Thank you Master at Arms, that was a well organised case. Kindly ensure that the ship's company is informed well in advance that lower deck will be cleared of all ratings not actually on watch after Stand Easy Wednesday.'

'It will be in tomorrow's daily orders sir, and will be added to a ship's broadcast on Wednesday morning.'

'Thank you Master at Arms; that will be all for now, I know you have much to do.'

'Aye aye sir.' The Master at Arms saluted his boss, turned smartly, and walked past the Royal Marine sentry saying, 'thank you Royal.'

The final thrust of the sword came from Gonzuella. As news reached her of the day's events, she played the part of the wounded female to the hilt as she ditched that 'orrible leetle man Smeeth!' His two working buddies were not at all worried, Gonzuella kept the bedroom, and paid a third share of the rent herself; anyway having a woman about the flat had distinct advantages to a couple of red blooded sailors.

Ironically, as Able Seaman Smith stood facing the ship's company of HMS *Rooke* that Wednesday morning on the first of May listening to his Captain read out the Warrant, Ordinary Seaman Miller and Ordinary Seaman Bennett had just faced their Commanding Officer to be rated Able Seamen. Commander Plowright gave them both a verbal pat on the back, each in turn as they stood smartly to attention in front of him. He had something else to say to Able Seaman Bennett before he left the table.

'Captain Dunbar-Naismith, Commanding Officer of HMS *Vernon*, has written me a letter commending Lieutenant Brown for his prompt action whilst Officer of the Watch at the time of the ramming. Lieutenant Brown, of course, is a product of the Torpedo and Anti Submarine Warfare School so it has a special meaning to his old Commanding Officer. He also asked after you showing great interest in where you go from here. I think, like all of us, he expects you to strive for your true station in life in the not too distant future.' Commander Plowright paused, looking directly into Wiggy's eyes expecting an answer.

'With respect sir,' Wiggy started seriously. 'I would like to complete the three week diving course in Malta first, and then I fully intend to present you with my request for consideration.'

Commander Plowright smiled at the direct, but respectful reply. 'Will I also be getting a diving course request from Able Seaman Miller?'

Wiggy grinned as he replied, 'most certainly sir.'

'Very well then Bennett, don't waste any time, we shall be in dockyard hands for at least another two months, so now is the ideal time to achieve this personal ambition. Well done Able Seaman Bennett,' he concluded the short conversation.

'Rated Able Seaman. Salute. About turn, quick march,' the Coxswain ordered loudly.

The two oppos rounded the corner of the galley flat together before relaxing.

'What shall we do with the three months' back pay for being really switched on sailors?' Wiggy grinned as he spoke.

'Oh!' Dusty exclaimed loudly. 'I suggest a few wets first, and the rest into the old savings book.'

'My feelings exactly, only I thought maybe a little prezzy for Felicity might be in order after all this separation,' Wiggy said thoughtfully.

'Oh flippin' 'eck yeah! That as well,' Dusty replied, swiftly covering his oversight.

Wiggy grinned at him knowingly, and thumped him playfully on the shoulder.

'Allo, what's goin on 'ere then?' Dusty said, as they were walking back to the accommodation block. HMS *Corunna* was being shunted into the next drydock, which had become available that morning.

'I was wondering when they would start on her,' Wiggy said. 'Obviously decisions have been made.'

He was right; the decision however was merely to cut off the hanging bow, fill the gaping space with concrete, and send her off back home to Blighty, never to return to the Squadron. A date had not yet been set for the court martial of her Commanding Officer, so with this cloud hanging over his head he had to sail his vessel back home wondering if fate had denied him any future command. He would have to sail his ship into Plymouth harbour with this ignominy hanging over his head under the watchful eye of his Admiral.

'I'll bet I'm called as a witness when the shit 'its the fan,' Dusty said as they were watching the docking procedure.

'Able Seaman Smith also,' Wiggy answered, pursing his lips as he prepared to add something else. 'I'll bet my back pay that he comes out of this smelling of roses, and gets a gong for keeping you afloat.'

Dusty frowned at his best friend's tone. "Ee did save my bloody life yuh know!'

'Yes my friend so he did. But one must not forget that just five months previously he tried to take it,' Wiggy answered, leaving Dusty in no doubt at all that his oppo was harbouring serious doubts about the navy's handling of the whole affair. In his mind justice had been clouded by events that could not have been foreseen.

Dusty did not reply to his friend's seriously delivered statement. In truth, he had no answer; he still had a picture in his mind of Smith leaning over his body giving him mouth-to-mouth resuscitation. He was sure in his own mind that his once-hated enemy had brought him back into this world, and for the life of him, he could not explain Smith's previous attempts to do him serious bodily harm. He was however, convinced that the fight in Portsmouth had brought the whole episode to a close, and whatever demons had been driving Smith had been banished forever as a result of the hard confrontation.

'Come on Dusty,' Wiggy's words broke into his thoughts. 'Let's get back to the windy hammers, and chip a yard of paint before dinner; but "that's life in a blue suit" innit,' he added, grinning widely, trying to bring his oppo's thoughts back to the present. He looked at Dusty for a reaction, but getting none he rabbited on, 'hey numbnuts, we have to fill in a couple of request forms for diving course tonight, so that's something to take your mind off Able Seaman Smith, and flying flakes of old paint!'

Dusty grinned at his pal's insistence, and replied, 'Yeah "deeps", that's life in a blue suit.'

THE END

A final word from the author:
'I used to be a sailor, but I'm alright now.'

GLOSSARY

264's: A sheet in one's service documents where personal attributes, or otherwise, are appended. It is not unknown for a drawing in the shape of a bone to have been one Divisional Officer's comment on one of his division. The comment 'uses the navy to transport his genitals from port to port,' was another comment that circulated naval lower decks.

Aggie Westons: Agnes Weston Royal Sailors Rest. A rather nice doss-house for sailors, where a bed and a bath could be obtained at low cost.

Andrew: Lower deck term for the Royal Navy. This stems from the name Andrew Miller, a zealous Press Gang officer who was said to own the Royal Navy during the Napoleonic Wars, due to the number of men he impressed.

A Right Jack Me Tickler Paper: Streetwise lower decker, wise to all the moves, and is navy through and through. More often than not, a very knowledgeable seaman.

Bagging Off: Lower deck term for sexual intercourse.

Belfast Betty: Author's invention.

Blank Week: Payday was every other Thursday, the in-between Thursday being 'blank'.

Breech: Blocks off the loading end, and houses the firing mechanism.

Breech Ring: The part of a big gun that houses all barrel parts at the loading end, including the breech block.

Broomstale: The handle of a long handled broom (believe it or not, there are people who have never heard the term).

Buff Stoker: A young and inexperienced mechanical engineer.

Burma Way: Nickname for main passageway.

Butcher And Tanky: Every ship has a seaman who is ship's butcher. A course with the army at Aldershot ensures that he is qualified for the job. The seaman generally working with the butcher is employed to get all the food stores from below to the galley. This seaman is traditionally called the 'Tanky'.

Cardiff Rose: Author's invention.

Cooks Of The Day: Two men daily, promulgated on a mess list to clean the mess before 0900 hours, and to collect the food for the mess at mealtimes, cleaning and returning all galley trays back to the galley on completion of mealtime.

Crushers: Naval regulators. Equivalent to Military Police.

Dabtoe: This is the popular term used by all branches of the navy to describe a member of the seaman's branch. The term has the connotation of being barefoot, and hence prone to dabbing one's toes against deck cleats, eyebolts and other things protruding from a ship's deck.

Deeps: Lower deck term for a diver.

Dockyard Matey: Sailors' name for a person working in naval dockyards.

Docs: Abbreviation for 'documents'.

Draft Chit: Official document assigning men to new ship or base.

Drip: Having a good old drip. Complaining about any presumed hardship.

Drum: Slang term for a Flat or House.

Duty Hands: Usually two ratings on Destroyers, delegated to carry out work after secure, where the whole duty watch is not required.

Fanny: Liquid container, e.g. rum fanny, washing up fanny. Also a non-derogatory term relating to the female gender.

Felipe: (Not the gentleman's real name.) A Spanish man of great agility and charisma. The author's last knowledge of this gentleman's whereabouts was in 1969/70, when he owned a bar named after him. He was still famous for giving his customers an entertaining exhibition of Spanish Dancing, although he was getting on a bit by then.

Flaked Down: Not rolled up. To 'Flake Down' means to lay cordage, or steel wire rope, in a zigzag formation across the deck, or if a fire hose, in a basket, ready to run out immediately with no chance of knotting or snagging.

Flat: Not living accommodation. This describes an area giving access to other compartments.

Flimsy: Thin message paper.

FXLE: Forecastle.

Gibraltar's Dakota Aircraft: This old passenger plane operated out of Gibraltar for years after the Second World War, running regular trips local to the Mediterranean. Heads always turned on ships in the dockyard to watch it claw its way into the sky.

Goffers: Soft drinks from the NAAFI shop. Also used to describe a large wave.

Have A Wet: Traditional request to rum bosun on messdecks for daily ration of rum.

Heads: Toilets.

Heaving Lines: Normally a sixty foot length of rope with a monkey's fist knot on the delivery end, and an eye splice on the inboard end, thrown from ship to jetty when coming alongside. If using ship's own berthing wires, the eye splice end is then passed through a Deck Cleat and attached to the berthing wire. The dockyard berthing party will then haul the berthing wire eye to the jetty and pass it over a dockside bollard.

Hoe: Traditionally calls a naval party of men to attention, e.g. gunner's party hoe.

Home Club: A navy pub, run on navy rules for the navy.

Jimmy: The First Lieutenant, in lower deck terms. Number One, to his Captain.

Jossman: Master at Arms. Jaunty is another sobriquet.

Jumping Ladder: Rope ladder with wooden slats that can be hung down the ship's side.

Kecks: Male or female underpants.

Kedge Anchor: On a Destroyer, a third anchor that is portable to the extent that it can be slung between two boats with hawser attached, and dropped in a pre-determined position away from the ship. Hauling in on the hawser will have the effect of 'pointing' the ship in a desired direction. Any picture of a fleet review will show ships' bows pointing in the same direction. Hence the term: 'To Point Ship'.

Limers: Citric powder that becomes 'Lime Juice' when water is added. Scurvy is not a problem amongst seafarers these days, but it is widely used in the Royal Navy, particularly when serving in foreign waters. The nickname 'Limey' is used by the Americans to describe anyone of British origin. Personally, I always retaliate 'yes, but I am a real Limey!'

Los Tres Cabaleros: Loosely translated 'The three fellows'.

Mackerel Line: With other thin cordage, collectively called 'Small Stuff'.

Marlin Hitches: The knots with which a hammock is lashed up.

Mick: Slang word for hammock.

Mousing: Pronounced 'Mouzing', and refers to a thin length of flexible steel wire rope, which is used to wrap around the end of a tackle hook, to ensure that it does not disengage from an eyebolt.

Nettles: The strings at each end of hammock.

Nomination Whist: The same as conventional whist, but the man who bids the most tricks gets to nominate a partner by card selection. He then has to find out who his partner is as early as possible as the game unfolds. If he has the lead, he will ask for his partner to make himself known, by leading a small card in the selected suit.

Non Sub: Abbreviation for a seaman's second and 'non substantive' job, e.g. Gunnery Rating, Tas Rating (Torpedo and Anti Submarine), Radar Plot Rating.

O.D: Descriptive of an Ordinary Seaman.

Old Joanna: Synonym for a piano.

O-Nine Dubs: 0900 hours.

Pas Boat: Port Auxiliary Service, e.g. Dockyard passenger craft.

POME: Petty Officer Mechanical Engineer.

Pompey Lil: A real Portsmouth character, famous along Commercial Road, and part of naval folklore now.

Ponders Ball: A metal ball, just above the lifting hook on a Crane wire.

POPTI: Petty Officer Physical Training Instructor.

Pot And One: Describes a paint-pot and one paintbrush.

Pun: Punishment.

Rec Space (Recreation Space): An area of the upper deck where relaxation is allowed when off duty.

Red And Blue Openings: Hatches on or below the waterline are marked with red paint, and permission has to be gained to open them. Hatches and doors above the waterline are marked with blue paint, and are kept open unless otherwise ordered. This ensures the watertight integrity of a ship at sea or in harbour.

Rum Rat: A sailor whose whole existence revolved around this major daily event.

Scuttle: Porthole.

Ships Husbandry: As the term suggests; the general cleaning and care of the ship.

Sin Bosun: Politely irreverent term for a Vicar.

Sippers: A sip of a man's tot of rum for a favour done. All favours had a grade of reward amongst old salts. Sippers: a small taste. Gulpers: a large mouthful. Halfers: speaks for itself. See it off: speaks for itself. 'Lighters' and 'Snifters' were terms preceding 'Sippers', but were not commonly in use by the time the fifties arrived.

Smokey Handbag: Typical lower deck jocular irreverence describing a priest's smoking basket.

Spithead Pheasant: Naval term for a kipper.

Sprog: Any young and inexperienced sailor. Also used when referring to one's own children.

Sticky Green: A cheap liquid concoction, the money for which is form of commission for a bar girl.

Still And West: An excellent public house in Old Portsmouth. Its history is told on a plaque positioned at the entrance to the many bars within.

Stone Frigate: Shore base.

Stroppy: Anyone who is loudly disagreeable or physical. Also used to describe inclement weather.

The Jack Tripod: The three legged support above the bullring at the tip of the bow to which the Jackstaff that carries the Union Jack is secured.

Three Badges Red: Rhymes with 'Nearly f***ing dead'. Indicates a man's seniority on the lower deck, up to a number of three; one for every four years of service from the age of eighteen.

Tiddly Suit: A made-to-measure sailor's uniform, the jacket of which has no buttons or zipper down the front, and is made to hug the body's definition. The trousers have no vertical buttons or zipper, and are made with a front flap. They were classed as legal wear, and were very popular among young sailors. Many lads would festoon the rolled up cuffs with unearned badges to impress mates and Mum and Dad when going on first leave.

Tide Spar: Prevents boat from going under accommodation ladder.

Toggle And Two: Navy expression for male genitalia.

Trampers: Tramp Steamers (very rarely carrying the British Red Duster), not always as watchful as they should have been whilst under way.

Trapping Valve: A sailor was said to have 'Trapped' if he had achieved a successful encounter with a female. The term 'Trapping Valve' as used in the story, means that the young man's natural instincts had not been aroused by the female/females concerned.

Trooped: Lower deck expression for a reported misdemeanour which resulted in punishment.

Trouser Python: Lower deck term for penis.

Twin Four Inch: Describes a double-barrelled gun mounting, each barrel being four inches internal diameter at the muzzle end.

Two Fold Purchase: Common block and tackle.

Two Inch Rope: Describes the size of a rope by diameter.

Upper Scupper: Any weather deck.

Utility: Reduced to 'Tilly' by naval personnel, and described a mini bus.

Washdeck Locker: A large metal box fixed to the weather decks, to house essential ready-use equipment.

Waste: Cotton waste in tangled mass made a good cleaning and polishing medium. It was barred from use on automatic gun mountings due to the tendency of even a small strand to cause the fast moving loading and ramming mechanisms to jam.

Watch And Station Bill: A huge broadsheet on a main notice board, detailing each man's position for action in all states of readiness. Also stating his job, his duty watch, his boat station, and even his hammock netting – where he must stow his hammock.

White Front: A sailor's 'T' shirt.

Windy Hammers: An air driven hammer that chips old paint off metallic structures far more quickly than a conventional chipping hammer. Another unpopular job that young seamen had to apply themselves to.

Yorkshire: A kitty. A bunch of lads going ashore in one group would put five shillings each (25p) into a kitty, which was either held by one of the party or placed in a glass in the centre of the table. Any member of the group requiring a spirit drink would pay for it himself; the kitty was only for beer.